MUTED

RACHEL HELZER

NEWMAN SPRINGS PUBLISHING
320 Broad Street
Red Bank, NJ 07701

First originally published by Newman Springs Publishing 2023

ISBN 978-1-68498-550-0 (Paperback)
ISBN 978-1-68498-551-7 (Digital)

Printed in the United States of America

To my friends and family. Thank you for believing in me!

PROLOGUE

Nobody knows. Nobody knows who I am.

Nobody knows who I am, because they don't bother to stop and ask. They always assume that I'm a poor, weak, helpless mute.

Well, I'll show them. I'll prove them wrong! I'll prove that I'm a person with feelings!

My mother would have yelled at me for such a rant and right now; I wouldn't mind. If that meant she was alive and well. That my baby brother wasn't dead. My twin wasn't lost. Had the Sickness never happened, I would have welcomed her yelling at me.

If it meant that I could have yelled back.

CHAPTER 1

The first wave of the Sickness came when I was four years old. There was some technical name for it, but as I had been four when it first came, I never bothered to learn it. Then as time went on the technical name slipped from everyone's mind, and it simply became the Sickness. (I'm certain if you went to the bigger cities, they could tell you and would tell you, the exact names the reasons behind it, but as I'm from a teeny tiny town where everyone knew each other, we all just tended to think of it as the Sickness.) Though the name seemed nonthreatening and mild, the Sickness was anything but. It came like a herd of thieves in the night. Refusing to discriminate between the rich and the poor. Between the mother and motherless. The evil and good. It was unforgiving, unrelenting, and as a child, it was traumatizing.

I watched as the world I had gotten know within my short four years began to fall apart. News stories were no longer about finding lost puppies; instead, there were reports of riots, and the death toll. In our small town people began to lock themselves inside their homes, battening down their hatches so to speak, but it was too little too late. I don't know who brought it to our town, but soon enough, it seemed like everyone was sick. Everyone but our family, but my mother had to go and help a family in our neighborhood that had kids that were affected by the Sickness. She had been a nurse once upon a time before she had her own children, and so she thought she could help. But despite doing everything she possibly could, the family still lost a child. She tried to revive him despite the family's protest to keep herself and my unborn brother safe, but she couldn't let this child go without a fight.

Ultimately though, she failed. She came home that night and fell asleep after crying in my father's arms. My twin brother, Zach, watched with me from the hallway just outside our room unable to truly comprehend why our mother was crying. Eventually, I had tugged at my twin's arm, and we ran outside to pick flowers for hoping that they might cheer her up.

Not two weeks later, Mother was confined to her room with the Sickness. Zach and I weren't allowed to visit her, and as I watched Dad rush back and forth out of her room, I wondered, why were we being punished? What had we done so bad that we couldn't see Mom? I didn't understand what was going on, and by the time I did understand, it was too late. At the beginning of the first wave of the Sickness, my mother was three months pregnant. My father worked in the city, and as soon as he realized how serious the Sickness was, he tried to get my mother to stay home. He tried to get her to stay away from everyone to protect both her and the baby, but my mother refused, saying, "God's will."

That's all she ever said. "God's will." She was a special type of person, my mother, and she had a special type of heart that got her to go out and try to help people infected with the Sickness in spite of being pregnant. It also didn't help that my father had been around sick people for many weeks before in the city but had yet to get infected. She thought that maybe God had protected him, and like him, she would be protected. That at the very least God would protect her child. Well, suffice it to say he didn't protect either my mother or the baby. They got sick. She became bedridden, and although I was so young, I could sense a feeling of dread on the house. Somehow my mother managed to make it through eight months of her pregnancy, and I was hoping that meant that she was going to be all right, but there was one night I couldn't sleep. I had walked downstairs for a drink of water. I had gone halfway down the stairs when I heard my father pleading with my mother about something, but it was garbled. I crept closer and made it just in time to hear my mother tell Father that she knew that she was going to die soon that it was God's will and that he should try and save the baby. My father tried to argue with her, but my mother silenced him with her gentle plea to try and save the baby. Needless to say, my father agreed, and the next day, Zacharias and I said goodbye to our mother.

Zach and I wanted to stay with her, but our father told us that we needed stay in the hall while he helped Mom deliver the baby. Before we left the room, however, my mother called to us asking us to wait. We turned back and she gestured for both of us to come to her. Obediently we walked to her bedside. As we lingered there waiting for her to say something, I kept my eyes aimed at the floor. Out of the corner of my eyes I saw her reach out and take my twin's hand. Vaguely I remember hearing her say that she would see him soon.

Then everyone was quiet for a long moment before I heard her say, "Mirda…look at me."

I didn't want to. I didn't want to look up at her only have to her taken away moments later. It wasn't fair I wanted to scream but how could I say no to my mother. So hesitantly I looked up at her, fighting back the tears. Over the last five months, her once wonderful golden-brown hair had turned dull and colorless. Her eyes were hollowed and sunken in. However, when she smiled at me, I could tell it was genuine and that this person lying on the bed was really my mother.

I remember her reaching out to grab my hand. Her hands were cold and clammy. "Mirda." I watched her whisper weakly, and that was when the little resolve had for a six-year-old vanished. Tears streamed down my cheeks as I threw myself into her arms, crying, "Mommy, don't leave." My tears soaked her favorite yellow shirt, but she didn't seem to mind.

She stroked my hair for a couple of moments longer before she stated firmly, "I'm sorry, Mirda, but it's my time."

"No." I cried, shaking my head in defiance. "I won't let you go."

I heard her chuckle weakly as she whispered, "So stubborn. Just like your mother." She chuckled again, weaker. "You'll need it to get through the challenges you have ahead of you."

I pulled away my forehead crinkling in confusion. I watched as the smile she had pasted onto her face fade as she said, "Mirda, you must promise me that you won't give up, ever. No matter what God sends your way. Promise me."

I nodded quickly; my only thought was that if I promised her that I wouldn't give up, then just maybe she'd stay. That my promise somehow had the pull she needed to keep on living, but it wasn't meant to be. I watched as her face relaxed, and a true smile appeared her face.

"Thank you… I love you, my Mirda… Don't give up… You're stronger than you know… Help will come when you need it…most."

That was the last time I ever saw or spoke to my mother. The next thing I remember was my father coming out of their room, a little bundle in his arms.

He knelt on the floor as Zacharias and I surrounded him, trying to see what was in his arms. He lowered the bundle to our eye level, and I found myself staring at a very small, pale, weak baby boy.

"Mirda. Zacharias. Meet your baby brother. Benjamin Ephraim Johnson."

I remember looking up at my father in surprise as I heard him choke on my baby brother's name only to frown in confusion in the next moment as I saw tears streaming down his cheeks.

"Daddy?" I asked quietly, placing a hand on his arm. Automatically he looked at me, and I saw a word I didn't know at the time of my mother's death, despair.

From there my memory jumped. Watching my father build two head stones. Then watching him as he pounded nails into two coffins. Before finally standing in front of two mounds of dirt. One mound much bigger than the other. I remember looking back at my father and brother as they lowered the bigger of the two coffins into the bigger hole. Tears stung my eyes as they finished, and I picked up my father's shovel and held it out to him before going to stand besides my twin. Hesitantly I reached out and grabbed his hand squeezing slightly. I remember it took him a moment for him to respond, and when it did, it was very faint. At the time, I had thought it was because he had just helped our father bury Mother, but I was wrong. I was so wrong. At that point, my memory jumped again.

We had just finished our schooling for the day, and per usual, Zach and I went to the woods to go exploring. We found daises and dandelions, a fat squirrel, and a slug. We were having so much fun, but at one point, I was separated from Zach. I don't remember when, but all of a sudden, I was alone. I called for him, yelling his name over and over. Telling him this wasn't funny, but he never responded. Eventually I turned and ran home to get Father.

Together, we searched for my twin, but we never found him. We called the sheriff's deputy as the sheriff just passed away from the Sickness, and despite the Sickness, the deputy and my father formed a search team. They combed the woods looking for any sign of Zach. Eventually they found him. Lying on a bed of moss like he had just stopped and curled up to take a nap. Only he didn't wake up when they touched him. So it was with a heavy heart that my father returned home that night and told me that Zach was gone.

I was devastated, of course, but not just because he was my brother. He was my twin. He couldn't just die. Not without me. We did everything together. I waited for days and days thinking it was all some big trick, but as I watched my father lower my twin's coffin into his own hole, I knew that he was gone. That we would never play again. That we would never pull pranks anymore or go exploring. He was gone, truly and utterly gone, and as my father stood beside me in our family's personal cemetery, I couldn't help but wonder when the Sickness was going to come and take my father. Little did I know that it wasn't coming for my father next; it was coming for me.

CHAPTER 2

Neither doctor nor scientist could explain why or how the virus came to be or why it disappeared for six years but then came back with a vengeance. There were theorists who thought that it was a worldwide terrorists' attack, or others thought it was a sign from God that they needed repent (yeah, right), but all anyone knew for sure was that each person the Sickness touched reacted differently. When my mother got the Sickness, it acted like the flu, and she lived for many months before she finally died. My twin, on the other hand, was infected by the Sickness rather suddenly and died hours later. For me the Sickness hit like the flu, but it was the flu combined with something else. I felt hot one moment, cold the next. I had migraines, and every time I opened my eyes, the world spun. It hurt to move, and it felt like I was trapped in a waking dream, but despite all odds, I survived. I survived the Sickness.

"It's a miracle from my God," my father had stated the night before my sixth birthday after he had taken my temperature and found out my fever was broken.

Tiredly I had smiled up at him and nodded. I had a really sore throat, and any speaking hurt, so despite my six-year-old impulses, I managed to keep my mouth shut as my father kissed my forehead and left the room. Uttering a small sigh, I rolled back over in my bed and fell asleep.

The morning of my sixth birthday, I awoke with a bundle of energy that I hadn't had since I had gotten the Sickness. I remember running downstairs to find my father cooking my favorite breakfast. Sausage, eggs, toast with grape jelly, and a glass of milk. I remember sitting at the table, and I had started to pick up my fork to eat when my father had stopped me with a look. Slightly hangry, I frowned in annoyance at my father before reluctantly setting my fork down, silently admitting that he was right, that I needed to bless my food before I ate it. Stiffly folded my arms then opened my mouth to say a blessing on the food before me, only, no words came. I closed my mouth then opened it again trying to say, 'God, please bless the food,' but my voice didn't come. Frantically I had looked to my father, who was frowning. We tried to figure out was wrong, thinking my throat was still too sore from getting sick, but it didn't make sense. I couldn't even feel the sounds I need to make to form proper words. I don't when I put it together, but it didn't take long for me to realize that the Sickness had just taken my family from me. It had taken my voice as well.

My father tried to help started using his contacts at works to arrange meetings with all the famous surviving doctors. However, just like with the Sickness, none of them had an answer to my unspoken question. Why was my voice gone? Where did it go? How could I get it back? The twenty-third doctor finally gave me an answer that I had dreaded since my father started dragging me to all these appointments.

He said that that it had most likely had something to do with my vocal cords being damaged from the effects of the Sickness; beyond that, there was nothing they could do. I was never going to get my voice. After his spiel, tears streamed down my face, and I had buried my face in my father's coat. My father begged them to try one more test. Just one more, but they regretfully informed us there was nothing they could do. So my father had gathered me up in arms said thank you before we went back downstairs to our rental car. We didn't speak during our ride back to our hotel, or on our flight back to our small town or even on the car ride home. There was nothing to say I was done. I was done with all the false promises and failed expectations. My heart had had enough.

I was exhausted and resigned to my fate, but my father wasn't ready to give up. When he had made me dinner, he told me that we would find another doctor. That there was someone out there who could fix my voice. God promised him that there was someone out there. At the mention of God, the food suddenly turned sour, and I snapped. I threw my silverware on the table before I pulled out the notebook my father got for me after I lost my voice. He taught me how to write and using that we had communicated for the last few years. Thought it was a gorgeous notebook with brown leather and crisp white pages, I hated that I had to use it as a substitute for my voice.

So with trembling hands I wrote, 'No, Father. You and both know that there's nothing they can do. So please, no more doctors.' Heartbroken, I set the notebook on the table. I turned toward the back door and fled from the house.

I was only eight years old.

CHAPTER 3

I ran to the hidden meadow, where my family was buried. I didn't stopped running until I almost right in front of the gravestones. Collapsing to my knees, I bitterly looked at the words written on the stone. Tears clouded my vision, but I knew the words written on them by heart. I tried to say them, but nothing came from my mouth. Grasping the grass in my fists, I tore it up, flinging the ruined grass to the sky. I wanted to sob, scream, yell, but I couldn't. No sound came from my throat. Silent, angry tears streamed down my cheeks as I searched for someone in my mind to blame.

It was my fault, I knew that for certain, and I was tired of blaming the Sickness, something that I couldn't see. Something that I was no longer sure had happened. No…someone had to be responsible for it.

Not my father. He was only trying to help. Not my mother. She was dead. Not my twin who had left me all alone. Not baby Ben, I mean, he was a baby. What could he have done? Not the doctors who with their endless supply of knowledge could not find a cure. Not the news people who did not emphasized the graveness of the Sickness. No. None of them were truly responsible. Sure, they all played a part in my trial but no none of them were guilty.

I stared at my mother's headstone as I realized that only one person was really responsible. Only one person had true control out of the situation, and He wasn't really a person. Not with all the power He had. My hands formed fists as the pieces of the puzzles started to fit into place.

The person had to have been someone with immense power. Someone who had an aerial view of everything. Someone who could show mercy whenever He wanted but chose not to. Someone so inherently perfect that His perfection got in the way of helping his children.

You see who I'm getting at don't you. The person who could not have fixed everything but chose not to, was God.

God abandoned me. He could have done something, like He could have sent a cure or allowed my family to escape the Sickness, or He could have allowed me to die with my twin instead of leaving me to suffer and go through life alone.

As this realization flooded my mind, my breathing became unsteady once more. Tears flooded my vision, and it was right then and there that I understood specifically what I was feeling. Hatred. *Hatred toward God.* God had abandoned me in the Sickness. In the moment when I most needed Him most. He left me and my family to suffer, and for that, I hated Him.

So that day as I left the cemetery, I also left God.

CHAPTER 4

That Sunday I told—correction, I *wrote* to—my father that I didn't want to go to church. I didn't tell him that I no longer believed in God (that would come later); for now I just told him I didn't want to go to church. I expected his reaction was going to be something akin to anger or, at the very least, demand why I didn't want to go; instead, he was silent.

He looked at me for several moments before he nodded and stated simply, "Okay. I'll see you when I get home."

Then he walked out of the house. Despite his obvious submission, I expected him to turn back. To realize he had just left his eight-year-old mute daughter home alone, but he didn't come back. He didn't come back until church was over at two o'clock, and when he got home, he didn't say a word.

The following week I expected a fight between the two of us or just something to happen other than this tense silence, but nothing happened. This became a pattern every Sunday for the next six months. My father would leave me at home while he went to church then come home and maybe have dinner with me. That was the pattern, at least until one random Sunday seven months later and he decided to change up our routine.

Just putting it out there, I didn't suspect that my father would change up our routine. He went to church by himself same as usual and came home at two o'clock, also per usual. I was sitting in the living room sketching (which was my usual), but this is where he decided to changed our routine. Now normally he would have gone up to his room and done who knows what until suppertime; however today, he stopped right in front of me. I waited for a few minutes expecting him to turn and go up to his room, but he never did. I looked up at him in confusion to find him staring sternly at me.

I glared right back at him and mouthed, 'What?'

He set his jaw forward before stating simply, "There was a new family at church today."

I nodded, expecting to receive a lecture about how great church was and how I should have gone, when instead, he said, "They invited us over for dinner. I said yes. We leave at five."

My mouth dropped open in shock as my father went to the kitchen. I sat there momentarily in shock then scrambled to my feet.

Slightly frustrated, I stood in the doorway of the kitchen, my arms crossed, as I watched him in silence as he pulled a mug from the cupboard and set it on the counter before he turned and saw my expression.

He sighed tiredly and said, "Mirda, you're the one who said you didn't want to see any more doctors and attempt to get your voice back so you're going to get used to not having a voice."

My expression quickly transformed into a glare as he affirmed, "As such, you're going to have to get used to communicating with people without your voice. So you might as well start now."

I continued to glare hatefully at my father. He also glared back at me, only without the hatred. Eventually my glare broke, and I silently admitted defeat.

At five o'clock sharp, my father and I got into our little Honda and drove over to the new family's house, approximately two miles away. Feeling like it was taking forever, I stared out the window refusing to look at my father. My notebook clutched to my chest, almost regretting not going to church (honestly not for any spiritual aspect, just so that I could be there to kill my father before he said yes to this stupid dinner). Almost.

As we pulled up to the house, my father murmured quietly, "They have a son, who is in the same grade as you and could really use a friend."

I rolled my eyes as I set my notebook in my lap and wrote on the first line. 'A mute friend?' My father parked the car before looking over at my notebook to see what I had written.

He shook his head, his face expressionless. "Everyone needs some form of a friend. Mirda…even you," then he climbed out of the car, shutting the door soundlessly behind him.

I sat in the passenger seat for a moment longer, wondering, before I pushed open the door and climbed out, turning to face the house. The house on the outside was run-down, yes, but it had a rustic personality that called to me every time I walked by it. A kind elderly couple used to own it, but a year or so before the Sickness, the couple died, and the house was put up for sale. It had been for sale for the last four years. It was two stories tall, with a cellar and had three acres of land with a pool. I had never been inside, but I used to explore the grounds of the house with Zach. Being this close to it now, after he died…it was painful, but I forced myself to lock my chest of emotions before I marched, behind my father, up to the house.

We stood in front of the door for a few moments before my father reached out and rang the doorbell. I resisted the urge to flinch as I heard the bell echo throughout the house. We waited for a few moments before we heard from somewhere in the house, "Coming!" Another minute passed before the door opened to reveal a woman wearing an apron that said, "Don't Mess with the Cook!" The woman smiled as her eyes landed on my father.

"Adam! Hi! I'm so glad you could make it! Come in! Come in!" She stepped aside and my father walked inside with me trailing behind.

As the woman started to chat with my father, I stared at the grand staircase spiraling up to the second floor. My new artist eyes traveled over the perfect white walls and dark wooden floors. The only thing that disrupted the charm of the house were the moving boxes scattered around. Half were open and partially unpacked the rest were still sealed shut. I glanced back at my father only to lock eyes with the woman as she took a moment to pause in her speaking.

"Oh. Hello!" she said kindly before she stuck out her hand, and I shook it politely, "You must be Mirda. I'm Sheila Salem."

I nodded, and she smiled then said, "My son, Paul, is outside with his sister, Caroline. You're going into third grade, right?"

I nodded, and she smiled and said, "So is Paul. Would you like to meet him?"

I shrugged, and she smiled sympathetically before saying, "Come on."

She led me through the kitchen to the back door. She pushed the door open and beckoned me onto the back porch with her. As I walked out onto the porch, I froze as I heard laughter and shrieks of joy. Sheila gently pressed her hand to the center of my back, encouraging me forward. Hesitantly, I walked forward and looked over the back porch railing to see a little girl and boy with strawberry-blond hair playing in the grass, beyond the gated pool.

"Caroline! Paul!" Sheila called out to them.

In unison, they turned and looked up at their mother. The girl had softer, more baby-like features with blue eyes, while the boy was thinner and had green eyes that matched his green glasses. I watched as Sheila waved to Paul and Caroline, gesturing for them to come to the porch. I watched, my face blank as the two kids with strawberry-blond hair quickly stood and ran to the gate. They pulled it open and ran around the pool up to the deck, leaving the gate wide open.

Sheila walked to them and crouched beside them behind nodding toward me, "This is Mirda and her dad, Adam."

Paul smiled and said, "Hi!"

I started to open my mouth to respond when I remember I couldn't speak. So instead, I waved. Paul smiled then gestured for me to follow him, and I started to look at my father for permission when his sister ran forward. She grabbed my free hand and pulled me toward the stairs. Startled, I dropped my notebook onto the deck and stumbled forward as she dragged me down the stairs, around the pool, through the gate and back to the field of grass that she and her brother had been playing in only moments ago.

Once there she had me sit down, then without a word she sat down in my lap and began playing with my hands murmuring nonsense.

"Caroline." Caroline looked up as her brother sat in front of us. Without a word, he held up a little basket and Caroline cried, "Yay! Flours!" She jumped up and grabbed the basket before running to a patch of flowers a couple of yards away. She knelt and carefully began picking the flowers. A soft sad smile spread across my lips momentarily before I turned to see Paul holding my notebook out to me.

"You dropped this."

Frowning, I took the notebook and set it on my lap, averting my gaze. We were quiet for a few moments before he said, "My mom said you couldn't speak."

I shook my head, keeping my eyes on the grass in front of me.

"I'm sorry."

I shrugged, like it didn't bother me when all in actuality, my drawings were my only real form of expression now. I put all my thoughts, feelings, and words into them. Not even my dad was allowed to see them anymore. However, I knew from Dad's tone in the car he wouldn't be willing to leave just yet. So I pretended it didn't bother me and pulled out a pencil from the spiral side of the notebook.

"Your drawings are very pretty."

My eyes widened, and I looked up at Paul, further shocked to see him crouched behind me. My cheeks flushed with color as I pressed my notebook to my chest, *He had snooped through my notebook?* At my annoyed expression, Paul quickly defended himself. "When it fell, it opened to a page with a red bird on it. That's all I saw."

Raising a doubtful eyebrow but unable to not correct him, I obnoxiously wrote on a blank page, 'It's called a cardinal.'

I held it up to Paul so he could read it. Once he did, he muttered, "Oh. Cool."

Satisfied, I nodded and pulled my notebook away only for my eyes to widen once again as Paul commented offhandedly, "Your handwriting is really good."

Something sparked within me, and I found myself smirking as I turned to another page and wrote somewhat sarcastically, 'Thank you. My tutor found that this is the easiest way to communicate with me until my father learned ASL.'

Paul frowned at the last word, and I breathed out a frustrated puff of air before I wrote out carefully, 'American sign language.'

His mouth made a little o as he read my words before he looked back at me. "Can you do any of this American sign language?"

Rolling my eyes, I mouthed, 'Obviously.'

Unfazed by my sass, Paul leaned closer and pleaded, "Can you sign something for me?"

His plea seemed so sincere, and I was taken aback momentarily. Taking a deep breath, I hesitated then signed cautiously, 'Like what?'

Paul's eyes widened in surprise. "What did you say?"

I took a deep breath, calming my frustration at not being able to communicate before I wrote what I had just said in my notebook, and a smile broke out across his face.

"That's so cool! Do you think you can teach me sign language?"

I frowned, confused. Paul mistook my confusion for anger. "I mean if you don't want to, that's cool. I mean…I am the new kid. I shouldn't be asking you for anything."

Raising a doubtful eyebrow, I wrote, 'Says who?'

Paul blushed as red as a tomato, and a real smile spread across my face. Flipping to another page, I wrote, 'I was not offended that you asked for ASL lessons. I'm just confused.' As I finished writing, slight embarrassment filled me. I didn't know this kid, and I had just borne a portion of my soul to him. I didn't know if he'd make fun of me. Was it worth the risk? My father's words echoed in my head: *Everyone needs some form of friend, Mirda—even you.* And with that, my decision was made. I kept my eyes focused on the paper as I continued to write, 'Why would you want to learn sign language from a person who can't talk? Who has to write out everything she says… It's going to take you so much longer to learn." Biting my lip, I stared at the words, my notebook tilted so he couldn't see, as I considered whether I should rip them up; this kid genuinely seemed to want to be my friend, so why was I purposely blowing my chance? The simple answer was, he had the right to know.

I handed him the notebook and he read out before he said, "Because you seem cool, and though you can't talk, talk, you can still talk." He frowned then said, "That didn't make sense."

A real smile spread across my lips as I wrote, 'It's okay. I think I understand.'

He nodded before looking at me and stuck out his hand. "Friends?"

I hesitated only a moment before I shook his hand and mouthed the word. 'Friends.'

CHAPTER 5

Shortly thereafter, Paul and I became best friends. Rarely were he and I ever apart. He and I hung out nearly every day. On the days we couldn't hang out, we would text. Him on his Android, and me on my iPhone my father had gotten me when I was nine.

We got into so much trouble together and made sure that Caroline felt included. However, what I couldn't have expected was that overtime, Paul would end up being more than my best friend. He ended up being the older brother I had never had. Honestly, now that I look back, I don't think I would have made it without him and his sister in my years of silence. Thanks to Paul, I was no longer alone.

He did everything he could to make sure that I knew I wasn't alone. He and his sister learned sign language. He sat with me at lunch every day when I started going to school and made sure that when we had group projects at school my opinion was heard. He was the light in the dark days of my life. However, he was never anything more than that. We never advanced our relationship beyond older brother and younger sister. Early on in our friendship, we had both agreed that it would be weird and destructive for us to date ever. (Which was perfectly fine with me.) Paul was a nice guy, but I somehow knew that he wasn't the one. That I'd have to wait…for that special him. Which frustrated me to no end, but I later learned that the wait was worth it. However, before I could learn to appreciate waiting, I first had to learn to hate it. (Which I'm certain drove Paul crazy as I'm not a very patient person.)

I did manage to convince Paul to get rid of his glasses and try contacts. I don't think I've ever seen Paul smile so much as when his crush commented on how nice his eyes looked.

Score one for Mirda!

CHAPTER 6

Paul had a car, and as a kind best friend, he would come and pick me up most mornings of our junior year of high school, unless he had a big away game the night before. As he had no game last night, I knew he was coming to pick me up today, Monday. The dreaded day of the week. I grabbed my bag from off the floor and swung it on my back, before running downstairs. My father was eating a bowl of cereal at the kitchen table while reading the newspaper when I entered. I pulled back my hair and tied it up in a sloppy bun as I walked to the cupboard.

"Morning, kiddo."

I opened the cupboard and grabbed a granola bar.

"How are you?" my father asked as I walked across the kitchen to grab an apple from the bowl of fruit on the table. I took a bite into it as my father said, "That's good."

I rolled my eyes as I leaned against the kitchen counter.

My father turned to face me, "Mirda, I'm just making conversation. It's not like I'm asking you to reveal all my secrets."

I set down my apple before signing, 'I'm fine. How are you?'

"Swell. The office needs me at headquarters today, so I'll be home late tonight."

I shrugged before signing, 'Okay.' I picked up the apple and ate the rest of it before tossing the core in the compost bin by the back door.

My father sighed before he asked, "Are you all right?" I went to the fridge and pulled out my water bottle. I uncapped the bottle and took a drink. "Mirda."

I set the bottle down and signed, 'I'm fine, Father.'

Then I heard the car horn. 'That's my ride,' I signed to my father. 'I'll see you later.' I grabbed my bottle of water and cap the bottle before walking to the front door.

"I love you," my father called as I grasped the front door knob.

I hesitated then pulled the door open and walked out pulling the door shut behind me. I walked down the steps and to the edge of the driveway where Paul's blue Honda Civic sat idling. I pulled the front door open and slid into the passenger seat. I pulled the door closed and crossed my arms not bothering to buckle my seat belt as Paul drove off. We were silent for a few moments until Paul dared to break the delicate pace established in the car.

"How are you?"

I rolled my eyes before signing a couple of curse words.

"That good?" Paul asked, still looking at the road.

I pulled out my phone and clicked on my Voice App. My Voice App was a tool that I used to speak for me. It had certain phrases that I commonly used saved so that all I had to do was click on it and a computer automated voice that I programmed would say whatever I couldn't say. However, if what I wanted to say wasn't in my saved phrases bar, I could type what I wanted to say into the app and the computer would say it for me. It was not as satisfying as being able to speak for myself but it was more satisfying than signing all the time.

'Let's just say I'm annoyed at my father.'

Paul sighed as My Voice App read my message, "Oh no. What did he do now?"

'Nothing.'

"Mirda..." He sighed again then asked, "Are you okay?"

I hesitated before typing, 'No, I'm not, but do you really want to hear me complain about the father that I have?' He frowned and I typed, 'Sorry.'

"No, it's all right, and if complaining to me means you won't blow off school right away, then I'll listen."

'Serious?'

He looked at me for a moment, "That's always been our deal. Right?"

Clicking on one of my saved phrases I gestured to the road, 'Yes, but eyes on the road.'

Paul smirked then asked, "What did your dad do this time?"

Rolling my eyes, I finally typed out my frustration, 'My *father* started taking interest in me this morning.'

"Sorry?"

I gave him a look before typing, 'It's been how many years, and only now does he start to care? Paul he's barely said anything to me since my thirteen birthday.'

"Mirda, he does care for you."

Mentally I sighed before typing, 'Then why has it taken three-plus years?' Paul was silent for a moment before he posed a simple question.

"Why did you shut him out? After that last doctor's appointment, I mean."

I hesitated a moment knowing the answer but not wanting to admit that I knew it. "Mirda?"

I cursed in sign language before typing, 'Fine. Stubbornness.'

"Exactly, you're both stubborn, and so you block each other out. It's like having two negatives and you're trying to make a positive."

Rolling my eyes once more, I finally typed, 'Yeah right.'

Paul shrugged as he continued to drive, "You don't like my normal answer, so this is the best I can do without you kicking from the car after I finish driving."

I smirked, but inwardly, a twinge of guilt pricked me. Paul loved God and believed that God loved him, so to restrain that side of him was clearly a struggle. Nonetheless, I was grateful that he respected me and my wishes. After a long moment, I typed into my phone, 'I can't believe you compared my relationship with my father to a math problem.'

"Yep, nearly everything can be determined by math."

I smirked before typing, 'Except you.'

"Hey!"

With a satisfied smirk on my face and a smile on Paul's, I went back to staring, out the car window, at the passing trees.

CHAPTER 7

Although my face was a mask of boredom as we pulled into the school's parking lot internally, I was in turmoil. I didn't want to go to school both because school was stupid and because I didn't want to have to face anyone in that stupid place. However, I couldn't just ditch Paul, not yet, at least. Rubbing my eye briefly, I saw an available spot. Tapping Paul's arm, I pointed out the spot, and he quickly pulled into the spot before someone else could take it.

"Nice one," he said as he put the car in park. I smiled then pulled my bag onto my lap. As Paul turned off the car, I unzipped my bag and grabbed the small brown box sitting on top of my binder. Then as Paul went to open his door, I touched his arm.

He looked to me, and I held out the box signing with one hand. 'For you.' He gave me a look before he released his hold on the door and took the box.

"What's this?" he asked, looking up at me.

I smiled then signed, 'It's a gift.'

"I realize it's a gift, but why? It's not my birthday."

Rolling my eyes, I made a face that said, no, duh, before I smiled and signed, 'I know, but the baseball season is starting again, and I found the perfect good luck gift that I had to get you.'

He frowned then looked at the box confused.

I tapped his arm again and as he looked at me, 'I promise it's not booby trapped.'

He laughed before staring at the present a moment longer.

Unable to remain patient any longer, I signed fervently, 'Open it!' He sighed then opened the box carefully before gingerly reaching inside to pull out a baseball that had a screaming face drawn on it.

Paul chuckled then asked, "You found this?"

'Yes, I found the baseball. The screaming face was just something that came to me when I was staring at the ball.'

He smirked then flipped the ball around to read the back, "Knock them dead." He read before looking at me. "It's perfect, Mirda. Thank you!"

I smiled as Paul leaned over the center console and hugged me before I had the chance to sign 'You're welcome.'

After a few moments, we pulled away from each other, and Paul said, "Time to go."

I made a face, and he sighed. "Yes, you have to go to school."

Irked, I made a crude gesture with my hands before I pushed open the door and climbed out of the car. I sighed then pulled my bag onto my back not bothering to zip it up, then I walked around to the trunk of the car and pulled it open. Smirking as I saw Paul's baseball gear neatly organized in the back of the trunk, I grabbed Paul's baseball gear then slammed the trunk closed. Taking a deep breath, I adjusted my grip on Paul's bad when suddenly I felt something tug on my backpack. Glancing over my shoulder, I raised an eyebrow at Paul who was shamelessly zipping up my bag.

"Honestly, if I didn't know any better, I'd think you left your backpack unzipped on purpose."

I bit my lip as he finished zipping up my bag. Glancing up at me, I gave a small shrug before purposely letting a small mischievous smile play across my face.

As he glanced at me, his eyes widened with sudden realization. "You did it on purpose!"

I shrugged innocently before I started walking to school leaving Paul with his baseball gear. "Mirda! Wait for me!"

Briefly I slowed down as Paul caught up to me, lugging all his baseball gear. I used to offer to carry his gear for him, but his motto was, "I brought it, I lug it."

So I just quit asking and let him carry his gear. Our school was a one-story campus, so spread out that we had ten minutes between classes. Our school colors were blue and gold, which always reminded me of Boy Scouts, for some odd reason. There were nearly a thousand kids that attended campus, so yes, I knew everyone in my class, but funny enough, none of them knew about me. We reached the two front doors, and I stared at them not ready to give up my freedom for the day.

"You ready?" Paul asked beside me.

I shook my head before walking forward and pulling the door open. Paul walked in with his gear, and after a moment of hesitation, I followed him. He turned and waited for me as I catch up, "Thanks."

I nodded, and he said, "I'm going to go to the locker room to put my stuff in my locker. I'll meet you at our usual hang out spot."

Nodding once more, I made to leave when Paul reached out and touched my arm. "If you want, you can come with me?"

I shook my head, fiercely conveying with my eyes that I would be fine.

He nodded then said, "I'll see you soon."

I nodded once more then turned away. He went to the right as I went to the left. I walked down the hallway keeping my head down. I heard people talk around me but never saw them. I was too focused on my shoes, and they were too focused on their conversation to pay attention to a self-conscious mute. I was almost to the empty class-room that Paul, and I hung out in everyday before school started, when Jonah Haggart stepped in front of me.

"Hey, Mutey. What's up?"

CHAPTER 8

Now to put it simply, Jonah Haggart was a bully. In middle school, he gave me the nickname Mutey Mirda. For that and a few other things, I hated his guts, and although we were in high school now, he still tormented me. He would throw things at the back of my head in physics or purposely trip me in gym. Once he even thrown his smoothie out the car as he drove past me into the school's parking lot. Though Paul did his best to help, he couldn't be with me 100 percent of the time; and as a result, I continued to get bullied by Jonah. I could have fought back. I knew self-defense, but I didn't feel like bullying the bully, especially when he hadn't really physically hurt me, yet.

I took a deep breath then started to walk around Jonah and to the empty classroom when he grabbed my arm. I started to pull away when his grip tightened.

I gave him a look before signing, 'Please. Let go of my arm.'

Jonah laughed then said, "Oh, poor Mutey can't even scream for help." Then his free hand grabbed my neck and slammed my back into the wall. All the air flew from my lungs as I hit the wall with a crash! He laughed then started to lower his lips to mine when I kneed upward. He doubled over, releasing me, as my knee made contact with his groin. Dropping to the ground, I barely managed to land on my feet. Nonetheless, I was bent over, coughing for what felt like forever as I attempted to regain my breath. Eventually I regained it enough to stand up straight. Refusing to brush the stray moisture of water from the corner of my eyes, I looked around the hallway, ignoring the bystanders as I saw Jonah attempting to recover in the corner. I glowered at him for a moment, deciding how to best manage him this time.

Finally, a simple yet picturesque idea came to my mind. I walked forward, and as he stood to confront me, I punched his nose. Jonah stumbled backward, his hand going to his nose, clearly in shock. A moment later, he lowered his hand, and I smiled as I saw the blood trickling down his face. Grabbing my bag from where it had fallen when Jonah grabbed me, I turned and blew a kiss at Jonah before turning to walk down the opposite end of the hallway. "I'll sue you!" Jonah yelled behind me, feebly, as I walked away.

My smile faded, and I turned. 'I'd like to see you try.' Then because I wasn't in enough trouble as it was, I signed a not-so-nice name toward Jonah. The few people in the crowd that had gathered to watch us fight and that actually knew ASL gasped. I smiled then turned back toward the empty classroom. Unflinchingly, I opened the door to the empty classroom before walking in and shutting the door. Bracing my back against the door, I briefly closed my eyes suddenly exhausted. Eventually I opened them and focused once again on the dark classroom. Reaching over I flipped on the light then take off my backpack and set it on a desk. Taking a deep breath, I unzipped the main pocket and pulled out the bane of my existence my Math homework.

Taking another deep breath, I stood and walked over to the whiteboard, grabbed a whiteboard marker from a box beside the whiteboard, then began copying the homework problems on the board before starting from scratch and solving them. The main purpose of this exercise was to make sure I got the problem right and if I didn't get the problem right or the answer on the whiteboard didn't match the one my paper I would ask Paul (the not so secret math genius), what I was doing wrong. He would explain it to me whilst showing me what I did wrong and overtime I found myself getting better at math. Did that mean I was learning to enjoy math? No. No, it did not.

I was in the middle of the fifth problem when the door burst open. Turning around I smirked as I saw Paul standing in the doorway clearly out of breath. Capping my pen, I set the marker and my worksheet down, I asked Paul simply, 'Where's the fire?'

Paul took a few deep breaths before he exclaimed, "You punched...Jonah?"

Scooting over to the other side of the whiteboard, I wrote, 'Yes, but he attacked me first.'

"Well, he's claiming that you attacked him."

Beyond caring what Jonah "claimed" happened, I shrugged nonchalantly, 'Let him.'

Paul sighed in frustration. "You could get suspended, Mirda."

'Good. Now you won't have to cover for me.'

Clearly frustrated with my flippant attitude, Paul breathed out a puff of air before stating simply, "Fine, but you know I can't back you if you end up in the principal's office."

'Yes, but you'll try, anyways,' I wrote before turning to him and smiling at him. Daring him to argue with me. After several minutes, he cracked.

He smirked then shrugged, "You're right, per usual..." Paul frowned as he noticed my work on the whiteboard, "Except with that math problem. Do you want some help?"

CHAPTER 9

Paul helped me with my math homework until the bell rang to go to first period. At that point, we separated, as he had swim class while I had English class.

English class was both boring and easy. I suspected that if I decided to lay my head down on my desk and go to sleep, the teacher wouldn't care, and I honestly was about to do just that when the classroom phone rang. Showing only the slightest hint of annoyance at being interrupted, our teacher walked over to our wall to answer the phone. He picked it up answering loudly before finally frowning and hanging up the phone. Without another word, he walked back to my desk in the back row and told me that I needed to go down to the principal's office.

Unsurprised at the interruption, I grabbed my bag and strolled out of the classroom. There were a couple kids in the hallway, but no one waved hi or bothered to acknowledge me as I walked by. To pretty much everyone in this school excluding Jonah and Paul and a few exceptional teachers, I was invisible. I know I should be used to it by now. Not being noticed in class, or in the hallway, but it still hurt. I wanted to be seen as more than the bullied mute girl or the poor mute girl who sits in the back of the classroom waiting for the end of the day. I tried to be friendly, "speak up," but hardly anyone had the patience or time to listen to someone who had type or write or sign everything that she wanted to say. It hurt but it was the truth and the sooner I accepted that the sooner the pain would fade away. Or so I told myself as I walked down to the office.

I walked into the office and the first thing I saw was Jonas and his parents sitting off to the side. Jonas had a band aid over his nose and a bag of ice pressed to it. I resisted my automatic the urge to smile as the friendly office lady as she directed me to Principal Calvin's office before taking my backpack and placing it on a chair just outside his office. I put on my game face as I walked up to the door prepared for the usual lecture. Gingerly I placed my hand on the handle before pulling it open to see the Principal Calvin behind his desk and my father sitting in one of the two chairs in front of him. Neither of them looked very happy.

"Come in, Mirda," Principal Calvin said, gesturing to the open seat.

Inwardly I cursed before shutting the door and walking to the open seat. Swiftly, I sat down and put my hands underneath my legs, conveying specifically to my father that I had nothing to say. "So, Mirda…" I kept my eyes bored as Principal Calvin leaned forward in his seat and clasped his hands together on his desk, "Do you know why you're here?"

I shrugged before looking down at my legs. Deciding that I hadn't heard him, Principal Calvin repeated his question. "Do you know why you are here, Mirda?"

We were all silent as they waited for my answer.

When it didn't come, my father sighed then leaned forward, "Mirda, you need to answer his question."

Closing my eyes for a moment, I reluctantly removed my hands from under my legs and signed, 'Yes. I'm here because I hit Jonah.'

My father translated, frowning before looking back at Principal Calvin.

Principal Calvin nodded then asked quietly, "So you don't deny punching Jonah's nose or kneeing him in his groin?"

Ignoring my father's look of disapproval, I shrugged then signed, 'No, why should I?'

My father translated, and Principal Calvin raised an eyebrow before commanding in an ominous voice, "Explain."

I took a deep breath then signed, 'He was going to hurt me. There were no teachers around, so I had no choice but to defend myself. Just ask the kids who were there or look at your cameras.'

After my father had translated, both he and Principal Calvin frowned. "How was he going to hurt you?"

I took a deep breath, unwilling to voice the truth and risk that they wouldn't believe me, but as they looked at me expectantly, I decided it didn't matter to me. The worst they could do was expel me, which I honestly wouldn't have minded. So without any ceremony, I signed my entire story. I explained how I'd been going to class, and Jonah attacked me for no reason. At the conclusion of my story, my father's angry face vanished to be replaced by a disappointed one. Principal Calvin's face became hard and stoic.

A moment of tense silence later, Principal Calvin finally cleared his throat, breaking the tension. "And why did you not let anyone know before that Jonah was bullying you?"

I stared at Principal Calvin for a moment; disappointment filled me. He still didn't believe me. His words shouldn't have surprised me. I mean I had expected this, but somehow, they still did.

Disgusted, I shook my head before signing angrily, 'Because every time I communicate, I need a translator. It's annoying and pathetic. Besides, if I can defend myself, why should I need your help? I did nothing wrong.' I stood. 'I don't need this ———' I signed a foul word then turned on my heels toward the door.

"Mirda!" I heard my father snap, and I smirked as I grabbed the handle and pulled it open.

"What did she say?" Principal Calvin asked as I stepped out of the office and grabbed my bag.

"A word that I cannot repeat," my father said quickly.

You can but you won't, I thought darkly as I shut the door, interrupting his yells for me to come back into Principal Calvin's office. Rolling my eyes, I walked out of the office grateful that the office lady had taken this particular moment for a coffee break and that for whatever Jonah's family had disappeared. Taking a deep breath, I walked to the side office door pushed it open and escaped into the unknown.

CHAPTER 10

Well, unknown is actually a bit of a stretch. I had used this door to slip in and out of the school unnoticed several times before. As such, it was with the incredible ease that I ducked through one hallway before slipping out another side door out into the courtyard. Ignoring the stares from the cheerleaders practicing and the I kept my eyes focused on the destination; the football field.

The football field was the place where I would relax. There was something about being outside, up in the stands, toward the trees that made me feel, I don't know, free. I took a breath before I crumpled the drawing I was working on and tossed it on the pile beside me. I pulled out another piece of paper and looked up at the birds on the power lines. I let my mind go blank as I sketched what I saw. When I finished a couple minutes later, I studied the picture dissatisfied.

"Why am I not surprised to find you here?" I turned and looked down to see Paul standing at the bottom of the stands in his PE uniform. The rest of his Baseball Team was on the track behind him warming up.

Frowning I signed, 'Is it third period already?'

Paul gave me a look that said, check your phone. Pulling my phone from my bag I ignored the many missed twenty-five FaceTime calls from my dad and instead just checked the time. It was almost noon.

Unashamed, I looked back at Paul and shrugged. 'Whoops.'

Paul rolled his eyes then leaned against the railing. "How long have you been out here?"

I took a deep breath before I typed into the app on my phone, 'Since the last twenty minutes of first block.'

Paul sighed then asked, "What happened?" As he climbed up the stairs to sit in front of me. My fingers froze on the keyboard of my phone, "Mirda?"

Slowly, I shook my head before typing, 'You were right. Jonah blamed me…' I paused then continued, 'I got called down to Principal Calvin's office.'

"Mirda…I'm sorry."

I shrugged then typed, 'That's not even what bothers me. The Principal's office is the Principal's office, but…my father was there.'

"Oh."

My frustration began to boil to the surface as I continued on, 'He hasn't come to school for the last four years and this time he canceled all his meetings to come to school and listen to Jonah's lies.'

"Well, you didn't let Jonah get away with it. Did you?"

I smirked then shook my head before I typed, 'No, I told the truth. Then ran out of the room.'

"And they haven't come after you?" I looked up at him and gave him a look. "Well, I hoped they would, or at least your dad would."

I shrugged, unable to entirely explain my father's and mine's failed relationship. 'He stopped being my father a long time ago.'

Immediately, Paul turned cold toward me. Shaking his head, he insisted, "No, don't say that." I glared at him, and he sighed before saying, "You know what I mean."

I rolled my eyes then started to type on my phone when he grabbed it and tore it from my hands. I looked at him about to cuss him out in sign language when I found his green eyes glaring hard at me. "Don't ever say that you don't have a father, Mirda!" he said harshly before taking a deep breath. He tossed me back my phone. I caught it and held it gingerly as Paul stared me down. "You have a father, Mirda! I don't…" He sat on the benches just in front of me. His shoulders shook, and I took in a breath before standing. I come and sit beside him.

I typed into the app, 'I didn't mean that, Paul, and you know it.'

He took a breath before glancing at me, "Maybe not, but you've seen me struggle. You know I would never wish my fate on anyone." He looked back down, and I gingerly put my hand on his back, comforting him in the smallest way that I could.

Paul lost his Father to the Sickness. Just like I lost my mom. Paul and his dad had been best friends so when his dad died it was hard. Eventually his mother decided to move them halfway across the country with his sister. Then not a year later his uncle. His dad's brother came knocking on their door and his mother decided, not three weeks later, to marry him. To provide Paul and his sister with a father figure, she had told my father.

That night I snuck out of my house and ran over to Paul's to find him sobbing in his backyard. I stayed with him that night, made sure he stayed alive. Though I couldn't speak he understood that I was trying to convey to him that everything would be okay. That his mom getting remarried wasn't the end of the world. That it was another chance to connect with his Father and his new Father. It took him years to become comfortable around his new dad/uncle and when he started to connect with his stepdad, he started to become whole again. I know this doesn't work for everyone, but in this case, it worked for Paul. (So don't judge him.)

"I'm sorry," Paul finally said.

I turned on my phone with my one hand and typed, 'I'm sorry too.'

He looked at me then stated simply, "You haven't lost everything, Mirda. You still have me. You still have my family, and you still have your father." I stiffened. "He hasn't left you. He's still here, and he's willing to help. You just have to let him." I removed my hand and placed it in my lap, "Mirda." Fear filled me, and I glanced down at my lap. "Mirda, you told him the truth, right? He's got to believe you."

Helplessly, I signed, 'No, he doesn't.'

"He will, Mirda. I know he will."

Looking at Paul and the certainty in his eyes, I started to sign something when a barking voice came up from the field. "Salem! Johnson! Get your butts down here right now!"

We both snapped our heads up and looked down at the field to see Paul's baseball coach standing grumpily on the field.

Unable to take the grumpy coach seriously, I looked to Paul, smirking. Paul quirked a grin in return before saying louder, "Yes, sir!" He looked back to me and said, "Come on!"

CHAPTER 11

Paul's baseball coach was named Coach Peterson. Now Coach Peterson was an interesting person to say the least. He was the type of person who believed the world was black and white. Good and evil. Yes or no. No maybes. I didn't dislike him, but I didn't like him either. I respected him, and I believed he respected me, as well. Which must have been why he didn't care most of the time if I skipped class and come watch Paul practice. As long as I did a couple favors for him and ran cross country with his Team in the fall.

'Why me?' I signed to Paul right before he ran down to the field. He and Coach spoke for a couple minutes before Paul ran to his teammates, who were finishing their warmups.

"Johnson! Get down here!" Coach Peterson yelled.

I pressed a hand to my forehead before sticking my phone in my back pocket. I grabbed my backpack, swung it on my back, before I walked down the stairs and onto the field. I walked up to Coach, not entirely sure what to expect.

I stopped a few paces in front of Coach Peterson and signed, 'What's up? Coach.'

He sighed then pressed his fingers to the bridge of his nose, clearly frustrated with me. (Wasn't the first time and won't be the last.)

"Johnson. What were you thinking? Running out of the principal's office. You know he sent all of us to track you down, and you didn't even make it that difficult." He lowered his arms and crossed them. "I found you within fifteen minutes. However, I convinced the principal to let you lie low and calm down. Do you realize how difficult that was?"

'I'm sorry,' I signed. It took Coach a few minutes before he recalled his very little knowledge of sign language.

He sighed, frustrated. "You're sorry? You're sorry?"

I flinched at his raised voice.

"Johnson, we can't keep doing this. I can't keep covering for you. Every once in a while, yes, but not every day. You're better than that."

Knowing he was right, I gave him a curt nod, indicating that I understood. One long tense moment, Coach Peterson dropped some of his tough-coach act and sighed. "Look, I know it's not easy being able to talk, but you're strong, Johnson. Stronger than most. I know that we all need a day off here and there, but sometimes, we all must enter reality again, Johnson. Including you. Now come on, these boys really need to start practicing if they even want a chance at winning this season."

Unable to hold back my smirk any longer, I let it spread across my face as I gave him a mock salute, 'Yes, sir.'

Coach Peterson grinned as well before snapping to attention. "Good. Now pull out your art book and make yourself useful."

I gave him another mock salute before walking to the dugout.

There I set my bag down and pulled out my notebook and pencils before walking to the coach's box. There I stood as I watched each boy as they stepped up to bat. I memorized each of their individual stances before quickly sketching out their stance on my sketch pad before writing the name of the person at the bottom of the sketch. The reason I sketched the players was to help Coach narrow down what each player needed to work out. So oftentimes I didn't just sketch their swings. I also sketched their pitches, catches, and slides. Though my art was not a hundred percent accurate it was accurate enough that Coach could identify problems within each of the players and help them before the problems became habits.

I was in the middle of my seventh sketch when my phone buzzed. Pulling out my pocket, I saw that it was my father trying to FaceTime me for the fortieth. I hesitated for a second before I pressed the *Decline* button and shoved the phone back into my pocket. He had been trying to get a hold of me ever since I left the office, but I had nothing to say to my father.

I had said all that I had needed to say to him.

CHAPTER 12

At the end of third block I, willingly, went to my fourth block. My favorite class of the day by far. Art. Today we were sketching then using a painting technique called chromoluminarism and pointillism, developed by Georges Seurt, a famous French painter back in the late 1800s. Chromoluminarism and pointillism involved using only primary colors and using the tips of your fingers to dot the canvas and create your picture. No paint brushes allowed.

It was time consuming, but it allowed my mind to clear and focus on the painting rather than my problems in life. I got about halfway done with this painting when the bell rang signaling the end of the day. I left my painting where it was on its easel knowing it would still be here tomorrow when I had art class again. I stretched as I walked down the fine arts hallway and out a back door. I took in a breath before practically skipping to the student parking lot. Once there I started to head toward Paul's car, when the sight of a very pretty girl standing by Paul's car stopped me in my tracks. The girl had long curly black hair trailing down her back. She had a kind face that looked vaguely familiar. She wore ripped jeans, brown cowgirl boots, a plain brown shirt, and a jean jacket.

A name started to form in the back of my mind when the girl perked up. I watched as she raised her hand and waved at someone. I swiveled my head to see Paul striding across the parking lot toward the girl. I watched in absolute shock as the girl darted forward to meet Paul. She threw her arms around his neck and hugged him. I didn't know what to expect from Paul, but I was definitely not expecting him to wrap his arms around the girl and hug her back. I watched in fascination as they pulled away from each other. Paul never let go of her hand as they spoke rapidly for a couple minutes. I couldn't see the girl's expression very well, but I could see Paul's expression quite well. I had never seen Paul so happy as when he spoke to that girl and so when their conversation lasted more than five minutes, I turned away from Paul's car then walked out of the student parking lot.

I smiled as I pulled out of my phone and texted Paul as I walked. 'I'm walking home, so don't wait up for me.' Then I pocketed my phone and tugged on my backpack's straps before picking up my feet and walked the six miles to my home. At the house I dreaded the long walk up to the porch steps, but I mustered up all the courage I had left and walked up to the front door. I tried the handle to find it unlocked. I took a deep breath before I pushed the door inward. I stepped inside and shut the door behind me before I walked into the kitchen to see my father sitting at the table, a clear indication that I could not go outside until he had spoken to me. Inwardly I asked, Why me? Then I walked to the seat across from him dropping my bag besides the table. I pulled the seat out then plopped down indicating to my father that I wasn't looking forward to this conversation.

After a moment my father sighed, "Jonah is suspended for two weeks." Though I was annoyed at my father a shiver of pleasure coursed through me at the news that Jonah was suspended.

'Good,' I signed.

My father frowned then said, "Since when have you become happy because of the misfortune of others?"

I shrugged, 'It's only Jonah.'

My father gave me a look then sighed, clearly giving up on me, "The principal made it clear that because you were a victim in this case that you wouldn't be suspended, but he told me to tell you that if you hurt Jonah or anyone again, you will be suspended for three weeks."

"Even if it's in self-defense." He gave me a look. "Mirda."

Exasperation dripped from his voice, and it was all I could do to not roll my eyes. So instead, I shrugged and signed, 'Okay.'

I started to stand up when my father interrupted me, "We're not finished with this conversation." I flashed a glare at him, indicating that I didn't care, only to find his face a mask of anger. The last time I saw my father this angry, I was a young child.

Zach and I stayed out past the sun setting, to watch the stars come out. The beauty of the stars were interrupted by my father's concerned yells. We had run up to him, not understanding why he was yelling. I had never seen him so angry. Zach and I had pressed close to each other terrified of our father's wrath. Then my mother came out of the house and calmed Father down before telling us to go inside and go to bed. That was the first and last time in ten years that my father had gotten angry at me. Today he broke his record.

I warily sat back down in the chair.

My father took a deep breath then leaned forward and clasped his hands together. "There will be consequences, at home, for your actions." My eyes widened in shock. My actions? I did nothing. I just defended myself when Jonah attacked, so why should I be punished? At my expression, my father's brow furrowed. "Not for defending yourself against Jonah. No…but for one, leaving the principal's office in the middle of a meeting; two, not going back to class; three, not picking up your phone, and four—"

I rolled my eyes before signing angrily, 'Who cares? I was still on school's ground. I still went to one of my classes. Why didn't you pull me out of school then?'

"Because I was talking to the principal about your other offenses." He sighed then asked, "Mirda, how long have you been skipping classes?"

I shrugged then signed, 'Awhile, I guess.'

My father sighed clearly exasperated. "I send you to school to learn, but you disrespect the freedom I've given you and skip class."

I gave him an annoyed look before I signed, 'I learn, just not in the traditional sense.' He raised an eyebrow, and I took that as a sign that I could continue. 'If you had taken the time to notice my grades don't ever drop. They remain almost perfect. So why do you care that I've skipped a few classes?'

"Because it's not healthy, and it's not traditional—"

'There's nothing traditional about me, Father!' My hands stilled for a moment before I signed, 'There never has been. I've lost my mother. My brothers and now even my father only cares about me when I get in trouble. That's not traditional. Not even close.'

My father's face tightened, then relaxed. He reached out to touch my hand. I withdrew, and he froze, uncertain. He took another deep breath before he said, "I'm sorry. I've been so distant. It just…helps with the pain. You're not the only one who misses them." He sighed again. "This isn't the life I wanted for you."

Inwardly, I thought, *Duh*. No one wants this life. He opened his mouth then closed it, then opened it again as he attempted to convey his thoughts. I didn't care though. I was beyond caring. With that thought acknowledged I stood my chair screeching momentarily filling the empty silence as I raced out the back door. Faintly I heard my father calling after me, but like when I had left the principal's office earlier that day, I didn't listen. Instead, I blocked out everything except for the sounds of my pounding feet.

CHAPTER 13

My legs gave out sooner than I expected, and I fell to the ground only halfway to the family's graveyard, my lungs heaving. I took a took a deep breath and closed my eyes, blocking back the emotions pounding the barriers surrounding my heart. Gasping, I pressed my hands to my head.

'Go away. Go away.' I mouthed, my voice silent. Slowly reality faded back into the recesses of my mind, and I was able relax just slightly. Falling into the grass's embrace, I vaguely watched as the sun moved across the sky. I don't know how long I lay there before I heard my father's yells; I just knew by the time he found me the sun was going down.

I didn't try to run from my father, how could I? I was exhausted; besides, I hadn't run away from my father when I left that dining room. I had run from a dream that would never become real. I took a deep breath and closed my eyes. Eventually he found me in the field, but instead of insisting I come home or dragging me home, he simply sat down beside me. I opened my eyes and stared at the darkening sky.

"You know they say that if you wish upon the first star of the night that your wish will come true." I shook my head then pulled out my phone and typed, 'That's not true.'

"No but wishing upon a star can help people, whether they realize it or not."

'How?' I typed.

It was a long moment before my father responded softly, "It gives them hope. That their dreams might become a reality." I wanted to scoff at his silly notion, but the truth was I needed hope so desperately in my life. If I didn't find it, then I wasn't sure I'd find a reason to keep fighting for the life I had. Closing my eyes, I played with the grass tickling my fingers. My father sighed then murmured, "I know I haven't been the best father, but I'm trying to do better. Please, Mirda. You have three months of your junior year left. If you don't want to be in school your senior year, I won't force you to go, but please, just try and finish up this year. If not for me, then…for your mother."

My grip tightened on the phone in my hand before I forced my hands to relax, 'What about my punishment?'

"No punishment. You were right—it isn't fair to you for me to start being a dad when I haven't been one for the last…few years. So this is a reprieve. However, if you pull this stunt again, then there will be consequences. Okay?"

I closed my eyes a moment before typing, 'Okay.'

The next few moments were filled with silence as we stared up at the night sky.

Eventually my father sighed then stood. "I'm going to go back to the house. Come home whenever you're ready. I love you, Mirda, and so does God."

He turned then walked back to the house. I closed my eyes and let my hands rest against my chest. When I opened my eyes again, I saw the first star of the night. Biting my lip, I debated for a long moment, but considering I had nothing to lose, I finally cracked my stiffened fingers. Raising my hands toward the sky, I started to sign, 'I wish for the courage and strength to hope.'

I took a deep breath, and my fingers stilled as I thought about my wish and realized that there was more to my wish than that little sentence. Raising my fingers again, I continued, 'I wish to be more than who I am now. To be more than this husk.'

Taking a deep breath, I lowered my hands effectively ending my wish. Looking up at the sky, I watched as stars began to shine and dance around the single star I had wished upon. A soft smile touched my face and a glimmer of something swelled within in my chest.

It was silly to wish upon a star, I knew that, but the little girl inside of me couldn't help but wish there was someone up in the heavens or something that could help me. That would listen to my plea.

I had been a nobody for far too long. Though my father was partly to blame, God of course was to blame, and the tragedies that had happened in my life, but a lot of it was still my fault.

I realized that today, and I realized if I didn't change something in my life, then I would be a nobody for the rest of my days on earth. I had to fix this, I didn't know how, and I knew that alone I wasn't strong enough, but the one being who could fix this with a snap of His fingers was no help. He had never been any help, and for that I would always hate Him. He abandoned me to this miserable existence and now that I was trying to find a way out from the hole He dug for me, He wasn't going to help. So He wasn't an option. There was always my father, but our relationship was currently a balancing act, so he wasn't available to help me. Paul was an option, but I couldn't do that to him. He had already helped me so much. I couldn't ask him for more help. I know he was my best friend, but I couldn't, it just wasn't within me. I breathed a shaky breath before signing my wish one last time, before I stood and walked home by starlight.

I awoke late the next morning with no desire to get out of bed. Eventually, my stomach growled, and I got out of bed. I walked downstairs and saw a note on the fridge. I walked over and pulled it down before reading it.

"Mirda, I went to the city to work today, because I left early yesterday. You don't have to go to school today, but starting tomorrow, if you miss one more day of school for no other reason than you don't want to, I'm taking away your art books. I love you! Enjoy your last day off. Love Dad." I frowned thinking grumpily, *That's cold, Father.* I set the note aside before walking to the fridge. I pulled the door open and grabbed the eggs.

CHAPTER 14

For the most part, I had a pretty chill day. I mean…I really did nothing but sit on the front porch of my house and draw, so there was nothing to report—well, until around four o'clock.

I was sketching away and just happened to glance up at the sound of displaced gravel only to drop my pencil as I saw Paul storming down the driveway, still in his baseball uniform.

I didn't know if this was Paul being funny or if something had happened that I should be concerned about, but I knew I would find out soon enough. Setting my notebook aside I stood and met Paul. He panted glaring at me, "Where were you?" His voice was crisp barely above a whisper, but to me, it was a death sentence. I was in trouble with my best friend, and I didn't entirely know why.

Raising my hands, I started to sign an answer when he barked, "There were rumors going around school today that Jonah was expelled, and some people speculated that since you weren't at school either then you were expelled too. I texted you thirty times, each of which I know you saw, but you never responded. Do you have any idea how worried I've been?"

I gave a slight shake of my head.

No, I hadn't known how worried he had been, when I saw his texts, I just didn't have the strength to respond. Now I realized that was a mistake. Paul took another deep breath before saying in a steely undertone, "So I ask you again…Where have you been?"

I took a breath then signed, 'I've been here. My dad cornered me last night, we fought, then talked, and somewhat reconciled. It drained me and I just didn't have the strength to come to school today. Also, Jonah wasn't expelled, just suspended for two weeks.'

Paul stared at me in stunned shock. Then without a word, he walked forward and pulled me into his arms, hugging me. I had expected every outcome to this conversation, but not this one. I knew he would be mad for me ignoring him, but I didn't think his anger would dissipate so quickly after I told him the truth.

Tears threatened to spill down my cheeks as he whispered, "I'm sorry I snapped. I was just worried about my best friend. You've been so distant lately, and after yesterday and your nonchalant attitude...I didn't know what to think."

Pulling away I quirked a slight grin at him as I signed, 'Not anymore. I'm going to try to get better.'

He frowned at me. "Why now?"

My weak attempt at a smile failed, and I looked across my front yard briefly as if it contained the words that I so desperately wished I could say. Hesitantly I raised my hands then signed, 'Because I don't want to spend the rest of my life like this.' I gestured to myself. 'A mute, nobody. I don't want to be her. Jonah helped me realize this when he hit me the other day, ironically enough.'

Paul smirked then said, "Well then, I'm grateful you go into that fight with him the other day." I punched his arm, and he yelped then rubbed his arm.

'I'm sorry for ignoring you.' Though my words were meant for today, I also meant for all the time in the past when I had purposefully ignored him. Paul had been the only one keeping me afloat even if I hadn't realized it, and I was sorry for dragging him down as he tried to pull me up.

"I'm sorry for yelling at you."

'Friends?' I signed.

He smiled then shook my still slightly outstretched hand. "Friends."

After a moment we pulled away from each other, slightly awkward, until Paul asked if I maybe wanted to go on a walk. Given that I hadn't really been out of the house at all that day, I agreed.

Ten minutes later, we found ourselves walking along the road Paul talking, me signing my response. Eventually, I found the courage to ask about the girl he had met after school yesterday. I watched as he processed my question then he smiled. His smile was pure joy and as if it were contagious, I smiled too.

"She's a friend." I raised an eyebrow, and it only took a few moments of me staring at him before he responded, "She's in my ancient history class." I gave him a look just before he said, "Her name is Ebony. We did a project at the beginning of the year together. She was a good friend, and just a month ago, I asked her out on a date. She liked the first date enough that the second time she asked me if I wanted to go somewhere. I said yes, and we've been dating ever since."

'So you like her?'

"A little bit." He blushed.

I smirked then frowned as he frowned. 'What?' I signed, concerned.

"It's just…" He sighed. "She's pretty and smart and cool. And I'm just me."

A small sad smile danced across my face at the expression on Paul's face. Guess I wasn't the only one who need a little glimmer of hope in my life. Regaining a serious expression, I shook my head getting Paul's attention before signing, 'Paul, you're amazing. You've put up with me, your best friend, for the last seven years. You're always positive, super funny, very smart, talented—'

"Give it a rest, will you…" Paul muttered as an embarrassed blush spreading across his face.

Shaking my head, I firmly signed, 'Not until you realize that just as you think she's perfect. You are perfect, and if she can't see that then having a crush on her is pointless.' He frowned and I took a breath, 'It sounded better in my head.'

He smirked then rolled his eyes and shook his head. "Well, thanks for that pep talk."

'You're welcome.' I signed back.

We were silent for some time, just enjoying each other's company. It was interesting coming back to life. It wasn't like snap, I'm back. No, it was going to take time. However, each moment that I tried, I felt slightly happier. However, the honking of a truck interrupted my happy thoughts, and I looked up in time to see a moving truck driving the opposite way besides us. Casually I turned around and started walking backward to see the moving truck drive down a little side street.

Trying to remember what was down that side street I looked to Paul who with one eyebrow raised looked faintly surprised. "Looks like the McCollen place finally sold."

My mouth opened to form a little *o* as I remembered that the McCollen place was what was on that side street.

The McCollen place used to belong to an elderly couple who had passed away in their sleep a year back. The house had been on the market for the last six months, and honestly, I thought it was never going to sell. Looks like I was wrong, again. "Do you want to go check the new family out?" Paul asked.

I shook my head before I signed, 'Not really. Let's let them move in first before we go over and freak them out.'

Paul smirked before sighing and saying, "Okay. Well then, you wouldn't want to go back to your house and play some soccer... would you?"

A genuine smile touched then signed, 'Absolutely!'

I was going to lose, but when you're hanging with your best friend, did it matter who won or lost?

Simply put yes, yes, it does.

CHAPTER 15

Swiftly, we walked back to my house, and I let Paul run inside to grab the soccer ball that I kept by the front door for such occasions. He ran back out a second later, set the ball down, then kicked it over to me.

Darting over to the ball I stopped it efficiently with the base of my foot.

Blowing a strand of hair out of my face I signed, 'First to seven?'

Paul nodded then pointed to two rocks beside him. "My goal." Then he pointed to two trees behind me, "Your goal."

I smiled then signed, 'Let the games begin.'

Now I'm not a soccer pro, and compared to Paul I am downright terrible, but even a pro can be stumped by the newbie every now and then, or so I've found. So as I started this game with Paul, I knew there was no way I was going to win, but I wasn't going to go down without a fight. As he came running at me, I tried to fake left but he guessed what my plan was. He went right and stole the ball from right under my nose, by the time I noticed he had already scored the first goal.

"1-0," Paul commented smugly.

Annoyed, I frowned, then grabbed the ball from the bushes. I tossed him the ball. He let it drop in front of him before he reached out and snagged it with his foot. He smiled as he dribbled the ball. I rolled my eyes then darted forward with surprising speed. I tried to steal the ball back, but Paul made sure I never got the chance.

"2-0." And so the game went until he had scored six and I had scored none.

I was breathing hard, but I wasn't going to let him win without scoring one point of my own. I took a deep breath then as Paul set up to take his seventh goal, I darted in front of it. It hit my chest with a dull thud. I let it bounce back down then as Paul came running at me, I took a couple steps back aimed then ran forward. My foot collided with the ball sending it over Paul's head and between the two rocks.

'Heck yeah!' I signed, pumping my fist in the air. I had gotten one goal. He could win the game now, and I wouldn't care, I had gotten one goal.

"6-1." Paul grumbled as he ran over to grab the ball.

I smiled when I heard the crackle of leaves. I whirled around to see, standing at the end of my driveway a boy about my age. He was tall, handsome with light golden-brown hair and a perfect tan. I looked to Paul to find him reaching for the ball. I ran up to him and tugged on his arm. He looked down at me and I jerked my head to where the boy stood.

Paul looked up and frowned when he saw the boy. "Who is he?" I shook my head, shrugging. I didn't know. Paul had an odd expression on his face, "You want to go find out?" My eyes widened with fear, and I looked at him, horrified. Was he crazy? No, I didn't want to go introduce myself to someone who I didn't know or whom he didn't know. Paul smirked then said, "Mirda. If you want to start coming back to the world, this is a good time to start. Introducing yourself to someone is a basic human skill that we all must know." I gave him a look, and his smile faded. "Please, Mirda."

I debated mentally for a moment before I took a deep breath and reluctantly signed, 'Fine.'

We turned, and I crossed my arms before marching forward toward the boy, internally deciding that if this went wrong, I would kill Paul later.

CHAPTER 16

I walked with Paul up to the boy. As I got closer, I saw that the boy was staring intently at me. I adverted my gaze and stepped closer to Paul. We stopped just in front of the boy, and I glanced up to see his gaze move from me to Paul.

"Hello." His voice was gently yet firm.

"Hi." Paul responded.

Joseph stuck out his hand, "I'm Joseph Wilson. I just moved here."

Paul shook Joseph's hand before he pulled away and gestured to me. "This is Mirda, and I'm Paul."

"Hello," Joseph said to me.

I nodded to him, and my eyes locked with his hazel ones.

We were quiet for a moment before he cleared his throat, "I saw you both playing soccer and was wondering if maybe you wanted a third player."

"Sure," Paul said coyly, and I looked at him to see him eying the two of us. I shook my head, and he smiled before he looked at Joseph, "You any good?"

Joseph shrugged. "I'm decent, better at baseball."

"Cool. You planning on trying out the baseball team at the high school or are you homeschooled?"

"Not homeschooled, and I was thinking about it. However, try-outs are over, aren't they?"

"Technically, but I'll talk to Coach. He's understanding like that." Paul said excitedly. I smiled at him then looked back at Joseph to find him staring at me again.

"Mirda, right?" I nodded. "Do you play any sports?" I shook my head. "Oh." At the look of disappointment on his face, I sud-

48

denly wished that I did play a sport, but I quickly scolded my way-ward emotions then listened to Paul.

"Yeah, I keep telling her that she should try out for at least one of the teams, but she's busy with her other talents."

"What other talents?" Joseph asked curiously, glancing at me for an explanation.

I started to shake my head when Paul blurted out, "She's an artist."

My eyes widened as shock filled me momentarily freezing me in place before I turned and flashed a glare at Paul.

Really? I mouthed, and he gave me an innocent shrug before mouthing back, *Just go with it.* Shaking my head at him, I started to come up with a defense as to why I do art instead of sports when Joseph completely undermined my efforts.

"Really?" Joseph inquired as he looked back at me.

I nodded then pulled out my phone to reveal a picture of the painting I had been working on in art class yesterday. "That's incredible!"

I gave a small smiled as I slipped my phone into my back pocket before I unconsciously signed, 'Thank you.'

As I realized what I did, my eyes widened and inwardly I started to panic.

Joseph either didn't know didn't care for he signed back a second later, "You're welcome."

My mouth dropped open in utter shock.

He smiled, and I signed hesitantly, 'You know sign language?'

"A little bit." Joseph signed back before saying aloud, "Since Paul isn't signing what I said, I presume that you aren't deaf."

I shook my head.

"And you're obviously not blind, but maybe you have a stut-ter. Then again, I wouldn't actually know if you do since you hav-en't talked yet..." His voice droned off, then he snapped his fingers, "You're dumb."

"What?" Paul asked, startled.

I smirked as Joseph turned bright red then frantically responded, "I didn't mean that...I mean...I meant it...I just didn't mean it like how it sounded…" Paul glared at him, and I raised my hand to cover my mouth as a grin stretched across my face. Joseph sputtered for a few more minutes before he said, "Look. I'm sorry. I talked without thinking, and it came out sounding all wrong—"

"You could say that again," Paul muttered.

"She's mute," Joseph finally said simply. "She has no voice." He locked his piercing hazel eyes with me, "Right?"

Startled, I lowered my hand and nodded before vaguely remembering to sign, 'That's correct.'

He frowned then glanced at Paul. "I don't know what that sign means."

"It means 'you're right,' pretty boy."

Joseph frowned, clearly annoyed. "Really?"

Paul grinned mischievously, "It's just a nickname. Don't get so excited over it."

"I'm not," Joseph protested. "I just don't like being called pretty."

"You don't have to like it, but it's obvious from the way Mirda is looking at you she thinks you're pretty too."

My eyes nearly bulged out of their sockets, and I swiveled my head to give Paul a look. He smiled in satisfaction. *Really?* I mouthed. He smiled then shook his head before he looked at Joseph, "You're right. Medically speaking, she is dumb. I just forget that's the term for it sometimes."

I punched Paul's arm, knowing that I couldn't actually do anything to make it hurt, but needing to get his attention.

He looked at me and I signed, 'Who's the dumb one here?'

Paul rolled his eyes then looked back at Joseph, who frowned confused. "Anyways. She has no voice, and at least whenever I talk to her, she prefers to be labeled as a mute."

"Really? So what's it like? To be mute, I mean," he asked, looking back and forth between me and Paul.

Paul glanced at me, ready to translate, but I had had enough.

I shook my head then pulled out my phone, opened my app, and typed. 'It sucks.'

Joseph's eyes widened as he saw me type into the phone, "Is that an app?"

'That I created to speak for me, yes.'

"That's super cool. I mean, it's not cool that you had to lose your voice to develop the app, but it's cool that you created the app to talk for you since you're mute…I'm going to stop talking now."

I smirked then typed, 'It's all right, and thank you, Joseph.' I stuck out my hand.

He shook my hand. "You're welcome."

CHAPTER 17

We ended up playing soccer with Joseph for almost three hours. Afterward, I sat on the porch and watched the two boys as they passed the soccer ball between the two of them.

"So you're in eleventh grade too, right?" Joseph asked Paul as he kicked the soccer ball to him.

"Yeah. As is Mirda, so hopefully, we'll have some of the same classes together, so you won't be completely alone on your first day of school. By the way, how are you getting to school? You taking the bus? Or…?"

"I have a vehicle, but I'm still not entirely sure how to get to school." Paul stopped the ball under his foot.

"Well, I'm sure Mirda would be happy to give you directions." He looked at me and I shook my head before pointing at my mouth.

'Mute. Remember?'

Paul sighed then said, "Fine. I'll give you directions, and, Mirda, would you be willing to drive my car to school?"

I nodded then looked back down at the sketch pad that I had retrieved from inside. It was of Paul and Joseph playing soccer obviously, but as I studied the drawing, I realized that the details on the sketch of Joseph were more well defined then any sketch I did of Paul. I looked back up at the two boys to find Paul had gone back to dribbling the ball. Joseph though seemed to be staring at me; nonetheless, as soon as he saw that I had noticed him staring at me, he looked away.

For some odd reason, disappointment rose up in my chest, and I had to fight the urge to tell him so, which made no sense as I had just met him. I barely knew him, but for some insane reason, I felt drawn to him. I shook my head, telling myself I was being ridiculous.

I was the mute kid, who should be focusing on staying out of trouble, not on some boy.

Only my gut told me he wasn't just some boy.

He was someone special.

CHAPTER 18

The next day I woke up early for school. Every ten minutes or so, I would peek out the window looking for Paul's car. But as a watched pot never boils, a watched Paul never comes. It was only after I had just finished eating a bowl of cereal when I heard a car horn. I stood and grabbed my backpack before I walked to the front door.

I had barely taken more than five steps when my father said from the living room couch, "Remember, no punching boys today."

Turning I was tempted to snap at him, but instead, I let a smile spread across my face and signed, 'Yes, Father.'

Even though I was still annoyed at my father, I had come to a realization yesterday. He was still here, even though Mom was gone, he was here. Hearing the honk of the car horn I signed, 'I love you!' to my father before I turned and grabbed the front door handle. Pulling it open, I paused before stepping out, just in time to hear my father say I signed before I walked back to the front door.

I pulled it open as my father said behind me, "Love you too, sweetheart."

A genuine small smile touched my lips as I shut the door and stepped out on the porch. Taking a deep breath, I imagined for a moment that the day was actually going to be perfect when I heard the honk of a car horn again and realized that wasn't the sound of Paul's horn. Frowning, I turned to face my drive way only to have my jaw drop open. I had expected Paul's older blue Honda, only that wasn't waiting in the driveway for me.

Instead, it was a 1964 red Mustang, if my knowledge of cars served me correctly. I had read about it in my history book. As such, I didn't think any of them were still around, but obviously, I was wrong. I walked forward in utter shock as Paul pushed the passenger door open and stepped out. I glanced to the driver's seat to see Joseph sitting there, hands on the wheel, a grin on his face. A smile started to stretch across my face, and I quickly raised my hand to my mouth to cover it. As soon as I had my facial expression under control, I lowered my hand and walked up to Paul.

'What is this?' I signed in absolute confusion.

The deal was for Paul to bring his car so that I could drive to school. Joseph and Paul weren't supposed to pick me up.

"My mom said that she wanted pick me up after practice, so Joseph offered to give me a ride to school to save gas. I'm sorry I didn't forewarn you," he explained swiftly before asking tentatively. "Are you mad?"

I looked back at Joseph in the car behind the wheel. He quirked a grin at me then gave me a wink. I felt my cheeks warm, and for whatever reason, I couldn't find a reason to be mad at Paul or Joseph.

My lips curved up in a slight grin as I looked back at Paul, shaking my head. 'Nope. Let's go.' I started to push past him when he stepped in my path, 'What?'

"So no protests? No complaints?"

I breathed out a puff of air to convey my annoyance before I signed, 'If we hadn't met Joseph yesterday, and talked for most of the afternoon then I definitely wouldn't be this compliant. Now come on. We have to go to school.'

Paul smirked then murmured, "Okay."

I nodded in contentment before I pushed past Paul without another comment. I opened the passenger door before I slid the passenger seat forward and climbed into the back seat. I set my bag on the seat beside me as Paul pushed the seat back and climbed into the car shutting the door.

"Morning, Mirda." Joseph said as he shifted the car into reverse.

I glanced at the mirror to find him looking at me.

Nodding, I signed, 'Let's go to school.'

Joseph smirked and even though I was pretty sure he didn't understand all of what I signed he got the gist of it.

"Yes, ma'am," he murmured then shifted his car into reverse before he backed the car out of the driveway.

On the way to school, the boys talked, and I found myself staring out the little side window at the trees we drove by. Eventually the school comes into view, and I barely heard as Paul told Joseph to pull into his parking spot. I closed my eyes briefly as Paul and Joseph climbed out of the side.

"Mirda?" I opened my eyes to see Joseph had moved his seat forward so that I could get out, "You coming?"

Taking a deep breath, I nodded mostly to myself before I climbed out of Joseph's car and into the sunlight. Briefly I allowed myself to absorb the sunshine when I felt someone's eyes on my back. As Joseph closed the car door, I turned to the forest beyond my school's parking lot to see Jonah standing there leaning against a tree. I sucked in a breath and clenched my fists as I watched him point at me then at his eyes, then back at me. Anger filled my bones at his, oh so obvious message. What happened between us was far from over. Narrowing my eyes at him to make it clear that I would never allow him to get close to me again. Jonah smirked, which obviously meant that he doubted my skills, but before I could retaliate, he turned away.

"Who was that?" Joseph asked beside me.

I flinched, startled by the sudden sound of his voice. I glanced at him to find him squinting at the forest trying to see Jonah again. He glanced down at me, and I looked away sharply. "Mirda?"

'No one,' I signed, then I turned back to the school.

"Mirda?" Joseph walked quickly to stand in front of me.

I glanced up at him, 'What?'

He sighed then said, "Look, I know we only met yesterday, but I do want to be your friend."

I nodded, glancing away. I knew that, and I was trying, but seeing Jonah had rattled me. He was supposed to be suspended, so why was he here. Why? "So I'm letting you know that you can trust me. Okay?" I blinked and saw Joseph staring at me, concerned. I forced myself to give a curt nod before glancing at Paul who was staring at the few cars in the parking lot. I smiled knowingly before tapping Joseph's arm and signing Paul's name. Joseph looked at Paul and frowned as he saw the intense look on Paul's face.

"Paul?" Joseph called.

For a moment Paul was distracted, and he glanced at Joseph, and I was confused. Joseph took a step toward him, "You okay, man?"

Paul smiled then nodded.

"Course."

I studied him and, as his best friend, knew that he wasn't all right. I glanced to the spot where Paul had been looking and saw Ebony talking to a group of girls. I smiled, reassured that there wasn't anything seriously wrong with him. He was just lovesick. I bit my lip then took a few steps forward and touched Paul's arm.

He looked at me, confused as I signed, 'How about I take Joseph to the office, and you can meet us there?'

An incredulous smile stretched across his face. "Seriously?" Rolling my eyes briefly, I smiled. Paul smiled back, then said, "Okay."

"What's going on?" Joseph asked, walking forward to stand beside us.

Paul smiled as he said, "Mirda offered to take you to the office and help you get things sorted since I have something to do really quickly. I presume you haven't gotten a schedule or your papers in order?"

"No, not yet. I was honestly about to ask if you could help with that so thanks."

Paul nodded then said, "It was all Mirda, man. Can you pop the trunk?"

"Right."

They both go to the trunk, and I took a few steps to the side shifting my backpack straps as I looked back at the forest. No one was there. I took a deep breath then turned to see Paul saying good-bye to Joseph. He looked up and waved bye to me before running off toward Ebony.

I smiled as Joseph closed the trunk and slung his backpack over his shoulder. He turned as I walked forward smiling as Paul ran up behind Ebony. I crossed my arms satisfied as Ebony turned and threw her arms around Paul. I bit my lip trying to control the grin spreading across my face as I turned to see Joseph staring at Paul in shock. He looked at me then back at Paul.

"I knew he had a girl," he murmured as he started at them. "I just didn't imagine her."

I smiled then looked at the happy couple and thought, *Neither did I, Joseph. Neither did I.*

CHAPTER 19

Eventually I looked away from the happy couple and tapped Joseph's arm once more. Immediately he turned and looked at me expectantly. I felt my cheeks warm, for no logical reason, and I awkwardly gestured toward the school. 'Let's go,' I mouthed.

Joseph nodded, and I started walking toward school. Every so often I would glance to my side to see Joseph keeping at pace with me. Internally something sparked and I found myself blushing once again for absolutely no reason.

"Mirda?" Joseph asked beside me.

'I'm fine,' I signed, waving his concern away. We walked up to the front office, I started to reach for the door handle, but Joseph beat me to it.

His hand caught hold of the handle and pulled it open. "After you, my lady."

I gave him an odd look before signing, 'Thanks?'

He smiled and I rolled my eyes before I walked inside. I froze as I saw Jonah's father standing at the front desk. As he heard the door opened, he turned and locked eyes with me. Even though terror filled me as I saw how angry his eyes were I knew that I couldn't do anything about it. So I turned and grabbed Joseph's arm. Come on, I mouthed pulling him toward the counselor's office. He followed without any resistance and as we leaved Jonah's father's angry glare I relaxed.

"Who was that?" Joseph asked as I let go of his arm and walked ahead of him.

I turned to him and shook my head before I turned around the corner to see the counselor's door was closed. I breathed out a puff of air in frustration. It was almost seven why wasn't she here yet. I walked to the opposite wall and leaned against it as Joseph walked in front of me. "Mirda?"

I glanced up at him, annoyed. What? my gaze asked.

He hesitated before he asking, "Are you okay?"

I shrugged then started signing my patience finally spent, 'Joseph, I barely know you, and as such, how I'm doing is none of your business. In fact, Paul barely has the right—'

Joseph interrupted my signing rant by clearing his throat. I glared up at him and he hesitated a moment before he said, "I can't understand you. You're going too fast."

Taking a deep angry breath, I finally shoved down my pride and signed, 'Sorry.' Then I whipped out my phone and typed, 'I don't want to talk about—' His hand covered my phone screen. I looked back up at him and found him staring at me intently. My face suddenly felt warm, and I started to look away when one of Joseph's hand came up, holding my chin in place.

"I didn't say you had to talk about it. I just was asking if you were all right. That's all I was asking. I wasn't asking about your past or your life story. I just wanted to know if you needed or wanted backup." I stared up at him in utter confusion. Why did he care? He barely knew me. Before I could ask him why Paul showed up.

"Hey, guys!" Joseph pulled back from me and I glanced away embarrassed.

"Hey, Paul. How's your girlfriend?"

"She's not my girlfriend…yet."

They laughed and high-fived one another.

Crossing my arms over my chest, I smiled despite the nerves I felt in the pit of my stomach. However, despite my best attempt to hide them Paul saw, at least somewhat, through my act. He took a step closer to me.

"You all right?" His voice was hushed, and I looked to see Joseph trying to appear inconspicuously as he fiddled with the zipper on his bag. I hesitated for a moment unsure what to do when suddenly the school education counselor's door opened to reveal a short, charming woman wearing three-inch-tall heels.

She beamed up at the teenagers as she said, "Mirda! Paul! To what do I owe the pleasure?"

"Hello, Mrs. Sanders," Paul said as I gave a small wave. "We are actually just helping Joseph out. He just moved here yesterday and needs a schedule."

Mrs. Sanders turned to Paul and shook his hand. "Well, how do you do? My name is Roberta Sanders, and I am a guidance counselor here at Freedom High."

I rolled my eyes and smirked as she mentioned our high school's name. It was a bit ironic actually. Freedom High, and we aren't free to make our own choices.

"Step into my office, and we'll get you sorted." Mrs. Sanders turned and walked back into her office with Joseph right behind her.

I started back down the hallway when Paul grabbed my arm.

"Oh no, you don't, missy." I turned back and glared at him. He glared right back. "What's wrong? I thought you two were hitting it off."

I took a deep breath before uncrossing my arms and signing. 'It's not him. It's me and…Jonah.'

"What? But he's suspended?"

I shrugged before signing and explaining what had happened. He gave me a sympathetic look, "Mirda…I'm so sorry." I gave him a look and he sighed then enclosed me in his arms for a tight hug. "Don't worry I won't let him come close to you."

Pulling away I gave a small sad smile before I signed, 'Too late.'

He smiled back at me. "There's my girl."

I nodded, and he pulled away before walking to the counselor's office.

He paused at the doorway then looked over his shoulder at me, "You coming?"

I gave a small nod. He smiled encouragingly at me before turning and walking into Mrs. Sanders's office. I crossed my arms and took a deep breath before dropping my arms by my side. With the slightest of hesitations, I turned back to Mrs. Sanders office and walked in.

CHAPTER 20

I walked into the office right behind Paul. He gestured to the only available seat, and I shook my head. I go to the back wall and lean against it glancing at the pile of magazines in the corner.

Hesitating for only a moment, I reached out to snag the one on top when Mrs. Sanders called, "If you knock over that pile of magazines again, Mirda, you're cleaning them up, and I won't give you a late pass to class."

Glancing at her to see if her threat was serious, I resisted the urge to smile as I saw her glaring at me over her reading glasses. "I'm not stupid. You may have everyone else buying that silent-little-girl act, but you and I both know better."

Smirking, I shrugged then nodded.

She smiled back then gestured to me. "Now come over here and help me out, will you?"

Nodding once more, I walked around the desk.

She pointed to her filing cabinet. "There should be folder in there marked *New Student Paperwork*. Find that for me, will you?"

Acknowledging her with a nod, I walked to the filing cabinet. I started at the top drawer then worked my way down. Eventually, in the very back of the third drawer, I found it! Triumphantly, I turned and handed it to Mrs. Sanders.

"Aha! Thank you, Mirda."

I nodded then stood and walked back to my wall. Mrs. Sanders handed pieces of the paperwork to Joseph and started to explain what each one was to him.

They looked like they were going to be busy for a while, so I pulled out my phone and texted Paul. 'You know...the magazines falling last time were your fault.'

He turned around his chair and gave me a look, "My fault?"

I nodded then signed, 'Yes, you were the one who bumped it.'

"Well, you were the one who failed to catch it," he retorted.

"Mirda! Paul!" Mrs. Sanders snapped sharply, glaring at the both of us, before returning her attention back to Joseph. Paul and I looked back to each other.

'Clutz,' I mouthed.

Paul rolled my eyes before mouthing back, "Weirdo."

I smiled then texted him, 'But you still love me.'

He read the text and chuckled, "Hermano."

'Et soeur.'

"Best friends."

'Forever.' We smiled at each other, individually amused by our cheesiness, before I texted, 'What do you think of Joseph?'

"He seems nice," he texted back.

I gave him a look, and he sighed before texting back a more explicit answer. "He's definitely different than most newcomers we get who survived the Sickness, but he's still a good person."

At the mention of the Sickness, my fingers stilled, and I looked up at Joseph. He was asking Mrs. Sanders a question. His face seemed kind, yet worn, as if he was tired from putting up an image.

I raised an eyebrow before I looked down at my phone and typed, 'Do you know if he was affected by the Sickness?' I looked up at Paul as he read the text.

He hesitated typing back, his thumbs hovering over his phone before he finally looked up at me and shrugged then looked back down at his phone. A moment later my phone buzzed with a new message. Glancing down, I read, "He hasn't mentioned anything about the Sickness."

'Well, if he was indeed affected, he probably wouldn't be so happy,' I texted back, thoughtful.

"Or maybe he's just trying to make the best of a bad situation. You forget, Mirda it's been over five years since the last bout of Sickness. People have had time to grieve and move on."

At his words, my heart clenched. How could people move on? How could people forget what happened to us? What we lost?

Just as I started to typed out an angry retort Paul sent another text, "Everyone deals with grief differently." My fingers stilled over the keys as I read his text.

Finally, I took a deep breath then deleted my angry words. 'Yeah,' I sent back before shoving my phone in my back pocket and pulling out my math homework.

I started to go over it again when Mrs. Sanders said, "Mirda, Paul."

We looked up, and she gestured to both of us to come close to her desk. She placed a piece of paper between all three of us.

"I tried to put him in a couple of classes with each of you."

Startled by Mrs. Sanders's admission, I fought against the sudden rise of joy filling my heart.

"Thank you," Paul said as he examined Joseph's new schedule.

Unable to do more, I nodded my thanks to Mrs. Sanders before looking back at the schedule.

"English, math, gym, chemistry," Joseph read.

"Only on A-days," Paul interrupted as he read the rest of Joseph's schedule.

I looked up to see Joseph frowning. He didn't know what the A-day, B-day schedule was, I realized. I jabbed Paul's side, and he looked up at me, annoyed. I pointed to Joseph, and as Paul saw the confusion on Joseph's face, his annoyed look softened.

"We go by A-day, B-day schedule here at Freedom High. Every other day we switch the classes. So since yesterday was a B-day, we attended our B-day classes—in your case..." Paul looked back at Joseph's schedule, "you would have attended Spanish, history, computer programing, free block...and dance class?"

Paul gave Joseph an odd look, and Joseph shrugged, muttering, "We all have our hobbies."

Paul nodded then shrugged before saying, "Anyways, today is an A-day, so your first four classes are the ones you'll be attending."

"English, math, gym, and chemistry," Joseph read again more confidently this time.

Paul nodded.

"It's not that hard to grasp once you get into the swing of things. It will help with Mirda being in your first two classes, and me in your second and third block."

Joseph looked at me. "You have English and math your first two blocks too."

I nodded then signed, 'Unfortunately.'

Paul translated with a slight grin. Mrs. Sanders waved a pencil at me then said, "Don't go all unfortunately on me, Miss Mirda. I did my best to put you with the best teachers. It's not my fault that you won't give them a chance."

I frowned at her, and she gave me a knowing look. "Now don't you go glaring at me, Mirda. You know I'm right. Now you all better get. Some of us have actual work to do."

Paul let a snicker loose before he could cover his mouth. Mrs. Sanders turned her glare to him then pointed at the door, yelling, "Out!"

"Yes, ma'am," Paul muttered before standing, grinning like the Cheshire cat.

I grinned back then waved bye to Mrs. Sanders before walking out into the hallway as Joseph thanked Mrs. Sanders for her help. As soon as Paul and I were in the hall, we lost our composure. He doubled over laughing, and I couldn't hold back the broad smiled spreading my lips apart. Joseph pulled Mrs. Sanders office door shut as Paul continued to laugh.

"What's wrong with him?" Joseph asked, pointing at Paul.

I wiped tears of mirth from my eyes before pulling out my phone and typing, 'Nothing. Absolutely nothing.' Joseph gave me an odd look and I smiled.

He smiled back before asking, "How long should he keep laughing?"

'Not long,' I typed before crossing my arms and looking at Paul still doubled over.

True to form, only a few moments later Paul stopped laughing. He stood taking a few deep breaths to calm himself. "We should get to class. The bell is going to ring soon." I nodded, and he said, "You can get him to English?"

I nodded then signed, 'I'll see you in math.'

Paul grinned, glancing between Joseph and me, before he turned and walked off.

"What was that?" Joseph asked beside me.

Paul being Paul, I thought, but physically I shrugged, then turned to Joseph and signed, 'Ready for English?'

He sighed then shifted his backpack on his shoulder. "Lead the way."

CHAPTER 21

I walked into English with Joseph, my head down. I walked up to the teacher and handed him a note I had written while I was walking.

He read it then said, "Welcome, Joseph. You can take a seat besides Mirda in the back. If that's all right with you, Mirda."

My eyes widened slightly, but I nodded then turned and walked toward the back of the classroom. I had almost reached my seat when someone stuck out their foot. I stumbled over it and nearly fall on my face when someone grabbed my arm pulling me back onto my feet.

"Sorry," a girl the desk in front of mine said as she faced forward. She must have been the one that tripped me.

Rolling my eyes, I pushed myself up then turned and saw that the one who had grabbed my arm and saved me from humiliation was Joseph. Startled by this revelation, I stared at him in shock. A small bit of color touched his face as I continued to stare at him.

"It was not a big deal," he whispered, and I felt my cheeks grew warm because, to me, it was a big deal.

No one ever helped me—the mute girl—but he did without even thinking about it.

"Ms. Smith and Mr. Johnson, please take your seats," our English teacher said.

And I felt my cheeks grew hot with embarrassment. Pulling my arm away, I signed, 'Thank you,' to Joseph before turning and sitting down at my desk just as the bell rang. Shrugging my backpack off, I set it on the ground beside my desk, only to hear a similar thunk on the other side of my desk. Looking up, I saw Joseph sitting down at the desk beside mine. I felt my mouth drop open and barely managed to close it in time as he turned and winked at me. Knowing my cheeks must be on fire then, I reached down and unzipped my bag. Grabbing the notebook on top of all the others, I pulled it out onto my desk, along with a pen, and started sketching when the teacher stood up and started teaching. However, not even a minute into my first sketch, a piece of paper slid onto my desk, disrupting my sketching. I turned and looked at Joseph who was staring at the board pretending that he hadn't just passed me a note. How old was he? Five? I took a deep breath then opened the note.

"Class just began, and you're already bored?"

Against my better judgment, I wrote back, 'Yeah, this class is super easy.' I passed the note back to him. Out of the corner of my eye, I saw him read it. I watched as he smiled then wrote on the other side of the paper.

He slid it back to me, and I read, "Then you wouldn't mind helping me, if I get confused."

'I'm certain you don't want help from a mute person.' I passed the note back to him, and he frowned as he read the note, then he tore off a new piece of paper from his notebook. He scribbled something then passed the note back to me.

"Just because you can't speak doesn't mean you aren't good at English. Besides, I'm good at Spanish, not this English stuff."

I turned in my seat and gave Joseph a doubtful look. He gave me an affirmative nod before looking back at the board and scribbling a note down. Shaking my head in disbelief, I slipped the note he had passed back underneath my sketchbook. I then pulled out my pencil and began sketching a very detailed raven.

By the end of class, it looked almost alive; but as I noticed the lines I had drawn for the wings, I couldn't help make a face of annoyance at their severity. Knowing this wasn't something I wanted to erase and fix didn't help either, then as my eyes glanced over the rest of the picture, I began to see even more wrong things with it, and I knew there was only one thing to do. Fisting the page in my hand, I tore it out of my sketchbook before crumpling it up and shoving my book in my bag. Pushing myself to my feet, I swung my bag over my shoulder before walking toward the class exit and started to throw the picture away when someone grabbed my hand. Startled, I looked up to see Joseph. He shook his head then grabbed the paper.

"You didn't mess up."

Startled at his ability to read my thoughts, I frowned and nodded in defiance of his statement.

He shook his head. "Just because you think it's a flaw doesn't mean it actually is. To me it's just enough imperfection to make it real." He gave a slight tug then pulled the picture from my hand. Annoyed, I frowned, then walked out past him.

Who was he to judge art? It wasn't good. I reminded myself as I walked. I should have just thrown it away. Instead, I let him taking it from me. What was wrong with me? I was still deep in my self-depreciating thoughts when we reached our Math class.

"You ready?" Paul asked, placing a hand on my shoulder startling me.

I jumped slightly before turning to glare at him. 'Don't scare me like that,' I signed at him angrily.

He cracked a smile. "Then you need to stop being such a stiff."

I frowned at him then pushed past him and Joseph into the class room. I go to the back right hand corner and sit down annoyed. I pulled out math notebooks and glared at the problems.

"Mirda, is everything okay?" Paul asked as he sat beside me.

I glanced up at him then jerked my head at Joseph as he sat in front of me as if to say, *Ask him.*

Paul sighed. "Joseph, would you mind explaining?"

"Not at all. I just grabbed one of Mirda's drawings that she was about to throw in the trash. Here."

I heard paper crinkle, and out of the corner of my eye, I saw Joseph hand Paul the raven drawing. I frowned then focused on my math problems once again.

"Mirda. We've talked about this. There are no mistakes in art."

I turned and glared at him.

"Don't give me that look. You know I'm right. Besides, if you were going to just throw it away, why are you mad at Joseph for taking it? That is if you truly don't want it?"

'I don't,' I signed. 'And it's trash, so he shouldn't want it either.'

"Well, he does. So now it is his trash, Mirda. Deal with it."

I stuck my tongue out at him, and I heard Joseph snicker in front of me. And my face suddenly felt hot, so I turned and faced my math problems. I started to go over them again when a hand covered my paper. I looked up ready to punch someone to see that it was just Joseph.

"I'm sorry for laughing, Mirda, but I'm not sorry for taking the picture. It's really good, and I'm just forewarning you if you throw away another drawing, I'll most likely take that one too."

I gave him a pleading look, and he shook his head. "Not a chance, luve."

My nose crinkled at the word *love*. He smiled before turning back to Paul and talking to him about the techniques of soccer. I stared at him, in utter confusion, until the bell rang and for the rest of class.

Most people for me, since I spent so much time watching and listening to them, were easy to read, but Joseph…he was different, very different.

CHAPTER 22

My next class was physics, and honestly, I barely concentrated on it. I kept thinking, wondering about what Joseph was doing. I knew he had gone with Paul to gym, but it still made me wonder. Were they practicing baseball? Running laps? Conditioning? Or talking about me?

Get a hold of yourself I told myself as I worked on a problem. He's just another dumb boy. *Nothing special*, but a nagging though in the back of my mind scoffingly stated, *You're wrong.* I was tempted several times to sneak out and go watch the boys practice, but more often than not I noticed the teacher would glance at me. I breathed out in slight frustration knowing that either the principal, my father, or Coach Peterson put them up to it. I rolled my eyes slightly before returning to the problem at hand. I finished my physics homework well before the bell rang for lunch and decided to pull out my notebook. I began to sketch and let my mind wander when the bell rang. I flinched, startled, then looked at my drawing to see I had drawn Paul and Joseph running down a field. I smirked then closed the sketchbook and decided that I was going to skip lunch today. Instead, I went straight to art class.

I gave a little wave to my teacher before going to the back corner where my easel stood. I pulled it out slightly before uncovering the painting. I smiled as I saw that it had dried exactly how I wanted. I smiled then spread some paint on my finger, enjoying the cool feeling on the paint before lightly dotting the edges of the canvas. I lost myself in the painting and forgot about Joseph. Forgot about Paul. Forgot about all my problems when the bell rang startling me out of my trance. I smiled as I saw my painting. It was of a field on my property. It was secluded by trees, and when you were in the center of it you felt completely secluded.

Alone. I sighed wishing I could be there now when my phone buzzed. I pulled out my phone and read from Paul, "Reminding you to set down paint brush and that Joseph is giving you a ride."

Unconsciously I smiled then typed back, 'Yeah, yeah. I'm going.' I clicked Send before standing and stretching. I covered up my painting then placed it back in the corner before washing my hands. After all the paint was gone from my hands, I snagged my bag and walked outside to the parking lot. I blinked as the sunlight blinded me for a moment, then I spotted Joseph's car next to the curb. I walked up and climbed into the front seat.

"Hey!" he said as I shut the door. I gave a curt nod, and he smiled before asking, "How was school?"

I shrugged as I pulled on my seatbelt.

"That good?"

I took a deep breath before signing, 'It was school. What more do you want?'

Joseph frowned then said, "I presume you're annoyed about something?"

I shrugged. I was annoyed, but not at him. I was annoyed with myself. As soon as I saw his car, I got this insane urge to run up to the car, be a cheerful, friendly…girl. I had to remind myself that that wasn't who I actually was. I was Mirda, the mute girl. No more. No less.

Just as I reminded myself, this Joseph said, "You know what you need?"

I raised an eyebrow as he turned onto the main road away from our neighborhood.

"You need some ice cream. When I first drove through town the other day, I saw a rolled ice cream place, and it looks amazing. I've always wanted to try it, and now we both get to."

I rolled my eyes. I knew all about rolled ice cream. I grew up here. Whenever I skipped school, I would make sure to stop by the shop and order some ice cream. The owners actually knew me so well that they had my order down, but I wasn't going to tell Joseph that.

At least not yet. I smiled to myself as we pulled into the parking lot. I climbed out and shut the door. Joseph locked the car before walking around the front to stand by me. I looked to him and nodded toward the door. A little awkwardly, he cleared his throat then nodded. I rolled my eyes again and walked up to the door. I started to reach for it when Joseph's hand covered the handle. I looked up to him, as he pulled it open a grin on his face. "Ladies, first."

Surprised by his gentlemanly behavior toward me, the mute, I hesitated for only a moment before nodding and walking inside.

CHAPTER 23

"Mirda!" Moses called from behind the counter as I walked into the shop. "It's good to see you." He ducked out from under the counter and came over to hug me. Moses was the Supreme Rolled Ice Cream King in my mind. He was from Thailand and, as a result, had a thick accent that was sometimes hard to understand, but I did understand because I was determined to understand everyone, even if they didn't understand me. However, in his own way, Moses understood me. Somehow. Maybe it was my facial expressions or my body language or his own apt way, he knew when I was having a bad day and what type of ice cream I needed. He sighed then pulled away. "You just missed Lita, who severely misses you, by the way. Stop by later this week, and keep her company. With just me and the boys, she gets lonely."

I nodded, understanding. Lita was Moses's wife, and as the only woman in the family of four boys, it was a lot sometimes. So when I started showing up at the ice cream shop more and more, I became the daughter Lita never had. Moses looked over my shoulder then asked, "Mirda, who have you brought with you into my store today?"

I turned and saw Joseph, realizing that I had completely forgotten he was there. I quickly pulled out my phone and typed into the app, 'This is Joseph. He just moved into my neighborhood yesterday.'

"Wow. So you brought him to my shop. I'm honored."

I smiled then typed, 'Technically, he brought me.'

Moses shrugged and said, "Potato, tomato," before he stepped forward and shook Joseph's hand. "Pleasure to meet you."

Joseph nodded. "Likewise."

Moses pulled away and turned ducking under the counter again. "Have you ever been to a rolled ice-cream shop before?"

Joseph shook his head.

Moses chuckled then said, "Most people haven't, so here's what we'll do…" He turned to me. "Mirda, I'm going to talk him through getting a rolled ice cream, and you are going to make your own ice cream."

I nodded then ducked behind the counter, washing off my hands. Sometimes if it was busy, Moses would call me back to help him, or if there was no one, he and I would try making new flavors. The worse flavor we've ever tried was probably sauerkraut in ice cream. (PS, NEVER DO THAT! EVER!) Anyways, I pulled a pair of gloves on, then prepped my station before turning to the fillings. Now typically, at Moses's store, he has the customer pick the flavor of the ice cream—birthday cake, pumpkin, strawberries, etc.—before he would dump the flavor onto a freezing metal plate, which was kept at a constant temperature of thirteen degrees Celsius.

He would then add either vanilla cream base or chocolate base, depending on the customer's preference, before he would blend the topping and flavor together. He would mix them up, getting lots of air into the ice cream before spreading it out across the sheet. He would let it freeze for a minute before use a metal scraper to roll up the ice cream. After you learn how to do this, regular ice cream from the store looks wrong and boring.

I took a deep breath before grabbing a cup and choosing cookie dough and Oreo. I dumped some into the cup before grabbing the vanilla base. I dumped the flavor onto the freezing plate before grabbing a cup measure and pouring out the vanilla base into the cup. I then set the base aside and pour the vanilla base that was in the cup onto the tops. I then set the cup aside, grabbed the scrapper, and began mixing the flavors together. Two minutes later, I was staring at a cup of perfectly rolled ice cream and toppings. I finally decided on chocolate syrup and peanut butter. A satisfied smile spread across my face as I sighed then took off my gloves and tossed them into the trash before I walked out from behind the counter with my ice cream. I grabbed a spoon from a cup before walking up to Joseph's side. I smiled as he stared his ice cream that Moses was rolling out.

"That's incredible," Joseph muttered a few moments later as Moses began to put the rolls of ice cream into a cup.

"Thanks," Moses said. "The machine comes from Thailand, and my papa taught me when I was very young how to make it."

Joseph shook his head in astonishment before looking at me as I ate my ice cream.

"And you know how to make it as well?"

I gave him a look that said, *Obviously.*

Before taking another bite of my ice cream, he stared at it then asked, "Would you mind if I tried a bite?"

I frowned at him.

"I'll let you try a bite of mine. I got peanut butter cup," he said proudly.

After a second, I shook my head and protectively hugged my ice cream to me.

"Mirda!" Moses snapped from behind the counter. I looked up to him as he said, "Let him try a bite. He's willing to offer you some of his."

I breathed out a puff of annoyed air before holding out my ice cream to Joseph. He smiled then grabbed a spoon and stole a bite. His eyes widened and he clapped his hands together once before saying, "Okay that's amazing."

I rolled my eyes again before taking another bite of my ice cream as Moses handed Joseph his ice cream. Joseph really quickly took a bite, sighed before holding it to me. "Your turn?" I frowned in confusion, and he sighed before saying quickly, "You let me have a bite, so it's only fair that you get a bite of mine."

I started to sign, 'No, thank you,' when Moses interjected, "Now don't go refusing Joseph's offer, Miss Mirda. It means a lot when a boy is willing to share his ice cream with you."

I gave him a look before turning back to Joseph who shrugged then said, "It's true."

I sighed then used my spoon to scoop out a little bit of ice cream. I looked up at Joseph to find his gaze fixed with mine. Quickly adverting my gaze, I stuffed the bite of ice cream into my mouth. I had tried peanut butter cup before, but this time, it tasted different. Sharper, more distinct, which was ridiculous—I know—but somehow, it did.

"So what do you think?" Moses asked as he cleaned his workstation. "Good?"

I hold a thumb up whilst nodding to convey my satisfaction before returning to my ice cream, more than a little confused. I ate a bite more before Joseph said, "It's amazing. Thank you, sir. How much—?"

"First one is always on the house," Joseph interrupted before saying, "After that, three bucks for a small, five for a big one, and seven for the couple's cup." As Moses said couple's cup, I inhaled a breath and started coughing uncontrollably.

"Mirda?" Joseph and Moses asked, concerned, as I grabbed a cup by the water jug. I poured some water into the cup and wave away their concern before taking several gulps of water. "What's the couple's cup?" Joseph asked as my coughs subsided.

"Well, it was an idea my wife, Lita, had when we were opening up the shop. If a couple comes here on a date night and doesn't want two different flavors or they want to share a cup, we give them the couple's cup."

"Wow. Have you ever done that, Mirda?" Joseph asked innocently.

I felt my cheeks burn red as I shook my head and took another bite of my ice cream.

Joseph shrugged then said, "Well, you'll most likely try it before me—"

My eyes widened, and the bite of ice cream that I was about eat suddenly froze to my spoon. I glanced at Moses, and he bit his lip as if trying not to laugh before nodding, officially giving his approval of Joseph. My mouth dropped open, and I looked back at Joseph as he continued to talk, not noticing Moses's and my reaction. "So when you do come out here with a date, let me know how it goes."

At that point, Moses lost it. He doubled over laughing, and my blush became a dark-crimson color. Joseph looked up from his ice cream and asked, "What did I say?"

"Nothing, boy. Nothing." Moses wiped tears of mirth from his eyes as I glared at him. He smiled then mouthed, "That one is a keeper."

CHAPTER 24

We stayed for another fifteen minutes. Joseph talked to Moses I listened. It was fascinating watching Joseph behave. He was kind and honest but never out of line. He was humorous but also serious and so wonderful. Although it was evident from the way he fumbled throwing away his ice cream cup he wasn't perfect, but he was perfect enough for me.

I shook my head, startled. *He was perfect enough for me!* Where had that thought come from?

Still trying to figure out the origin of that thought I vaguely heard Joseph ask, "So you've been there before?"

Glancing at him, I signed, 'What?'

Joseph chuckled then asked again, "You've been to Moses's shop before?"

I gave him a look that said, *Obviously*, and Joseph chuckled again. "Sorry, dumb question, I know, it was just the only way I could put it without making things awkward."

I rolled my eyes then pulled out my phone, typing into the app, 'Too late.'

A crimson brush touched his cheeks, and he muttered, "Sorry."

Shrugging, I typed, 'It's all right.'

Turning toward the car I froze as Joseph said, "I've never seen you so comfortable with not having a voice." My body stiffened, and I bit my lip. Was I that obvious? "Either that or you're in love with Moses." That broke me from my stupor.

Whirling around, I signed desperately, 'No!' However, as I saw Joseph's smile, I realized he was teasing me.

Rolling my eyes, I went to open the car door when suddenly Joseph asked, "What makes Moses's shop so special?"

I hesitated then turned back to the shop, almost as if I had to be reminded of why I loved it.

A small smile touched my face, and I typed, 'It was the one place I never needed my voice. Moses does all the talking, and though he's tried'—I smirked as I typed this next part out—'he's awful at sign language.'

Joseph laughed briefly then murmured, "Really? Well, with how fast he makes ice cream, you would think he would be a pro at ASL."

Shaking my head as a smirk danced across my face, 'No. That's all forearm strength—his hands are just there to grip the tools.'

"Ah." Then he reached across me and opened my door. "At the very least, do you feel better?"

I smiled then nodded.

He grinned. "Good. Now let's get you home before your father shoots me."

Smirking, I rolled my eyes before climbing in the car. He shut the door then walked around to the other side. He buckled his seat belt before shifting the car into drive and back out of the spot before pulling onto the road.

"You think if I asked Moses that, he would teach me how to make rolled ice cream?" Joseph asked suddenly breaking the silence.

I nodded, pulling out my phone. 'Absolutely.' Then hesitantly I typed, 'Or if you want, I could teach you.'

Joseph stared at me clearly in shock, and I worried I made the wrong assumption.

'Or Moses could teach you. He can speak, after all, and I—'

Joseph's free hand covered my frantically typing fingers, and I glanced up to see him smiling down at me before looking back at the road. "I would love for you to teach me to make ice cream. You set the date and the time, and I'll be there."

My eyes impossibly wide, I stared at him as Joseph briefly glanced back at me. "If you want, you can even invite Paul and tell him to bring his mystery lady." He smirked, looking back at the road before giving a little shrug. "But only if you want to."

I hesitated then closed my mouth and nodded silently. We rode in silence for the rest of the drive, and as we turned into my driveway, I unbuckled and got ready to get of the car.

"Mirda." Joseph's hand covered mine before I could get out of the car. I turned to look back at him to find him staring intently at me. "It was just an idea. Paul doesn't have to come."

Jerking my hand away, I signed, 'I know that.' Which of course I didn't actually know, but I wasn't going to let him know that I didn't know that. (Excuse the teenage brain.)

He nodded and continued, "And you don't have to teach me if you don't want to. I can ask Moses."

I gave him a look then signed, 'I already said I would.'

"I know, but you just look so upset."

'I'm not upset,' I signed the admitted, 'just confused.' Then I turned and opened the car door climbing out. I started walking up to my porch when suddenly Joseph was in front of me.

"What are you confused about?"

I bit my lip then signed, 'I shouldn't have offered to teach you. I can't speak. I can't help you, and yet you said yes. Why did you say yes?'

He stared at me signing his eyes had glazed over. Taking a deep breath, I pulled out my phone and typed, 'Why did you offer Paul and his mystery girl to come? Was it so that Paul could translate?' Joseph shook his head. 'Then why?'

He sighed then shoved his hands into his pockets. "Although you were clearly more comfortable in there than anywhere else, you still seemed awkward around me, so I thought maybe having Paul with us when you taught me would help me, would make you more comfortable." He shrugged. "It was an idea, but if you don't want to and if you don't want to teach me, you don't have to, but if you do it, I don't want you to teach me because you feel obligated because you offered." He took a step forward and was suddenly less than half a pace away from me. His breath caressed my face as he stated simply, "I want you to teach me because you want to teach me."

I stared up at him, my heart beating erratically then shook my head trying to get my head out of the gutter. He was just being nice because I made a fool out of myself no more, no less. I unlocked my phone intending to click on one of my stereotypical responses when Joseph interrupted my thought process.

"Mirda."

I looked up at him, a question in my eyes.

His gaze soft, he reached out and took my phone. "The truth please."

I stared at my phone his hand then stared down at my hands, trying to figure out what I should say.

Hesitantly, I raised my eyes to Joseph's then signed, 'I want to teach you.'

After a moment of translating, Joseph smiled then nodded. "Awesome. Let me know the day and time, and I will be there."

I couldn't help it. I smiled back at him, and for a moment, we just stood there in silence, smiling at each other. If I was one of my neighbors passing by, I would have thought that something was very wrong and might have stopped to ask if we were okay, and if it was any other person, it would have gotten awkward real fast, but not with Joseph. For whatever reason, the silent moments I had with him were nice. Most people I had observed, and at times even Paul couldn't stand the silence. However, Joseph seemed to thrive in the silent moments. Like me, it seemed it gave Joseph the time he needed to think and to breathe, then he was ready he would speak.

Eventually Joseph broke out the eye contact and glanced down at the phone in his hand. "I suppose you'll be wanting this back." He held it out to me, and I reluctantly took it from his hands. Cradling my phone, I was tempted to offer him my number, but considering how well me offering to teach him how to make ice cream, I decided against it.

'I'll see you tomorrow,' I signed, and Joseph nodded then pulled out his phone.

"Actually, can I get your number? Just in case you need a ride to school or ride home."

I raised an eyebrow, a half smile playing on my lips. *How did he do it? How did he read my mind?* Completely misinterpreting my half smile, Joseph asked, "Did I say something wrong?"

I shook my head then signed, 'Yes,' before signing my number.

Joseph quickly inputted into his phone before shooting me a text that stated simply, "Hi, this is Joseph."

I gave him a thumbs-up as an indication that I had gotten it, and he grinned before shoving his phone in his pocket.

"I should probably get going."

I nodded and shoved my hands in my pocket to keep me from saying anything embarrassing.

Joseph hesitated then blurted, "Thanks for hanging out with me and getting ice cream with me. It was way more fun with you than without you."

Shrugging, I gave him a look that said that it would have been fine either way. It was Joseph's turn to raise his eyebrow at me. "You really think I didn't have a good time with you."

I gave him a look before taking my hands out of my pocket and signing, 'I didn't talk.'

Joseph gave me a look that said, *I know you didn't talk*, before he took a deep breath and stated simply, "Oftentimes when people hang out, they don't need someone to talk to them. Rather, they just need support or company. Besides, I can do enough talking for the both of us."

At that comment, I cracked a small smile. Joseph smiled back before taking another step forward and reaching out to place his hands on my shoulders. "I want you to know that even if you could talk in the traditional sense you don't need to if you don't want to. It's not a requirement for me. However, if you ever do want to talk just as you were here to listen to me today, I'm here to listen to you too. About anything and everything. I promise." As he finished his declaration of promise, I stared at him in shock as understanding filled me. He had known me for less than a day, but he had already determined that I was a person. Not just someone he could ignore or walk over but a real person that he valued and wanted to include. It was a kindness few, if any, had offered me lately.

Truly touched, I glanced down so that way Joseph couldn't see the tears gathering in my eyes, but then I felt a tap on my chin, and

I had to look up at him. Concern evident on his face he asked, "Was I really that bad? Did you have an awful day?"

My eyes widened, and I frantically shook my head as I realized that he must have interrupted my tears as tears of anger.

He smiled at me then brushed away the tear trickling down my cheek with the pad of his thumb. "Then why are you crying?"

I shrugged. I didn't know why. I mean I did, but at the same time, I didn't.

Joseph sighed then pulled me into a small hug before leaning down and murmuring, "My mom used to say that hugs made everything better."

My body naturally stiffened and as much as I wanted to relax into his hug I couldn't. I was too nervous and too unused to people touching me, but I did manage to place my hands on his arm and lean in slightly before pulling away. Joseph smiled down at me then took a step back to his car. "See you tomorrow."

Hesitantly I nodded then raised my hand and waved bye before turning and walking up my porch. I opened the front door with a slight twist of the handle then walked inside kicking off my shoes before tossing my bag on the couch and shutting the door. Leaning my back against it I let out a breath, closing my eyes briefly, when I heard the rev of Joseph's car engine. My eyes snapped open, and I ran to the couch, throwing myself on it then pulling the blinds of the window open slightly.

Peering out, I watched as Joseph backed his car out the driveway then drove away. Taking a deep breath, I slowly sat back on my haunches as I turned away from the window. Pressing my hands to my heart I willed it to stop beating so erratically, but it wouldn't stop. I didn't understand what was going on with me. I hadn't felt anything like I was feeling now in a long time, and as I sat there trying to decipher what I was feeling, a smile spread across my face.

It was only after that smile that I realized what I was feeling, and as I glanced back out the window to where Joseph's car had been parked, I admitted to myself that what I was feeling was the gift of life.

I felt alive.

CHAPTER 25

That feeling of life didn't suddenly up and vanish when I did my homework or when I texted Paul. Or when I made dinner. When I went to bed. I definitely expected for it to be gone the next morning, but for whatever reason, when I woke up the next day, I literally felt like I was walking on air, like today actually had possibilities. It was strange and felt like the only thing I could do to channel the feeling filling my chest was smile, so I did. I smiled as I cooked breakfast then as I ate my eggs.

When my father came down, he did a double take on the stairs, and after giving him a brief look, I decided I didn't care what he thought. Shrugging my shoulders, I went back to eating my eggs with a smile. Slowly my father came over to the table and sat down, folding his hands.

"Mirda?" Glancing up at him, I raised an eyebrow, and my father took a deep breath before asking simply, "Did you skip school yesterday?" Giving him another look, I shook my head. My father raised on doubtful eyebrow then looked down at his clasped hands briefly before looking back up at me. "I'm going to give you one last chance to tell me the truth."

At that statement, I snapped. I set aside my fork and signed, 'I'm telling you the truth. I went to school yesterday. You can ask Paul.'

"Paul has covered for you before."

Clenching my hands into fists for a moment, I resisted the urge to strangle my father. Just because I was actually in a good mood today did not mean I skipped school. Couldn't he just be happy that I was happy? Why did this have to be an interrogation? Thankfully, I heard the honk of horn and knew Paul was in the driveway. I stood and put my plate in the sink before grabbing my bag.

Turning back to my father, I signed, 'Believe whatever you want, Father. I was at school yesterday, and I'm going to school today.' I walked to the front door, and I heard my father sigh behind me.

"Mirda." I stopped my hand on the door handle. Normally I would have just walked out the door but the feeling in me demanded I gave my father a chance. Turning back to him, I gave him a look, and my father, clearly resigned, stood and said, "You just look very happy, and normally, when I force you to do something, you're not happy."

Compassion for my father filled me, and I allowed my body to relax as I turned and signed, 'Am I not allowed to be happy?' Such profound relief filled my father's face that I suddenly realized why he had gotten so mad at me the other day when he found out I was skipping school. He was concerned for me just as a father should.

A smile touched my face as my father said, "No, it's not that you can't be happy…it's just been a while since you've been this happy, and I was wondering what prompted this change."

Not willing to tell my father about Joseph yet, I gave a small shrug of my shoulder before signing, 'It's a new day. I'm giving it a chance.' Another honk of the horn and I smiled before I turned back to the front door and twisted the handle of the door. Pulling it open, I started to step outside when that feeling inside of me got me to pause. Tightening my grip on the door handle briefly, I realized I couldn't leave like this. Turning back to my father, I signed, 'Bye, Father. Have a good day at school.'

My father's eyes bulged, and I bit my lip to prevent another smile from spreading across my face. Turning back to the front porch, I started to pull the door shut when I heard my father murmur, "All right, darling. Have a good day at work."

This time I couldn't prevent the smile that spread across my face as I pulled the door shut. Walking down the steps I practically skipped to Paul's' car. Tugging at the door handle, I pulled open Paul's passenger side door before sliding into the car. Looking to Paul I saw his eyes were impossibly wide too. A smirk stretched across my face, and I signed briefly, 'Hey!'

It took him a moment of moving his mouth before he finally managed a "Hey" back. Shaking my head, I turned and grabbed the door and shut it before pulling on my seat belt. Knowing questions were bound to come spilling out of Paul at any moment I reached into bag and pulled out my phone. Looking back at him I found him still staring at me and not for the first time I wished I could laugh. Just as melancholy for my lost voice began to fill me Paul finally found his voice.

"Mirda?"

Blinking at him, I raised one eyebrow.

He stared at me a moment longer before asking somberly, "You, okay?"

Another smirk threatened to appear across my face, but I forced it back as I typed into my phone, 'Why wouldn't I be?'

He stared at me in shock before saying, "Because we're about to go to school and you skipped to the car."

'I didn't skip.'

"You totally did!" His voice was so full of shock that I worried for a second that he was going into shock from my sudden change, but the next second, Paul was speeding through all the things that I had every right to be mad at him about, and I knew he was going to be just fine. "I abandoned you yesterday to hang out with a guy you barely know. I still haven't introduced you to—" At that statement, he cut himself off and I bit my lip before finally interrupting his rant.

'Paul, it was fine. Joseph and I had a good time, and besides, you had practice there wasn't much you could do about it.'

"So you're not mad?"

Shaking my head, I typed, 'Not even close, and I think I'm actually going to try and tolerate school today.' Silence filled the car, and slightly startled, I glanced at Paul to see his mouth hanging wide open. Giving him an incredulous look, I raised my hands and signed, 'What?'

"Who are you and what have you done with Mirda?"

I grinned then signed, 'Still me, Paul. Just a bit more hopeful.'

He closed his mouth and turned to face the steering wheel. "Remind me to thank Joseph." He mumbled as he backed out of my driveway.

I punched his arm, and he made a face as he shifted his car into drive.

On the way to school, I typed into my phone, 'So when will I meet your girl?'

Paul blushed before clearing his throat, "Soon, I hope."

'I would like that,' I typed. 'Until then, you want to tell me about her?'

Paul smiled then launched into a detailed description of his girl, of Ebony. I smiled happy then heard a car horn honking. I turned around to see Jonah driving the car behind us. My eyes widened as he locked eyes with me then slid his finger across his throat. I frowned then thought, *Mature. Real mature.* Then he sped up by about twenty miles and jerked his car around ours into the opposite lane before passing by us then cutting in front of us.

"What the—?" Paul yelled as he slammed on the brakes. We screeched to a halt, and we both watched as Jonah sped away. "Rude. That guy should get a ticket. Did you get his license plate?"

I hesitated then typed into my phone, 'It was Jonah.'

"What?" Paul asked, looking at me. "Are you sure?"

Nodding, I typed into my phone, 'I saw him, Paul.' Then anger filled my bones as I typed, 'Just because he's suspended doesn't mean he's going to stop tormenting me.'

Paul shook his head. "That's it. You're going to come to practice with us. It's not safe for you to be walking home by yourself or driving home." I turned and glared at Paul. He glared back as he said, "I'm right and you know it."

'Fine, but we can't tell Joseph about this or about Jonah,' I typed into my phone as Paul continued to drive to school. 'This is a need-to-know information. If he asks what's wrong, we have to just change the topic.'

"Are you certain that's a good idea?" Paul said as he pulled into the school's parking lot.

Shrugging I typed, 'I don't know but we barely know the guy, and I don't want him to put in the place that he has to choose a side. He has the right to choose.'

"He also has the right to know being our friend."

I took a deep breath before typing, 'Not yet.'

Paul pulled into a spot parked the car before turning and glaring at me. I glared back, and eventually, he caved.

He rolled his eyes, knowing he had lost the battle. "Fine. We'll do it your way."

I nodded my thanks then turned to open my door to see Joseph running up to the car. I watched as he stopped just in front panted for a second before pulling my car door open.

"Morning."

'Morning,' I signed before grabbing my bag and stepping out of the car. Joseph shut the door behind me as I throw my backpack over my shoulder, 'Thanks,' I signed.

Nodding, he hesitated then said nervously, "I would have picked you up, but Paul called dibs."

I blushed slightly before signing, 'It's all right. I needed to bother my best friend, anyways.'

Joseph frowned then nodded. "Sorry it took me a second."

I nodded then looked over as I heard the car door slammed. I looked to the other side of the car to see Paul looking distractedly looking around the parking lot.

I smiled then as Joseph said, "Paul?"

Paul blinked then looked to Joseph, "Hey, Joseph. How are things?" Joseph smiled then looked down at me.

I smiled at him before looking at Paul. 'Go,' I signed. 'I'll help Joseph figure out his B-day classes. We'll be in the usual classroom.'

Paul grinned then said, "I so owe you. Thank you." He rushed forward and gave us both a hug before turning and running off.

Joseph and I grinned as we watched Paul run off to a spot in the back corner.

"Do you think we're bad friends encouraging Paul to chase after a crush?" Joseph asked beside me.

I smiled then shook my head before grabbing his arm. He looked at me, and I gestured to the school.

He nodded then walked with me into the school.

CHAPTER 26

I led Joseph to an empty classroom and wrote my schedule on the board before writing, 'Pull out your schedule please.' Stepping back, I let him read the board before erasing what I wrote. Turning back to Joseph, I watched as he rummaged through his bag before finally pulling out a folded piece of paper. Handing it to me I opened it before scanning is b-day schedule.

First block, Spanish. Second block was computer programing and history. Third block was a free block, and his last block was a dance class. I looked up at him, surprise on my face.

"What?" he asked. "Is something wrong?" I shook my head as he crossed his arms. "Well, what is it then?"

I hesitated then signed bluntly, 'You take dance?'

He nodded sheepishly then asked, "It's a hobby of mine. Is that weird?"

I shook my head then signed, 'Unexpected.' He frowned, and I turned and wrote the word on the board before turning back.

He nodded then said, "That's a kind way to put it."

I shrugged, and he smiled. I felt myself blush slightly and quickly scolded myself before gesturing him over. He uncrossed his arms and walked over.

I handed him his schedule before turning and writing on the board. 'So you have a completely different schedule than Paul, but the same lunch.' I turned and took a step away so he could read the message. He read it then afterward nodded. I took that as a sign that I could continue writing. I walked back to the board and wrote, 'However, we do have the same second block class together and, afterward, the same lunch.'

I took a step to the side as he read a smile crossed his face. "Sweet." I gave a small smile until he turned and looked at me.

At that I quickly clear my face of any emotion before signing, 'Can I see your schedule again?' He frowned, and I pointed to the schedule in his hand. He looked down at it then up at me.

"You want it?"

I nodded, and he quickly handed it over to me. I took it then looked at his third block again. A free block with Mrs. Waltman. Paul knew her, and if Joseph wanted, he could have his study hall transferred to somewhere else. Say the same art class with me and Paul. I bit my lip then looked at Joseph, who was staring at the schedule over my shoulder.

"Is something wrong?" he asked as he saw the look on my face.

I shook my head then walked to the board and erased the previous messages before I wrote, 'How attached are you to your free period?'

He read the message then shrugged, "Not much."

I nodded then walked back to the board as a hopeful smile crept over my lips.

'Paul and I have the same art block. Would you like to come join us? Our art teacher won't mind. You can do homework or whatever in the back of the class while I paint, and Paul learns about what art project they're starting.' I took a step back and read the message before stepping to the side biting my lip. I watched Joseph's face as I capped the marker in my hand. I tried to read his expression, but he kept it closely guarded as he read. Then at the end he looked at me and smiled.

"You wouldn't mind me watching you work?"

I shrugged. If this was the price, I had to pay to spend more time with him then I would pay it.

"Then yeah. I would love to do that. What do I have to do in order to come and barge in on your class."

I smiled then turned and signed, 'Leave that to Paul.'

Joseph hesitated until he saw Paul's name and nodded. Even if he didn't understand the symbols I signed, he got the message. Paul would take care of things.

"Okay."

I nodded then walked over to a desk and sat crossed legged on top of it. "So how are you from the last time I saw you?"

I smiled then signed, 'Good. You?'

He smiled then said, "Got home, and Dan was painting the kitchen."

Frowning at his oddly worded statement I hesitated then signed, 'Dan?'

He nodded then said, "He's my guardian."

Nodding wordlessly, I hesitated a moment more before asking, "Why?"

Joseph smirked, "He was attempting to appease his wife. It worked sorta. She was happy that we were painting, but she didn't like the pale blue we chose and wanted a sky blue, so we went back to the store got new pain and redid the entire kitchen." He chuckled, and I smiled briefly before raising a hand. He raised an eyebrow as I lowered my hand then signed, 'Can I ask a question?' He translated in his head then nodded. I hesitated prepared to sign my question when I realized he might not understand it.

So I hopped off the table and walked to the board. I uncapped the pen and wrote, 'What do you mean by guardian? Where are your parents?' I turned back to Joseph to watch a flash of pain cross his face before a mask covered his face in the form of a sad smile. 'Joseph?'

"They passed away from the last wave of the Sickness."

I put a hand to my mouth as I realized that in the city, with so many people, the Sickness lasted much longer than it did here in the country. Then I remembered waiting at one doctor's office watching the news as they reported about how the Sickness hadn't stopped. I was so worried about my voice that it didn't register to me that people were still suffering from a strand then an active virus. I was just trying to comprehend that I would never get my voice back and that it was God's fault. I never thought of all the other people suffering like Joseph's parents.

With my heart in my throat, I limply signed, 'I'm so sorry.'

Joseph shrugged. "It's all right."

However, I could see in his eyes that it wasn't all right. Tears threatened to spill from my eyes as the sudden emotion invading my chest, and I turned to the whiteboard. With my hands trembling, I raised my dry erase marker and wrote, 'I lost my mom and my brothers to the Sickness."

Stepping aside so Joseph could read my words, I brushed away the moisture to prevent the tears as I added numbly, 'Paul lost his dad.' Capping the pen roughly, I turned and walked to my usual table. Forcing myself to act naturally, I sat on the table and looked down at my hands unable to look at Joseph.

I couldn't believe I had thought he had been unaffected by the Sickness; it was so obvious that he was. From his actions, his words… and…I just judged him…before I really knew him. However, before the shame could really sink in, I felt a hand on my shoulder. Looking up I saw Joseph smiling weakly down at me.

"I'm sorry too."

My heart ached momentarily but then faded as Joseph sat on the table next to me. He took a deep breath then stated simply, "At the time of the Sickness, they…Dan and Sharol…they were my next-door neighbors. However, they lost their children to the Sickness, and I lost my family. We were a perfect match." He took a deep breath, and I saw a hint of a sad smile on his face as he murmured, "I haven't always treated them right, but they've always been patience and kind to me. They even took me with them when they decided to move and start anew."

I found myself smiling for no particular reason, and I looked down at his hands resting on his lap. With new found courage, I reached out and took his hand and turned it over so his palm was right side up.

Slowly, as for him not to miss a single word, I traced on his palm the words 'Well, I for one am glad they decided to move here and that you were able to come with them.' My hands stilled, and I wanted to look up at Joseph to see his reaction, but the burning in my cheeks prevented me from doing much more than taking little nervous breaths.

After what felt like forever, I felt a finger touch my chin, encouraging me to look up. Despite my nerves, I glanced up to find Joseph smiling down at me. "Thanks." A small, helpless smile touched my face, and I acknowledged his thanks with a curt nod. (Which I want to smack myself for now, but at the time, I didn't know how else to respond.) We sat in a comfortable silence until first bell rang at which point. I walked to the board and erased our work before turning to grab my bag only to find Joseph holding it out to me.

'Thanks,' I signed, taking it. He winked at me before walking to the classroom door and holding it open for me.

Taking a deep breath, I nodded then walked out with Joseph into the throng out of bustling students.

CHAPTER 27

After I directed Joseph on where to go for his first class, I turned the opposite way and walked to my first class. ASL.

As I was already pretty much an expert at ASL I didn't really need to take this class, but as it was an easy class and the teacher actually attempted to include me, so I kept taking the class.

Giving my usual curt nod to the teacher, I swiftly walked to the to my usual spot in the back of class before pulling out my sketchbook. I had just gotten out my pen to start sketching when I heard a loud thud. I looked up to see a girl with black hair sitting in the seat in front of me. She looked very familiar, and as she turned to face me, I recognized her as Paul's girlfriend, Ebony, and I recognized her as the girl in ASL who knew nearly as much ASL as I did but sat in the front row answering all the teacher's questions. Today however she had uncharacteristically moved to the second to last row. Why?

Then she turned around and said, "Hi."

I signed back, 'Hello."

She smiled then stuck out her hand. "We've never been properly introduced. I'm Ebony Ezekiel."

I shook her hand before pulling back and signing, 'I'm Mirda Johnson.'

She smiled then said, "Paul talks about you a lot."

'Probably not as much as he talks about you,' I signed back.

She blushed before saying, "Paul said that you needed a ride home from school today, and I don't have cheer practice, so...?"

'Sure,' I signed.

She nodded. "Cool."

We sat there in awkward silence for a few minutes. "So it's a little sad that we've been in the same class all year and never introduced ourselves to one another to until I started dating Paul."

Shrugging I signed, 'Well, as you can see, I don't talk much.'

She smiled then signed back, "In this class, we don't have to."

I gave a small smile, and she smiled back before facing forward as the bell rang. During class Ebony never let me fade into the background when we had to do partner work without any encouragement she would turn around and start signing. In between activities and the teacher talking, we would sign questions to one another. I learned that her favorite color was indeed ebony. I also learned that she had been the one to peruse Paul not the other way around. Paul had never suspected a girl like Ebony would go for a guy like him, so she surprised him one day in their ancient history class by asking him to be her partner on a project. He said yes and as soon as they started doing the project they just clicked. Ebony blushed every time she talked about him, and a smile lit up her face. I managed a smile as I realized that she really did like him. I didn't know if it was love yet, but I knew that she didn't have plans to break my best friends heart anytime soon.

Toward the end of class, I turned to her and signed, 'Has he told you much about his family yet?'

Shaking her head, she murmured, "Not really." She cleared her throat then murmured quietly. "He's told me about his sister and the that his mom remarried, but other than that, not much."

I nodded then signed, 'A word of advice: have an open mind when he opens up to you about his family. It's a sensitive subject for him, and he is still a little…worked up about it.'

She nodded then said, "Thanks. I'll try to keep that in mind."

I smiled then waited about thirty more seconds before the bell rang signaling the end of class. I stood and gathered my notebook. "You know, you really are good," Ebony said as we walked out of class.

'What?' I signed.

She gestured the notebook I was carrying with her free hand. "Your art. You have a gift."

I shook my head and clutched the notebook to my chest.

She smiled then said, "Okay. Well, if you ever change your mind, I happen to know a few people who wouldn't mind helping you to publish some of your work."

'Thanks,' I signed before turning my head to see Joseph at the end of the hallway looking around.

Ebony elbowed me. "Is that the new kid? Paul mentioned him." I nodded, and she grinned. "He's cute."

I blushed, and she gasped shock evident in her gaze. Concerned that something was wrong, I signed, 'What?'

"You like him." I shook my head, denying her accusation. "Yes, you do. Admit it." I shook my head more fervently before moving slightly toward Joseph. She sighed, frustrated. "Fine. Don't admit it, but this conversation isn't over." She unexpectedly moved forward and hugged me. "Have fun and stay safe. Though he's cute, you never know." Then she backed away and smiled. "Bye, girl!" She turned and walked down the hall out of sight.

I stared after her in confusion.

"Was that Paul's girlfriend?" Joseph asked and jumped as suddenly he was next to me. "Sorry," Joseph muttered.

I shook my head before signing, 'It's fine.' I turned and started walking to the computer lab.

"So was that Paul's girlfriend?" Joseph repeated as he caught up to me.

I nodded.

"What's she like?"

I gave a small smile before turning to him. 'She's sweet.'

CHAPTER 28

Joseph and I walked into class right on time. Bravely Joseph walked up to the teacher by himself while I took my seat in the back corner of the class. Since I had created my own app and apparently was a genius with a computer, the teacher let me sit in the back corner and block most of what she was saying out. I took a breath as I signed on to the desktop when suddenly Joseph sat in the seat beside me.

I frowned at him in confusion as he pulled out a piece of paper and typed what it said on it into the username and password section. Joseph looked up at me and asked, "What?" I turned back to computer and pulled up word. I typed into the top line.

'Typically, the teacher doesn't sit anyone in the back row.'

"Well, I guess I'm special," he murmured to me before the teacher started talking. I listened briefly to what she said before pulling up the assignment she had me doing to pass the class. I was creating a complex landscape that employed movable features. It was slightly difficult especially since I was adding in layers to the detailing of the trees in the background, but I was getting it done. It was worth the extra time I had added to the project. I typed a few more pieces of code before looking over to see Joseph staring at the code intently.

I pulled up the word document and typed, 'What?'

He frowned the pointed at a line of code that I had written a few days ago. "This isn't right."

'Why?'

He bit his lip then asked, "Can I use your keyboard?"

I looked up at the teacher to see her still focusing on the rest of class. I frowned in confusion then looked back to Joseph in confusion and nodded. He reached out and took my keyboard. He went up to the line of code and deleted about half of it before retyping it. My eyes widened as I read what he had typed.

"Try that," he said.

I nodded then clicked Apply Code at the bottom of the screen. Suddenly the detail in the third tree I had been struggling to code was perfect.

My mouth dropped open, and I looked from Joseph to the teacher to the computer before back to Joseph.

"What?" he asked modestly before returning back to his own computer.

I shut my mouth and looked down at my lap as the pieces clicked together in my mind. The teacher let Joseph sit in the back row, even though he was brand-new. He wasn't overwhelmed by the prospect of joining a computer class toward the end of the school year. How he was able to help me with code. I looked back up at Joseph to find him starting on the project the class was working on: a simple game. He was flying through the code, and it confirmed my suspicious. He glanced over at me and paused in typing a line of code.

"What?" he asked.

I turned slightly and typed into my word program, 'Did you take an AP computer course before coming here?'

He nodded. "Yeah, and I've always had a knack with comput-ers." Then he frowned then said, "I hope you weren't offended by me helping you with that line of code. I mean your code—it was good, but it was just overly complicated."

I shook my head then typed, 'I'm not offended. I'm just no lon-ger confused as to why the teacher put you in the back row. Thanks, by the way.'

He grinned then said, "You're welcome." Then he pulled up his own word program and typed, "I still want details about Ebony and Paul."

I frowned then typed, 'Your project?'

"Will get done, but details now please."

He gave me a pleading look, and I breathed out a huff of air before typing, 'Fine.' I took another breath before typing, 'They really like each other. That much is obvious, but Paul is still holding back, meaning he's hesitant about getting close.'

"So he needs encouragement?"

I bit my lip then shrugged. 'Probably.'

"I got you." I turned to give him a look, and he nodded before typing, "Bro power." I made a face then shook my head, smirking. "What?" Joseph typed.

I wiped a tear from my eye before typing, 'I'll let you encourage him as long as you don't say bro power ever again.'

"Deal," Joseph typed, chuckling.

I smiled at him then looked up to see the teacher glaring at us.

I averted my gaze and typed, 'Teacher glaring. We have to get back to work.' I let Joseph read what I typed really quickly before I exited out of the Word document and worked on my project. I had worked on it for a couple of minutes before I felt a tap on my shoulder. I looked to see Joseph staring at me.

'What?' I signed glancing at the teacher to see her focusing on a student.

He smiled at me then signed, 'Thank you.'

Nodding, I signed back, 'You're welcome. Now work.'

He smiled then muttered, "Yes, ma'am."

CHAPTER 29

For the rest of class, Joseph and I worked in a comfortable silence. Occasionally we would help each other, but we both knew what we were doing so there was no point. The fact that we were there supporting each other was enough. At the end of class, I shut off my computer and cracked my neck. I stretched then turned to Joseph who was still working on his project. 'Joseph,' I signed in front of his face. He blinked as if he didn't see me. I took a deep breath then touched his hand that was lingering on the keyboard. He flinched then looked at me. I pulled my hand back, 'Sorry. It's just class ended and lunch—" Then his hand covered the both of mine stopping me from signing the rest of my sentence.

"It's okay. You just startled me." Then he turned back to his computer and let go of my hands. I lowered my hands to my stomach as he quickly saved his project then turned it off before turning back to me. He smiled at me before reaching down and grabbing his bad.

"So lunch?" I nodded then grabbed my own bag and stood up.

He looked down at my hand and I quickly crossed my arms hiding my hand from sight. *Note to self* I thought *never do that again.* I jerked my head to the door, and Joseph cleared his throat before nodding. He followed me out into the hallway. I walked to the corner and signed to Joseph. 'Paul will meet us here.' He nodded and looked around nervously at the crowd of students. I gave a small smile as he stepped closer to me to avoid a boy holding his workout gear.

"Who knew high schools were so dangerous?" he muttered sarcastically. I shrugged my shoulder then saw Paul walking toward us. I waved and he quickly walked over.

"Hey you ready for lunch?"

I nodded as Joseph said, "Absolutely."

"Cool then, follow me."

We walked into the lunch room, and I pressed myself toward Paul ensuring that I didn't get swept away with the crowd. Then I felt a hand on my arm and quickly looked to see Joseph holding onto me. He gave a sheepish shrug, and I raised an eyebrow then faced forward. *No one wants to get swept away in the crowd*, I told myself as we walked to the cafeteria.

We go to the back left hand corner near the bathrooms and set our stuff down.

"So what do you recommend for lunch?" Joseph asked as we walked to the lunch line.

I shrugged. I didn't typically get lunch. I would maybe get a water then would steal some fries off of Paul's plate. The reason I didn't get lunch from the school wasn't because the lunch was bad, it actually was really good I was just never really hungry at lunch time.

"For your first time, I recommend a burger." Joseph nodded then said, "Burger it is then." Then Joseph looked at me. "What are you getting?"

'Nothing,' I signed.

He frowned and at first, I thought he didn't get what I said but then he asked, "Why not? Forgot your lunch money?"

Paul snickered as I rolled my eyes, 'No. I'm not hungry.'

"Then why are you standing in line with us."

'Because I am thirsty,' I signed as I moved to the front of the line. I walked up to the lunch lady who smiled kindly at me. I smiled back then pointed at a water bottle. She nodded then grabbed one and set it on the counter. I handed her a dollar and took the water. I waited off to the side as Paul ordered a hot dog and fries, then we both waited together as Joseph ordered his burger.

'I need a favor.'

I signed he nodded. "Anything."

'Can you talk to Joseph's study hall teacher and getting him transferred into our art class?'

'Sure. Ms. Long won't mind.' I shook my head and signed, 'She's always complaining about how she wished her class had less students in it.' Paul made a face, and I signed. 'I listen.'

He nodded and said, "And one day you're listening is going to get you into trouble."

I made a face and signed, 'I don't know if that's possible.'

"Trust me anything is possible when it comes to you, Mirda." I blushed then shook my head before looking back up at Joseph to find him looking back at me. As our eyes met, he smiled, and I gave a small nod before looking back to Paul.

He gave me a weird face, and I signed, 'What?'

He started to say something then shook his head. "Never mind."

'Okay.' I gripped my water bottle tightly in my hands before Paul touched my arm gently. I looked up at him and quickly he pointed to Joseph who was still paying for his food.

"Has your opinion of him changed?" Paul asked quietly.

I shook my head then signed, 'Not really. I just want to know more.'

Paul smiled then asked, "What about your opinion of Ebony?"

I grinned.

"She told me that you two 'signed' today."

I nodded then signed, 'I approve.'

"You do?" he asked incredulously.

I nodded once more then gave him a look, 'You should really trust her.'

He took a breath then looked down, "You're right...I just... don't know how yet."

I touched his arm getting his attention. 'You will when the time is right.' He nodded his thanks at my reassurance, and I smiled before turning to see Joseph had just finished putting ketchup on his burger.

I made a face as he walked over, "What? You don't like ketchup?" I wrinkled my nose and shook my head. "Why?" Joseph asked in confusion.

Paul laughed then said, "An unfortunate accident from when we were younger."

"Oh?" Joseph asked, looking at me, and I quickly glanced away as my cheeks turned bright red.

"Yeah!" Paul exclaimed before he launched into the story that was the cause of why I didn't like ketchup as we walked back to the table.

CHAPTER 30

After Paul finished the story Joseph turned to me, "So you don't like ketchup because Paul's dog threw it up and you thought it was blood and just automatically assumed that his dog was going to die?" I nodded, and he grinned. "That's hilarious."

Frowning, I signed, 'It's not funny. It's embarrassing.'

"It kind of both," Paul said, chuckling as he ate his hot dog.

I rolled my eyes before I reached out and snagged his entire cup of fries. "Hey!"

I eat a fry before setting them down in my lap and signing, 'Just for that these are all mine now.'

Paul made a face. "That's cold."

I ate another fry before signing, 'No, they're actually still pretty warm.' I grinned as Paul glowered at me. I ate another fry before picking the cup up from lap and set it in the center of the table. He raised an eyebrow, and I signed, 'I'm not that mean,' before I stole another fry and pulled my sketchbook from my bag.

I pulled out a pen to start sketching when Joseph asked, "Do you do anything but sketch?"

I looked to him sitting beside me and nod, 'Sometimes yes.'

"Like what?" I looked to Paul, and he shrugged helplessly.

I rolled my eyes before I signed, 'I listen.'

"You listen?"

I nodded then signed, 'Two tables down from us a girl just confessed to her friends that she thinks her boyfriend is going to break up with her. The table across from them are studying for a Science test and the two kids with glasses are disagreeing whether the answer to number 6 is Plutonium or Boron.'

Joseph frowned, and Paul quickly translated.

As soon as he did, Joseph's jaw dropped. "How?"

I shrugged. 'It's just one of my many skills, I guess. Just like your skill to pester me with boring questions, pretty boy,' I signed before stealing another fry.

Joseph nodded. "You're right, but I was asking so that maybe I could learn how to listen better, like you obviously do. I mean God did give us two ears and one mouth for a reason, right?"

My face paled then as he grinned at me the color returned. My eyes narrowed, and I clenched my fists under the table as the word God echoed inside my head. *God.* I took several deep breaths and fought the emotions rising up within my chest. Slowly Joseph's smile faded as he noticed that something was very wrong with me.

"Mirda?" I averted my gaze and grabbed my bag. I turned to get from the table and leave when Paul grabbed my arm. Momentarily pausing my escape, I looked at him. He shook his head, and I saw in his gaze a plea for me to stop running, to face what I had been running from for so long.

I jerked my wrist from his grip and shook my head. 'No.' Then I shouldered my bag and walked out of the lunchroom.

CHAPTER 31

I stormed into the art room and threw my bag into the corner. Running my fingers through my hair, I paced the back of the classroom. No one was there of course; it was still lunch. I had another half an hour alone to myself. Turning around, I tried to control the desperate urge I had to throw something. However, the emotion inside of me refused to me contained.

Unable to hold back any longer, I turned to a box of paint on the table and grabbed a jar of black paint. I uncapped the lid, throwing it aside before stalking over to the canvas that was already conveniently over a tarp. With a single thrust of my arm, I threw the paint inside the jar toward the canvas. The paint splattered against the canvas as I slammed the empty jar on the table. I turned away from the canvas needing to do something with my hands still.

My eyes landed on a basket of paintbrushes on a nearby table. I rushed over grabbing a random brush before turning back to the box of paints. Glaring at them for a moment, I finally grabbed a much smaller jar of white paint. I uncapped the lid then jabbed the brush into the soup of white. I pulled the brush before setting the white paint back down on the table. I turned back to the canvas and pulled the bristles of the paintbrush back until they were taunt. I held them there for a moment before letting then going the drops of paint flew onto the canvas to form stars among the sea of darkness.

Frowning, I turned tossing the white brush back into the white jar of paint before turning and grabbing a jar of red paint from the box. I uncapped the jar and set the lid aside before grabbing a wider brush out of the basked. I stabbed the brush into the mass of red and pulled it out wiping the brush on the jar. Then I turned, briefly remembering set the jar aside as I faced the canvas again. I raised the

106

brush and rotated it briefly in my hand before placing the tip against the corner of the still wet canvas.

Hesitantly, I drew a circle before mixing in the red paint with the still wet paint. Turning back to the basket of brushes, I grabbed a thinner brush and dabbed it back into the red paint. I turned back to the canvas and placed the tip of the brush against the edge of the circle, letting drops of the red paint to trickle down the canvas. Once I finished, I turned back to the jars and set the brushes on top of them. Exhausted, I spun back in a circle and looked at the canvas, at my creation. A blood red moon on a star filled night.

"Not bad," I heard behind me.

I whirled around to see Mrs. Anna, my art teacher, looking at the canvas. She walked forward her arms folded. "Not your best, but not bad. Now this…"—she walked up to the piece I had been working on for the last couple of days—"this is something special." It was presently a sketch of my favorite field, my place of peace, of solace. She smiled then looked back at me. "What's gotten you down, Mirda?"

I shook my head and began cleaning up my mess. Mrs. Anna sighed, and as I turned to grab the empty black paint jar, she picked it up. "Do you know why I love black paint?"

I nodded; she had told this story hundreds of times to all her classes.

She smiled then said, "Of course you do, but let me remind you, anyways." I nodded, and she smiled. "Most people consider black paint boring and dull. However, I find it rather magical. The color black can represent so much—darkness, death, loss of hope— but without it, we would never see the light at the end of the long tunnel. We would never be able to high light on our work. Why without black our images would be boring and static. So the fact that you tend to use so much black in your work makes me really happy, Mirda." She smiled then said, "Because even though you don't realize it, you see the light in the dark and you are fighting your way toward it. No matter what it takes." She set the paint jar down before walking up to me, taking my hands in hers. "Now do you want to tell me what's really wrong, or are you going to force me to decipher another one of your paintings?" I give a small smile and she grinned before leading me to the table. She set a piece of paper and pen in front of me.

I hesitated before I write, 'You know my feelings about God.'

"Yes, as you know mine."

A sly smile crossed my face for a moment before I wrote, 'I still can't believe that you believe in the Bible but not in God." Mrs. Anna made a face as she recited a sentence she had said so many times to any missionary that came knocking on her door.

"I believe events in the Bible happened but not by the power of God."

'Then how did they come about?"

"Mother Nature," she answered before quickly adding, "That's not the point. What happened? Did Paul preach to you about God again?"

Shaking my head, I swiftly wrote, 'He knows my feelings and respects my wishes.'

Mrs. Anna read then made a face, "Well then, who did?"

I hesitated then wrote, 'A new kid."

"Kid?"

Looking at what I had written, I quickly realized my error that caused Mrs. Anna's confusion. Quickly, I crossed out the word kid and wrote above it 'Boy.'

"Oh." Mrs. Anna commented. "Is he a cute boy?" A blush spread across my face, and she smiled. "Oh, so he's very cute." I smiled then bit my lip and nodded. She smiled back at me before saying, "So this boy mentioned God, and you reacted poorly, I imagine."

I nodded before writing, 'He basically said that the loss of my voice was a gift from God.'

"And he didn't know of your hatred toward God." I shook my head and after a moment she sighed before saying, "Since he didn't know you should forgive him this once."

'I know,' I wrote, 'but if I threaten to never 'speak' to him again if he brought up God again, like I did to Paul, I'm not entirely sure I could keep that promise.' Mrs. Anna made a face as she read the words, and I took a breath before I wrote, 'This boy makes me feel alive. The last time I felt this good I had just become friends with Paul, and even then, the feeling diminished after some time. However, the feeling he gives me has yet to dissipate or slack in anyway.' I hesitated before I wrote the next few words, 'And because of that I want to be around him all the time and would have difficulty keeping my promise.'

Mrs. Anna read my words before nodding. "Yeah, that would be a problem. However, I don't think it's as serious as you might think." I made a face, and she said, "If he truly is as wonderful as you say then you probably won't have to even make a threat." I made a face and she leaned forward. "Five bucks says at the earliest convenience he's going to find you and apologize for making you upset."

Confused, I made a face then wrote, 'Why?'

Mrs. Anna shrugged. "Just a hunch. Now stop worrying and help me clean up. We were going to use that canvas today, but obviously we can't now." She gave me a look, and I gave a sheepish shrug. She smiled then reached out and patted my hand. "Just teasing you darling. I have more in my car. I'll go grab it if you want to clean up." I nodded and grabbed the paper I had been writing on and tossed it in the trash can before walking to my painting of anger. I went to throw it away when Mrs. Anna snatched it from me. I turned to her giving her a look of outrage, and she smiled mischievously.

"Just because it's not your best doesn't mean it's a bad painting. There's a lot of symbolism that my first-year art students can study." Then she turned and walked off being very careful not to drip paint as she went.

I stared after her my eyebrows raised in question before shrugging and turning to look at the mess I had made. *Fun,* I mouthed before walking over to the table and grabbing the empty paint jars and used paintbrushes. Then I turned and walked over to the sink and got to work cleaning up my mess.

CHAPTER 32

Mrs. Anna and I had just finished setting everything up for Paul's class when the bell rang signaling the end of lunch. I looked to Mrs. Anna who nodded, and I took a breath before grabbing the canvas that I had been working on for the last few weeks and set it up in the back room to start painting. I was in the middle of setting up my station when there was a knock at the door. I looked to see Joseph standing sheepishly at the entrance.

"Hi."

'Hi,' I signed back.

We stood awkwardly like that for a few seconds before he said, "Mrs. Anna is really nice and seems to like you a lot."

Giving a small nod, I signed simply, 'She's an amazing teacher.'

He nodded, and there were a few more minutes of awkward silence before he said, "I'm sorry." I made a face, and he winced before continuing, "I just presumed since everyone in this town is so religious and was so open of talking about God—" I winced, and he hesitated a second before continuing, "That you would be too, but obviously, I was wrong, and I'm really sorry. I didn't mean to offend you or bring up any bad memories. I'm really sorry."

I stared at him in absolute shock four words echoing in my head. Mrs. Anna was right. I slowly nodded, and he took a breath. His shoulders relaxed. "May I give you a hug? It's just something I've been taught to do after one apologizes," he said awkwardly as he rushed to provide an excuse for his odd but cute request.

I gave a small smile then walked forward and hugged him first. He stiffened slightly startled that I initiated the hug but then wrapped his arms around me drawing me to him closer. Even though it was a little awkward, it was nice. It was what I needed.

I closed my eyes for a moment before pulling back and signing, 'Class.'

Joseph nodded, clearing his throat.

"Right. Is there anything I can help you with?"

I shook my head before gesturing to the chair in the corner. Joseph looked to it then back at me.

I took a breath then signed, 'You can sit there.'

He grinned then said, "I figured as much I just wanted you to say it."

Then he pulled up the chair a few feet behind from where I was painting and took a notebook from his backpack. I stared at him in shock as he pulled out a pen then looked at me. "What? I write you draw."

I made a quizzical face at him, and he shrugged before looking back down at his notebook. I shook my head then looked at the canvas and sat down. I began layering the picture and adding texture. Slowly the trees I drew came to life, and I was in that field with Joseph. Just simply enjoying each other's presence. It was wonderful. Then I felt someone tap my shoulder, and I looked behind me at Paul entering back into reality.

"Class is about to end," he said, gesturing toward the art room.

I looked up and saw that everyone was cleaning up which meant I had to clean up to and go to gym. *Ugh.* I sighed then stood and started gathering my things when I heard laughter not too far from me. I looked up once more to see Joseph and Mrs. Anna talking and laughing together like they were old buddies. I made a surprised face just as they looked at me.

"You good, Mirda?" Mrs. Anna asked.

I nodded averting my gaze as I cleaned up my station.

Mrs. Anna walked forward and examined my latest painting. "Good job, Mirda, per usual. Are you going to add further detail to it?"

I gave a little nod, and Joseph remarked, "Well, this is already amazing. I can't possibly imagine how it could get more amazing, but you're the expert, Mirda."

My cheeks turned a little pink as I picked up my brushes and headed for the sink. The bell rang just as I finished cleaning up.

"See you all later!" Mrs. Anna called as we left her room.

"Where are you headed next?" Joseph asked Paul and me as we walked.

"Gym and computer programing," Paul supplied. "You?"

"Dance class."

"Well, have fun. I'll see you at practice?"

Joseph nodded then looked to me and asked, "Dance class is near gym, right?"

I nodded and gestured for him to follow me.

'So you on the baseball team officially?' I typed into my phone before handing it to Joseph as we walked.

Joseph read the words then handed the phone back to me before saying, "Not officially. Coach Peterson wants to see what I can do first before adding me to the team, but in his email, he said that if I was good enough, I could join."

I smiled then typed into my phone, 'You can do it!' Once again, I passed the phone to him, and this time, Joseph grinned as he read the text.

"Thanks for the moral support."

I gave a little nod and signed, 'You're welcome.'

"Sorry I can't give you a ride home today."

I shrugged then typed, 'It's all right. Paul's girlfriend offered me a ride.'

Joseph read the text then said, "Oh, cool."

I shrugged then started to point out where the dance room was when he grabbed my arm, stopping me.

'What?' I signed.

He took a deep breath then said quickly, "Do you want to come to practice? Then I can give you a ride home after, and we can get ice cream either to celebrate my failure or success." I hesitated and he said, "Of course, Paul and Ebony can come get ice cream too." My mouth formed a slight O in shock. He had just guessed what I had been thinking and calmed my one protest in a single bound. "What?"

I shook my head and wiped the expression off my face before signing, 'Nothing.' Then the bell rang, and my eyes widened. I was so going to be late. I turned to leave when Joseph grabbed my hand stopping me. I looked back to him.

"You didn't answer my question. Will you come to my tryout?"

Pushing aside the rational side of me for just a second, I signed, 'Yes.'

He smiled at me before saying softly, "Thank you."

Then he gave me a quick hug before he turned and into the dance room. I stared after him in complete shock when the late bell rang. Shoot, I cursed inwardly before turning and running down the hall to gym.

I realized after class that I could have ditched gym, but rather I accepted the consequences of being late (running three extra laps around the track), and actually tried. Which was a new thing for me but something I think I could greatly grow to enjoy.

CHAPTER 33

As promised, I went to Joseph's tryouts and silently cheered him on from the stands. (Ebony was needed at home, so she couldn't stay.) He did extremely well, and Coach Peterson was impressed, to say the least, so it was no surprise when after practice Joseph came up to me and told me that he made the Team.

"And the fact you were here supporting me made all the difference," he remarked just as Paul came out of the locker room. It should have bothered me, what Joseph said, or I should have tried to deny it, but if I could speak, I wouldn't have found the words.

So instead, I simply signed, 'You promised ice cream.' I didn't think my remark was such a big deal until after we left Moses's shop and Paul drove me home. (I know Joseph had promised, but Paul had emphasized how important it was for him to talk to me. So Joseph gave in.)

He had driven me back to my house and parked in my driveway before turning to me, "Mirda, are you freaking kidding me?"

I shrugged my shoulders, and he pursed his lips, frustration evident in his expression as he clasped his hands together. "When a boy gives you a compliment or says something like what Joseph did you, don't just respond with 'You promised ice cream'!" I gave him a look, and he took a deep breath before saying slowly, "You respond with either 'thank you' or 'anytime' or something else that shows you're interested in him!"

I blushed before shaking my head and signing, 'I'm not interested in him.'

Paul shook his head, truly annoyed now. "No. Don't you dare give me the 'I'm not interested' response. It may have worked with all the guys I tried to hook you up with in the past, but not this time."

He leaned closer and said, "Mirda, you like him. You're not even dating yet, and I can already tell that you're different around him. A good different. He's not a bad guy, and he's not going to break your trust. Mirda…I bet you five bucks right now that he's the one."

My eyes widened in absolute shock at Paul's declaration, and I shook my head. 'You can't know that.'

"Oh, can't I?" He sighed then said, "Okay, no five bucks, but I will be telling you 'I told you so' at the wedding."

I rolled my eyes. 'You're forgetting several things. First and foremost, he believes in God, and I don't.'

"So do I, and yet you put up with me."

I made a face before signing, 'After you promised you wouldn't try to convert me ever again.'

"After you wouldn't talk to me for over a month. You didn't even last forty minutes with Joseph, thus once again proving my point he's different. Give him a chance."

I raised an eyebrow before signing, 'He's happy and content with life. You really think he wants a broken, voiceless, cursed girl to come ruin it all.'

"First off, you're not cursed. Second, the broken can be mended. Third, you're not voiceless. You've proven that much." I gave him a look, and he sighed. "My point is…you're not a girl anymore. You are an intelligent woman who wants to be someone and mean something to people. Though you've helped me and those closest to you, you could be so much more if you had someone else to help you, help others." I gave him another look. "Think about it." He pleaded. I sighed then nodded before turning to get out of the car when Paul said behind me, "Pinkie swear." I turned back to see him holding out his pinkie finger to me.

I sighed the wrapped my pinkie finger around his and mouthed, 'Pinkie swear,' before I withdrew my pinkie from his and climbed out of the car.

"See you tomorrow," Paul called before backing out of the driveway.

I waved bye before going to the mailbox. I grabbed all the mail and skimmed it as I walked inside. Only one thing caught my eye. A note in plain black ink.

"Only one and half more weeks, Mirda. Though I've promised to stay away from you, it doesn't mean I still can't rattle you every now and then." It wasn't signed but I knew it was from Jonah. I sighed and knew this note should rattle me but for once I wasn't afraid, I was angry, and I decided then and there that I would never be afraid again.

I grabbed the lighter from kitchen drawer and held the note over the sink as I light it. Entranced, I watched as the note went up in flames. Only after it was completely gone did I allow a smile to cross my lips. Turning on the sink, I extinguished the flames before going up to my room to work on homework the smile still on my lips. Maybe Paul was right.

Maybe I was changing.

CHAPTER 34

Nothing really happened within the next couple of days. It was just school, baseball practice, and ice cream. I tried to be more open with Joseph as Paul suggested, but it didn't really result in anything substantial other than Joseph learning a ton more sign language. Which I couldn't tell if he enjoyed or was just tolerating. He didn't tell me to stop teaching him, so I guess that was something. I had expected the weekend to myself, but it turned out the assistant base-ball coach was sick, and Coach Peterson really needed my help. So instead of having a Saturday off from school like a normal human being I got up early and went to the school and coached the boys to the best of my capability. Even got a few cute sketches in of Joseph.

We finished practice around three in the afternoon, and Joseph suggested that we should go to the library to work on homework. As I had no other plans and a small mountain of homework, I agreed. Paul agreed and said that he would invite Ebony. She ended up being able to come, and the two lovebirds decided to hang in a private corner of the library, leaving me and Joseph to fend for ourselves. It wasn't necessarily awkward ... Okay, maybe it was a little awkward, but eventually, Joseph and I pushed past it. He ended up helping me with math, and I helped him with his English essay.

Now that I looked back on that moment, I realized that Paul and Ebony were maybe giving us a chance to be alone and develop a relationship, but at that time, I wasn't ready. I was still just trying to get used to being in my skin and being human being again. Sure, Joseph helped me a lot, but there were aspects of it that both he and even Paul couldn't help with, and I soon came to learn that were les-sons I still had to learn on my own.

Sunday came and went. I didn't go to church or to whatever family's house my father went to for dinner. Instead, I stayed home and skipped rocks at the pond. It was a normal boring Sunday and an even more boring week at school. The only excitement I had to look forward to was the fact that Paul and Joseph had their first big game on Saturday. Luckily, Coach Peterson's assistant was feeling better, so he didn't need my help, and I got to sit in the audience with Ebony. I watched as the boys ran to their places (opposing team was up to bat first). My eyes locked with Joseph's, and he gave me a small smile and nod before looking at the guy on the plate. I watched as Joseph wound up then suddenly release the ball. I saw the catcher's mitt close around the ball and watched as the guy swung at the air.

"Strike one," the pitcher called.

I watched as Joseph wound up again. Saw the catcher's mitt close around the ball.

"Strike two."

I looked at Joseph one last time as he wound up then release the ball.

"Strike three. You're out."

Fans in the stands cheered, and I clapped my hands as Joseph looked at me, winking. I smiled then released the breath I hadn't known I was holding. The game continued splendidly from there. Joseph got one more batter out before the last batter actually matched to hit the ball to the first baseman who promptly tagged him out. I stood and clapped with the rest of the fans as the boys ran into the dugout and watched the other Team warm up briefly. They were good but our Team was better that I was sure of.

Ebony and I watched silently as Paul walked up to the plate. "He's got this."

Ebony muttered, and I looked at her in confusion. She looked at Paul a bit longer before looking at me, "He's got this, right?"

I gave a small smile then nodded. She smiled then looked back at Paul. I looked at Paul and smiled as he relaxed into his stance. I knew he would ignore the first pitch whether ball or strike but then the second is when he would swing. His strategy worked most of the time and thankfully this time he did. He watched the first pitch then on the second he swung and fowled. He swung a second time, also fowled. But when he swung a third time, he hit the ball hard. Unfortunately, not hard enough, and he only got to second base. The game progressed steadily from there. One boy hit the ball; he got to first, and Paul got to third. One boy did strike out, but as it was our only our first out, I wasn't too on edge. Then Joseph was up.

'Come on,' I mouthed.

Joseph looked the pitcher dead in the eye before making a final practice swing. Then he stepped up to the plate and watched as he raised his bat. His grip loose. I made a face as I saw his footing shift. What was he doing? Then just as the pitcher wound up, he shifted his hold on his bat so that he was prepared to bunt it. My eyes widened as the ball connected to the bat rolling forward just past the pitcher toward first. The pitcher ran snagging the ball, but it was too late. Just as he threw it to first, Paul stepped on home. We all stood clapping and cheering. (Obviously, I just clapped.) Joseph was tagged out, but we got our first point.

CHAPTER 35

Our team didn't get any more runs that inning, so the boys came back on the field. This time two boys from the opposing team managed to hit the ball and one even stole a base, but no one got a run, thankfully. That meant our boys were back up to bat, and this time, we scored one home run and two runs. It was awesome, and I was super proud. The first game of the season was starting off great. The other team made it to the fifth inning without any runs, but after the fifth inning, they got two runs. Not enough to threaten or even really worry, but my anxiety levels started getting up there, and maybe it was because my senses were hyper active that I saw something I would have normally missed. I was watching the other Team throw the ball around, and I noticed the coach swapped out the pitcher. I made a face as I studied him and saw him throwing the ball with his left hand.

It was nothing new there were pitchers who threw leftie all the time, but it was how he did it that worried me. He had a flick to his wrist that caused the ball to curve just slightly and throw off the angle at which it would normally hit the bat. All the players need to raise their bats up just slightly if they wanted a good solid hit and not just a foul ball. This was confirmed after the first boy went up to bat. He got two strikes then kept fowling before finally striking out.

It was in the moment that I turned to Ebony and signed, 'I'll be back.' Then I turned and ran to the back of the dugout. I banged on the gate and one of Paul's teammates called Paul over.

Paul rushed over, and I quickly signed what I had just seen before asking, 'Who's up to bat?'

"Joseph."

My eyes widened, and I gestured to the field. 'Go tell him.'

"Right." He ran from sight, and I ran to the other side of the dugout where I could see the plate. Joseph was looking at someone in the dugout, presumably Paul. Then he looked and locked eyes with me.

"You're certain?" he seemed to ask me.

I nodded, and he looked back at the pitcher adjusting his hold on the bat, raising it slightly higher. I looked to the pitcher and watched him wind up then throw the ball. I looked back to Joseph as he swung the bat and struck the ball. I watched as it arced through the air then over the fence. A home run. I smiled as I watched Joseph casually jog around the bases tap them all before finally arriving at home. He looked at me smiling as he ran across. I smiled then ran to the back entrance of the dugout, where Coach Peterson was already standing.

He tipped his hat to me and smiled. "Nice one, Johnson."

I smiled then signed, 'Just doing my job.'

Coach frowned, and I knew he didn't catch what I said, so I raised my hands to wave bye when I heard Joseph say, "She's just doing her job."

Then he stepped into the doorway from behind the coach, and he winked at me. A small smile touched my lips, and I glanced at Coach, who had cleared his throat.

"Two minutes, you two."

"Yes, sir," Joseph responded, and I nodded in confirmation.

Clearly satisfied, Coach walked off to presumably finish watching the rest of the game.

Glancing back at Joseph, I saw him leaning against the gate door, and hesitantly, I raised my hands to sign, 'Thanks for translating.'

"I should be thanking you."

I smiled then walked forward and signed, 'You did all the work.'

"Well, if you hadn't told me about his technique, I couldn't have gotten that home run. Thanks, Mirda."

'Anytime,' I signed back before hearing the crowd cheer. 'I should probably get back to my seat.'

Joseph nodded then pushed off the gate and shoved his hands into his pockets. "See you after the game."

'See you then.' I signed before turning and walking back to where Ebony and I sat.

"Where did you go?" Ebony asked. "You just missed Joseph's amazing home run!"

I smiled before signing, 'Don't worry, Ebony. I saw it.'

CHAPTER 36

Unsurprisingly, our team won the game. It was five to three. To say I was proud of my boys would have been an understatement, and I was almost tempted to join them at the town's local diner for milkshakes, but I knew that I would just end up getting in the way. So after congratulating Joseph and Paul, I bid farewell.

"Wait, you're leaving?" Joseph asked in the middle of me signing goodbye. I took a deep breath then nodded. Joseph shook his head as Ebony asked in confusion, "But what about milkshakes? Are milkshakes still a thing?"

"They are. It's just typically, Mirda doesn't come and get milkshakes with us," Paul explained before looking at me. "Be safe and text me as soon as you get home." I nodded and fist bumped him before turning and walking toward the parking lot.

"Mirda! Wait!"

I turned back to see Joseph running after me. I stopped as he stopped before me, panting. "Let me give you a ride home."

I frowned in confusion. 'Milkshakes—'

"I can get them after I get you home. Please, Mirda, just accept the ride."

I hesitated, biting my lip before nodding.

He gave a quick sigh of relief before saying, "Awesome. Let me just get my bag, then I'll be back."

'I'll meet you at the car.'

He nodded before turning and running back to the dugout. I took a shaky breath before facing forward. I walked to the parking lot and looked around for Joseph's car. I found it in the back and started walking toward it when I saw him at the opposite side of the parking lot walking toward me. I froze briefly before reminding myself that

I had nothing to fear. I continued to walk to Joseph's car ignoring Jonah as he sidled up beside me.

"So was it a good game, Mutey? I heard we won, so it must have been." I kept my eyes facing forward refusing to acknowledge him. "Yesterday was my last day of suspension, Mutey. How do you feel about that?" I signed nothing, just kept walking. Jonah growled then said, "Are you deaf now as well as mute, Mutey?" I kept walking. "I'm talking to you." He reached out and grabbed my arm, but I jerked it from his grasp. "Don't you dare just walk away from me. Not after everything you've put me through." He grabbed me from behind lifting me up, stopping me. My mouth dropped open in silent outrage, and I quickly elbowed back once, twice.

After the second elbow to the gut, Jonah set me down to fix his grip on me, but before he could do that, I stomped on his foot, then tore away from his grasp. Whirling around, my fists raised to protect my face, I couldn't help but smirk as I watched as he grabbed his foot, cursing momentarily before dropping it and looking at me, "You think that this is funny, Mirda. Causing me pain." Titling my head to the side, I raised an eyebrow as he continued to rant, "You're going to regret this night, and all those other times you hurt me, because someday soon I'm going to hurt you back ten times harder."

Rage filled me, and for a moment, I lowered my guard to sign, 'You've already hurt me more then you know, Jonah. Why can't you leave me alone?'

Jonah cruelly mocked me with his hands as I finished signing, "Oh, I'm Mutey Mirda, and I don't know words and can't talk like a normal person."

Forcing my fury down, I signed, 'Maybe not, but I can whoop your butt with or without a voice.'

Jonah glared at me then growled, "You know I don't speak your stupid hand language." Jonah growled, and I watched as his fist curled into a punch. Resisting the urge to ask 'Why me?' to the universe, I raised my fists prepared to defend myself again when I heard from behind Jonah.

"Hey!"

Looking up, I looked up to see Joseph running toward me from being Jonah. My eyes widened in fear as he ran past Jonah and stopped beside me. "You ready to go?" he asked me, and I looked to Jonah. He glared at me, his fists still clenched.

Joseph looked to Jonah and stretched out his hand. "Hello, we haven't had the chance to meet. I'm Joseph."

Jonah glared reproachfully at his hand before saying, "So you're the new kid who has the crush on Mutey?"

"What?" Joseph asked.

Jonah smirked then said, "Don't you know that what she truly is, is a freak, nothing more. You would be better off dating a fish than Mutey over here."

I winced as his words stung me, and I glared at Jonah. 'Leave him out of this,' I mouthed as Jonah glared back.

However, with Joseph there, he didn't try anything else. Clenching his fists, Jonah growled at me, "You brought this upon yourself, Mirda. Remember that."

Then he turned and stalked off.

CHAPTER 37

I drew back from Joseph and looked up at him. He was staring after Jonah with something that I had never seen on his face before. Rage. I hesitantly reached out and touched his arm. He flinched then looked down at me.

I asked him silently with my eyes, 'What was wrong?' He was fine. I was fine. Jonah unfortunately was fine. Everything was fine. If anyone should have been mad, it should be me, and I was but for Joseph's sake. I forced my anger back into its box, so why was Joseph furious?

Despite my very obvious unspoken question, Joseph ignored it and instead asked, "Are you all right?"

I hesitated for a moment tempted momentarily to push Joseph further, but instead, I remembered that I wanted him out of the situation. Pulling back even further from Joseph I signed, 'I'm fine.'

Doubtful, Joseph gave a once over before nodding his agreement, "Yeah. You're fine." Then he turned and started walking toward his car. "Let's get you home."

Automatically I started to follow him, but then I stopped as I remembered Jonah's words. "Don't you know that what she truly is. She is a freak, nothing more. You would be better off dating a fish than Mutey over here." Flinching at the truth behind his words, I reluctantly realized that maybe what was best for Joseph was to stay away from me. Biting my lip to prevent the sudden swell of emotion rising in my chest, I prepared myself to reject Joseph for good.

"Mirda?" Looking up, I saw Joseph had opened the side door for me to get in, but when he had noticed I wasn't there, he had turned around to look for me.

Sweet boy, I thought numbly as I raised my hands to sign words that would truly cut Joseph once and for all, 'I had things under control. You shouldn't have intervened.'

Joseph raised an eyebrow. "Really? You had things under control," he scoffed before shutting the passenger door shut and walking up to me. Resisting the urge to step back, I held my head high as Joseph stopped right in front of me. "Then if you have things under control, you won't be afraid to tell me who that was just now?"

My jaw tightened, and I signed, 'I'm not, but it's not your problem, Joseph. Not now, not ever.'

I started to turn away when he called out, "Actually it is. You're my…friend, and any problem you have with someone becomes my problem." I noticed the slight way he stumbled over the word *friend*, and had I been of clear mind, I would have addressed it, but I didn't care. All I cared about was keeping Joseph safe and away from my problems.

They weren't his burden to bare. I shook my head turning back briefly to sign my one-word answer, 'No.' Then I turned and started walking down the road home. I must have walked for a good five minutes before Joseph finally caught up to me.

"Mirda." I kept walking. "Mirda!" Still I kept walking, then someone grabbed my arm, and as I stopped to pull away, Joseph used my momentum to pull himself in front of me. "Mirda, stop." I stopped, glaring up at him only to falter as I saw his eyes full of concern. *Who was the last person who looked at me like that?* I started to ask myself when Joseph broke the spell. "Mirda?" Forcing my eyes down, I stared at my shoes as Joseph sighed. "Mirda, please. Tell me what's wrong?" Shaking my head, I tried to pull back, but Joseph was too strong, or I didn't really want to leave him because I barely moved more than an inch. Joseph leaned closer and quietly pressed, "Who was that kid? Why was he hurting you?" I shut my eyes tight, and I shook my head fervently trying to pull back. This time I almost broke his grip on my arms; but then Joseph tightened his grip just a little more, and I couldn't break free. Desperation filled me, and I looked up at Joseph only to have my will to leave crumble.

The sincerity of his concern was written plainly on his face, and I saw a bit of my own desperation reflected back at me, confusing me. I thought breaking away from him would free but maybe… Joseph must have seen me falter because he quickly pressed his luck, "I saw him grab you. You defended yourself, yeah, but you shouldn't have had to. You don't have a mean bone in your body." My body stiffened as Joseph's spell lost hold over me. Shaking my head, I pulled back the slightest barely perceptible distance. The confidence in Joseph's face fell, and I watched as he looked down trying to figure out how he had lost me yet again. Finally, he just looked up at me and asked, "Please. Tell me. Tell me who that kid is. Tell me how I can help."

My resolve fortified once more. I pushed his suddenly limp hands away from my arms. 'You can't help, Joseph. The only way you can is to stay away from the situation to not ask questions.'

I go to walk by him, but he took a step to match me. "Why?" His voice was calm, but underneath it, I sensed a storm that I wasn't ready for. In a desperate attempt to abate the storm, I glanced down, and he lifted my chin with the touch of his fingers. "Why do you want to protect me? That's what you're doing, right? By not telling me what that was about. Or why you're mad that I intervened." I made a face, and he said, "You're an open book, Mirda, when it comes to your emotions…or at least to me you are."

I glanced down, blushing.

"Just tell me. Please."

I hesitated before finally caving. Pushing aside his hand, I signed, 'You're still new, so you don't know…but you deserve to know that… that I'm the most unpopular girl at school, and the only way I've survived is by keeping my mouth shut.' I looked up at him then away to keep the little confidence I still had. 'However, some bullies weren't satisfied by that. Jonah especially. Over time the rest of the bullies faded away, but Jonah remained. He always stayed to torment me, and I dealt with it silently, but one day the teachers caught us. They asked for my side, and I didn't want to give it. I could handle it, but my dad was there, and I just lost it. I told them everything, and Jonah got suspended for two weeks.'

"And he hates you for it."

I nodded in confirmation. "For the last two weeks, he's left notes, watched me from a distance, almost got Paul and me in an accident, and now—'

"The ambush in the parking lot," Joseph whispered.

I nodded then signed, 'I told Paul not to tell you because it occurred before you got here, and you deserved a chance to get to know everyone without my bad rep looming over you.'

"Mirda, I don't know if you noticed but I don't care about what others think of me."

'Well, I do,' I signed angrily, looking up at him, 'Maybe not about my own reputation but about my friends. I didn't even want to tell Paul about Jonah, but like you, he saw Jonah and me fighting, and I couldn't prevent it any of it. Then you came and I hoped this was the chance to fix my mistake, but I messed up just like before. So thanks for the offer to help, but I got this, Joseph. Really, I do.' I brushed past him, walking away.

"Mirda!" Joseph called, but I kept walking forward.

Even in the dark, I knew my way home.

CHAPTER 38

I made it home in record time.

Anger fueled my walk, thus causing me to go much faster and take more reckless chances. (Like darting in front of a car that was maybe five feet away from hitting me to get across the street "quicker.")

Stomping up the front porch steps, I grabbed the doorknob and shoved the door open. Throwing my bag to the side, I slammed the door shut before marching to the stairs.

"How did the game go?" my father asked from the couch reading the newspaper. Rolling my eyes, at his obvious lack of sincerity in asking that question, I sped past him up to the stairs. "Mirda?" My father called again, but I was already half way up the stairs. Ignoring any further yells, I pushed open my bedroom door weakly, shutting it before walking over and throwing myself onto my bed.

Physically trying to soothe myself I stroked my pillow as I mentally beat myself up internally. Everything had been going so well. For the game for Joseph and me, then Jonah had to come and ruin it. Granted he was going to ruin it sooner or later, but why did it have to be today of all the days?

I wanted to scream, but like always, I couldn't. Silent tears threatened to drip down my cheeks, but I forced them back as I felt my phone buzz.

Taking a deep breath, I pulled it out of my back pocket to see a text from Joseph. "Mirda, we need to talk."

Furious at his cheating ways, I typed back, 'No, I already said all I needed to say.'

"Well, I didn't. Please let me in."

'No!' I punched into the phone then threw it off to the side of my bed. *You'll just try and change my mind, and I can't let you get hurt.* Resting my head on the pillow that I had been stroking a moment, I closed my eyes taking a deep breath preparing to force myself to try and get some sleep when suddenly my phone began ringing. Reaching over, I lifted it up to see Joseph's contact lighting up the screen. Sighing I let me phone fall back to the bed, and I turned over intending to let it go to voicemail. Besides even if I did pick it up, I couldn't answer him anyways. Tears began to trickle down my cheeks at the unfairness of it all when I suddenly I heard Joseph's voice, "Hey, Mirda. It's me."

Startled I sat up my first assumption that Joseph had somehow gotten into my bedroom, but no one was there. Looking down at my phone, I saw it playing the voicemail. Confused, I picked it up, intending to turn it off when Joseph said, "Look, you don't have to talk. I just want you to listen. I'm grateful for what you've tried to do for me, but I know bullies…and the best way to take care of them is with friends. Not by going off on our own." He sighed, and I lay back down on my bed, setting my phone besides my head as he stated simply, "Look, I want to keep being friends, but you're going to have to trust me just as I'm learning to trust you. Please, Mirda. Just give me a chance." He was silent for a minute before he said, "I'll keep asking you until you see reason." Rolling my eyes, I mouthed, 'Yeah, right.' I reached over to turn off the phone when Joseph said, "I'm right outside and will stay here all night if I have to." Then he hung up.

Startled by Joseph's announcements, I lay on my bed momentarily in shock, *He was on the front porch? What did that mean?* Then as the obvious hit me I sat up, scrambled out of bed, and ran to the window. Pulling back the curtains, I peered outside to see Joseph sitting on the porch steps, two milkshakes beside him. He was here.

My knees suddenly weak, I collapsed on the edge of bed as I began to analyze the pros and cons of the situation.

He had come, despite me pushing him away. It seemed that he was even more determined than Paul, but why? What was his end game? Then I realized maybe Paul was right, maybe he liked me like the way Paul liked Ebony, and maybe I liked him like that, but I would never know if I stayed away from him. I looked back out the window, and a soft smile traced across my lips as I looked at Joseph. All I knew was that he was here and that was more than enough… for now.

Taking a deep breath, I silently opened the window and slid out reaching for the low hanging branch of the tree shadowing our house. Shimming along the branch, I lowered myself to a lower hanging branch before dropping to the ground and walking out of the darkness to stand in front of Joseph. My sudden appearance had the desired effect I wanted on Joseph, and I was tempted to smirk as I saw the surprise in his eyes. However, as much fun as it was teasing him, I was here for a reason. Crossing my arms, I let the one question I had appear on my face, praying in my heart he would understand.

Joseph set the milkshakes aside then stood and walked toward me. "When I moved here, I was running. I didn't realize but then, but I know now. I was running for my life. For an explanation that I wasn't sure I wanted. Then I got here…and got my explanation." I saw his hands fist momentarily at his side, then they relaxed as he reached out gently taking one of my hands from its folded embrace. He took a deep breath then stated simply, "And now that I've conquered many of my demons, I want to stand beside you and help you conquer your demons. Whether it be your lack of faith or even if it's a skinny twirp who doesn't know what he's talking about." He reached out his other hand, and I stared at it then hesitantly placed my hand in his. Joseph took a deep breath of relief then said, "I want to help you conquer it all."

Taking another deep breath, he firmly declared, "That's why I keep sticking beside you, because you matter to me. You're part of my purpose here, and I don't know where that will lead me, or what will happen to me if I keep going down this road, but I intend to see it through. If you'll have me."

I stared at him in shock then looked down as I fought back the tears. He had answered my question. I didn't say a word. I didn't sign. I didn't do anything beyond giving him a look, but he knew my question and he answered it. Taking a deep breath, I temporarily pulled my hands from his wrapping them around my side as I attempted to regain control of my emotions, but I realized it was pointless. Looking up at Joseph, I saw his eyes full of disappointment, and I knew he thought from my reaction that he had failed in winning me over. Well, that was simply not true, and he needed to know the truth.

So after a moment of hasty decision making, I took several steps forward and threw my arms around his neck with the intent of never letting go. A moment later, I felt him hug me back, and I melted in his embrace. Although I knew he probably would never know how much this hug meant for me, I knew and that was enough for now.

Eventually we pulled away, and he led me to the porch, where he handed me my milkshake and he talked while I signed. It was a special night and moment that I would never forget, for that night I fell for Joseph.

I fell hard, and I fell fast.

CHAPTER 33

Though Joseph and I hadn't admitted anything verbally, it was evident from the way we acted around each other that there was something between us. We were more accepting and more tolerant of each other. Even Paul remarked to me that we seemed a little subdued and was worried that something was wrong. I reassured him that everything was all right and that we had just come to accept each other and more importantly our differences. I refused to admit that my refusal to sign around Joseph some days wasn't because I was unsure of myself but because I was unsure of what he might think of me. Though I knew he wouldn't care, I didn't trust myself not to mess up.

Well, as it turned out, I did slip up, but it wasn't entirely my fault. You see, after Jonah returned to school, we were at an impasse of sorts. He didn't get in my way, and I stayed out of his. However, each day I awoke in fear wondering if this was the day? Was this the day that Jonah would get revenge for that night in the baseball field parking lot? For the first time in a long time, I hoped. I hoped that he would just let go, that he would see what he was doing was wrong and would leave me alone. However, he didn't and all those feelings that I had locked inside of me came spilling out.

It was about two weeks after Jonah had gone back to school and a little over two weeks since Joseph and I had our little talk. The boys had just found out that baseball practice was canceled and were debating what they were going to do with their free time. Joseph wanted to get together and play a game, while Paul wanted to take a nap. They were trying to get me to pick between the two when reached Joseph's and Paul's cars, who were parked side by side.

Paul's car was just fine, but Joseph's was covered in a neon-pink spray painted words BOY TOY!

"What the—?" Paul asked in shock.

"Boy toy?" Joseph muttered in absolute confusion. As soon as Joseph said those words, I lost it. I whirled around and examined the parking lot before I saw Jonah and his goons in the corner laughing and point at us.

"Mirda?" Paul asked.

'I'll be back,' I sighed before marching over to Jonah's car. As I got closer, Jonah elected to ignore me, so I had no choice but to march straight up to Jonah and get right up into his face.

I stabbed my finger into his chest as I mouthed, 'Leave Joseph out of this. This is between you and me.'

He glared at me, "Fine, but only if you say please."

I glared at him then mouthed the word, 'Please.'

He smirked then cackled, "What was that? I didn't hear you."

'Please,' I mouthed again with more emphasis.

He and his goons chuckled as he laughed, "Still can't hear you, and if you don't say please, then your boy toy will never be safe."

I glared at him, and he met my gaze. It was then we both came to an understanding. He knew I could never truly say please, and he would never agree to leave Joseph alone so the only thing to do was to speak to him in his language. My hand clenched into a fist as Jonah and his goons continued to laugh. Jonah turned away for a second then turned back and I saw my opening. I swung my fist at his jaw. It collided with a loud thud. Jonah took a few steps backward before looking back up at me his face filled with shock. I saw a line of blood trickling down his chin.

'Leave him alone,' I mouthed before turning and walking back toward Joseph's car. I knew he would take a swing at me so as I walked, I dropped down under his punch, and I pushed him from behind. He fell to the ground unbalanced, and I took a couple of steps back, ready for anything when I heard behind me.

"Johnson." I turned to see Coach Peterson stalking up from the field. By the look on his face, it was clear he had seen what had just happened. He looked to Joseph's goons still hanging by his car ready to jump to their leader's aid no longer. "Get lost," Coach Peterson stated before looking at Jonah still lying on the ground. "On your feet, Haggart." Jonah stood as all his boys fled. Coach Peterson looked Jonah up and down before asking, "So what were you two arguing about this time?"

"Nothing," Jonah muttered. "She just walked up and attacked me."

"Oh, I highly doubt that, Jonah." Jonah looked up in annoyance as Coach Peterson said, "Johnson always has her reasons for doing something even if sometimes they are stupid," he muttered toward me. I gave a small nod, and Coach Peterson smirked before looking at Jonah. "So you want to tell me the truth, Haggart? Or should I tell you what I just saw?"

"Sir?"

"I saw Wilson cleaning off his car windows as they were covered in spray paint. Now who would do a thing like that? You want to tell me?" Jonah, being stubborn, kept his mouth shut. Coach Peterson gritted his teeth before saying, "Fine." He turned to me. "Johnson, since we are still on school property, I have to punish you. Come by my office tomorrow after school, and I'll have work for you."

Then he turned and glared at Jonah. "Attempt to bully any of my players again or Johnson, for that matter, and I won't let you off the hook so easily next time. Understood, Haggart?" Jonah mumbled something. "Haggart!" Coach barked.

Jonah flinched. "Yes, sir."

Coach nodded and muttered, "Good," before gesturing to me.

I followed him back toward Joseph's car, rubbing my fist. My knuckles weren't bleeding or anything; they were just a bit bruised. A small price to pay if it meant Jonah would leave Joseph alone. Coach stopped us just before we reached Joseph's spot.

"You all right, Johnson?" I nodded, and he said, "If he ever pulls something like this again, don't go after him. Come to me. I'll take care of him. Got it?"

I nodded and signed, 'Yes, sir.'

Coach Peterson nodded, and we started walking toward Joseph's car once more, "By the way, Johnson…" I looked to him curiously as he nodded approvingly. "Nice left hook."

CHAPTER 40

With Coach Peterson's words echoing in my head, I walked back to Joseph's car; however, before I could get there, the boys rushed up to me, asking, "Are you okay?

"What were you thinking." Joseph reached out and snatched my left hand. "Let me see your hand."

I withdrew my hand, rubbing my knuckles before signing, 'You guys saw that?'

They nodded, and I looked down ashamed, waiting for them to correct me on what I had done.

When I head Joseph say with pride, "Yep, we did, and personally, I'm really grateful I wasn't Jonah."

I looked up at him, confused, then my eyebrows furrowed in more confusion as I saw the huge grin on his face. "That was incredible!" he stated simply before looking to Paul, who gave him a look that apparently told Joseph to keep going, for in the next instance, he said, "I mean normally, I don't support violence, but Jonah was being absolute…"

"Pig," Paul supplied.

Joseph nodded before resuming, "Yeah, so your response was exactly how I wanted to respond, only I…we weren't expecting it, and I wanted to charge in after you, but Paul held me back."

I flashed Paul a look, who simply shrugged. "You had things handled."

I gave a slight nod of thanks before looking back at Joseph.

"Anyways, your response was perfect. You tried to be diplomatic, but when that failed, you didn't hold anything back, and man, am I glad that when you got mad at me about God, you didn't punch me because that looked like it hurt."

I gave a slight smile before asking, 'You're not mad or disappointed in me?'

Joseph frowned until Paul translated the third word.

He shook his head. "How could I be? You stood up for me when I was being bullied. Honestly, I should be thanking you."

"So do it."

We both looked to Paul, who we had honestly forgotten was there. He looked back and forth between us before muttering, "Oh, for crying out loud." He looked to Joseph. "Thank her so that way we can go to my house and try to wash the spray paint off your car." I looked to Joseph, whose cheeks were a little pink, which caused mine to redden a bit as well.

He stood awkwardly across from me for one moment before signing, "Thank you." Then he walked forward and hugged me.

I froze, confused for a second before I hugged him back. Despite my loss of temper, he didn't judge me. Rather he accepted and encouraged me to show him who I was. I hadn't lost him; rather, I had somehow become more connected with him.

As he pulled away, he whispered in my ear, "On three, we run to the car and race Paul to his house. Okay?"

I gave the slightest of nods before he reached down and snagged my hand as he pulled away. He pulled me with him as we ran toward Joseph's car. "Race you there, Paul!"

"What? Mirda! Joseph! Ah!"

I didn't look behind us as Joseph ran with me around to my door. He pulled it open, and I slipped inside. He slammed it shut before running to his side and hopping in.

"Get buckled!" I quickly did, smiling as he buckled and shoved the keys into the ignition.

He twisted the keys to start the car, and my grin widened as the car started. We pulled out of the parking spot just seconds before Paul did and drove to his house. Though Joseph knew where it kinda was I did have to remind him about a couple turns. However, Paul took a shortcut and beat us to his house.

"What the heck, man?" Joseph yelled as we shut our doors and climbed out. "How?"

Paul grinned before winking at me. "Shortcut."

I rolled my eyes as Joseph looked to me in confusion.

'Dirt road. Paul doesn't take it that much because it can flood super easily, and honestly, your car is too nice to go on it.'

Joseph gave me a look before shrugging in resignation. "That's fair."

We looked back to Paul who rolled his eyes and said, "On the way here, I called Ebony, who will be coming over to help soon. I'm going to run inside and grab supplies. Joseph, you want to help with that?"

"Sure." Joseph let go of my hand which somehow had happened again.

He walked with Paul to the house, who at the last second turned and said, "Mirda, can you get Caroline? She should be in the back-yard and would be disappointed if we left her out."

I nodded before going around to the side entrance and opening the gate. I walked to the back and saw Caroline hanging out by the side of the pool.

As I walked up, she turned and shouted, "Mirda!"

I smiled then opened my arms as she ran into them.

I hugged her back tightly before pulling back and signing, 'We need to clean some spray paint off a car, you want to help?'

She grinned and said, "Who wouldn't?"

I smiled then gesture for her to follow me. She did and we waited out in the front playing a couple of hand games while we waited.

"So whose car?" she finally asked after we had finished our third round of lemonade.

I took a deep breath before signing, 'A guy from school, Joseph. Super cool and brand-new.'

She nodded and said, "And this is his car?" I nodded, and she asked in confusion, "And he accidentally sprayed Boy Toy across the side?"

I shook my head, smiling before signing, 'Nope. Jonah did.'

She frowned before saying, "I don't understand. Isaac is so nice to me. Why is his brother so mean to you guys?"

I shrugged before signing, 'I don't know, but on the bright side, I stood up for Joseph and me today.'

"Really?" she asked excitedly. "What did you do?"

I started to sign a response when we heard from the doorway. "She punched him."

We looked up to see Joseph and Paul exiting the house with the supplies needed to clean off the spray paint and wash off Joseph's car.

Caroline looked to me excitedly. "Really?" I nodded, and she frowned before asking, "Did it hurt?"

I shrugged then signed, 'A little bit.'

"Can I see your hand?" I held out my hand in response, and she examined the bruises and my bloody knuckles.

"That's so cool," she murmured, admiration evident in her voice.

"But..." Paul spoke up and we looked to him, "beating up someone is not the answer, Caroline. Mirda got lucky that it worked out so well. Don't expect it to work out for you."

Caroline rolled her eyes. "I'm not stupid, Paul."

"Really? Could have fooled me." Paul teased and Caroline pushed him as he walked by. "Hey!" Paul exclaimed as he regained his balance before setting the tools we needed on the car. "Okay, we're ready to go just waiting on Ebony..." Then we heard the honk of a car horn, and all look to the curb to see Ebony pull up to the curb in her bright hot pink car.

She hopped out and ran up to us, "Sorry I'm late."

"You're actually right on time." Paul smiled as we all looked to him for direction. His cheeks went red for a minute before he cleared his throat. "All right, let's get to work. Ebony and Caroline, water bucket duty. Joseph and Mirda, scrubbing, and I'm going to figure out which soap gets the spray paint off."

I signed, 'Okay.' While Joseph shrugged, agreeing. I glanced at Ebony and Caroline just in time to see them exchanged glances before giving Paul a look. *Uh-oh.*

"Sure, but while you guys experiment, we're going to wash your car, my car."

"And Dad's car," Caroline added. "We're not going to sit around and be bored." She walked up to Paul and snagged the buckets and the sponges before walking over to their dad's car and getting to work.

I smiled then glanced at Joseph, who was smirking, and as I locked eyes with him, he winked at me before glancing at Paul, "Let's get to work."

CHAPTER 41

Washing the spray paint off of Joseph's car was way more fun than I initially suspected it would be. By the time we managed to get the spray paint off Joseph's car, Caroline and Ebony had finished washing Paul's dad's car and had started on Ebony's car. However, I think they got bored halfway through because as I was washing the windshield with Joseph they ran up behind Paul with the hose and nailed him in the back with a spray of water. I froze in shock for a moment as Joseph jumped down from the hood and hid behind me as Ebony ran around the car throwing a bucket of water in my face. I stumbled back spluttering, sprayed then as Joseph ducked behind me as I got sprayed. I spluttered covering my face with arms before turning and pulling Joseph to the front as Caroline threw a sponge at us. It nailed Joseph in the chest leaving a dark wet splotch.

Pleasant surprise lit his face and he laughed as he said, "So not fair!" I smiled then looked at Paul as he snuck around behind her past Caroline. He grabbed Ebony around her waist and stole the hose from her hand turning it on his sister then her.

I looked to Joseph, 'Should we join in?'

He shook his head. "I think it would be more fun to hide and let them think we're gone."

I smiled then gesture for him to follow me. I led him around the back, of the cars to a clump of trees lining Paul's house. Paul and I had discovered during an intense game of hide and seek when were kids. From the house you couldn't see us, but we could see the house and driveway just fine. It was perfect. I smiled as I sat down and leaned against the tree to see Caroline grab the hose from Paul and spray him. He still had hold of Ebony, so he was attempting to use her as a shield and failing. I smiled then until I heard Joseph chuckled. I looked to find him staring at me.

My cheeks go slightly pink as I signed, 'What?'

He shrugged before commenting, "You really support them, don't you? Paul and Ebony?" I looked to them messing around with Caroline, and I nodded. "Even though you could lose your best friend in the process."

I shook my head before looking to him and signing, 'I'm not losing Paul. I'm gaining another friend.'

He smiled before nodding.

"That's a wonderful way to look at the situation." I gave a slight nod before he blurted out, "Do you want to play twenty questions?" I gave him a look and he shrugged sheepishly, "Even though I know you, it feels like I barely know you." I raised an eyebrow and I saw his cheeks slightly redden as he cleared his throat, "I know you like math, and that you're a very good artist. You like ice cream, specifically strawberry ice cream." I gave a slight nod to indicate he was right. He took a deep breath before pressing onward, "You don't go to church, and I'm going to presume Paul is a really good teacher, since you don't play any sports officially but can coach very effectively."

I nodded then signed, 'Paul's a good teacher, but when I was younger and had my voice, I did play a sport. Soccer in fact.' Joseph gave an appreciative nod as I continued explain, 'I enjoyed it especially since I got to play with...' My hands hesitated before finally stilling. I wasn't ready yet to tell him about Zach. It hurt too much.

However, although Joseph must have been insanely curious at my dropped sentence, he just let it slide. "So was your lack of a voice the only reason you stopped playing?" I shook my head my hands clasped in my lap unable to continue my side of the conversation.

Joseph sighed before asking, "Do you like to read?"

I nodded. "Favorite book?"

I shrugged. '*Pride and Prejudice.*'

He smiled. "So you're a hopeless romantic?"

I gave him a look, and he held up his hands in defense. "You're not the only one. My favorite book is *The Highwayman of Tanglewood.*"

I gave a small smile before reverting back to my normal face. "Sleep or no sleep?"

Once again, another look, and he nodded encouragingly.

I thought for a second before signing, 'Somewhere in between.'

"Relatable and exactly what I would have said."

I gave a small smile before asking, 'Odds or evens?'

Joseph gave me an odd look, and I gave a sheepish shrug. He grinned before answering with confidence, "Evens. You?"

'Odds.'

"Why?"

I hesitated then signed, 'The sound and when I could speak, the feel of them as you say them was cool.'

He nodded then asked, "I presume you like music."

I nodded, and he asked, "Well then, what's your favorite song?"

I shrugged. "'Songs without Words.'"

"So you like soundtracks?" I gave a small nod, and he smiled. "That's cool. I like listening to the reruns of the band We the Kingdom." I gave him a look of confusion, and he said, "I'll show you it later."

I nodded, and he asked, "Are you always this shy?" I glanced up at him and saw that he was grinning.

I offered a small smile before signing, 'Being unable to talk and refusing to talk are two very different things.'

"Yes, but which one are choosing to do in this moment?" He prompted, scooting closer to me.

My hands froze and I hesitated before signing, 'Fair point, and just for that I'm going to choose the third option.'

He raised an eyebrow. "There was a third option?"

I nodded. 'I was listening.'

He chuckled. "Okay then, while you were listening did you think of any questions for me?"

I hesitated then nodded. 'Were you the popular jock at your old school?'

He gave a small smile. "I wouldn't exactly say popular, but I was totally a jock. Also, a nerd, and the Christian boy and a couple other titles that I refuse to say aloud." I gave a small smile and glanced down at my hands in my lap. He tapped my chin just slightly so that I would look at him. "I wasn't always the jock. Or this happy person you see now." I raised an eyebrow in surprise, not sure if I actually believed him. He nodded. "It's true. The first few years I was in school, I was absolutely terrified, and I dreaded going to school, but then my dad gave me this." He pulled from under the collar of his shirt a cord with a metal ring on it. "It was his class ring. He told me if I wore this, I wouldn't necessarily be braver, but I would have the power to face my fears and become braver. I started wearing it, and he was right. It took some time of course, but eventually, I became the person you see today."

I reached out and gingerly touched the ring before pulling away and signing, 'And all because of this.'

He smiled then tucked it under his shirt. "It's my secret and what keeps me going." I gave a small smile before it faded. I started to hide behind my hair again when he asked, "And what's your secret, Mirda?"

I glanced up at him in surprise.

"What keeps you going?"

I hesitated before shrugging and signing, 'My art.'

He smiled then said, "I've seen it. You're incredible. Have you done any art shows?"

I shook my head.

"Well, you should show those pros what real art looks like."

I smirked then shook my head. 'That's not how it works.'

He chuckled before stating simply, "Course it is."

I shook my head, rolling my eyes before asking, 'Are you any good at dancing?'

He shrugged. "Is there a school dance coming up?"

I frowned and shook my head.

He shrugged. "We'll figure out something else. Maybe with Ebony and Paul...or...hey! There's a church activity coming up. We're learning how to ballroom dance. You should come. It would be more fun with you there."

Quickly I shook my head. I had declined all offers to attend church activities before I wasn't going to start accepting them now even if it meant I wouldn't end up dancing with a cute boy who was willing to dance with me. Joseph's smile faded, and I started to apologize when he raised his hand. "No, it's okay. If you're not comfortable with going to church activities, I understand." With that quick yet kind reply, he once again surprised me.

How he kept surprising me, I would never be able to understand, so instead, I simply signed, 'Thank you.'

He nodded, signing back, "You're welcome." Briefly he looked to Paul, Ebony, and Caroline still fighting over the hose before looking back at me and tentatively asking, "Earlier when we were talking about soccer, you never finished your sentence. Who did you play with?"

This time I didn't hesitated before signing out, 'My brother.'

"Is this one of the brothers that died during the Sickness?"

Unable to find the energy to sign, I simply nodded.

He sighed then scooted closer to me, pulling out his phone. He pulled up his photos and clicked on one specific photo. It blew up on the screen, and I examined it to see Joseph standing in the middle back surrounded by who I could only presume was his family.

He pointed at the screen and said, "That's my sister, Emma; my brother, Jacob; my mother, Sariah; and my dad, Samuel. Emma died during the first wave of the Sickness. Everyone else died during the second wave." I gave him a pained look. I had heard about the second wave, but it never hit our small town. My dad was told to work from home for a year when I was like thirteen because of it but besides from that the second wave of the Sickness had never affected us. Yet if the Sickness had affected him like this, where he had lost his entire family how could he be so happy all the time? Joseph stared at the photo and said quietly, "Some days it feels like the Sickness had never happened, and if I went downstairs, they would still be there."

I nodded before signing, 'I know what you mean. I miss my mother so badly. Even though we lost them in the first wave of the Sickness, the second wave didn't affect us.'

"Oh, I'm sorry."

'I'm sorry too. They probably would have liked you.'

He smiled then it faded as he asked, "So is your dad still around?"

I nodded but then shrugged. 'Yeah, but we don't really get along.'

"Oh, sorry."

I shrugged before signing, 'And you? How are you getting along with your guardians?'

He offered a small smile. "My guardians/stepparents, Sharol and Dan, are actually really awesome." He smiled sadly as he said, "They were our neighbors before the Sickness hit, then during it, they lost all their kids, and after since, I had lost my family. They offered me a home with them. Having nowhere else to go, I accepted."

'And they brought you here.'

He nodded.

'Did you want to come out here?'

He frowned before saying, "At first no, but then I prayed…" he said hesitantly, looking at me as if he was trying to judge my reaction. I purposely let my face go blank. I was starting to realize just because I didn't believe something didn't mean that someone else wouldn't believe it. "And I got the answer that I should come out here, and that's when I started to want to come out here. I know it's cheesy."

I gave a slight nod. 'It is, but if it's what made you happy to come out here, then I'm willing to look over its cheesiness.' I offered him a small smile, and he sighed with relief before looking up.

His eyebrows furrowed for a moment before he smirked. "I think they might be missing us."

I looked up and peered out of our hiding spot to see Paul, Ebony, and Caroline looking around in confusion. A small smile touched my face before I looked back to Joseph and signed, 'Maybe.'

"Should we return?" I shrugged leaving that decision up to him. He thought about it for a second before standing and holding his hand out to me. I took it and let him help me up. "We should return, finish what we started, but this conversation is far from over."

CHAPTER 42

True to his word Joseph led me back to the driveway. Paul teased us a bit, and both Ebony and Caroline gave me suggestive looks, but collectively they said nothing substantial. Instead, we just finished washing all the cars Joseph making polite conversation with them. Afterward, Joseph opened the passenger side door to his car, and I slid in. Glancing back at Paul, Ebony, and Caroline, I saw them all giving me a thumbs up. Blushing slightly, I glanced down at my lap before Joseph got into the car.

"Hey." I felt his hand cover mine, and I glanced up to him. He smiled at me, squeezing my hand gently before shifting his car into reverse and pulling it back onto the road. For whatever reason, that made me blush even further, and I glanced out the window, a small shy smile touching my lips as he drove. Joseph drove me the block and half back to my home before parking in my driveway. I reached out to grab the door handle when I heard him snap, "Don't even think about it." Glancing back at him, I saw him giving me the stink eye. Frowning, I took my hand off the door handle before giving him a look that said: *Now what, pretty boy?* Joseph grinned held up a single finger before he opened his door and ran around the other side of his car to where my door was. He reached out tugging on the handle then opened my door.

"My lady," Joseph said, grinning giving me a mock bow. A smile touched my face, and I snagged my bag before climbing out of the car. Throwing my bag over my shoulder, I signed thank you. Joseph grinned then shut the door as I walked up my front porch. Setting my bag down I turned back to find Joseph standing at the bottom of my porch smiling up at me. Biting my lip, I looked around briefly then jerked my head to the woods.

'Want to go for a walk?'

He gave a small nod before holding out his hand. I looked down at his hand then hesitantly I took a deep breath before placing my hand in his. Looking up at him, I saw that his eyes were encouraging as I walked down the porch steps and toward the woods. The path narrowed not long after we started walking, so I let go of his hand to focus on where I was walking before the path started to widen again.

"So where did we leave off?" Joseph asked as we walked through the woods.

I glanced to him and shrugged.

He chuckled then said, "All right. Have you lived here all your life?"

I nodded as I jumped over a fallen tree.

"Do you like living here?"

I froze midstep then took a step forward as I thought about that question. Did I like living here? I mean, there were times I felt trapped or secluded, but would I ever dream of leaving? No. No, I don't think I would; this is my home. Besides from that, it was the most beautiful place that I could imagine. So did I like my home? I glanced at Joseph and nodded again.

"Why?"

I smirked then brushed aside some leaves to reveal a small valley with a beautiful river flowing through it. He walked forward to stand beside me. His small gasp and wide eyes caused a small smile to appear on my face.

'This is why.'

He nodded before looking back at the sight. I glanced back at it then turned and started walking on a new path. Joseph followed me as we left the woods and entered a field teaming with wildflowers. I smiled then ran my hands along them as we walked through a path I had already made. The smile faded as I felt him step up beside me and brush his shoulder with mine.

I pulled further away before signing to him, 'Any more questions?'

He cleared his throat then asked, "I'm going to take a gander and say your favorite subject is art." I nodded, and he smiled triumphantly before asking, "Why?"

I shrugged then signed, 'I'm good at it, and I don't need words to express myself in art. I can paint whatever I'm feeling. Whatever I can't get out, I draw.'

He smiled then said as we walked, "You make it sound so poetic."

I smirked. 'I wish. My first attempts at art were failures.'

He smiled then darted forward before turning around and walking backward as he said, "You should show me."

A small smile touched my face, and I shrugged. 'As soon as you show me that band you were talking about earlier.'

Grinning he stated simply, "Deal."

A small blush on my cheeks, and I glanced down in part so I wouldn't trip but mostly so I could gather my thoughts. Eventually we started talking again, and although I worried it would be hard for us to keep up a conversation, it turned out to be no problem. Joseph kept the conversation going, and although I couldn't speak, it never made things awkward between us. He actually began to treat my lack of speaking like a game, as if I wanted him to guess what I would say before I gave my actual answer to his question. He was right maybe 20 percent of the time, but he never got mad; he would just shrug off the questions he got wrong before briefly inquiring as to what he got wrong. Eventually he started to get more and more questions right and pride swelled in my chest as he gave me fist bump after fist bump. It was as he did this that I saw the light glinting in his hair and couldn't help but think he was even more attractive than when I first saw him.

"Sunny days or rainy days?"

To that question I simply shrugged. I liked both.

"I personally like sunny days more because they chase away any gloom. Heart or mind?"

At that question I gave him a confused glance.

With that very mild prompting, he went onto to explain, "Like which one do you use to decide more. I try to use the spirit…I mean my heart, but I mean sometimes, I'll simply make the logical choice and up being right, which is always nice. So which one do you use more?"

I shrugged before lacing my fingers together and unlinking them and signing, 'My mind…I guess.'

"Cool toast or french toast. I have a feeling you'll probably choose french toast because it is the best, but I have to make sure." I gave a small smile before I gave a small nod to show that I agreed with him. He pumped his fist excitedly before taking a deep breath, "Okay. Another question movies or books?" So the questions continued. He occasionally threw a serious question in, but for the most part, it was something ridiculous and simple, which I appreciated. However, when we took a break from walking and sat on my favorite hill overlooking the valley, he decided to start asking them.

"So is it true that you would skip school all the time?"

Pausing momentarily, I looked to him and raised an eyebrow. *Who told him I used to skip school?*

Joseph raised his shoulders sheepishly. "Paul."

Making a small *o* with my mouth, I finally nodded, confirming Paul's words. As if unsure how to respond to my confirmation, Joseph also nodded before asking, "Where would you go?"

Shrugging, I raised my hands and signed, 'The ice-cream shop. Or the field. Honestly, anywhere but my classes and home.'

"Why?"

I shrugged before explaining, 'Home was boring, and class was equally boring…' then after a moment of debating, I finally added, "and easy.'

"So why not take harder classes?"

I made a frustrated face before signing, 'Because in those harder classes, I have to give presentations and—'

"Talk," Joseph interrupted. I looked to him, and he nodded, understanding, "If it makes you feel better, a lot of people who can actually speak still get scared when giving their presentations, so they refuse to give them, which is why they drop out of those classes." It didn't make me feel better, not really, but it was sweet of him to care.

"Did you ever try a translator?" I gave him a look, and he went onto to explain, "Someone who can speak for you."

I nodded before admitting, 'When I was younger and hadn't created the app on the phone that talks for me, I did. Her name was Charlotte. She helped me during my first year of middle school.' I smiled. I had fond memories of running away from her and hiding.

"Mirda?" I sat up straight and looked at Joseph.

'Yeah?'

"I just wanted to make sure I understood the last part of what you said." I nodded, and he pressed onward, "You had a translator your first year of middle school?"

I nodded.

"So sixth grade?"

Shaking my head, I corrected, 'No, seventh grade.' He frowned, and I started to pull out my phone, thinking that he hadn't understood my signing when his hands covered mine.

Looking up at him, I saw his brows furrowed as he processed something. Almost to himself, he muttered, "No, I understood what you said. Seventh grade, but if your first year of school was seventh grade…" He snapped his fingers as he realized, "You were home-schooled up until seventh grade." I gave a small nod, and he said, "That explains why you're so smart and why you're so good at studying on your own. That's really cool."

I shrugged, then bent down and pulled a couple of blades of grass from the ground and began braiding them together.

"But I'm guessing you don't think that way."

I shrugged again. I knew that was every kid's dream not to go to school and stay home. It was the perfect life from the outward appearance, but with no voice and no friends except Paul and Caroline, it was lonely and boring. Wandering these fields on end by myself, after my studies were over. You get used to it after a while, but when things were constantly the same, never changing…it made me wonder how I bore it for so long.

How did I slip and become the shadow of a person I was for so longer, but then again, how did I change? Just as I started to wonder that Joseph said, "I've always gone to regular school except for during the Sickness. Then my parents tried their best to homeschool me, but it wasn't long before they got sick…and… yeah." I glanced up to see him looking away from me. Sensing it was because of the pain from the loss of siblings rather than something I did, I reached out my hand and placed it on his shoulder. He looked back at me, and I smiled sadly before I started to withdraw my hand to say something, anything to comfort him when he reached out to snag my hand. "You don't need to say anything. I know that you understand more than most." He looked back at the field and said, "In places like these, unmarred by the Sickness, you would think it never happened, but the scars on us are still there, so we'll always remember." He paused for a moment, clearing his throat. "Always."

We sat in silence for the reminder if the hour eventually though Joseph cleared his throat and said that he had to go home if he wanted any dinner. So we stood and walked silently, hand in hand, back to my house then to his car. I stood just in front of the porch as I watched Joseph unlock his car and open the door. I waited for him to climb in and drive away, but he didn't. Instead, he paused then turned back and took a step away from the car gesturing to me. I took a couple of steps toward him, and he stood still unconsciously playing with his car keys. He hesitated for one more moment before stating, "One last question for today." I raised an eyebrow in surprise before nodding at him to continue. "What's your favorite color?" In shock at the simplicity of his question, my mouth dropped open then closed as I thought for a moment.

Eventually, I simply signed, 'Gray.' He raised an eyebrow in surprise or judgment, I wasn't sure.

"Just plain gray?"

I gave a small smirk then shook my head before signing fondly, 'No, like the calm-before-the-storm type of gray.'

He smiled. "Cool. Mine is red." I pointed at his Mustang silently questioning his statement. He grinned then said, "Yep, exactly like that." I smiled then turned to leave when he called, "Mirda?" I turned back and said, "I'll see you tomorrow?"

I nodded and waved before turning again.

"Mirda?"

I turned back to find that he had taken a step away from the car. He gestured with his keys before clearing his throat and saying, "I like it when…you have a pretty smile."

I glanced down, blushing before looking up to him and smiling. 'Thank you.'

He grinned then turned and ran into his car door. I covered my mouth as an even wider smile spread across my face.

He turned back, his cheeks slightly red from embarrassment, but still smiling, and said, "I meant to do that."

I crossed my arms then nodded, giving him the look of *Yeah right*.

He shrugged then said, "See you tomorrow."

Then I watched as he climbed into the car. I took a deep breath as he started his car, and I turned, walking up the front-porch steps, only to turn back and watch as he backed out of the driveway, then drove home.

CHAPTER 43

The next day Joseph picked me up again and this time he had a present with him.

I hadn't walked more than five paces to the car before Joseph said, "I have something for you."

I glanced up at him raising an eyebrow in surprise. He smiled and held out a folded piece of paper to me. I took it from gingerly from his hands; as if it could explode then slowly, I unfolded it. What was on the page was a crude sketch of a girl's face. It was black and white and had very little depth, so I couldn't really tell who the picture was supposed to be of, but it was evident by his use of long tender pencil strokes that he admired this girl. That whoever she was was special to Joseph. I looked back up at Joseph and tried to convey my admiration of his drawing.

His smile wavered, and he frowned. "You don't understand, do you?"

I furrowed my brow then desperately shook my head to admonish that I did understand. Joseph chuckled then said, "Mirda, I thought we agreed you'd stop keeping things from me. Besides, it was my fault for not pointing out what appears to me as obvious."

He leaned closer to me and gently moved my fingers a little lower on the paper to point out a soft gray flower tucked behind the girl's ear and it's only then that I remembered telling Joseph yesterday that my favorite color was gray. My mouth formed a little o, and I suddenly held the drawing with a bit more reverence.

"I know it's nothing like your paintings or sketches, but as I could find no gray flowers in my yard this morning, I figured this would have to do. Do you like it?"

I glanced up at him then picked down at the sketch lightly tracing it with my fingertips. I gave the smallest of nods as I reverently folded it up and clutched it tightly to my chest. I looked up at Joseph to see him sighing in relief.

"Good. I was so worried."

I smiled then walked the rest of the way to his car. I go to open the door, but he beat me to it.

"So since you're keeping one of my drawings now, will you let me keep all the drawings you toss into the garbage?"

I smirked before signing, 'I'll think about it.' Then I slid into the car and smiled as I heard his laughter before he closed the door. As he walked around to the other side of the car, I unfolded the drawing once more and smiled at the simple drawing. A blush darkened my cheeks, and I folded up the paper before placing it in my pocket. By the time I had done that, Joseph had gotten into the car, started it, and buckled himself into his seat. I glanced over at him to find him staring at me.

I gave him a look, and he said simply, "Shall we be off?"

I gave a slight nod, and he shifted the car into reverse before backing out of the driveway. We got to school rather early leaving ample time for me to practice my math and for Ebony and Paul to join us. I glanced over my shoulder as I looked at the two lovebirds. I turned back to Joseph and rolled my eyes he smirked then shrugged simply in return. I sighed and looked back at my equations expecting the next few weeks to be long and dreadful, but they weren't.

I attended Paul's and Joseph's practice, and when required, I would coach them, but for the most part, I stayed up in the stands sketching or listening to Ebony as she talked and talked. It was nice; I felt sort of normal, especially after practice when we would go out with the boys and get ice cream or to the Dollar Tree or some other place in our small town, and though I hardly signed when we were out, Joseph made sure that after when we went on our daily walks that I would sign or type the words in my phone. He made sure to remind me that though I didn't have a voice I had a voice. Okay, that didn't make sense. Let me try again. He made certain that I remembered that I had a mind and a right to express it even if I didn't have a real voice.

He truly was an incredible person, and he was so very thoughtful of others. Always putting others first, stopping to help a poor freshman on the way to class, staying after or coming early to help a fellow teammate. He was someone to look up to that's for sure but occasionally when we walked, I saw a hint of regret, typically only when he talked about his family and no normal person would have noticed. Only a person who relied on making facial expressions her entire life, who would practice in the mirror to make it as obvious as possible what she was trying to say.

I never brought it up to him. I trusted if it was important, he would bring it up in his own time. After all, he respected my wishes about God, gave me time to adjust to his strong belief and love of such a being. I owed it to him. Didn't I?

CHAPTER 44

Nothing significant happened until a couple of weeks later. Joseph and I were walking to our respective PE classes having already said goodbye to Paul after art class. I expected Joseph to go straight into dance class per usual, but instead, he paused and glanced back at me.

I frowned then sighed, 'What?'

He hesitated then took a step closer to me, reaching out and grasping my hand as if he was afraid I'd leave him before he said all that he needed to. Mostly to prove him wrong, I took a step closer to him and looked up at him making sure the trust that I had for him was evident in his eyes.

His breath caught, and he stared at me for a moment more before clearing his throat. "Would you mind coming to our youth activity?" Joseph asked softly.

My immediate reaction was no, and he must have seen it on my face for he tightened his grip on my hand as he went on to state, "It's next Wednesday. We're making cards for the people in the neighborhood."

My face started to relax from its determined not as he continued to placate me.

"No emphasis on God, I promise."

I took a breath, glancing at Joseph. I knew this was important to him, but I didn't want anything to do with God. Including being a part of his church in anyway, but this was for a good cause. I bit my lip then nodded, and he smiled before rushing me in a hug.

I hugged him back briefly before he pulled away, saying, "Thank you, Mirda. I'll pick you up at six?"

I nodded as the bell rang.

"These transitions between classes are never long enough," Joseph muttered before saying, "I'll see you later."

I nodded then watched as he rushed off to dance class before turning and going to the locker room. I got changed slowly, ignoring the gossip echoing around me. What was I thinking? Going to a youth activity? Just because Joseph promised that it wasn't centered on God didn't mean there still wouldn't be talk about God. These people loved him, I hated him. I would be a pariah, but the fact remained that Joseph wanted me to come and if he wanted me to come, I would be there. He was special to me, and if this was important to him, then I would be there. I told myself as I ran around the track, ahead of the rest of the class.

What if Paul had asked you? He's important to you too, an internal voice of mine asked. I probably would have, hopefully, given him a polite no. *Then what makes Joseph so different from Paul, your best friend?* I don't know. I admitted to myself as I stopped running, but the fact remained that I couldn't say no. If it was something horrible, I would have the courage to say no, but as it was so simple and arbitrary, I couldn't say no. I didn't want too. I took a deep breath then sat down and began stretching, before smiling. I had just realized that if I wasn't careful this boy would be the one to convert me. He'd be it, but if I remembered and recited to myself why I hated God, his gentle smile, his heartwarming eyes, and smooth words would have no effect on my hatred for God. With that plan in mind, I went throughout my week, content. I did crack a smile when I told Paul that I would be going to the youth activity with Joseph. He had been drinking some milk and ended up choking on it. It had been pretty funny. Even Joseph, who was sitting within earshot, was chuckling.

After Paul recovered thought and shot a look at Joseph, he looked to me and smiled, "Well, I'll be there too, and so will my sister and Ebony."

'So the five of us?' I signed.

He nodded before taking a bite of his pizza. "Yep, which should be interesting." And in fact, it was. You would think writing cards, to people in the neighborhood, would be pretty fun and simple. What could go wrong?

Well, it turned out we weren't just writing letters. We were also decorating them. So after the initial shock that I showed up to a church event, the other youth asked me for help with designing their cards. It got to the point where a leader had to stand up and tell the kids to go back to their own tables, and that it didn't matter how they looked, it just mattered that they were doing this good deed. The rejected kids went back to their table, and I looked to Joseph, who was sitting beside me, smiling.

I gave him a look, and he shook his head. "I was worried that you would be by yourself for most of the night, and that I would have to stick up for you, which would make you mad at me, and I would get mad at myself for making you mad, etc. Obviously, I was wrong, and instead, I will have to defend you from the massive hordes swarming you. Who knew you were so popular?"

I swatted his arm then shook my head before looking back at my card at the bunny I had drawn. I had so far written nothing on it. I bit my lip and was staring at it, frustrated, when Caroline, Paul's sister, reached over and stole it from me.

Quickly she wrote in calligraphy, "Hoping that you'll get better soon, Mrs. Peters!"

"She's been sick for a while and in the hospital. I hope you don't mind."

I shook my head as she took the card and placed it in the basket at the center of the table before snagging another piece of paper. She passed it to me and asked, "Can your draw a rose on this one?"

I smiled then nodded before quickly sketching out a rose and coloring it. Then I passed it to Caroline, who smiled brightly before whipping out her pen and writing another note. This time it was to Mr. Emmanuel. Apparently, he had just lost his wife. "Their favorite flower was a rose," she told me as she placed it in the basket.

I looked at Caroline in awe before reaching for another piece of paper.

'What else do you want me to draw?'

We fell into a pattern after that. I would draw a picture that Caroline told me to draw, or I would come up with something cute. Then Caroline would write something sweet and simple while telling me the story of the person she was writing to. I learned about a lot of people in the neighborhood. Many of whom were going through hard trials of their own. Others were just fine, but a bit lonely or a bit of a recluse. So thus, the letters. However, her comments about each of these people made me start to wonder. Eventually I touched her shoulder.

She looked at me smiling as I signed, 'How do you know all this?'

She started to open her mouth to respond when Paul spoke up, "In all her free time, Caroline goes around making deliveries to most of these people that we're writing to."

'Deliveries?' I signed.

"Cookies," Caroline explained. "Sometimes bread too, but only when Ebony or my mom helps."

"Don't forget me," Paul muttered as he colored in a picture of a pumpkin on a card.

"Yes. How could I forget you, big brother? Always sneaking into the kitchen when I take a break and stealing a dozen cookies."

"Hey! I do more than that. I help you bake them."

"Helping them does not include standing at the oven and asking every five seconds if they're done, big bro," Caroline stated as she placed another card in the basket.

"How is that not helping?" Paul asked as I put my hand to my face to hide my smile.

I glanced at Ebony, who winked at me before saying, "Don't worry, babe, you're a big help when you want to be."

"Thank you—hey!" Joseph, Ebony, and Caroline laughed while I smiled.

(Believe me when I say I was laughing on the inside.)

After the laughter died down, I turned to Caroline and signed, 'I want to help.'

Her eyes widened and asked, "You sure, Mirda?"

I nodded. 'How can I?'

"Um…well, usually for some of the people I draw pictures because they love art. It takes up a lot of my time, because I'm not that good or not as good as you are. If you took over that part, that would free up a chunk of my time and I might be able to make other desserts besides cookies."

I nodded then signed, 'Done. What else?'

Her mouth dropped open, and she glanced at Paul before back at me.

"Um…our oven just broke. Do you mind if I come over to your house this week in the evenings and make cookies?"

I shook my head then nodded. 'Yeah. In fact, everyone should come over and help bake.' I looked around the table at each person in turn. 'Everyone.'

They all stared at me in surprise, and Paul leaned forward, asking, "Are you certain, Mirda?" I gave him a look that said, *I wouldn't be offering unless I was certain*, and he sighed. "All right. What day would you like us to come over?"

I thought for a moment before signing firmly, 'Thursday. Rarely does anything happen on Thursday.'

Paul smirked as he thought about it. "You're right. I've never thought about it before, but it does seem that Thursdays don't have a lot going on."

"Except baseball practice."

Ebony pointed out as she placed a card in the basket, "Well, that's every day!"

Paul protested as I smiled, and Joseph chuckled besides me.

CHAPTER 45

Thursday came, and right after school, Ebony took me home so that way, we could prep the kitchen for the hours of cooking we had ahead of ourselves. She then left for a short time to pick up Caroline and all the special ingredients that she needed for her recipes. I smiled as we brought in the bags, and Caroline began to direct us on where to put things. Afterward, she explained that we were making three different versions of the same recipe. One was normal, one was gluten-free, and the final couldn't have any chocolate. It was a bit confusing, but with Caroline directing Ebony and me on what to do, it was very easy for us to do our jobs. Eventually we all got into a rhythm as we worked around the kitchen, and both Caroline and Ebony agreed that the place was too silent. They turned on music and began dancing their way around the kitchen as we worked, occasionally pausing the music to hear each other without yelling. Though I didn't do much to encourage them, the little I did do would set them into fits of laughter as I kept having trouble with electric mixer that Caroline had brought over.

"I don't understand how you're having this much trouble," Caroline said as she fixed the mixer yet again. "You're an amazing cook, and aren't you always cooking in this house?"

'Because I do everything by hand,' I signed as she stepped aside so I could pour a cup of flour into the bowl.

She smirked then reached into the bag of chocolate chips besides me and stole a couple before turning to Ebony, who was cleaning off some of the dishes in the sink.

"Are you doing all right?"

"Surprisingly yes," Ebony said as Caroline popped a couple of chocolate chips into her mouth then as the oven's timer went off, she said, "First two dozen cookies should be done."

"No, duh," Caroline said, brushing off her hands on her pants before grabbing a towel. She then opened the oven and used the towel remove the trays from the oven and onto the counter. "Perfect," she said as she examined the freshly baked cookies. "Ebony, after you finish doing the dishes, do you mind putting these on the rack to cool."

"Nope, not at all."

"Cool. I'm going to throw the next two trays of cookies into the oven…" Her voice drowned off, and Ebony and I both turned to her. She was standing in the middle of the kitchen tapping her finger to her chin. I glanced to Ebony, who frowned at me, also confused by Caroline's sudden silence.

"Caroline?" Ebony asked, setting the dish she had been washing aside.

Caroline turned to us. "It's going to take us forever to cook all these cookies by ourselves."

"So?" Ebony asked, leaning against the counter glancing at me to see if I had an answer to Caroline's cryptic sentence. I gave a silent shrug before glancing back at Caroline.

She sighed then breathed in exasperation. "So where are those boys?"

A smile tugged at the corner of my lips as Ebony rolled her eyes before turning back to the sink.

"Baseball practice isn't done for another hour, Caroline. Be patient."

Caroline made a face before putting the cookies in the oven. I bit my lip, trying to hide my smile as Ebony grinned at me before going over to the cookies that Caroline had just pulled out of the oven and began using a spatula to scoop them onto a cooling rack. We worked for another half an hour, and I had just finished my batch of cookie dough when there was a knock on the door.

"I got it!" Ebony said, swiftly moving through the kitchen before going to the front door. She opened it, and both Caroline and I smiled when we heard her cheer. "Paul!"

"Hey, babe. Still need help?"

I rolled my eyes, easily imagining what was going on at the front door when an arm encircled me from behind. Surprised, I whirled around, fisting the cookie dough still in my hands, to see Joseph looming over me.

I frowned up at him, and he grinned. "Surprise." I made a face shaking my head at him, pretending to be mad when really, I was simply delighted that he was here and that Coach had let them out of practice slightly early.

He smiled at me and let me turn back to the cookie dough. "So how can we help?" he asked Caroline as he casually stole a piece of cookie dough from the bowl. I glanced back at him to see his face pucker in confusion as he ate the piece. "Where's the chocolate? I thought we were making chocolate chip cookies?"

"We are, but that one can't have any chocolate because most of the family is highly allergic. They still like the taste of the batter, so I simply make it without chocolate chips."

I grinned as I saw Joseph's horror at the thought of not being able to eat chocolate.

"That poor family. How do they survive?"

Caroline giggled. "They make do. Now finish helping Mirda roll the dough out onto wax paper, and I'll go get Ebony and Paul to help me roll out the gluten free cookies."

She marched off, yelling behind her, "Don't forget to wash your hands, Joseph."

I bit my lip as I saw Joseph frowned in pretend exasperation.

"She's even bossier than Paul," he muttered as he went over to the sink and washed his hands before coming back over to stand by my side.

I scooted over so that there would be space for him, and he stepped right up to the spot I had been.

He reached into the bowl and got some cookie dough before turning to me as he rolled it. "How was school?"

It had been an A-day today, so I hadn't seen him for the last part of the day. As my hands were covered in cookie dough and incapable of signing or typing anything at the present moment, I simply shrugged.

He frowned. "Decent?"

I nodded my head once, and he gave a small smile before setting the perfectly rolled ball aside and grabbing another handful of cookie dough, "Jonah didn't bother you?"

I shook my head, as I thought about it. Though I had seen Jonah he had made sure to keep his distance from me, hopefully, that was a permanent change and not a temporary one. I nodded at Joseph, and he somehow understood my expression. "My day was great, except that my chem teacher assigned a paper on what is the proper definition of a chemical reaction?" He rolled his eyes. "I mean, it's not hard, but honestly, it feels a bit like busy work."

I smiled a gave a slight nod, affirming his suspicion.

I had taken the class last year and had the same teacher Joseph now had. The teacher was good, yes, but he didn't really know to connect with his high school students, and as a result, he gave lots of busy work.

He sighed then said, "You're so lucky that you're taking physics."

I smirked then shook my head. Though I was passing physics with an A, it was a bit more difficult and tedious that it appeared on first inspection. He sighed then reached into the bowl and grabbed the last handful of cookie dough when Caroline came into the room pushing Paul and Ebony.

Joseph and I grinned. "What took you?" Joseph asked innocently.

I smirked as Paul glared at him before turning to his sister.

"Okay, we're in the kitchen, happy now."

"Yes," his sister said, thrusting the bowl of cookie dough at him before walking to the oven as the timer goes off.

In a bit of childlike fury, Paul stuck out his tongue at his sister's back before nodding, satisfied, and turning with the bowl to Ebony, who was trying not to laugh. A tear came to my eye, and I brushed it away with my sleeve before going to the sink and washing off my hands, grateful for once that I could not laugh.

CHAPTER 46

Eventually we finished rolling out all of cookie dough and was able to take a break. We all crashed on the couches in my living room. Ebony and Paul cuddled on the sofa. Carolina sat in the middle between Joseph and me. We were watching the movie *Footloose*, and since we had all seen it before, we didn't bother pausing it every time one of us had to get up and take the cookies out of the oven and put two new trays in. However, when the last song came on, I was in the kitchen placing the last of the second batch of cookies on the cooling tray when Ebony ran into the kitchen.

She grabbed my hand, tugging me toward the living room. "Come on. You have to see this."

I frowned and set down the spatula before walking with her to my living room to see Joseph and Caroline swing dancing to the song footloose. My mouth dropped open as Joseph spun Caroline around, then I grinned as Paul stepped in, to dance with Caroline. I grinned as Joseph stepped toward us, then it vanished as Ebony pushed me from behind. I stumbled forward right into Joseph's arms, and I started to pull away completely awkward and embarrassed, instead of letting me go like expected Joseph pulled back to him and into a loose grip.

I stared at him in shock as he smiled then said, "I promised I'd show you my dancing skills."

I offered a small shy smile as he encouragingly pulled me along to the beat of the song, my feet moving in sync with his as I got a handle of the swing style. I smiled as he began spinning me in circles and swinging me out then in. He laughed as I tripped over my own feet, and he was forced to catch me; however, he turned it a smooth dip. I smiled up at him, then wrapped my arms around his neck as he pulled me back onto my feet. I smiled as he pulled me into a simple box step.

"So am I a decent dancer?" he asked me as we danced to the credits song.

I smiled then nodded.

"Though I'm not classically trained." I grinned and shook my head, indicating that it didn't matter.

He chuckled then looked up and said, "They gave us the room."

I turned to see he was right. Ebony, Paul, and Caroline had disappeared.

I shrugged then pulled away to sign, 'Probably just finishing up the cookies.'

He nodded then reached out and tugged on my arms, guiding me to wrap them around his neck. I did so and he wrapped his arms around my waist.

"I don't think Paul has caught onto us yet."

I gave him a strange look, and he said, frowning, "Maybe he's not the only one. Mirda?"

I didn't know what to think of his gaze, so I lowered my eyes to the floor as I lowered my arms to my side, and he slid his hands from my waist to my hands. "You know I never thought one person could surprise me so much, but here you are, surprising me yet again."

I glanced up at him to see in his eyes that he wasn't just toying with me or playing with my emotions he was telling the truth so that prompted me to express a truth of my own.

I pulled my hands away from his and signed, 'This change... you inspired me.'

Joseph raised an eyebrow and said, "I hope in a good way."

I nodded before taking one of his hands in mine. I pulled him toward the stairs, and he followed me up the stairs, to my room. With a hesitant smile on my lips, I pushed open the door to reveal my private domain. As we entered, I let go of his hand and walked to a shelf in my room. I pulled out my latest completed drawing book and turned to hold it out to him only to find him riffling through canvases that I had painted at school. I walked up to him and watched his face carefully, "These are incredible," he finally whispered as he finished looking at them. He looked up at me. "Incredible," he repeated.

I nodded then tucked the drawing pad under my arm, 'Well, those are all before I met you.'

He frowned then asked, "Is there a difference?"

I shrugged then held out the notebook, giving him the look of 'You tell me.'

He took the notebook then flipped it open. He didn't say anything as he flipped through just simply turned and walked to sit on a chair I had at my art desk. I hesitated then walked to my bed and sat on the edge, staring at my hands as I rubbed them together nervously. Occasionally I would look up at Joseph to study his face, to ascertain what he was thinking, but his face never gave anything away. Just as I thought he wouldn't say anything, that I had been wrong to reveal myself to him he flipped to a certain page and passed the art book back to me.

"This one is my favorite."

I glanced down at it to see that it had been the one I had drawn while we had been sitting around the campfire a few weeks back. It was all of us. Paul had been feeding Ebony a marshmallow, Joseph and Caroline were blowing out a burning marshmallow, and I was drawing them. It was a picture within a picture. It was one of my favorites as well, especially since I didn't have to draw my face.

I glanced up at Joseph as he said, "You're right." He cleared his throat. "There is a difference, and I'm honored to have helped make that difference, but that difference, Mirda...that's all you. That's your choice, and I believe if you continue to make the choices like the ones you've been making, you'll become the person you want to become."

I glanced down as emotions I didn't know were possible flooded me. I raised my hand and brushed at some moisture gathering there.

"You'll become a person you'd want to draw in your sketchbook and make permanent."

I exhaled a sharp breath and started to shake my head when he stood and walked over to me. He knelt in front of me and murmured, "Promise me that you won't ever give on yourself. That'll keep make these changes, whether I'm...or any of us are in your life. Please."

I hesitated then nodded, as I made a silent promise to keep changing.

CHAPTER 47

I hadn't told my dad that we were going to bake cookies, so when he came home and saw us packaging cookies in the kitchen, he was very surprised yet recovered quite quickly by calling the town's Five and Dime and ordered two pepperoni pizzas and one cheese. Each of us, equally exhausted, gave a weak hurray (though I signed mine). Shortly after pizzas arrived, we finished working, relieved we all crashed on the couch.

"Thanks, guys!" Caroline said from where she lay on the floor. "That normally would have taken me three-plus days to do."

"No problem, sis," Paul said from the couch where he had his arm wrapped around Ebony's shoulders.

I smiled then closed my eyes as I lay my head on the side of the couch. The next thing I knew I was being shaken awake.

"Mirda?" I opened my eyes to see Joseph sitting down on the other side of me. "We're about to start doing deliveries. You want to come?" I shrugged, and he smiled then stood. "I'll go tell Paul."

He headed for the kitchen as I figured combed my hair out of my face before I headed to the kitchen. There Caroline was directing Paul, Ebony, and Joseph on whom they should make deliveries to.

"I'll head with Ebony. We'll take the east side of the neighborhood. Paul, you take two of the nonchocolate plates to the Grinlows and the Verns at the end of our street. Joseph, you go with Mirda and take the west side. Everyone cool with that?"

They all chorused their assents, and Caroline looked around Joseph to see me. She gave me a look, and I nodded assent.

"Awesome. It's almost seven. We'll meet back here around eight?"

"Yep. See you soon, sis," Paul said, grabbing his two plates, and turned to the front door. "Can you open it for me, Mirda?"

I nodded then go to the door and pulled it open. He started to walk past me then looked at me. "You'd tell me if something is going on between you and Joseph."

I frowned then shook my head, signing, 'Nothing is going on.' At least not at the moment.

He sighed then said, "Maybe not now, but whenever it happens...you'll tell me?"

I nodded. 'Of course. You're my best friend.'

He smirked then said, "Even though my sister invaded your house and forced you to make cookies."

I smirked. 'I volunteered, and you of all people should know that no one can force me to do something.'

He smiled then said, "Yep. I know that all too well."

I rolled my eyes as I sensed his tone then signed, 'Get going. I'll see you in an hour.'

He smiled then turned with the cookies.

"See you soon."

He looked over my shoulder and nodded at Joseph. "Be careful driving, Joseph."

I whirled around to see Joseph coming up behind me with a basket I was certain was full of plates of cookies.

"Yep. See you later, Paul." He nodded then turned and walked to the car.

I looked to Joseph, who smiled and said, "Don't know why he's worried, since I probably won't be the one driving."

I frowned, and he said quickly, "I was going to ask if you wanted to drive, so that way you wouldn't feel obligated to talk...when you can't..."

His voice droned off, and he said, "I'm just going to stop talking now. I'll meet you at the car." He started to walk past me when I reached out and grabbed his hand.

He looked back at me as I signed, 'I can drive. Thank you.'

He offered a small smile before reaching into his pocket and handing me the keys. I took them and walked around to the driver's side of the car. I unlocked it then slid in and buckled my seatbelt before sliding the keys into the ignition and starting the car. It roared to life, and I grinned before glancing at Joseph.

He read my expression and nodded. "Yep, Caroline gave me directions and addresses."

I gave a thumbs-up before backing out the driveway and onto the main road.

CHAPTER 48

It didn't take Joseph and me an entire hour to make all the deliveries, but it did take an hour to break away from the families. Each one we visited just kept talking and talking. Joseph wasn't at all helpful; he kept talking and encouraging them. At first, I had just stayed in the car, but eventually, I got out each time and had to practically drag him to the car. Although each time I was asked if I was his girlfriend and each time my cheeks flushed, I softly shook my head. As I did so, the family would glare at Joseph before demanding him why I wasn't his girlfriend. Joseph would give a meek shrug before glancing at me and saying something about timing and that we needed to go; however each time, right before we went to the car, one of the family members would take my hand and say thank you. I would nod, unable to speak, and look to Joseph, who would say, "You're welcome," for me, then I would pull away and walk with him to the car. The first couple of times, I could handle it, but the third time, it just hit me different. We had delivered cookies to an older couple, only I learned they weren't a couple at all. They were brother and sister. Twins, like Zach and me.

She had lost her husband a few years ago, so her brother moved back in with her. It was painfully sweet watching them interact, and I wondered if this is what Zach and I would have looked like had he… had he lived long enough. Finally, I managed to force Joseph out the door and held my fake smile in place until we got to the car. There my smile fell, and my fingers fumbled with the car door. Suddenly Joseph was there, his hand covering mine. Startled at the physical contact, I jerked my hand away, taking a step back.

Vaguely, I heard Joseph sigh before he opened the driver door. Walking forward, I started to get into the car when I heard Joseph murmur, "Sorry I took so long. They just started talking, and I…"

Pushing back the tears, I shook my head, not meeting his eyes before getting in the car. Jerkily I pulled the door shut before buckling my seatbelt. Out of the corner of my eyes, I saw Joseph walk around to the other side as I fumbled with the keys finally shoving them into the ignition.

With a shaky breath, I started the car before moving my hand to the gear shift, my hands still trembling.

"Mirda?" Joseph's hand covered my own and asked, "Do you want me to?"

I shook my head. I was strong enough to do this—at least I was, up until we pulled into my driveway. Paul, Ebony, and Caroline weren't here yet, and I was glad. I shifted the car into park and turned off the car before I wrapped myself in my arms.

I stared at nothing for several long moments and Joseph eventually whispered, concerned, "Mirda."

Shaking my head, I shut my eyes as the tears, which kept threatening to spill, started to trickle down.

"Mirda. What's wrong?"

I opened my eyes and unbuckled my seatbelt. I threw open the door and ran out. I ran to my field, where no one would bother me. No one ever bothered me…but just as I arrived, I felt someone grab me from behind. I fought against them beating their chest. Soundlessly telling them to let me go.

"Mirda! Stop!" It was Joseph.

I froze and my moment of hesitation gave him the opportunity to set me down and spin me around to face him. "Mirda?"

I glanced away, putting my hands on his chest pushing him away. He only tightened his hold on my arms.

"I'm not letting you go. Not until you tell me what's wrong. What's got you running?"

I shook my head. I couldn't answer him. He would think I was selfish jerk, which I was, but I couldn't admit that. At least not to him. I shook my head, stubbornly refusing when he whispered, "I'm not Paul."

At the statement, I looked up at him, confused. He held my gaze as he said, "I can't read your mind."

I frowned, not understanding. He could read my mind. Even better than Paul could. Paul could read my mind; he couldn't explain it. Joseph could do both. Guessing what I would say before I would even have a chance to sign, but now he was claiming that he didn't have that power. Before I could form an argument in his defense, to tell him he understood me better than Paul, he started talking again, "I don't understand why you're freaking out right now, but I want to. Please. I'm sorry I got stuck talking each and every time, but I know them. They're good people. You can trust them."

I shook my head, and he nodded. "They won't judge you. Your past is yours, and if you still don't want to come to church, you don't have to."

I shook my head, desperately trying to convey to him what was wrong. He just stared at me with confusion, and frustrated, I pushed him away. He let me go, and I felt the absence around his arms immediately. I sank to the ground, wrapping my arms around my knees. Joseph knelt beside me and waited patiently for me.

I sighed then took a deep breath before signing, 'It's not you. I'm glad you made me come and get you. However, I went to church until I was six, and at one time in my life, I knew all of them. All of the people we visited today, and after listening to them, I'm starting to realize how much I missed. How much good could I have been done had I not been so selfish?' My hands shook so much that I had to stop signing for a few minutes.

Joseph was patient though and didn't push me he just sat there waiting for me to respond.

Taking a deep breath, I closed my eyes enjoying the wind on my face before I opened my eyes. 'I had a twin once.'

Joseph inhaled a breath.

'His name was Zach, and he was my best friend.' Looking down, I shut my eyes as the memories that I had of Zach assailed me.

"What happened to him?"

My lip trembled, and for a second, I didn't think I could do it. It's not that I didn't want to tell Joseph I did, but something inside of me prevented me from opening my mouth. Then I heard the sigh of the wind and felt it propel me toward Joseph.

"Tell him, Mirda."

My eyes widened, and I looked around for the voice that I was certain I heard, but besides Joseph, there was no one here. Momentarily frightened, I looked to Joseph and saw him looking at me patiently.

"Tell him," the voice said again.

Hesitantly, I raised my trembling fingers and suddenly found myself signing, 'He died…from the Sickness, and I'm pretty sure I got it from him.' Glancing down, I signed, 'I don't know why it took away my voice and it killed him. I've never heard of case like mine before, and it should have killed me too…but I'm still alive. I'm alive, and he isn't, and I squandered the extra time I was given… but Zach. He wouldn't have wasted it. He would have gone out to be with those who were suffering. He would have gone to church with my dad. He would have-—' My hands stiffened then fell to my lap as the tears started to stream down my face and silent sobs racked my body. Turning away from Joseph so he couldn't see my tears, I curled into a ball, hoping he would leave me alone.

However, the next thing I knew, he was pulling me into his arms. Automatically, I stiffened and started to resist, but Joseph tightened his grip. "Hush." His mouth was right next to my ear, and I can't help but relax as I felt him press a soft kiss to the top of my head. Slowly my tears slowed, and I stopped trembling.

Once I did, Joseph murmured, "He isn't here, Mirda. Although you think you know what he would have done had he been in your shoes, you couldn't possibly know, so stop blaming yourself. You made mistakes, Mirda… We all have." At that statement, I felt his body tense, and I knew he was talking about more than just my mistakes. He had his own story, but I knew if I asked him tonight, he would just brush it away and want to focus on me so I promised myself next chance I got I would talk to him about it.

So instead, I listened to him as he murmured, "Mirda, this fear you feel…we all feel it, even when we trust God, this fear still comes to us. What if we are doing the wrong thing? Why are we saved even though other people who are better than us died?" He sighed, and I felt his hands rub my back briefly before he dropped his hands to hold mine. Rubbing his thumb across the back of my hand, he murmured, "I can't give you a reason. You have to find that out for yourself."

I watched as he lifted one hand then titled my head up as I felt his hand tap my chin. Blushing at the intensity of his gaze, I managed to hold my head there as he said, "But I can help encourage you to find it and to have hope and faith over this doubt that plagues you." He shrugged then dropped my hands. "That's the best I can offer."

I stared at him before looking away at the woods as I pondered his words.

Blinking, I saw what I thought was a person amongst the dark trees, but he was glowing white. Pushing myself to my feet, I looked to where I saw the person. I couldn't make out much, but among the white, I saw some blue and his hand. He was waving to me, no not waving, beckoning. He wanted me to follow him. Startled, I stiffened and blinked again. Opening my eyes, I saw nothing, and I dismissed it as the reflection the moon in my eyes. "Mirda?" Joseph whispered behind me, startling me from my confusion stupor.

Taking a deep, shaky breath, I started to turn around when I felt Joseph's arms encircle me from behind. Leaning back against Joseph's powerful chest, I closed my eyes and let him hold me as we listened to the sounds of nature. Eventually I felt him press a soft kiss to the top of my head before whispering something. Twisting in his arms, I looked at him in the dark. As he locked eyes with mine, I gave him a confused look, and he leaned closer to my ear as he said, "I think it has been more than an hour."

I pulled back so he could see my smile, and it only broadened as I watched him smile. Then silently I lifted my hands from where they rested on his arms.

Slowly and precisely, I signed the words, 'Thank you.'

Joseph grip tightened on me as he whispered, "My pleasure."

Then he surprised me and lifted me up off the ground. Startled, I locked my hands behind his neck and looked at Joseph in surprise. He smiled then said, "We have school tomorrow, chica. Plus, your dad and Paul are probably wondering where you are."

I rolled my eyes, and he shook his head at me.

"They both care about you, Mirda. Even I can tell that, which is why I'm praying that they won't shoot me."

I rolled my eyes once more, pretending I didn't believe a word he said, but inwardly, a spark of hope flooded my chest. A spark of hope that kept reappearing every time I was around Joseph. A spark I never wanted to die again.

CHAPTER 49

Joseph managed to get me back to the house with dropping me, and no, my father did not kill him. After he got over the shock that Joseph had carried me back to the house, he managed to tell us that Paul had called the house saying that since Caroline and Ebony were tired that he was going to drop Ebony off at her house then take Caroline home before walking back to my house and snagging Ebony's car. It sounded all very complicated to me and like a whole bunch of extra work, but honestly, I was so tired that I didn't care one bit.

My father looked at me, and after a moment of hesitation, he nodded then walked up the stairs, calling behind him, "Good night."

As my father glanced at Joseph, Joseph smiled then murmured, "I probably should set you back on your feet."

Nodding against his shirt, I withheld the breath of regret as Joseph gently dropped me to the ground. Then he turned and started going toward the front door when I grabbed his hand holding him there. Joseph looked back at him, and for a moment, I held his gaze, trying to convey all that I wanted to say but couldn't.

Eventually my gaze fell as it became increasingly apparent that even I had my voice I couldn't convey all the gratitude I felt for Joseph for being there with me not only tonight but the last few weeks. He was someone special and even I could say all the words in the world I would never be able to convey how much he meant to me. So finally, I took a deep breath then walked forward so that way our hands were no longer stretched between us. I pressed myself against his chest and briefly closed my eyes. I felt Joseph's hand brush the back of my head and comb his fingers through my hair briefly before he pressed a kiss to the top of my head.

"I'll see you tomorrow," I heard him murmur, and I took another deep breath before pulling back and looking up at him nodding. He smiled down at me then winked before letting go of my hand and reaching for the door knob. Grasping it firmly, he pressed down, and the door swung inward. I heard Joseph sigh and walk outside pulling the door slightly shut behind him before he turned back smiling, and I couldn't help but smile back at him.

"Bye, Mirda."

'Bye, Joseph. Don't die driving home.'

He smirked. "So little faith in me, but"—then gave a mocking bow—"as you command, my lady. I will strive not to die as I drive home."

Grinning, I bit my lip as he took a step back and nearly fell backward down the stairs. Walking forward, I placed my hand on the door as Joseph regained his footing. "Totally meant to do that."

Raising a doubtful eyebrow, I gave him a knowing look.

Shrugging, he turned walking down the steps. "Can't blame a guy for trying." Then as he reached the bottom of the porch steps, he looked back, and with a serious look on his face that conveyed all that I had been trying to convey to him, he said, "Goodbye, Mirda." Then he turned away and walked toward his car.

Taking a step forward, my heart in my throat, I leaned against the porch railing as I watched Joseph climb into his car, start it, then backed out of my drive way.

'Be safe,' I mouthed, taking a deep shaky breath before turning and walking inside my house.

Pulling the door shut behind me, I leaned against it momentarily before standing up straight and walking reluctantly up the stairs toward my room.

"I'm going to presume he was a gentleman the entire time?"

Turning around, I saw my father standing in the doorway of his room wearing a bathrobe.

Briefly, I rolled my eyes before I finally nodded, smiling. 'Yes, Dad. Joseph was a gentleman the entire time.' As I signed that, a fluttering filled my chest, and I realized that Joseph was more than just any gentleman; if I had my way, he would become my gentleman before our junior year was done.

My father cleared his throat, interrupting my imaginings, and I glanced up at him to find him staring at me, love—and something else I couldn't quite place—in his eyes.

'What?'

A small smile touched my father's face, momentarily distorting the emotion I had seen in his eyes. Before I could sign anything, my father softly said, "Nothing. Good night, Mirda."

Not convinced, I gave a small nod before turning to go into my room when I thought better of it. Turning back to my dad, I walked up to him and threw my arms around his neck. Surprised, it took him a second to hug me back, but after he did, I pulled myself back.

Smiling up at him, I signed, 'Night,' before going back to my room and shut my door.

Exhaustion overwhelmed me, and I wanted to collapse right where I stood, but I forced myself to throw on some sweatpants before crashing onto my bed. Five seconds later, I was out. To say I slept like a rock would be an understatement, and it seemed only minutes later I was waking up to the sound of car horn.

Annoyed at being awoken so abruptly, I pushed myself up off the bed and look over at my alarm to see that it was almost half past seven, on Friday. On Friday! *School! Crap!* I cursed in my head, throwing off my blankets.

Rushing to my closet, I grabbed clothes and, in record time, got changed. Turning around in my room, I looked for my backpack only to remember I threw it downstairs when I had gotten home from school yesterday. Running downstairs, I started to rush to the living to grab my backpack when I saw my father and Joseph standing in my kitchen talking. Instantly my legs switched direction, and I ran back into the kitchen, rubbing the tiredness out of my eyes. My mouth dropped open as I blinked open my eyes again and realized that I wasn't dreaming. My father and Joseph were talking, in my kitchen. Taking I step forward, I held out my hand then retracted it as my father and Joseph turned toward me.

Joseph's face instantly lit up with a smile, and he waved, saying simply, "Good morning."

My mouth suddenly very dry, I closed it and glanced to my father, who was smiling. Forcing a smile of my own to my face, I raised my hands and signed, 'Morning. Sorry I'm late. I overslept.'

Joseph smirked then said, "So did I, actually. Paul called me and woke me up."

I raised an eyebrow in surprise, and Joseph shrugged. "His car battery died, and he asked if I could give the both of you a ride to school."

My mouth made a little *o*, and a real grin came to my face as I heard the car honk again. Raising an eyebrow, I bit my lip then signed, 'And let me guess, he's still in the car?'

Grinning, Joseph nodded. Smirking, I shook my head, no longer annoyed and just content, but as I glanced at the kitchen clock and saw that school was going to start in twenty minutes, my face paled. Turning back to Joseph, I signed, 'We have to go.'

Joseph frowned. "What about breakfast?"

Resigned to my fate of an empty stomach, at least until lunchtime, I shrugged as I walked backward toward the front door. 'Don't have time.'

I turned, placing my hand on the door handle, prepared to leave when my father's voice stopped me in my tracks, "Yes, you do."

I looked back at him, my eyes narrowed. Briefly my father held eye contact with me, letting me know that he wasn't budging in his decision. In answer, I raised my eyebrow, asking what his decision entailed. A small smile touched his lips before he looked to Joseph. I watched as he locked eyes with him, and an understanding passed between them.

Joseph nodded. "Yes, sir, we do."

Then he looked to me. Raising an eyebrow, I asked him silently what was going on. Joseph walked forward and placed his hand on the doorknob, pressing down and pulling it open before leaned down and murmuring softly, "I'll explain in the car," then louder, he turned to my father and said, "Have a good day, Mr. Johnson."

"It's Adam to you, Joseph."

My mouth dropped open as shock coursed through me. My father, who barely knew Joseph and was a Southern gentleman through and through, was letting Joseph call him by his first name!

"Yes, sir," Joseph replied before gently placing a hand on my back and practically pushing me out the door.

As he closed the door behind him, I turned to him, raising one eyebrow in question. Joseph started to say something when a car horn interrupted him. We looked to see Paul leaning over the back-seat and pushing on the car's horn. I shook my head suddenly very annoyed again and marched to Joseph's car. Joseph quickly got up to me, and as we got closer to his car, he leaned down and murmured, "Don't kill him."

I flashed him a look, and Joseph pointed out, "We don't have time to hide a body before school and get breakfast."

I gave him an *Are you sure?* look.

Joseph nodded emphatically before adding, "Besides, how do you plan to explain it to Ebony?"

I shrugged before signing, 'She'd understand.'

Joseph chuckled, muttering as he opened the passenger door to his car, "Maybe you'll feel better after you've eaten breakfast."

'Funny.' I slid into the car and let Joseph shut the door.

"Took you long enough," Paul muttered from the back seat as I buckled my seatbelt. "What took you so long? Brushing your hair?"

I rolled my eyes before turning around and signing, 'Overslept. Thanks for the wake-up call.'

"My pleasure," Paul said, grinning as Joseph opened the driver's door and slid into the car, shutting the door behind him.

I glanced at him as he put on his seatbelt and shifted the car from park into reverse. He pulled out of the driveway before saying, "Here's the plan. Paul, I'm dropping you off at school so you can have a bit of time to chat with Ebony. Mirda, per your father's instructions, we're getting breakfast. As I have actually eaten once this morning, I don't have a preference as to where we go to eat. Plus, I still don't know this town like you do, so you get to pick the restaurant. Any questions?"

I stared at him, my eyes bulging out of their eye sockets in shock. That's what my dad had meant by the look he had given Joseph, that Joseph needed to take me out to get breakfast, but what about school? I mean, I honestly couldn't care one way or another, but this was technically skipping, and my father had made it very clear his thoughts on me skipping. However, if my dad was really giving me permission to skip, I wasn't going to question it. Apparently, Paul didn't feel the same way.

"Yeah, one question. You planning on coming back to school?"

"Yep," Joseph said, his eyes glued to the road.

"How are you going to pull that off?"

Joseph glanced at me before looking back at the road. "I'm not. Mirda is."

A small corner of my mouth twitched upward in a smile as I realized his plan.

Still lost Paul spoke up again. "How is she going to pull sneaking back into the school…?" His voice droned off, and I smiled, knowing that he had finally realized Joseph's plan. "You can't be serious."

"Yes."

"But if she gets caught, she'll be in more than just trouble. She could be expelled."

"Yeah, but considering how often you told me she skipped school, five bucks says we'll be fine."

"But…"

I took a deep breath before turning around in my seat and signing, 'Dad gave us permission.'

Paul's eyes widened, and he said, "You're joking. Adam gave you permission?"

"Don't sound so surprised," Joseph stated, pretending to be offended. "I'm actually quite charming when I want to be."

"Right," Paul muttered, rolling his eyes, "and I'm president of the United States." I smiled as Paul winked at me before saying, "Just don't do anything stupid, you two."

It was my turn to roll my eyes before facing forward as Joseph murmured as we pulled into the school's parking lot, "No promises."

CHAPTER 50

As soon as Paul and Joseph had done their bro-hug thing and Paul had given me a side hug, I pulled up my seat so he could jump out of the car, then he ran across the parking lot to where Ebony stood by her car, waiting patiently for him. I smiled then shut the door before turning to Joseph and signing, 'What now?' Joseph smiled then said, "Now breakfast.

Where are we going, Chief?" I wrinkled my nose at the nickname, and Joseph laughed before saying, "Seriously, where to?"

I sighed then signed, 'The Roadside Diner.'

"Where's that?"

Quickly I gave him directions, and after I made certain he understood where we were going, he pulled back onto the road. It wasn't too far from school, maybe a ten-minute drive or thirty-minute walk. They had the best pancakes in town, and I had fond memories of Mom and Dad taking Zach and me early on Saturday mornings before the Sickness came.

As Joseph parked his car in the parking lot, he turned to me and asked, "Dining in or to go?" I smiled at him grateful he had given me a choice.

I raised my hands and signed back, 'Dining in. Please.'

He nodded then said, "Of course."

Then he opened his door and said, "Wait a second before getting out."

I rolled my eyes but did as he requested and simply unbuckled my seatbelt. He walked around the car and opened the door before offering me his hand. I took it and let him help me out of the car. He pulled me forward a bit before shutting the door and murmuring, "Thank you."

I nodded and led him into the diner. After a quick glance around the diner, I saw that my usual booth in the corner was open, so I tugged Joseph forward toward the book. As we approached, I let go of his hand so he can slide in the booth across from me. I grabbed a crayon and a coloring sheet from the center of the table. Quickly I flipped it over and wrote a quick message for the waitress. I then set the crayon down and looked at Joseph.

'Stay,' I mouthed before standing and walking to the counter. I flagged down a waitress, and as she walked over, I passed her the paper waited for her to nod before walking back to the table. Joseph raised his eyebrow as I sat down. I took a deep breath before signing, 'I've been here often enough that we figured out a system.'

He nodded then said, "What did you order?"

I shrugged. 'Double the usual. Pancakes, bacon, eggs, hash browns, and hot coco.'

Joseph smiled, "Sounds wonderful." He looked around briefly. "So you come here a lot?"

Nodding, I glanced around briefly before looking back at him. 'I used to. When I started skipping school, this was one of the first places I came to. Eventually, it became too painful, so I started going to Moses's ice cream, but even though it hurt, it was the only way I could remember and still feel somewhat happy. This place…' My hands stilled for a second before I finished signing, 'It got me through some hard times.' With that my hands stilled once more as I remembered the times I had come here. The good days and the bad. The few days where I had everything under control or the more frequent day when all my emotions were out there, and I… I was unstable. This place…this diner…it got me through some really hard times. I'll never forget how often it pulled me back from the brink. Just sitting here at this table listening to the people and families around me. Imagining my family sitting across the way happy, my brother besides me stealing my crayons. It hurt yes, but it hurt more not to think about them, to forget. I lowered my lashes as a tear trickled down my cheek, and I raised a hand to brush away when Joseph's hand covered my other. I looked up at him in surprise, and he smiled at me before reaching out and cupping my cheek wiping away the tear.

"Thank you for letting me in." He ran his thumb across the back of my hand once before he pulled back settling his hands in his lap. "It really is a nice place. A place my family would have loved too." I gave a small smile when I heard, "Order up."

I turned to see the waitress bringing out the food. I pulled my hands into my lap as she placed the food and drinks in front of us. She glanced at Joseph then at me, smiling. "Have him holler if you need anything, honey," she said to me before winking and walking off.

"What was that about?" Joseph asked as I placed the napkin in my lap. I shook my head and smiled before reaching for my utensils. Joseph's hand covered mine, and I glanced up at him, and he hesitantly asked, "Would you mind if we said a prayer before we start eating?"

I hesitated for a moment considering if I would mind, then surprising myself I shook my head. I wouldn't mind. I wouldn't be offended. He smiled then whispered, "Thank you."

Before folding his arms and bowing his head, I bowed my own head out of respect and listened to his prayer, "Dear Lord, we thank you for another wonderful day you've given us. Please bless this meal before us that it might strengthen and nourish our bodies. Bless we'll have a wonderful day and that with your help we might overcome any trials you place in our path."

Just as I thought he was going to finish the prayer, he added, "And please bless Mirda to know how important she is to your plan and for her to know that she can take her time. That a full recovery takes time. We love you Lord and are grateful for the blessings you've bestowed upon us. In the name of our Savior Jesus Christ. Amen."

'Amen,' I signed opening my eyes and unfolding my arms to see Joseph avoiding my gaze as he grasped his utensils.

He started playing with his food and I started to reach for my utensils too when he spoke up, "I hope you don't mind me adding you into the prayer." He glanced up, and I could tell he was surprised to find me smiling at him.

I raised my hands, signing, 'I don't, and though I don't wish to ask God for anything, I'm honored that you added me into your prayer.'

That got him to smile at me. "I was hoping you would say that, but still, next time, I'll ask for your permission."

'Thanks,' I signed before grabbing a utensil and pointing at the food. A silent command to eat.

"Yes, ma'am."

We didn't talk much during the meal other than Joseph remarking how good the food was.

After we had finished, he leaned back and said, "I can see why you come here so much."

I smirked then take the last bite of hash browns before setting my fork down. I reached for my bag only to remember I had left it in the car. I went to stand and get my wallet from the bag when Joseph reached out stopping me. "I got the check."

I frowned at him and shook my head, and he smiled. "Well, technically your dad got the check, but I have the money he gave me to pay for yours and mine's breakfast."

The frown immediately turned into a raised eyebrow.

"What?"

I shook my head, shrugging conveying that it was nothing, only it wasn't. My father trusted Joseph enough to let me spend half the night with him, skip school, and give him money for breakfast. I shook my head thinking to myself that my father must be losing it. Or maybe I was? Losing it for Joseph. As that satisfying thought passed through, a smile touched my lips, and I took a final sip of coco. The dinner bell rang, and automatically I looked up, only to wish I hadn't. Jonah was walking into the diner, a smirk on his face.

Averting my gaze before Jonah could see me, I waved to Joseph, who was getting out the money my father had given him. He glanced up, and I quickly signed, 'Bad news,' before pointing over his shoulder.

Frowning, Joseph glanced around, and I watched as his jaw clenched. Looking back down, he started counting the money in his hands as he muttered under his breath, "Shouldn't he be at school?"

Shouldn't we? I thought, flicking my eyes up once more to see Jonah looking at me. Forcing my eyes back to Joseph, I reached across the table and tugged on Joseph's arm. He looked back at me, and I nodded to the door. He nodded, placing the money on the table before standing and holding out his hand to me. Reaching out, I placed my hand in his and let me help up. Lowering out entwined hands we quickly walked toward the exit. As we passed Jonah, Joseph tugged me in front of him so that way, Jonah would get the idea to stay away, but apparently, he didn't care. Just as we reached the exit, Jonah cut us off and placed his hand on the door handle just as I was going to open it. Looking up, disgust filled me as I saw an evil grin on Jonah's face.

"Well, well…what are you doing here, Mutey? Last I checked, you were supposed to be in school."

Glaring at him, my muscles tensed, prepared for a fight, but I felt Joseph's hand tightened momentarily in mine, and I looked back at him. He shook his head, a clear indication that this was not the place to start a fight. Taking a deep breath, I nodded before leading Joseph to the side exit. We walked out, Joseph briefly letting go of my hand to hold the door open for me.

Nodding in gratitude, I took his hand as we rushed toward the car. Out of the corner of my eye, I saw Jonah's grin grow and he walked out the exit he had been blocking toward Joseph's car. My eyes widened, and I glanced to Joseph. He shook his head again, and I saw a hardness in his gaze I had never seen before, so I didn't protest when Joseph opened the passenger door for me.

I started to sit inside when I saw Jonah coming up behind Joseph. Automatically, I stood back up, grabbed Joseph's arm, and pulled him behind me. Stepping in front of him, I glared defiantly at Jonah. I didn't care if he hurt me but hurting Joseph, which was crossing a line.

A smug smirk spread across Jonah's face, and he gave a low yet piercing whistle, "So you and the boy toy are an item now. Congratulations, Mutey."

My body stiffed, and I clenched my fists, asking Jonah slightly what he wanted.

Mirthlessly, Jonah chuckled. "You never answered my question, Mutey. What are you doing here?"

Refusing to dignify his question with a response, I shook my head before pointing back at the diner. Once again, Jonah chuckled before shoving his hand in his pockets.

"Nah, I think I'll stay out here awhile, Mutey. It's a little stuffy inside."

Clenching my teeth momentarily as rage filled me, I relaxed slightly as I felt Joseph's hand wrap around my waist.

"Mirda, let's go."

Taking a deep breath, I let Joseph guide me back to the passenger side of the car as Jonah taunted us, "Are you chicken as well as mute? Mutey."

Despite Jonah's taunts, I forced myself to slide into the car.

"So Joseph is your new boy toy. Have you told him that you're just toting him around until something better comes along?"

I felt Joseph's body stiffened beside me, and I glanced up to reassure him that it wasn't true, only to stop as I saw him with a tight smile on his lips. A smile that I said "I know" and that everything would be all right. A small smile spread across my own lips, and I nodded before pulling on my seatbelt.

Joseph nodded, and just as he went to close the door, Jonah threw one last insult. "Honestly, I don't know what he sees in you, Mutey. You're pathetic waste of space."

Briefly his words affected me, and my muscles tightened as doubt filled me. Maybe what Jonah was saying was true, maybe I shouldn't be here, but Joseph's slam as he shut the car door told me otherwise. Snapping my head up, I watched as Joseph marched up to Jonah. He was yelling something; the car door muffled it, but I knew it wasn't kind. Jonah fired back a response, and I watched as Joseph suddenly reeled back and punched Jonah in the face. My mouth dropped open, and I rapidly unbuckled my seatbelt and pushed open the passenger door. Rushing to Joseph and Jonah, I watched helplessly as Joseph punched Jonah again and again.

My first reaction was to shout to Joseph to stop, but I couldn't. So instead, I rushed forward, and before Joseph could throw his next punch, I grabbed Joseph's arm, momentarily looking back to Jonah, who, despite having blood streaming down his face, was grinning. He wanted this fight. Rage filled me, and it took all of my self-control not to give Jonah exactly what he wanted. Instead, I turned and put a hand on Joseph's chest, pushing him back toward the car.

"What are you doing?"

Looking up at him, I pleaded with my eyes for him to calm down and not let Jonah win. Joseph hesitated for a moment then took a deep breath and stopped fighting me. Turning back to his car, I walked him to his side before walking around to my side.

Looking back at Jonah, who was still recovering from Joseph's last punch, I mouthed, 'Stay away from us!'

Then we climbed into the car and shut the door, before Joseph finally peeled out of the parking lot.

CHAPTER 51

Joseph drove us to school at a speed that had we passed any cops would have gotten us pulled over, but I didn't care. Joseph was safe, and that was all that mattered. Jerkily, Joseph pulled into the school's parking lot and into a spot. Hesitantly, I looked up at him to see his jaw clenched. We hadn't spoken the entire ride, and although I knew that he wasn't mad at me and that he was mad at Jonah, it still hurt me to see him hurting. Reaching out, I touched his hand that was lingering on the gear shift. He flinched, and for a moment, I worried that he was indeed mad at me, but as I pulled my hand away, he reached out and took it, lacing his fingers with mine.

A breath of relief escaped me, and I looked up at him to find concern evident in his gaze. He reached out and, with his hand, brushed a strand of hair behind my hair before cupping my face. "You all right?"

I nodded, and he pulled back his hand, and I momentarily saw the back of his hand. It was red and covered in splotches of blood. Whether it was his blood or Jonah's, I wasn't sure. "Mirda." Distracted from my obsession over the wellness of his hand, I saw Joseph looking up at me intently.

'What?' I silently asked him.

"You know what," he responded back silently.

Retracting slightly, I tried to play ignorant, but I did know what. He had to know more about Jonah and me—the origin of our rivalry—but that didn't concern him! Shaking my head, I denied his request. He already knew that Jonah didn't like me. He didn't need to know anymore! I felt Joseph's hand on my face again. I looked up to see him nodding and mouthing please. Shaking my head, I pulled away from him, opening the car door and climbing out. Shutting the door, I bit my lip and leaned against the car. I wasn't being selfish. I told myself I was protecting him.

Joseph climbed out and walked around to my side and stood in front of me murmuring quietly, "Mirda."

Shaking my head, I placed my hands against his chest as he boxed me in against the car. "There's more to the story than what you're telling me."

Shaking my head desperately, I tried to convey what I couldn't say aloud. I didn't want to bring him more into this mess more than he was already. It wasn't his problem; it was mine. Gently, he reached forward and placed his hands on my shoulders. Caving, I leaned forward into his chest, the tears I hadn't known I was holding back releasing.

He held me for who knew how long before his grip tightened slightly, reminding me that he was here waiting for an answer. Sighing, I pulled back slightly still not meeting his gaze. Joseph sighed then leaned down and murmuring, "I don't think your dad will mind us skipping class for a little longer."

Shaking my head, I leaned back, trying to sign, to explain to Joseph that I wasn't worried about my dad, but in reality, I was worried about him. However, I saw the look in his gaze and knew that even if I refused to tell him, he wouldn't run; he just wanted this to be my choice. Glancing back down, I saw his knuckles still bloody, and for a moment, my heart clenched. I wanted to tell him I did, but I knew better. Pushing away from him, I told myself that he could still be saved. He could still escape me. Hardening my heart, I looked up at him and signed, 'Then we're even. I saved you. You saved me.'

Turning away, I reached to open the car door to grab my bag when Joseph's hand covered mine.

I felt his breath on my neck as he murmured, "Yes, as friends, but…" He hesitated then said, "But if we want to be anything more than that, you have to let me in. All the way."

I squirmed and tried to pull his hand off mine, but he was too strong.

So I was helpless as he whispered, "Please, Mirda."

At those two simple words, my internal defenses started to fall. I wanted to tell him. More than I wanted to tell anyone anything before, but what would he think of me after I told him the whole truth about what happened between me and Jonah? Squeezing my eyes shut, I continued to struggle with my doubts and fears when through the darkness, I heard that simple yet very magical word once more, "Please."

With that one word, the last defenses fell, and I heard myself exhale before I turned around and looked up at him. His eyes were questioning but so full of care and understanding that I fell for him all over again. Reaching up, I touched his cheek. His eyes closed momentarily, and I smiled at the effect I had on him. Pulling my hand down, I twisted my hand on the handle of his car door and laced my fingers with his.

Opening his eyes, he looked at me as I mouthed, 'Come with me.'

Silently he followed me as I led him to the back way onto the field before finally leading him up into the bleachers. We sat on the highest bench in the shade. Out of sight from anyone and everyone practicing on the field. Nervously, I glanced at Joseph to find him staring at the field. Taking a deep breath as the nerves filled me, I let out the nerves as I let out the breath of air. *This is good. This is a good thing.* Taking another deep breath, I shut my eyes for a second before I heard Joseph sigh. Opening my eyes, I saw him turn and sit on the bleacher in front of me.

"Okay. I'm ready. What's the full story? What happened to you and Jonah?"

I hesitated for a moment, so unsure, but as I saw Joseph nod encouragingly, I found the courage to pull out my phone and type into the app I so rarely used nowadays, 'You know that most of these people, including me, grew up here.'

Joseph nodded, so I continued, 'Jonah didn't. He moved here when I was eight. I had already lost my voice, lost all my family. I was broken. Paul tried to help, but I wouldn't let him in. Even though we had agreed to become friends, I still held him an arm's length. Him and his sister. Maybe if I hadn't, things with Jonah wouldn't have gotten so bad.'

I took a deep breath, not meeting his eyes as I typed, 'I met Jonah at the park. I was sitting on the swings listening to the kids running and laughing around me. It hurt to be around them, to be reminded of what I lost, but I wanted to forget the pain, to remind me that I was still alive. Jonah was playing with his new friends from school when suddenly he broke off, came over to me. Sat on the swing next to me and started talking. Distracting me, when suddenly from behind, I'm shoved to the ground.

'I turned around to see one of the bigger boys, which Jonah had made friends with, standing behind me. I got to my feet ready to defend myself when Jonah put himself between us. Started talking the bully down. The bully ignored him, pushed him aside, and came after me. I had been taking self-defense courses for two years. So I was fine, but after everything, the kids came up and started congratulating me. I shrugged them off and went to walk off, to walk home, when I saw Jonah lying in the mud. He had anger on his face, as if I stole his moment. I didn't think of it at the time, but I noticed as I went to the park from then on, he never came to my rescue. He stayed away. Then the first day I joined real school, he made it clear which side he was on. He pushed me down told me he knew my secret. Why I couldn't come to school. He told everyone I was mute and told me to prove him wrong. I couldn't, of course, and he laughed at me. Paul was standing right beside him and did nothing, only I learned later that wasn't true.' I took a deep breath. 'After I ran and skipped my first day of school, Paul found me. Took me home and apologized, told me that he had been searching all day for me. He said that if Jonah wasn't going to be nice to me, then obviously, he shouldn't hang out with him. I don't think Jonah ever got over that betrayal, and I have a feeling he blames me.'

"Well, that's just ridiculous. Jonah should know it's not right to push others around, and he has to accept the consequences of his actions." I gave him a look. "You know it's true."

I shrugged. 'Maybe, but—'

"Paul was right to leave him. If Jonah can't be nice to you, then I wouldn't want to hang out with him either. Besides, Jonah's a jerk, who would want to hang out with him?"

'You don't get it,' I interrupted with my hands. 'Paul was his only friend, in his gang. Paul was the only one who cared, and then I took him away from Jonah. Him and his stupid pride.' I signed bitterly, resisting the urge to curse before signing furiously, 'As a result, he hates everyone around him but especially me, and he does everything possible to make my life miserable. Including beating me up. Though most days, I win our stupid fights.' I smirked, but then it faded as I signed mostly to myself, 'I wish I could turn back time and done something differently. Maybe then he wouldn't be the way he is.' My hands clenched into fists, and I placed them on my lap.

Joseph was silent for a moment before he said, "You're wrong."

I looked to him, and he held my gaze for a long while before stating firmly, "It's not your fault. Sure, you could have made different choices, but so could Jonah. The way he is right now, and the way he acts, that's a result of his actions, not yours. However, what you do as a result of his actions will determine who you are." He took a breath and looked at the field before looking back at me. "You were the one who walked away from a fight today, granted I didn't, but still you did good. You pushed me back. So no, it's not your fault Jonah became who he is. It's his, and I'm sorry he ever made it feel like it was your fault because it's not." I stared at him in shock for a moment before he held his arms out to me. "Permission to hug."

I rolled my eyes then signed jokingly, 'When have you ever asked permission to hug me?'

Grinning, he shrugged, and I rolled my eyes once more before throwing my arms around his neck. He pulled me close, and I can't help but smile as I heard his heart beat against my chest. I didn't deserve him. I knew that much but I was too selfish to care. Joseph was mine, even though he didn't know it, yet I knew it. He was mine, and I would do anything to make it happen.

Our hug was eventually interrupted by the bell ringing. With a sigh of annoyance, Joseph pulled away and asked, "Can you sneak us in still?"

I nodded then signed, 'It's actually the perfect time. Come on.'

We snuck back into the school no problem, blending in with crowds, and after listening to a bit of gossip, we figured out it was third period on a B-day. A small smile played across my lips as I tugged Joseph toward Mrs. Anna's class.

From past experience, I knew that Mrs. Anna would totally cover for me, and she knew that I liked Joseph and so would most likely cover for him too. Joseph and I slipped into the back of the class waving to Mrs. Anna, who smirked before wagging her finger at us. Shrugging unapologetically, we went to the back room. I got out my newest painting, and Joseph pulled out his homework. Nothing happened until halfway through art class when Mrs. Anna's phone rang. Setting down my paint brush briefly, I looked to Joseph as we both listened to Mrs. Anna as she reassured Joseph and I were in class and that we hadn't snuck in.

Glancing back at Joseph, I couldn't stop the smile that played on my lips as I saw his shocked expression. "How?" he mouthed, and I gave a mock little bow before picking up my paintbrush.

Leaning over my dark landscape, I gently blended the paint already on the canvas. A moment later, I heard a soft chuckle emanating from Joseph. Glancing up, I saw him shaking his head at me in wonder. "No wonder it took them so long to bring you in," Joseph muttered as I worked on my newest painting.

I smirked as brushed out my storm clouds. "All the teacher's love you and are willing to cover for you."

Rolling my eyes, I smirked knowingly. *Not all of them.*

Glancing back at my painting, I frowned then took a deep breath and stepped back, tilting my head to get a better angle on my painting. I smiled, knowing it was progressing exactly as I designed. I had to fill in a few more of the minor details, add in a bit more shading, but I was actually happy with this one. It was an abstract with the clashing of lights and darks. From one angle, it looked like a storm that was brewing; from another, it was a storm that was in full force. One couldn't really tell which side was winning, the light or the dark, but I felt like that was part of the abstractness of it all.

I took another deep breath before turning and going to the sink. Gently I cleaned off my brushes in the sink briefly glancing over my shoulder as I heard a knock at the door. Paul was standing there examining my painting. Frowning, I turned as I dried off my brushes. This was normal Paul looking at my paintings, but the expression on his face, I had never seen it before. It was not just awe; it was something more…maybe entrancement.

Looking to Joseph, who was packing up his things, I signed, 'Would you mind?'

He nodded, understanding, and paused in his packing. "Paul. Paul!"

Paul blinked once and briefly looked at me, then he turned and walked out of the room.

Furrowing my brow in confusion, I turned to Joseph, glanced down at Joseph, who was still sitting at a table. He shrugged, then his eyes widened as he saw someone behind me. Whirling around, my mouth dropped open as Paul walked back into the room with Mrs. Anna. Now strictly speaking, Mrs. Anna didn't come and look at my art until after I had left or if I asked her advice. So the fact that Paul went "behind my back" and got her was big.

Biting my lip, I hesitated for a moment, debating whether or not I should get mad for Paul doing this, but then I felt Joseph slide his hand into mine. Looking up at him, I saw him smiling down at me. Unable to not smile back, I grinned at him before looking hopefully at Mrs. Anna. She was still studying the painting and I noticed that she had pretty much the same expression Paul had on his face. The only difference was the critical look she gave my painting, an obvious sign that she was the art expert not me. My limbs tensed, and I found myself attempting to control my breathing. I shouldn't be nervous, I told myself; this was Mrs. Anna, but I was nervous. Just as I was worried as I was about to burst at the seams with the amount of tension in the room, Mrs. Anna glanced at me, a soft smile on her face. Letting go of Joseph's hand, I took a step forward, clasping my hands together, waiting for her critiques. Only none came.

"It's good," Mrs. Anna stated simply, looking back at the painting. "Really good." Then she picked it up from the stand, "I'm keeping this."

My eyes widened, and I looked to Joseph as I signed, 'Tell her it's not finished.'

Joseph translated for me, and Mrs. Anna shook her head. "Mirda Johnson, that is load of phooey. It is finished. You're just putting off the inevitable."

I raised my hands to deny her claim but slowly lowered them as I looked back at my painting. She was right. It looked pretty awesome. Maybe I could make it more awesome, but beauty was in the eye of the beholder. Right?

Glancing up at Paul, he shrugged, clearly leaving the choice up to me. Turning back to the man standing close behind me, I saw him nodding encouragingly before taking a step back, also clearly leaving the decision up to me. Taking a deep breath, I looked back at Mrs. Anna before I finally shrugged, admitting defeat. She was right, the painting was hers if she wanted it. Vaguely I heard Paul try to stifle a snicker across from me, and I snapped my head up to glare at him.

Evidently not caring about my glare, he grinned then signed, "I love you" from behind Mrs. Anna's back.

Rolling my eyes, I looked back at Mrs. Anna, who had resumed looking at her painting.

"This is beautiful," she murmured, mostly to herself, then looked at me with a smile that brightened the whole room. "All that's left is for you to sign it."

Taking a deep breath as she placed the painting on the table, I walked over to the stack of dry paint brushes and dipped one in some of the leftover gray paint. Taking care not to drip any paint, I walked over to the painting before leaning over it and signing my name in the left corner of the painting, *Mirda Johnson*. Once I finished, I looked back up at Mrs. Anna and nodded, confirming that I indeed was done.

Somehow after I did this, her smile widened. "Thank you. Oh, don't forget to remind me to write a check for a thousand dollars," she said before she abruptly turned and walked from the room.

My eyes widened, and I looked at Paul to see if I had heard Mrs. Anna properly. He grinned then nodded, confirming that I had heard Mrs. Anna correctly.

"Congratulations. You just sold your first painting."

My mouth fell open, and I covered it still in disbelief. However, before I could get my wits about me, the bell rang, and he straightened up.

"Well, that's the end of class. I'll see you both after school at baseball practice."

Then he shouldered his backpack before he turned and exited first the backroom then the art room. Dropping my hand from my mouth, I turned to Joseph, asking him, with my eyes, the same question that I had asked Paul.

He chuckled then shook his head still, smirking. "Yep. That was real, all right," he confirmed before he turned and grabbed my bag. He held it out to me expectantly, and I took one more deep breath before I accepted what had just happened.

A smile spread across my face as I tossed the paint brush that I had used to sign my name into the bucket of water in the sink then turned back to Joseph and took my bag.

Shrugging it over my shoulder, I signed, 'Thanks.'

Joseph nodded before reaching out and taking my hand. Quickly he led me from the room at almost a breakneck pace, weaving in between people like a pro. Smiling, I practically ran to keep up to him. Despite my running, though, my pace was obviously still too slow for Joseph.

Glancing over his shoulder, he smiled at me before declaring, "Come on, Miss Artiste. If we don't hurry, we're going to be late for class!"

Rolling my eyes, I smiled as I hurried my pace to match his.

CHAPTER 52

Joseph said goodbye to me at the locker-room doors per usual before rushing off to the dance studio. I walked into the locker just as the bell rang and shrugged off the warning the female PE teacher gave me as I threw on my PE clothes. PE was nothing special. The kids played basketball, while I was allowed to do free throws in the corner. I didn't much care for basketball, but being pulled aside like this, even if it was for practical reasons still kind of hurt; however, it was a dulled kind of hurt. I didn't particularly know why until I had shot my fifteenth free throw. I was content with my lot. I knew that though things would never be fair for me because I was mute, I still was able to be happy and was able to find joy in the little things. I smiled as I threw my next shot, knowing the reason I was able to feel this way was that a certain someone convinced me to change my tune.

After that realization, class passed by quickly, and before I knew it, I was back in the locker room throwing on my PE clothes, alone. Everyone had finished, and the bell had rung, but I was content to take my time. I was just going to the field to watch the boys play baseball and hang out with Ebony. Despite myself, I smiled again as I pulled on my T-shirt. I started to stuff my PE clothes back in my locker when my cell phone buzzed. I grabbed it from the bench in front of the locker and smiled as I saw that it was from Joseph. "Practice was canceled today. Want a ride home?"

My smile broadened, and I started to text back, 'Sure, give me five minutes,' when a sudden shrill scream caused me to freeze in place. Why would a girl scream in the locker room unless she slipped by the showers? However, that didn't make sense. There was no thump sound to indicate the girl had fallen, nor did the scream sound like a startled scream one might expect from slipping on water. No, this was a scream that conveyed pure terror. My memory flashed back to when Jonah slammed me against the wall and being unable to scream. I blinked and took deep breaths, trying to calm my racing heartbeat. Then my head snapped up as I heard the scream again.

Shoving my phone in my pocket, I darted forward, down the aisle of lockers. I reached the end and looked up and down the rows—no one. I go to the next aisle as I heard another scream, then I froze midstep as a girl ran past the aisle of lockers I was in. I fought the urge to run as not a second later two boys and Jonah casually walked past me, after the girl. My eyes widened as I heard the girl scream again, and I ran to the end of the aisle of lockers. I peered around the corner to see the boys had cornered the poor girl by the showers.

For a few moments, I debated with myself, then I whipped out my phone and deleted the text I had started to type to Joseph, then I quickly typed, '911 Girls Locker Room.' I sent the text just as I heard a loud smack! My eyes jerked up, and I saw the girl doubled over her, hands trying to cover her face. Jonah stood over her, his hand an unusual shade of pink. I tried taking a deep breath, but it was pointless. For once I wasn't afraid of Jonah. I was mad. Anger filled my bones as I whirled around and saw a book about Constantinople lying on the floor. A sudden idea struck me, and I smiled as I grabbed it before I ran to the end of the row of lockers. Stopping briefly to catch my breath, I lifted the book up over my head then threw it against the lockers with a satisfying clang.

Running back down the aisle of lockers, I arrived just in time to hear Jonah say to his boys. "Go check it out. If it's a girl, invite them to join in the fun. If it's a teacher, just give me a holler."

I reached the end of the aisle as both boys nodded then walked off, each taking a separate route. I took a deep breath as I watched Jonah kneel before the girl and grabbed her hair.

'Oh no, you don't,' I mouthed as my mind frantically swirled with another idea to distract Jonah. Glancing around once more, I looked around, this time for something to throw and potentially hit Jonah. My eyes scanned the vicinity, and my nose wrinkled as my eyes landed on a pair of dirty gym shorts sticking out from underneath the lockers, then I heard the girl cry out, and I knew I didn't have the luxury to be picky. Darting forward, I snagged the shorts before whirling around to see Jonah's lips inches away from the girl's. My eyes narrowed as I raised my arm like I was throwing a baseball and pitched them at Jonah. The shorts flew through the air perfectly then landed on his head just as his lips were about to brush against the girl's; he spluttered and drew back from the girl, releasing her to grab the shorts from off his head. He glowered at them then stood and whirled around. I stood my ground as his eyes scanned the room and landed on me. I gave a little wave, as an animalistic growl resonated his throat. *Time to go*, I thought as he started for me.

Whirling around, I ran down the aisle as Jonah chased me. My immediate thought was to head toward the exit, but I knew if I did that, then most likely Jonah and his two friends would run off before I could come back with the teachers, so I knew I had to stall. Veering to the side, I made a sharp left then ran straight for a couple of rows of lockers before I made another sharp left and almost ran into one of Jonah's friends.

Despite the almost collision, my feet kept moving, and shock froze him in his tracks as I casually slipped past him, and he said, "What the—?"

Behind me, I faintly heard Jonah say, "Get her!"

Their pounding feet were loud in my ears as I ran down another empty row of lockers, my eyes scanning every which way as I attempted to avoid the third boy, when suddenly he appeared in front of me. I stumbled to a halt then made a sharp right toward the exact same place they had first cornered the girl. Luckily the girl was gone, and I hoped she had been able to get out of here before Jonah and his goons caught her.

"There she is. Don't let her get away."

Rolling my eyes at Jonah's command, I thought bitterly, *Where can I go? Y'all have me cornered.* Only option I had was to stand and fight, which hypothetically was a very bad idea. I knew I could most likely take Jonah in a fight, but him and his goons? That was a different question entirely; however, I had to stall for time until Joseph got here. I reached the corner and whirled around to face Jonah and his two friends.

They glared at me as Jonah said, "Well, that was rude. Besides, if you wanted to join in the fun, Mirda, all you had to do was ask."

I glared at him and clenched my fists.

"What was that, Mutey?" Jonah asked, laughing. "You don't want to start a fight? Well, it's too late. The fight has already begun." He cracked his knuckles, walking forward. "I'm going to enjoy this."

No, you're not, I thought, just before I punched his nose. He stumbled back, startled at the force behind the punch. Despite the raging emotions behind the punch, I allowed myself a small smile as Jonah stood back up and glared at me.

"Get her!" he commanded his goons.

They hesitated for only a moment before they started forward. I wouldn't hurt them, I promised myself. I would just stop them from hurting me until Joseph showed up. I put my arms up and blocked the first punch one guy threw at my jaw. It hurt, but it could have been worse. I kneed up and hit the boy where the sun didn't shine, then as he doubled over clutching his balls, I placed my hands on his head and slammed it down on my knee. He collapsed to the floor when suddenly I was grabbed from behind. The other goon started dragging me backward as Jonah started forward. I wasted no time. I swung my legs out and up before elbowing back into the boy's side. His grip relaxed just enough for me to turn and step on the instep of his foot. He yelled, grabbing his foot, letting go of me. I darted forward and punched Jonah's nose again before turning back to the boy still clutching his foot. I punched him in the nose too before kicking him in the balls. He fell to the ground, doubled over, and I almost smirked when someone grabbed my arm from behind and twisted. I made a face then stepped toward Jonah under his arm, twisting out of the grip to face him with my fists raised. He stared at me fiercely, blood running down his face.

"Okay. You're dead, Mutey!" Instead of throwing a punch at me like I expected, he ran at me.

He caught me around my middle and used the force from his run to slam me into the wall, thus stealing the air from my lungs.

I gasped for air as Jonah pressed me up against the wall, but I still couldn't breathe. Taking a gasping breath, I slammed my elbow into the small part of his back. He pulled back slightly, and I attempted to knee him whilst he grasped my leg. However, I must have missed because Jonah's hand held steady as he looked up at me. "I don't think you've ever been this close to a man before, Mutey, or have you?" I glared at him then banged my forehead against his face. He gasped and stumbled back, dropping me. I landed crouched and started to get up when someone grabbed the back of my hair. I opened my mouth to give a soundless shriek as my hands reached back to grasp the base of my head.

"I got her, Jonah," one of Jonah's goons said as he pulled my hair even more.

Tears streamed down my face as Jonah recovered and walked in front of me. Mad would only begin to describe the expression on his face, but considering the amount of blood streaming down his face, I felt a swell of pride rise up inside of me despite the pain in my skull.

"Nice try, Mutey, but you are and always will be a little helpless mute girl."

Even though it hurt, I opened my mouth and mouthed, 'Liar.'

Jonah frowned, and I wasn't sure if the fact that he couldn't understand me or that he didn't like being called a liar caused him to hesitate. However, he must have decided that what I thought of him didn't matter because he shrugged then rammed his fist into my face.

CHAPTER 53

I don't know how long Jonah and his gang beat me. All I knew was the pain in my face and chest. Eventually, they let go of my hair, and I fell forward, curling myself into a ball, praying that I would last the torment when suddenly through the pain, I heard shouting. Opening my one good eye, I saw Jonah grappling with someone, then he was pulled from my line of sight. I stared blearily at the person who was my rescuer as he knelt before me.

"Mirda?" It was Joseph. It was his concerned face in front of my bruised one.

Tears streamed from my good eye, and I signed weakly, 'What took you so long?'

He sighed with relief then reached out and pulled me to his chest. I vaguely heard him saying "She's okay" to someone before he lifted me up and carried me somewhere. When I next came to, I was lying on a bed. Joseph was leaning over me, holding a bag of ice on my bad eye.

"Hey!" he said. "How are you feeling?"

Weakly I raised my hand and signed with a wince, 'So. So.'

He frowned then asked, "You're in pain?"

I hesitated then nodded.

"Where?"

I gave a small shrug then winced again. Everywhere hurt, and I meant everywhere. However, I was also sore, like I had been sleeping in the same position for a while. I realized then that I needed to sit up. I raised my hand and grabbed Joseph's wrist. He stared at me in confusion, but at the slight tug of my hand, he pulled the ice away from my face. I then removed my hand and placed it on the other side of the bed. I then pushed myself upward. "Mirda? Are you sure you should be doing that? You just got beat up. We don't know what type of internal damage you have."

I glanced at him then signed. 'I'm not at a hospital, am I?'

"No, the nurse assures me that you'll be fine."

'Then I'll be fine enough to sit up,' I signed as I started to push myself up again.

He sighed then stood and turned to stand beside me. He placed a hand on my back and helped me sit up the rest of the way. I took a deep breath as pain traveled up my ribs. A tear trickled down my cheek and averted my gaze as embarrassment filled me. I felt awful, and I had a feeling I looked it too.

"You know I wanted to kill Jonah." Joseph's voice startled me out of my thoughts, but despite his startling revelation, I still couldn't look up at him. "He molested a girl, and he tried to do the same thing to you." Disgust filled his voice, and I bit my lip, unsure of whether the disgust was aimed at me or— "I can't believe any man would do that to a woman, and I promise you, Mirda, that I will never do that to you." I felt his hand on my chin, and he tilted it up, so his eyes met mine. "Never."

A smile touched my face, and I mouthed, 'I know.'

He nodded. "Good, because I have never been more scared in my entire life when I got your text." He dropped his hand from my chin and looked away, clearly in thought.

Leaning forward, I wearily leaned against Joseph, entwining one of my hands with his.

Joseph ran his thumb over the back of my hand before murmuring, "I didn't think. I just got out of my car and ran to the locker room. As I ran there, I intercepted the girl who Jonah had molested, and she told me what was going on. What you had done. I was mad mostly at Jonah, little bit at you," glancing at me, a small smile on his face.

Raising an eyebrow, I mouthed, 'You were mad at me.'

He nodded then reached out and stoked my hair. "Although heroic, you shouldn't have taken that risk."

Shrugging, I conveyed silently that I had no choice. It was either me or her. Joseph sighed then rubbed my back, pressing me slightly closer to him. "You still shouldn't have taken that risk, but you gave me the time I needed to get teachers and"—a small chuckled escaped—"even though when we arrived and saw Jonah was on top of you, it was obvious from the amount of blood still streaming from his nose and other places that you gave him a run for his money."

Offering him a small, tentative smile, I nodded before raising my hands and signing, 'Well, that was the goal.'

A small smile touched his own lips for a moment before it faded. "Still, you could have been—"

I placed my hand to his cheek and mouthed, 'But I wasn't.' Then pulling back my hands, I signed, 'And nothing happened that won't be healed in time.'

Although I couldn't say it with my voice, I did my best to convey with my eyes that I was all right. That the bruises I had would heal in time. The important thing was that I had saved that girl and revealed Jonah's true intentions to the school. He sighed then wrapped his arms around me, pulled me into his lap, and hugged me close. Letting my eyes drift close, I relaxed against Joseph, and in that moment, neither of us needed a voice.

CHAPTER 54

Eventually my ribs started to hurt, and despite me pithy attempt to hide the pain from Joseph, he saw. Releasing me, he gently helped me lie back down then went to and got a bag of ice from somewhere. Setting it on top of my ribs Joseph took one of my hands and let me squeeze it until the pain died down and my eyes closed. Sleep overcame me, and I slept like a log until what felt like a few moments later, Joseph was gently shaking me awake.

"Mirda." I opened my eyes to see the school nurse and Principal Calvin standing beside my bed.

I sat up, and the adults in the room started to protest. Joseph knew there was no point trying to stop me, so he helped me sit up fully and lean my back up against the wall. I rested an arm across my chest as I looked at the adults.

They stared at me for a moment before the principal said, "How are you feeling?"

I gave him a look, and he sighed, "Joseph, would you be willing to translate?"

"Course. She's fine, in pain, but fine."

The principal nodded. "Okay. I called your father. He'll be home as soon as possible, but he went to the city today and—"

'I know,' I signed, interrupting his explanation.

Joseph translated, and the principal nodded before looking at the nurse. She took a step forward then looked at me.

"You've got lots of bruises, darling, a split lip, sprained arm, but nothing too serious. Possibly a slight concussion, so if your head really starts hurting, you let me know, but other than that, you should be fine."

I gave a slight nod, and she walked forward, holding out some ice. I started to reach out when the pain made spots dance in my eyes.

"I got it," Joseph said beside me.

I withdrew my arm as he grabbed the ice and handed it to me. I placed it on my wrist, which was starting to throb.

The nurse nodded. "If you need anything, anything at all, I'll be in my office."

I signed. 'Thank you.'

Joseph translated. The nurse nodded again before walking back to her office. Only after she shut the door did the principal start talking again.

"Mirda, I need to know what happened. Chief Baymont is talking to them, but they won't say anything. Leah gave us an account, but it was only part of the story. We need your part."

I hesitated then looked to Joseph. He nodded, and I signed, 'If I tell you, will you believe me?' Joseph translated and looked at the principal with stern eyes. The principal nodded.

"I saw the security cameras. I heard Leah's account. I know you are not at fault. All you did was defend yourself and that girl."

Nodding, I raised my good hand to touch my face, only to have my hand come away wet. I lowered my hand and looked at Joseph.

He read my eyes then looked at the principal. "I'll translate."

Principal Calvin nodded. "I wouldn't have it any other way."

I moved the ice to the side and shakily raised my hands. I signed my story, having to pause every now and then to spell out a word or phrase that Joseph wasn't familiar with. When I was done, Joseph sat on the bed beside me and held me. My shuddering slowly eased, and briefly I relaxed in his arms before looking up at Principal Calvin.

He sighed. "Thank you, Mirda. I know that was hard for you as such. I'll take care of everything, and I'll make sure Jonah gets the consequences he deserves."

I nodded slightly.

He gave a slight grin before he said, "Hang in there, kid."

I nodded as he left.

"Hang in there?" Joseph muttered into my hair.

I pulled away then signed, 'It's the thought that counts.'

Joseph rolled his eyes. "Oh, please."

I gave a small smile, and Joseph smiled a triumphant gleam in his eye. "You ready to go back home?"

I hesitated then nodded before remembering I left my stuff in the locker room. I started to sign when Joseph shook his head. "Your art teacher tracked down Mrs. Sanders to break into your locker." He pointed to the corner chair where all my stuff was. "Come on."

He stood up and held out his hand. I placed my hand in his and let him help me stand. We walked to his car in silence. He didn't let go of my hand until I had to get into the car; however, as soon as he got into the driver's seat, he reached over and took my hand from my lap, squeezing it gently. I gave him a weak smile, and he smiled back before backing out of the parking lot.

On the way home, he played no music, and we just sat in the silence, enjoying each other's company. He pulled into my driveway, and though I knew my dad most likely wasn't going to be home yet, I was still disappointed not to see his car in the driveway. Joseph parked the car, and I looked at him as he looked at me.

He held my gaze for a few moments before he said, "Do you want to go for a walk?"

I nodded quickly. I didn't want to be alone, but more importantly, I didn't want him to leave. Not until he had to.

CHAPTER 55

Joseph and I left our bags in the car and walked the property behind my house. Sensing my tension, Joseph started telling stories from his childhood. Before the Sickness. Like when his brother fell on his face in front of his crush. About the time that his sisters used him as a test subject for their makeup. Then he started talking about his guardians, how once Derek and Sharol were making a pie and thought it was a good idea to let him turn on the oven. Instead of turning on the oven, though, he turned on the gas stove. He chuckled as he told me Sharol's expression as she realized the kitchen suddenly smelled of burning gas. He didn't burn the house down, thankfully, but he came rather close.

'Thanks for not leaving me alone,' I signed as we walked.

Joseph grimaced then said, "Well, after seeing you beaten and unconscious, this is much preferred." I gave a small smile, then it faded. "Whatcha thinking about?"

I shrugged then signed, 'I didn't think. I just responded. It was stupid, but…I couldn't stop myself. Then when I was lying there being beaten, all I could think about was that this is how I would die, and for some stupid reason, I prayed. I prayed to a God I don't believe in.'

"Are you sure about that?" I looked up at Joseph, and he shrugged before he said, "Maybe you don't hate Him as much as you think you do."

I shook my head in shock. 'No, I've hated Him since I was six. I still hate Him.' *Because it was His fault*, I thought bitterly.

"Mirda, you don't hate Him. You can't."

'Why not?'

"Because He saved you. Then and now. You prayed to live. You prayed to survive the pain, and you did with His help."

'You can't know that for sure,' I protested. I shook my head in weak protest.

He took my hands in his. "No, but I can feel it. You believe. You just need to accept that fact and come home."

I shook my head, pulling my hands away. 'I don't know—'

Before I could finish what I was saying, he grabbed my hands, interrupting me.

"I know I'm not supposed to do this, but I had to."

I glared at him but nodded for him to continue.

He sighed with relief before asking, "When was the last time you prayed?"

I frowned as he let go of my hands so I could sign again. 'Right before I lost my voice. Why?'

"I want you try something for me." I gave him a look, and he took a deep breath. "I want you to pick a place, any place, and pray. It doesn't have to be now or tonight, just soon. Within the next week."

'Why?'

"James chapter one verse five," he stated simply.

I gave him a look and shook my head. Did he really think I would know the scriptures? I hadn't touched a bible in over seven years, and the last time someone (my dad) gave me a bible, I threw it out the window. Joseph took a breath and recited, "If any of you like wisdom, let him ask of God that giveth to all men liberally, and upbraidth not and it shall be given him."

Crossing my arms, I gave him the look, 'And I should care why?'

He sighed then said, "Look, I think you're so resentful against God is because you were never able to see the full picture. The full reason why you lost your voice and why you lived."

I gave a small shrug. That was part of it, sure.

He smiled, more confident now. "That scripture basically explains that if you want to know why, all you have to do is ask. He'll answer."

'You sure about that?'

"I'm willing to bet my life on it."

After a moment of hesitation, I signed, 'Fine. I'll do it, but that's it. If I don't have the spiritual revelation you want me to have, don't be disappointed.'

Joseph shrugged then took my hand in his.

"That's all I can ask." Then he pressed his lips to my cheek, causing my heart to skip a beat. "Thanks," he whispered, pulling away.

I gave a small nod before pulling away my hand to sign, 'Would you mind staying with me until my dad got home, then possibly for dinner?'

He smiled then said, "As long as you don't mind me taking a break to do homework."

Blushing, I shook my head. 'No, I don't mind, but before homework, I want to show you something.'

He frowned but nodded. I took his hand and led him over the plains and through the woods to where three headstones stood in a clearing. I heard Joseph's breath catch as he read the headstones.

"Who else knows?"

'My dad,' I signed one handed.

"You didn't show Paul?"

I shook my head weakly. He turned back to the graves then pressed his fingers to his lips then touched them each individually just as I did whenever I came here. Putting a hand to my mouth, I fought fiercely to hold back the tears that threatened to stream down my cheeks. Eventually he stood and walked over to me, taking the both of my hands in his.

"Thank you, Mirda." He glanced back to the graves, then gently gathering me into his arms, he murmured, "I'm honored."

I shrugged. It wasn't about honor; it was about me. I was finally opening myself up. After everything. I finally was willing to start living again. Pulling away from Joseph, I walked forward. I picked a small dandelion and placed it on top of Zack's grave before I glanced back at Joseph. He was staring at Benjamin's grave, a pained expression on his face. He knew the pain that I felt deep inside because he had dealt with it too. I stood and walked back to his side taking his hand again.

We were stronger together and together nothing could stop us.

CHAPTER 56

When my dad came home, I was sitting with Joseph on the couch. He had his arm wrapped around me as I leaned back against his chest. One of my hands was tangled with his; the other was lying at my side, occasionally used if I wanted to sign something. We were watching some obscure Hallmark movie with a happy ending, I was casually putting off making dinner, when I heard the door open then shut. Joseph reached out and grabbed the remote, pausing the movie. A second later, my dad walked into the living room, on his face a strained expression. I smiled kindly as he looked me up and down.

"Are you all right?"

I nodded then gestured to Joseph with my head.

Joseph looked at my father and gave a slight nod. "She's fine. The school nurse and principal recommended that she stay home from school tomorrow." I looked to Joseph and made a face. He frowned. "I thought I told you…or she…?" I made another face, and he said, "Sorry."

He pressed his lips to my forehead briefly before letting me go and standing up. "I'm running to the restroom," he stated, giving me a pointed look before he turned and left the room.

I looked back to my father, who was still looking at me. I signed, 'Dad, I'm all right." I stood and walked forward and hugged him.

I felt him release the breath he had been holding and sigh. "I'm sorry I couldn't get down here sooner. The office—"

I pulled away and signed, 'Dad, I'm okay, really, I am. Joseph…" My hands stilled on his name as I fought to convey through my signs what he had done for me. My father chuckled, and I looked up to see him smiling. 'What?'

He shrugged. "I'm just surprised this event hasn't made you two official yet. Or has it?" he asked, eying me with a truth seeker's eye.

While blushing, I casually signed, 'No.'

He groaned then said, "Why not? You two would be a perfect couple!"

I smiled then, pretending to be outraged, signed, 'Dad!'

"What? Can I not be excited for my daughter's first boyfriend?"

'He's not my boyfriend yet.'

"Yet being the operative word." I rolled my eyes as he laughed then said, "I'm glad you're all right."

I smiled then signed, 'Me too.'

He sighed before he reached out and hugged me one more time. "I love you, Mirda."

For what seemed like the hundredth time that day, tears came to my eyes. After I had them mostly under control I pulled away and signed, 'I love you too Dad.' We heard the door to the bathroom shut and I turned to see Joseph walking back into the living room. I sat back on the couch, and he sat down behind me. My dad looked at the two of us smiling before turning and walking to the kitchen. "So what do you kids want for dinner?"

I looked to Joseph and signed, 'Breakfast?'

He nodded and smiled. "Sounds good."

"What sounds good?" my dad called from the kitchen.

I smiled as Joseph called, "Breakfast."

"Sounds great. You kiddos just keep watching your movie."

Joseph made a face and said, "Shouldn't we go help him?"

Shaking my head emphatically, I signed, 'No. When it's Dad's turn to cook, especially breakfast, you stay away from the kitchen.'

Joseph quirked a grin then asked, "Should we be worried?"

Once again, I shook my head. For a moment, he raised his eyebrow, conveying his doubt in my father's cooking, skills but after a reassuring nod from me, he sighed. "All right then. You want to finish that movie?"

I shrugged then signed, 'Why not?'

He grabbed the remote and pressed Play before leaning back up against the couch. He wrapped his arm around my shoulder, and I lay my head against his shoulder before he takes my free hand in his. Eventually, my dad finished cooking and he brought the food over to the coffee table. He had made my favorites: sausage, eggs, toast with grape jelly, and a new favorite French Toast. We all ate until we were full and until we had finished a second Hallmark Movie. Afterward, though, Joseph admitted that he had to go. I offered him to walk him to his car, so that was where we ended up. Hugging each other besides his car. I didn't want him to leave. I knew he had to but that didn't make it any easier. I felt him press his lips to the crown of my head, and I closed my eyes briefly before opening them. I took a step back, and he held my hands in his, refusing to let me go.

"Promise me I won't see you at school tomorrow." I made a face, and he said, "You need the rest."

Taking a breath, I tried to think of a way to weasel out of staying home alone, a second later, an idea popped into my mind. Pulling my hands back, I signed, 'Fine, I'll skip school tomorrow, but you have to skip with me.'

"Mirda—"

'That's the only way you'll get me to stay away.'

He shook his head then said, "I can't believe you used to skip school. Paul had to be kidding."

'Well, obviously I've changed.'

"Yeah, you've corrupted yourself, so now you have to corrupt others." Widening my mouth in mock outrage, I punched his arm. He retracted his arm, wincing while saying, "Hey! I'm kidding."

'I know,' I signed.

He smiled at me then reached out and tucked a strand of hair behind my ear. 'So?' I signed.

He sighed then said, "Okay. I hope you have a plan for tomorrow."

I smiled then signed, 'I think I can think of something.'

Raising an eyebrow, he nodded before saying, "All right. I'll text Paul so he doesn't freak out."

I nodded then signed, 'Thanks.'

He nodded then reached out and hugged me once more.

"I'll see you tomorrow," he whispered before pulling away and climbing into the car. He shut the door as I stood there with my arms crossed. He started his car then turned to me and waved. I waved back then watched as he backed out of the driveway.

'Tomorrow,' I mouthed before turning and walking back inside. I walked to the couch where my dad was sitting and watching the highlights of a baseball game.

"So did he kiss you?" he asked after a moment of silence.

My mouth dropped open as I snapped my head toward him. "I'll take that as a no."

Shaking my head, I signed furtively, 'No!'

He made a face then said, "Do you want me to go beat him up?"

'For not kissing me?'

He nodded, and still half in shock, I shook my head. 'No, Dad!' He made a pouting face before crossing his arms and glaring at the TV.

"Party pooper."

Smirking, I rolled my eyes. Dad laughed before opening his arms. Scooting over into his embrace, he held me in his arms for a time. "I love you, Mirda." He kissed the top of my head, and a tear trickled down my cheek as I tightened my arms around his arms saying with them what my voice couldn't.

'I love you too, Dad.'

CHAPTER 57

Turned out the plan was for me to teach Joseph how to make ice cream. (Woke up at like 3:00 a.m. with the idea!) Even though I was still a little sore, it was a lot of fun. Joseph protested my plan at first, but after a few minutes, he gave in. (After all, he was the one who wanted me to teach him how to make rolled ice cream to him in the first place.) Joseph was a quick learner, and I didn't have to guide him that long before he was making ice cream on his own.

Even Moses was impressed. "He's a keeper," Moses whispered to me, causing me to blush.

Afterward, we headed back to my house, and I sketched Joseph as he kicked the ball around, although eventually he stole my notebook and I had to chase him to get it back. I got it back just as Paul and Ebony pulled into the driveway with Caroline in the backseat. They jumped out and started unloading groceries. They refused my help as they took the food into my house and proceeded to make dinner.

I remember looking to Joseph for an explanation, and he shrugged. "They did this on their own." Then he kissed me on my cheek before running outside to help Paul with the rest of the groceries.

I looked to Ebony, who was making dinner with Caroline, to find them both grinning at me. 'What?'

They giggled, and Caroline asked, "I get to be a bridesmaid, right?"

My cheeks go bright red as Ebony elbowed her before gesturing to some broccoli that needed to be cut up. I looked away then back at Ebony to see her glancing at me and smiling. I shrugged my shoulders, and she gave me a wink before preparing the rest of the meal, which turned out to be a three cheese mac and cheese with steamed vegetables on the side.

Afterward we went to Paul's house and started a fire in his fire-pit. However, while we were waiting for the fire to catch, Paul "accidentally" pushed his sister in the pool, meaning I had to push Paul into the pool. Which meant Joseph had to grab me and pull us in. The only one who was saved was Ebony but only because she was tending the fire. However, as soon as she came to tell us the fire was going, Paul gave her a very wet hug before jumping with her into the pool, which promptly started a water fight between all of us.

Eventually the fight died down, but only because everyone was laughing too hard, even I was smiling so much that my cheeks hurt. I took a deep breath before lying in the water and looked up at the sky to see the first hint of darkness. A moment could never last forever. I took in another breath before sitting up and swimming to the stairs. Pausing for a moment, I sat on the edge of a stair and looked down my still healing hands. I didn't regret punching Jonah that was for sure, but I did regret having to resort to violence to get my point across. Taking a deep breath, I looked down to find another pair of hands clasping them a moment later. I looked up expecting to see Joseph, but instead I see Caroline.

She smiled at me. "Mirda, do you want to come and roast marshmallows with me?"

I smiled then nodded. She smiled then jumped up tugging on my hand. We got out of the pool to find Paul's mom had left towels for us on the chair. I smiled then snagged one before walking with Caroline down to the fire. I sat in a chair as Caroline got two sticks ready.

I stared at the fire until Caroline asked, "What you have with Joseph"—I looked up to her to see her handing me a stick with a marshmallow on the end—"is it like what my brother has for Ebony?"

I started to raise my hands when she said quickly, avoiding my eyes, "I know it's none of my business, but he's my brother, and though I like Ebony, I'm worried she'll break his heart." She glanced back at Paul and Ebony, who had just gotten out of the pool. "And I don't want to lose my brother."

I gave a small smile before resting the stick against the firepit and patting the seat beside me. She sat beside me, and I wrapped an arm around her before spelling out with my free hand, 'I have faith that she won't, and even if she does, he'll be okay.'

"Because he has you?" Caroline murmured, looking down.

I touched her chin with my free hand to get her to look at me before signing, 'And you. He'll be okay.'

She smiled then wrapped her arm around me, hugging me before looking back to the fire and exclaiming, "Oh my gosh, Mirda, your marshmallow is on fire!" I looked back to see that my marshmallow was truly on fire. I picked up my stick, intending to blow the flames out, when Joseph appeared out of nowhere and took the stick from me.

"Thank you." He blew it out, smiling, and we stared at him in utter shock. Looking back, he asked innocently, "What? You know that I like my marshmallows burnt. It's the only way you can know they're cooked properly."

Caroline laughed, and I smiled.

"That's not how it works Joseph," Caroline said.

Joseph winked at me before looking back at Caroline. "Says who?"

"The God of Marshmallows."

"Oh really. Well, how exactly does the God of Marshmallows say marshmallows should be cooked?"

"Golden brown," she said, grabbing her stick and showing the perfectly cooked marshmallow before handing the stick to me. "For you, sis."

I smiled then signed, 'Thank you.'

I pulled the marshmallow off the stick and eat it, before licking my fingers and smiling as I watched Joseph shudder in horror. However, when he saw my smile, he grinned back at me before going to the bag of marshmallows. He reached in and pulled out one then turned and tossed Caroline it.

"Thank you!"

"No problem," he said, turning back to the bag of marshmallows when he hesitated. Looking back at me, I saw a vague question in his eyes. In answer, I gave a small shrug, and he nodded then without a single comment, he stuck two marshmallows on the end of his stick before coming over to sit in front of me to roast his marsh-mallows. I smiled to myself as he leaned back against my legs as he and Caroline continued to debate about what was the correct way to cook a marshmallow.

I looked up at the stars, content when I heard behind me. "Who started marshmallows without me?"

I turned to see Paul walking with Ebony toward the table with the marshmallows.

I smiled, and Joseph said for me, "Your sister."

"What? Caroline!"

"You're just lucky I saved some for you," Caroline muttered beside me.

My smile grew, and I looked to Paul, who rolled his eyes before getting his own marshmallow and sitting with Ebony on a dual camp chair. Content, I leaned back in my chair and stared up at the stars. Later that night, Joseph took me home. We sat in his car in front of my house, neither wanting the other to leave.

"Who knew that skipping school was so fun. I can see why you did it so much." I smirked, and he asked, "Why did you stop? I'm certain it's not just because your father and the principal threatened you."

I raised an eyebrow, and he explained, "Paul."

I nodded then shrugged, smiling, 'Wouldn't you like to know.'

He opened his mouth in mock outrage, and I smiled before leaning over the middle and giving him a quick hug before pulling away, 'Thanks for hanging out with me. I'll see you tomorrow.'

I opened the door and climbed out as Joseph said, "See you tomorrow."

CHAPTER 58

The rest of the week went by faster than I would have liked. It didn't give me a lot of time to worry or talk myself out of the promise that I made to Joseph. Though I did try. Several times, but each time I was interrupted. Whether it was by one of my friends, by a teacher, by my father, or by the asparagus that caught on fire. (Don't ask!) Yeah, I wasn't left with a lot of free time to worry and now that I look back on it, I wouldn't have had it any other way.

I remember that morning I decided to try praying again very clearly. I had gotten up before Dad went to church. Made breakfast, he came down ate then gave me a hug goodbye. I had put away the leftovers, washed the dishes, then looked outside to see the backyard green and inviting. I took a deep breath before setting my washcloth down. I went to the door and pulled it open reluctantly. I stepped outside and closed it softly behind me before walking forward. I walked for some time before I stopped and looked around. This was the place.

I took a deep breath then knelt down on the grass. I was in the middle of my favorite field. It was Sunday, so no one would be home. I took another breath before closing my eyes and folding my arms. A second later, I realized that I couldn't pray like this. Or at least in the traditional sense.

So I unfolded my arms took another deep breath before I began to sign my prayer, 'Oh God who art in heaven. I come before thee today to ask...' My hands stilled, and it took me a moment before I could continue, 'To ask a question. God, I know you're there. I keep denying that fact, and I can deny it no longer.'

I took another breath as I felt my hands quiver. 'So my real question is, Why? Why did you afflict me with such trials?' My hands stilled as I collected my thoughts. 'I don't know if I ever hated you, but I tried so hard to convince myself that I did…that hating you would solve something. Would make you regret what you did, but all it did was make the pain hurt worse. It made my life so much harder. No longer. From this day onward, I won't hate you, but unless you give a good reason why this all happened, I can't like you, I can't, because without a reason for all this pain and misery, my life is pointless. So why did you let these things happen to me?' Silent tears streamed down my face as my strength gave way, and I fell to the ground, curling into a ball.

I don't know how long I lay there with my eyes shut, blocking out the world, but when I came to, someone was touching my shoulder. I opened my eyes to see a man with kind blue eyes kneeling beside me. Though I should have fled, saved myself, I remained where I was. The man smiled at me with no menace in his gaze he held out his hand. I looked at it then at him.

He nodded encouragingly. "Come with me."

I hesitated for only a moment before I placed my hand in his. He helped me stand then wrapped an arm around me and led me through the field high into the mountains where I could see forever. My breath caught in my throat, and I took a step forward away from him so that I might see more of the world that I had missed so much.

"Mirda Rebekah Johnson." I froze as he said my name then turned to see the man had remained in the same place. "You asked God a great question, and the only way he can answer it is in this great way. Are you willing to accept this price?" I slowly nodded and he smiled then walked past me and gestured to the world. "Then look." I turned back and walked to the edge and looked.

Before me the edge of the mountain disappeared, and suddenly, I was in a home. My home from when I was younger. My father was sitting at the table, his head buried in his arms. I heard the tears, and I felt his pain. Tears of my own trickled down my face as I realized this was just after I had lost Zach. Then I watched as I ran in holding a flower. My dad looked up as I showed him the flower. He smiled and said that it was the best gift he had ever gotten. He took the flower then hugged me. I hugged him back then proceeded to tug him outside where we played tag. Even though you couldn't hear my laugh or my little screams as my father tagged me you could see the joy on my face.

"Without you, your father would have given into his gulf of misery and never surfaced," the man said.

I stared at the memory in shock until it faded before my eyes. Suddenly I was facing a wall. I turned around and saw myself and Paul. Paul was sobbing, and I had my arms around him, my meek attempt at comforting him. All at once I knew where I was. I was in the old hideout that Paul and I had when we were younger. It was deep in the woods, a tree house, made by someone long ago. It was our place; it had been so long since we had last been there. It was probably destroyed now. I watched as Paul kept sobbing, and I kept patting his back telling him with my actions that everything would be okay. It was then I realized which particular memory this was. Paul had just learned his mother was marrying his uncle and Paul though that she had forgotten his father. Had forgotten him and sister. I spent all night convincing him that she hadn't forgotten them or his father. That she probably was doing what she thought best for her family and if he wanted the truth he just had to ask.

"If you hadn't convinced Paul that day, the next week he would have run away." I swallowed a sharp breath of air as if he didn't notice the man with blue eyes continued, "He had a plan all laid out, but because of this moment and how you included him in your life ever since he never put that plan into action. He never left. He found his purpose helping you, even if it didn't always feel like his efforts were helping much." I smiled as suddenly the memory changed, and I saw us in the car, then as I gave him his good-luck gift, aka the baseball. "You never needed your voice to speak your mind, Mirda." I looked back at the man with blue eyes. "You must realize that now. Don't you?" I slowly nodded, and he smiled kindly. "No. Not yet, you don't."

Then my surroundings changed, and suddenly, I was in a cemetery. I frowned, then turned around in confusion. This wasn't my memory.

Or if it was, it didn't look familiar. I looked to the man with blue eyes. 'Where am I?' I signed.

"You are currently twenty miles away, getting your vocal cords checked for the last time, but this memory is not about you. At least not at first."

'I don't understand.'

"You will." He pointed, and I looked to where he was pointing to see Joseph. A much younger Joseph, but Joseph, nonetheless. He had a bouquet of flowers in his hand and was staring at the graves surrounding him tears trickling down his face. I took a deep breath trying to calm myself as I walked to his side to see the headstones he was looking at. Samuel Isiah Wilson and Marie Elizabeth Sanchez-Cruz Wilson, beloved parents. I put a hand to my mouth as tears started to stream down my cheeks again. I looked to the right and left and saw four more gravestones with the last name Wilson, Joseph's siblings.

CHAPTER 59

Shamelessly, tears trickled down my cheeks as I watched Joseph place the flowers in front of his parents' graves before pressing his fingers to his lips then placing them on each of his siblings' graves individually. "Love you. Miss you," he murmured, and I saw tears of his own drip down his face.

Joseph stayed there for a moment, and I heard him whisper, "I tried everything, but I'm immune to the Sickness." He sobbed then said, "I can't bear this pain any longer." Then the memory faded.

My eyes widened in shock as in the next second I saw Joseph standing at the very edge of a cliff. Tears streamed down his face, and I realized what he was planning to do. I wanted to cry out, to stop him, but I had no voice, and this…this was just a memory. So I watched in fear and with heartache as he balanced on the edge. "God, now would be a really good time for you to answer my prayer. Should I do this?" The wind whipped his jacket, and even though I couldn't feel the wind's chill, a shiver ran through me.

Then suddenly I heard the words, "You are still needed, Samuel Joseph Wilson."

Joseph took a deep breath and said, "What do you mean needed?"

"You will see." Joseph hesitated for only a second before he took a step back.

I released the breath I was holding as I watched him back away from the edge, my mind still reeling from the fact that I just almost saw my love almost commit suicide. Wait, my love. Before I could ponder that thought, more the memory changed. Suddenly I was in a bedroom. Joseph was kneeling beside his bag, boxes surrounding him.

His hands were clasped together, and he was murmuring a prayer, "God…Derek and Sharol want to move. Start over and would like to be my stepparents. I want to know what I should do. Should I go with them? Join the system? Or just run away?"

He waited there for some time praying and pondering then the voice came again, "Go."

With tears in his eyes, he stood and left the room. I took several deep breaths, trying to control my recent heart, even though I knew what decision he would make fear still coursed through me. My surroundings changed, and suddenly I was next to a moving van. Joseph was standing off to the side holding a box. I walked over to see where he was looking, and I saw the backs of Paul and me as we walked down the street.

An older lady walked up to the other side of Joseph and said, "Go!"

"What?" he asked then turned to face her.

Clearly exasperated, she took the box and said, "Go talk to them. Make some friends."

"Sharol."

"Joseph!" She gave him a look, and I smiled as she snapped, "Go!"

Joseph sighed then said, "Fine, but I'll be back soon."

"I certainly hope not," she said as she turned and walked into the house. Joseph took a deep breath before he got up the courage and started down the road. Without a word, I started following him down the road. I followed him to my house, and I watched as he froze in both terror and awe as he saw our faces for the first time. However, his eyes didn't linger on Paul for long. His eyes followed me, and my movements.

It was then I realized that he had always seen me. Fresh tears trickled down my cheeks as I heard him murmur, "Astonishing. She…is she the reason why I'm here, God?"

Then I watched as he, with newfound courage, walked forward. Knowing him now, I could tell he was so nervous when he introduced himself to me, and as I watched myself hesitant and shy, I wanted to crawl in a hole. *Oh, Mirda.*

I watched as he would tease me and flirt with oblivious little me and couldn't help but smile, until I saw myself step to sketch and Joseph and Paul kept playing.

Curiosity filled me, and I stepped a bit closer, just in time to hear Joseph ask Paul, "So are you two dating?"

"No. We've been best friends since we were six, and nothing more ever since, but be warned, if you want to date her, you must be patient. Mirda has had a hard life and doesn't have God in our life like we do."

"How did you know I believe in God?"

"The cross around your neck."

Joseph glanced down, then looked back up smirking as Paul continued.

"And your mannerisms. You'd be a good influence for Mirda."

"And you aren't?"

Paul shrugged. "I've tried, but obviously, I alone am not enough, nor is her father."

"Wait, so she has had God in her life the entire time, but she does not believe."

"She lost her faith and testimony when she lost her voice and family."

"What?" Paul shrugged.

"If you want to know more, ask her, but just fair warning, this is what you're getting yourself into."

"I haven't decided anything."

Paul smirked. "Course you haven't, but that look she gave you said it all. She trusts you." He stopped the ball they had been unconsciously passing back and forth the entire time and said, "And the last time she trusted someone was over ten years ago." He kicked the ball back to Joseph.

He stopped it murmuring to himself. "This is my purpose. This is why I needed to live."

"What?" Paul called.

"I said I think I might just take that advice."

Before he kicked the ball back, the memory faded and suddenly, we were in the nurse's office. I turned and saw me lying on the bed. Joseph was pressing an ice bag to my forehead.

Tears streamed down his face, and he whispered, "If only I had gotten there sooner. You wouldn't be hurt. If I hadn't been waiting in the car." He looked away, taking the ice with him. I heard myself moan just slightly, and he quickly looked back and placed the ice on my forehead. "I'm sorry," he whispered. "I'm sorry I wasn't there. I'm sorry I wasn't here when you lost your faith. I'm sorry I almost ended my life and would have never gotten the chance to see you." He paused, shifting the ice to my bad eye. "I'm sorry for a lot of things, but the one thing I'm not sorry for is falling for you. You are amazing even without your voice. I think if you had had your voice, I would have never been able to approach you, talk to you, but even without it, I'm still amazed by you. Every day, every hour, every minute." He smiled, and a tear trickled down his cheek he brushed it away as he said, "You make everything seem a little brighter. I'm living in part because of you." He leaned down, then moving the ice bag to the side, he gently kissed the top of my head before he lightly placed the bag of ice back over my eye and waited in silence for me to wake up.

More tears streamed down my face as the image faded and the man with blue eyes turned to me. "Without you, Joseph would have given up on life long ago. You helped him to see one of his many purposes in this life."

I nodded then signed, 'Thank you.'

The man smiled kindly before answering, "You asked, and God answered."

CHAPTER 60

Unwilling to let this moment end, I held the gaze with the man in front of me. However, from the grin on his face, I had a feeling that he knew that I was stalling. Eventually he cleared his throat and said simply, "I hope you realize how much love God has for you, Mirda Rebekah Johnson." He took a step forward and held out to me my old bible—a bible that I had thrown out the window years ago once I had stopped believing in God. I hesitated, knowing as soon as I took this bible, my faith in God would start coming back. I took a breath then grasped it with both of my hands and pulled it from the man's hands. Suddenly my whole life flashed before my eyes and a single question rang in my head, "You've been without this most of your life. Are you sure you want it back?" I knew the voice was talking about more than just the bible, but it didn't matter to me, I had decided.

'Yes,' I mouthed, and suddenly, I was overwhelmed with His spirit. I gasped at the sheer power and stumbled backward as my knees gave way. Smoothly, the man with blue eyes caught me before I could fall and helped me stand upright as His spirit continued to pound me. Then a moment later it was over. I started to breathe again, and tears streamed down my face as I felt his spirit within my soul.

I looked up at the man with blue eyes and mouthed, 'Thank you.'

He smiled kindly then released me as I regained my balance.

"You are one of his special daughters, Mirda. Never forget that you are a daughter of God and that everyone around you is a child of God," he added as I looked back at him.

I smiled at him with tears in my eyes as the spirit within me testified of the truthfulness of his words. I nodded and watched as he smiled then turned to walk away.

'Wait,' I signed, and even though his back was turned, it was almost like he could hear my very thoughts. The man with blue eyes stopped and looked back at me. 'Who are you?' I signed. 'An angel?'

The man smiled and shook his head. "No. I'm something a bit more than that." Then he walked forward and pressed his lips to my forehead. "I'll see you soon, sister…" He pulled back. "In our Father's kingdom. Until then I bid you adieu. I love you." The man with blue eyes turned and for a moment the light that radiated from him blinded me.

I thought I had no more tears left to shed but a single tear rolled down my cheek as I mouthed, 'Christ?' He turned back slightly, smiling, and waved, before turning back and walking into the light.

The next thing I knew, I was waking up on the field. I sat up and looked around in shock. I must have fallen asleep while I was praying. I thought slightly puzzled as I looked up to see that the sun was setting. My eyes widen with shock, and I stood up only to find my knees were too weak to hold me. I collapsed back to the ground and as I lay there, I saw bunches of daisy's had popped up around me. I gasped then looked around and saw lying beside me on the grass my bible—the bible that I had thrown away so long ago. It looked perfect, no grass stains or yellowed pages. I pressed the book to my chest, as I felt the same warm spirit I had felt when talking to Christ, no to Jesus Christ. I realized then that my dream, my dream of Jesus Christ was real. God loved me. God had not abandoned me. On the contrary, he had used me to help others come closer to him who then helped me to find my way back. Tears streamed down my face as I fell to my knees and prayed once more in gratitude and with love to God before I stood and walked home. I reached home just as the sun set and I saw my father standing on the porch looking out at the woods pointing a flashlight.

"Mirda?" he called.

I smiled then waved as I came from the woods. He sighed as he saw me before exclaiming, "Where were you? I was about to send out a search team!" I shook my head as I stopped before him, 'There's no need. I'm right here. I'm all right."

"Are you?"

'Yes,' I signed, my smile broadening before I could restrain myself no longer. I rushed forward and threw my arms around my father's neck before pulling back and signing, 'You were right.'

My father frowned. "About what?"

'Everything,' I signed before hugging him again.

That night I told my father everything that had occurred in my vision, and tears streamed down his face as I concluded that my testimony was back. That I believed in Jesus Christ and God again.

CHAPTER 61

I couldn't sleep that night, or at least not for long. I was up by four making breakfast, then at five, I was out the door. I walked to school and sat in the parking lot for an hour and a half just appreciating nature and God's creation. At one point, I even pulled out my bible and began reading it. However, only ten minutes into my reading did I hear the squeal of tires. I looked up to see Joseph's Mustang pulling into its usual parking spot. I stood and watched as he parked and got out of his car. His face was full of worry, and he looked around the parking lot with such desperation that I almost felt it myself. I placed my bible in my bag then grabbed my bag and rushed over. Somehow, I snuck up behind him because he didn't notice me until I touched his arm. He whirled around, his fists raised, and I held up my hands to show that I meant no harm.

It took him a moment before he said, "Mirda?"

'Hey,' I signed.

He gasped and stumbled back a step as if I punched him, and I asked with concern, 'Joseph, what's wrong?'

He took a deep breath and bent over briefly before looking back up at me.

"Don't ever do that to me again."

I stared at him, not understanding. Sighing, he stood up straight before walking up to me and took my hands. "I showed up at your house to give you a ride only to find that you were missing. Your father presumed that I had already picked you up. I texted Paul, but Paul said that he hadn't picked you up and that he was picking up Ebony. Then I texted you only to receive no reply. Which after the Jonah…incident," he said, clearing his throat, "you dropping off the map for thirty minutes kind of terrified me."

I made a little o with my mouth before pulling my hands away, 'Sorry. My phone is on silent in my bag, and I just couldn't sit still, so I walked. I should have left a note.'

Humorlessly, he chuckled then said, "Probably." Then he pulled me into his arms. "At least you're safe."

I closed my eyes and leaned my head against his chest briefly before pulling back.

"What?"

'I did as you requested of me.'

His eyes widened as he mouthed the word *prayer*.

I nodded, and he asked carefully, "How was it?"

I smiled, unable to contain my joy any longer.

'It was amazing, and I'm sorry I waited so long to do it.'

As Joseph interpreted my signing, he smiled too.

"So you got the answer you wanted."

Shaking my head, I signed, 'I got the answer I needed.'

He smiled then said, "Good."

Momentarily distracted by his good looks, I felt a faint a nudging in my soul to ask about the cliff. Not wanting to ruin the good mood, I pushed the feeling aside and continued to smile up at Joseph when the feeling returned. Breaking the eye contact, I pulled back.

Sensing my mood, Joseph asked, "What is it?"

I took a breath, and I looked up at him then signed, 'Why didn't you tell me?'

Frowning, he asked, "Tell you what?"

As he stared at me, I felt the nudge again, and so I took one of his hands and wrote on his palm. 'About the cliff.'

Looking up at him, I saw the shame on his face, and I knew that he knew what I was getting at. Reaching up, I pressed a hand to his cheek only to have him pull away from me.

For a second, I worried that maybe the feeling I was getting was wrong, that I shouldn't have been pushing him, but then Joseph murmured, "I was waiting for the right time."

Reaching out, I hesitantly touched the back of his hand. This time Joseph didn't pull away, and I was able to lace my fingers with his. I waited patiently for Joseph to say anything, and after some time, I was afraid he wouldn't say anything at all, but then as I stood silently by his side, he finally looked at me. His eyes were full of moisture and saw the fear in his eyes. The fear that I would reject him. "It wasn't the proudest moment of my life."

Taking a deep breath, I prepared to share something I had never shared with anyone. Turning his hand over I smiled sadly at him before writing on his palm, with my free hand, 'Neither was it mine.'

Confusion filled his face, and I saw the silent question on his face. "Did you?"

Shrugging, I pulled my hands away and signed, 'After my twin died and left me alone, I wanted to die too. There were several times I thought about...thought about killing myself or letting someone else kill me, but I never could.'

Joseph's breathing quickened as he translated my words as I continued, 'Over the years, there have been several times where I planned and thought about trying, but I never could. Then the day before you came along, I decided to give into the little hope that was left inside of me. I didn't know why. I thought I was just tired of being lonely and that was probably part of it, but I have feeling it was because God was preparing me to meet you.' Smiling up at him, I continued, 'You saved my life in more ways than one.' Wanting to touch him but still be able to sign I took a step closer to Joseph, 'You are one of the reasons I needed to stay here, but more than that, there's still work for me to do. Work for us to do.'

As I finished signing, I reached forward and took both of his hands in mine. Then I looked up at him and did my best to convey all the love I had felt for him all the last couple of weeks. Even if I didn't realize it right away, I knew now that the feelings inside of me were indeed love. My only hope was that maybe he loved me back, and as he stared back at me, I saw my feelings reflected his eyes. However, more than that the moisture I had seen earlier had developed into tears. They were trickling down his cheeks, and I couldn't help but reach up and brush his tears back with the pad of my thumb. Smiling up at him to show that I wasn't embarrassed or hurt that he had emotions I saw the hope in his eyes. Unconsciously we both took a step toward each other leaning closer our faces only a few inches apart when we heard the squealing of tires. Fear coursed through my veins, and I whirled around to face the oncoming threat when I saw Paul's old car pull into a spot right beside Joseph's car. I released the breath I was holding in time to notice Joseph holding onto me tightly. I looked up at him to see him shaking his head.

"I forgot to text Paul that I found you."

Mouthing the word *Oh*, I grinned then signed, 'That explains why he was driving like a madman.'

Joseph chuckled, then we both looked at Paul and Ebony jumped out of the car and walking toward us.

As Paul approached, he wagged his finger at me. "You little punk."

Smiling, I took a step forward out of Joseph's comfortable embrace as Paul stopped just in front of me. Taking deep breaths, he spat out, "Do you know how much you scared me? Especially after that whole Jonah scenario."

'Sorry,' I signed sheepishly.

Shaking his head, Paul muttered under his breath something about me being impossible before Ebony cleared her throat and said louder, "So what's the big news?"

Startled by her question I made a face then signed, 'What?'

Ebony started to open her mouth to respond when Paul, clearly still annoyed by me, interrupted, "You didn't wait for Joseph to pick you up, and you have never willingly gone to school so early before. Thus, the only explanation I have for your strange behavior is that you must have some pretty big news."

Understanding filled me, and a small smile touched my mouth as I mouthed *Oh*. Biting my lip, I glanced to Joseph, who grinned at me. Grinning back briefly, I then turned back to Paul and signed, 'I guess I do have some news…' Paul rolled his eyes at me then gestured for me to continue. Although I wanted to tell him and Ebony the news, it was also really funny teasing my best friend, and I was tempted to keep teasing him, but I couldn't keep the secret anymore. So without further ado, I raised my hands and signed the sentence he had been waiting for me to sign since the day he learned that I didn't believe in God anymore, 'I believe in God again."

I watched as Paul started nodding after he interpreted my sign-ing, then as the meaning of what I signed hit, he did a double take.

He stared at me, shock evident on his face, and it took him two tries before he could murmur hoarsely, "What?"

A smile touched my face as Joseph chuckled beside me. Raising my hands, I started to sign again when Ebony cleared her throat and walked forward, placing a hand on Paul's shoulder.

"She believes in God again, mi amor."

Paul looked at Ebony, the shock slowly fading away as she smiled at him. "Take a deep breath and just let it sink in. She believes in God again." Then she looked up at me and smiled. "Congratulations."

I don't think Paul truly heard Ebony because when he turned to me, his face was starting to turn a bit red like he was still holding his breath. "You serious?" In answer, I let the smile inside of me out, and with that simple assurance, Paul finally took that desperately needed breath. "Well, it's about time." Then with a whoop, he ran forward, picking me up in his arm. Gasping as suddenly all the air was gone from my lungs, I attempted to breathe as he hugged me fiercely before setting me down and wagged his figure at me again. "I guess it's good news. What a bunch of baloney." Smiling up at him, I took a step back then hugged Ebony as she walked forward and threw her arms around me (much more gently than Paul). Pulling away, I turned to face Paul again, and he smiled at me then stated simply, "We should celebrate."

Not wanting any attention or celebration for doing something I should have clearly done a long time ago, I shook my head then signed, 'Paul, it's not a big deal. It's not like I'm getting baptized or anything.'

Paul rolled his eyes then said, "You're right. You're not getting rebaptized, but this is way better than rebaptism. My best friend has God in her life, after how many years! It's a big deal, and don't try playing it off."

I started to protest when he raised his hands. "No buts. We're celebrating. Where do you want to go?"

I glanced to Joseph and Ebony; they both shrugged, and I finally raised my hand in surrender then signed, 'How about the ice-cream shack?'

Paul grinned. "Sweet. Ice-cream shack it is."

I smiled then looked to Joseph, who gave me a small smile of surrender. Understanding filled me, and I started to turn to the school our conversation would have to wait. Then I felt Ebony's hand on my arm, and I looked up at her to find her smiling kindly at me. Confused, I made a face, and in response, she just winked at me before turning to look at Paul.

"Paul, would you mind coming with me while I talk to my English teacher and make sure I did the homework right."

Paul frowned then muttered, "No, I wouldn't mind, but Mirda is right here. She can help you."

"Nah, she needs to talk to Joseph."

"What?"

For the first time, Paul looked to Joseph and me, truly looked at us. I watched as he examined us, and I wondered if he saw how we were naturally gravitating toward each other, but it was like his eyes just glazed over us. Looking back at Ebony, he shook his head, "They seem fine to me."

Joseph cleared his throat. "I actually would like to talk to Mirda privately please."

"Oh," Paul muttered then said louder, "Why didn't you say so?"

Glancing to Joseph he looked back at me for an explanation so hesitantly I raised my hands and signed, 'We didn't want to be rude.'

Paul gave me a look and started to respond when Ebony interrupted, "That's very kind of you, Mirda. We will be on our way."

She grabbed Paul's hand and dragged him away. "See you in ASL, Mirda!" she called over her shoulder as they walked back to their car grabbed their stuff then walked up to the school, Paul occasionally throwing worried glances back at me. Nodding to confirm my safety, I watched as he and Ebony entered the school.

When the door shut behind them, I took a breath of relief and turned to find Joseph doing the same thing whilst combing his fingers threw his hair. When he caught me staring, he lowered his hands and shoved them in his pockets. With his hair tousled and him just standing there in the morning sun, the love that was blooming in my chest grew a fraction of a centimeter more. However, doubt plagued me. Although I liked and loved him, I wasn't sure if he liked me back, but I knew God would want me to be brave. So hesitantly, I smiled at him, and he smiled back. "Guess that moment's ruined."

Raising an eyebrow to convey my doubt, I signed, 'You sure about that?"

I had never really had the opportunity to flirt before, but I guess I did it right because Joseph's cheeks turned a delightful shade of pink after he translated my signs, and I heard him mutter under his breath, "Not anymore."

I smiled then took a took a step toward him. Joseph drew his hands out of his pockets then held out his hand. Taking a deep breath, I raised my hand and placed it in his before letting him pull me to him. He guided me to wrap my arms around his neck, and I found myself playing with the soft hair at the back of his neck. Briefly I saw the look of content in his eyes before he closed them and leaned forward pressing his forehead to mine. A single breath escaped me, and I found myself closing my eyes too.

"You know that I like you, right?"

Startled by his sudden admission, I opened my eyes and leaned back so I could look at him properly.

Fear was evident in his eyes, and he rushed to say, "Like really like you."

Happiness swelled inside of me. Happiness at the fact that the boy I liked, well, loved, liked me back. I couldn't help but smile back as I nodded then mouthed, 'I like you a lot too."

He stared at me a moment, and I worried for a second; they we were too close for him to have read my lips, but then a smile stretched across his face.

"You like me too?"

Eagerly I nodded in confirmation, and I watched as in the next second his smile broadened. He pulled me even closer into his embrace, and I heard him whisper, "Yes!" next to my ear.

I smiled, and a tear of relief trickled down my cheek. I couldn't believe it he liked me, and I liked him. Just as I was becoming overly comfortable his embrace his grip tightened on my waist, and he had suddenly lifted me up, spinning me around, shouting, "Yes!"

Even though I couldn't laugh, couldn't react beyond a smile at the true joy I was feeling, I didn't need to, because whenever I was with Joseph, I never needed to.

CHAPTER 62

Eventually, Joseph and I pulled away from each other. We walked back to his car never once letting go of my hand as he reached in to grab his backpack. He shrugged it over the shoulder, shut the car door, and locked it. Then he looked at me smiling. I smiled back and let him lead me to the school. We went through the front doors and to our usual math room. For once I didn't have any math homework so instead, we both sat on a table in silence. Joseph kept lacing his fingers with mine then unlacing them. It was a cute nervous habit; eventually though, I placed my other hand over the both of ours. He looked up at me, and I gave him a look.

Joseph sighed then took a breath as if he was stealing his nerves. "So since we've admitted our feelings to each other, would you like to go on a date with me this Friday?"

He rushed at the very end of his sentence then looked away as if he was actually worried. I would reject him, which, knowing Joseph, probably was his reason. I smiled then raised my free hand and touched his cheek.

Joseph looked back at me, and I smiled kindly before pulling my hands away from Joseph and signing, 'As long as you don't mind spending three days in a row with me, I would be more than happy to go on a date with you.'

Joseph made a face.

"Three days?" Joseph asked in surprise.

I gave a small cocky smile before signing, 'Date, baseball game, and church."

His mouth dropped open.

'What?' I asked innocently.

He closed his mouth then asked hesitantly, "You're going to church?"

I nodded, and he asked, "You're serious?"

I nodded once more before signing, 'Aren't I always?'

He smiled and put a hand to his mouth before lowering it. He looked at me, and I got the sense that there was something more behind his gaze.

'What it is it?" I asked.

He reached out and tucked a strand of hair behind my ear before reaching out and clasping both of my hands saying simply, "You've changed, Mirda. You're not the same girl I met when I moved here."

I pulled away and signed, 'I hope that is a good thing.'

"It is," he confirmed. "A very good thing."

Then he paled, and I made a face that asked, 'What?'

He grinned sheepishly at me before saying, "I forgot to do English homework."

A smile crept across my face, and he shook his head. "It's not funny."

I raised two fingers and pinched them slightly together.

He cracked a grin before reaching into his backpack and pulling out his book. "Would you mind helping me?"

I shook my head then got out my own book. That was what we did for the rest of the time before class just worked on English homework. No, we didn't do anything questionable, unless you count discussing if we really needed a soul to survive; other than that, we did homework then went to class. However, for the rest of the school day, we barely left each other's side, with the exception of the one class we didn't have together.

After class as promised, Paul did take us all to get ice cream. It was sort of a double date. However, since Joseph and I hadn't announced that we were together yet, I didn't really consider it a double date. It was just a fun activity between friends, I convinced myself whenever Joseph would wrap his arm around my shoulders or when he would take my hand just because. Despite the fact that we (he more than I) were so obviously together, Paul never caught on; nevertheless, Ebony knew. As soon as the "date" was over, Ebony volunteered to drive me home. The entire drive home she pelted me with questions, then we sat in my driveway for two more hours discussing our feelings about Paul and Joseph. I felt a little guilty about, but Ebony said it was a normal thing for girls to do. She called it "girl talk." Though I had never done this "girl talk" before, I had enjoyed it. It was really nice hearing Ebony's perspective as she described Joseph and mine relationship; however, at the same time, it was so embarrassing. She had managed to reveal some of my deep desires for Joseph and me the fact that I didn't want to kiss him yet. I believed very strongly that a kiss should only be between those in love and although I was confident that I loved Joseph, I was not confident that he loved me yet. It was a hopeless romantic's tale, I knew, but it governed my mother and father for all their dating life, and it seemed to work out for them just fine, so why shouldn't the same principle govern me. Ebony even admitted that I was probably right on that matter, but that she enjoyed kissing Paul too much to stop now. At that sentence a red blush spread across my cheeks, and I signed that I didn't to know that.

Eventually though she had to leave, and I had to go inside to make dinner. Once inside, though, I checked my phone and saw Joseph had texted me. "So Ebony knows?"

I grinned then tossed my bag on the couch before replying, 'Yep, and from our conversation, I think she knew before we knew ourselves.'

"Lol, and yet Paul still oblivious somehow."

'Haha. Somehow yeah, but don't worry, he'll find out soon enough. He's not that dense.'

"Lol. So we're still good for dinner Friday night?"

'Yeah. We're still good.'

"Good, make sure you were something you don't mind getting dirty in."

At that text, I frowned, my mind swirling, thinking of all manner of dates he could take me on, but instead of pestering him like I would normally do to Paul, I simply typed, 'Okay,' before putting my phone in my pocket and going to work on dinner.

CHAPTER 63

So it turned out my date with Joseph was going on a hike, then going to dinner, then lastly going to the park. It truly was a magnificent first date. I felt like an absolute queen when I was with him, and I did my best to make him feel like the king and not a foolish court jester.

I think my attempts were a success because at the end of the night when we stood on my porch saying goodbye, he pressed his lips to my cheek before pulling back and whispering, "I'll see you tomorrow."

Unable to do more than just nod, I stared at Joseph as he squeezed my hands briefly before letting them go. I watched as he went back to his car, and just before he got in, he waved goodbye. A smile stretched across my face as I waved back, and he smiled before sliding in to the front seat. I watched, my arms wrapped around my sides, as he backed out of my driveway and headed home. Releasing the breath I was holding, I turned and went inside. My father was sitting up on the couch reading a book.

"So how was it?" he asked as I took of my coat.

I smiled, and a blush rose to my cheeks.

My father chuckled then said, "That good, huh?"

I nodded, and my father smiled and muttered right before he returned to his book, "I approve of that boy."

So I guess that was my dad's take on me dating Joseph.

The next day I awoke early tense and ready to go to the baseball game; though I didn't have to couch, I was going anyway to support Paul and Joseph. My dad dropped me off at the school right by the locker rooms. Though I couldn't go inside, I didn't have to wait long before Joseph came running out, a grin spreading across his face as he saw me. I smiled back and ran to him. He picked me up and spun me around holding me tightly to him. Even though it had been less than a day since we had seen each other I missed him immensely, and by the way he was holding me I could tell he had too. He set me down and we waved bye to my dad as he drove out of the parking lot.

"So how are you?" he asked as we turned to face each other.

'Better now that I'm with you. How are you?'

"Honestly?"

I nodded.

And he sighed. "The same. I know it hasn't been very long since we have seen each other, but—"

I nodded, cutting him off. I knew what he was talking about. He took a deep breath, and I could feel his hands tremble as he held me.

I made a face the pulled my hands away and signing, 'You're nervous.'

He sighed then asked, "Is it that obvious?"

I shook my head. 'Just to me. What's the matter?" He looked at me for a moment before glancing down at his shoes.

"I just don't want to disappoint you. After all that time you spent with us, drilling us."

This game was a big one. We were to play against our rival team who currently, like us, were undefeated.

To me it was just another game, but to everyone else, it was a big deal, and that us included Joseph, so I swallowed my pride and pulled my hands away once more as I signed, 'You won't, Joseph. You'll do just fine. Besides, win or lose, I won't ever leave you.'

"Promise."

Lifting myself up on my toes I kissed his cheek before pulling back and signing. 'I promise.'

He smiled then pulled me in for another hug.

"I'm so glad you're my girl," he whispered into my ear.

My heart fluttered at the words "my girl," but I wouldn't let them distract me for long. He had a game to play.

So I pulled away and signed, 'As much as I appreciate the compliment, you have a game to play, mister.'

He smiled then nodded. "That I do, Miss Mirda, that I do."

He pulled away and walked backward toward the locker room. I smiled as he called, "Don't forget to look for number nine."

I nodded and gave him a thumbs-up. He grinned momentarily before he walked back into the locker room door. His grin vanished as he said, "Ow." I smiled then bit my lip. He smiled as he saw that I was smiling. "I meant to do that."

I nodded then signed, 'Right.'

He chuckled before turning and pulling the door open to the locker room and walking inside. I smiled to myself then turned to face Ebony and Paul. Paul stared at me; his jaw dropped wide open.

"What was that?" he asked simply, looking to the locker room then back at me.

I made a face then signed, 'Surprise?'

He shook his head, a perturbed look on his face. "What the heck, man?"

I shrugged then signed, 'Sorry?'

He shook his head once more, crossing his arms, frustration evident on his face.

"You and I are going to talk about this about this after the game. You understand?"

I nodded sheepishly, and he turned and gave Ebony a kiss good-bye before walking to the locker room, muttering something under his breath.

Glancing at Ebony, I was startled at the look she was giving me. 'What?'

"Really?"

'I was hoping he had figured it out by now,' I signed lamely.

She shook her head. "You've known him for how long, and you thought he would figure this out. Come on, honey. You're smarter than that."

I shrugged then signed, 'Apparently not.'

She laughed then shook her head before walking forward and hooking her arm through mine.

She and I walked toward the field as she said, "Paul's not mad, Mirda. Not really at least, just a little annoyed at himself for not seeing it sooner and a bit at you for not telling him. You're his best friend, Mirda."

'Well, I…we didn't know how to tell him.'

She laughed once more. "I know what you mean, but a little advice, next time, don't wait to tell him something this big. Okay?"

'Okay,' I signed just before we separated our arms so that we walk up to the stands and take our seats.

CHAPTER 64

Joseph and Paul won the game. I was so proud of the both of them and was smiling most of the night. Afterward, we went out for dessert, and there Paul grilled Joseph and me. He wanted to know every single detail. Whether we had kissed. When had we made this official? Had we always been in a relationship and just had never told him? Joseph did a lot of the answer, but before every answer, he would turn and look at me. Consulting me with his eyes on how he should answer, or if I wanted to answer this question. It made me feel like I was a part of the relationship and not just an observer or his submissive girlfriend. I was his partner, his equal, one of his best friends.

The next day at church we sat together. His parents and my father sat behind us. Ebony and Paul sat on my right side their families, in the two rows in front of us. It was interesting being back at church, and I had to admit, I felt a little guilty—for waiting so long, for not understanding everything but anytime I tensed up. Anytime I even contemplated leaving, Joseph's grip tightened on my hand and Paul would pat my arm, grounding me, reminding me why I was here.

After church I felt light, and happier than even when I had first hung out with Joseph. So when Joseph's parents invited me and my father over for dinner, I didn't even give it a second thought. I went home and changed out of my church dress and into jeans and a T-shirt. Around four, my dad and I drove over to Joseph's house. I brought a plate of cookies and double chocolate chips. I was nervous, but I was going to have dinner with Joseph's parents sooner or later, and I would do sooner rather than later. Dinner was lemon chicken, potatoes, and green beans. It was pretty good, and the meal was going really well until Joseph's stepparents brought up Joseph's birth family.

"Oh, I remember Joseph and his siblings would play outside together with our children every single day," Derek told my father.

"Yes, Joseph was so cute when he was younger. Would you like to see some of his baby pictures?" Sharol asked me.

Resisting the urge to smile, as I felt Joseph tense up beside me, I gave a small shake of my head before politely signing, 'No, thank you.'

"Maybe later, Sharol," Joseph said after he had translated for me, squeezing my hand under my table. Turning in my seat to look at him, I gave him a look, and he smiled at me gratefully.

A small smile touched my own face before I looked back at Sharol, who was somehow still smiling. "All right." She sighed then said, "Joseph tells me you're an artist. You must show me some of your work sometime."

Now it was my turn to shift uncomfortably in my seat. I was hesitant to show anyone my art work beyond my small circle but this woman across from me wasn't just anyone. She was Joseph's guardian. Practically his mother and perhaps one day my mother too. So hesitantly I gave her a small nod before signing, 'Sure.'

Joseph translated and said, "Sharol, you can't rattle her up too much. I still want her to like me after the night is over."

"Oh, I have absolute confidence that she will, Joseph." She looked to me, and if it was some big secret, she said quietly, "That boy can do nothing wrong, I swear."

Joseph shifted uncomfortably at his stepmom's compliment.

Smiling more for Sharol's sake than my own, I patted Joseph's hand under the table before signing, 'Believe me, he gets things wrong in English all the time.'

Joseph translated, and his stepparents and my dad chuckled.

"That's true," Sharol admitted, "but besides that, he is the most perfect stepson a parent could ask for, especially after the Sickness. Then moving and coming out here. He was always supporting us, always helping."

"He even went to the church and helped those who were infected with the Sickness every day," Dan added, and I glanced to Joseph as he looked down guilty at his plate.

I looked back to his guardians as they continued to talk absent-mindedly to my dad. "You would think after he had just lost his whole family to the Sickness that he would want to get as far away from it as possible, but instead, he chose to stay and help like the amazing young man he is."

"We're very proud of him," Dan said, placing his hand over Sharol's on the table.

Though it was sweet and cute, it was the last straw for Joseph. Abruptly he stood and pushed his chair from the table. Unsure as to what I should do, I watched him leave, avoiding everyone's gaze. Silence filled the room, and for a moment, I debated about going after him.

Eventually I realized that it wasn't a matter of if I should go after him, it was a matter of when. Looking at Joseph's stepparents I signed, 'Sorry,' then I looked at my dad. He nodded and translated my signing, 'Excuse me,' before I stood and ran out the door after Joseph.

Scanning his yard, I finally found him walking furiously toward the woods behind his house. He was already halfway there, and although I knew the woods well, I didn't know them that well. Taking a breath, I scampered down the deck stairs before breaking out into a full on sprint.

It took a bit, but I finally ran around in front of him. He tried to brush past me, but I grabbed his hands forcing him to stay in front of me. Once he stopped trying to escape my hold, I released one of his hands and press my free hand to his face, then with a slight pressure from my fingertips, I got him to look up at me, and I saw tears streaming down his face. He looked at me, broken, and I took a breath before wrapping my arms around him and hugging him. After a moment, he hugged me back, and I felt his tears drip down my neck as he buried his face in my hair.

Eventually he shifted, and I pulled back to see him looking at the ground again. Sensing that he had something to tell me, I took his hand and turned my eyes, searching the edge of the woods for a spot to sit. Spotting a fallen tree, I led Joseph to it before pulling him down beside me. We sat in silence for few moments, and as I started to feel him tremble, I tightened my grip on his hand. Doubt was the name of his gaze as looked at me, and I couldn't help but wonder if this was the same face, I made at him not so long ago. Returning the favor he did me, I looked back at him with complete and utter trust.

Nodding, he took a breath before looking to the ground and telling me the real reason he had gone to the church to help. He had gone to try and die. After seeing him at the edge of the cliff and hearing him say he tried everything, it wasn't hard to put the pieces together, but I didn't judge him. How could I? I was tempted to do the same thing, but this wasn't about me right now. It was about him. He told me that he had never told his stepparents whenever they brought of the subject of him helping at the church he had always managed to change the subject. He wanted to tell his stepparents, but every time they talked about him helping, they seemed so proud, and if he told them the truth, they would be ashamed. I assured him they wouldn't be, and if they were, he wouldn't lose me. I wouldn't give up on him ever.

He had hesitated for a brief moment before hugging me again. I hugged him back before pulling away and signing that we should go tell his stepparents the truth. He had been apprehensive, but he eventually came around.

It was nearly dark when we walked back to his house. I stood by his side as he told the stepparents what he had told me. They were shocked of course, but they were very understanding. They weren't ashamed of Joseph; rather, they felt awful that they hadn't noticed how much he had been suffering.

At that Joseph had looked to me and smiled. "You were right," his eyes said, and I couldn't help but smile back squeezing his hand briefly before letting go to let him hug his stepparents.

Later in private, he told me that I had been right. Though it meant a lot that he told me, I was right—what mattered to me more was that he had overcome his challenge, though I had helped he was the one who had done all the hard work.

I had just been there to witness his victory.

CHAPTER 65

We all went on with our lives, and man, I had a much happier life than it did a couple of weeks ago. Everything was perfect. Jonah was still in Juvie. Paul was still dating Ebony. I was still dating Joseph. I was acing all my classes, and I was still going to church. I settled into a wonderful routine of going to school and staying at school all day. Then going to the boys practice, sometimes with Ebony, and occasionally end up coaching. Then going to Mr. Moses's ice-cream shop. Before going home where Joseph and I would work on homework, on occasion, he would stay for dinner, or I would go to his house for dinner, but usually, I just hung out with my dad in the late evenings. It was a wonderful routine, and I even got to see Paul's sister every other day to help her with her art class. I felt useful, loved, and most importantly, in my mind, heard. However, I soon realized that maybe living in the background wasn't as bad as I thought.

I had been eating lunch in the cafeteria with Joseph, Paul, and Ebony, when the girl I had saved from Paul and his goons, Ruth, came up to our table and sat across from me.

Despite my curiosity as her sudden change of luncheon habits, I smiled kindly at her and signed, 'Hi, Ruth.'

"Hi, Mirda," she stated stiffly after Joseph translated before clearing her throat, "I have a proposition for you."

I made a face as she produced, from seemingly out of nowhere, a stack of papers. She passed them across the table to me, and I leaned over and read them briefly. They were a list of accusations and witnesses to convict a one Jonah Haggart. My mouth dropped open, and I tapped Joseph's arm, distracting him from his own skimming of the document.

Startled, he looked at me, and I signed hesitantly, 'Can you translate for me? Please.'

He nodded, and a breath of relief escaped me before I looked to Ruth. Looking at her then at the stack at papers, then back at her, I signed carefully, 'So if I'm reading this right, you want to take Jonah to court for harassment and attempted harassments?'

Joseph translated, and I watched Ruth's face very carefully as she formed a response.

"Yes. He hurt me and you, and I won't feel safe until he is behind bars for the rest of days at high school. You shouldn't either."

At her blatant tone, shame filled me. I hadn't even thought about Jonah since his arrest, much less him being released from prison and coming back to school. Recalling the lesson from church on Sunday that I knew Ruth had attended, I signed slowly, 'What about forgiveness?'

"Forgiveness?" she scoffed after Joseph once again translated. "After what he did? No, what he did and almost did deserves no for-giveness. It demands justice."

I took a deep breath as I processed what she said, then I further clarified and signed, 'Justice. Not revenge?'

She nodded then said, "Yes. I want him to serve the time for the wrongs he has committed and no more. Which is why I need you." I gave her a confused look. She sighed then said, "He harassed me, but nowhere near the extent he harassed you. If you come to court, then our win is guaranteed."

Glancing down at my lap, I knew my decision should have been simple. I should have wanted to prosecute Jonah, especially after everything he did to me, but ever since that day in the field, my heart didn't have room for anger or blame. All it had room for was peace and love, and the desire to share that, even with Jonah. So although the decision should have been easy for me, it wasn't, and I knew I had to give an answer that Ruth most likely wouldn't like. Taking another deep breath, I looked up at Ruth and signed, 'I'll think about it.'

Joseph translated my words, and Ruth's eyes nearly bulged from their sockets.

"You'll what?"

Resisting the urge to return to my old habits, I leaned forward and looked her dead in the eye before repeating myself once more. 'I said I'll think about it.'

Ruth glared at me, her gaze furious as she started to argue. "You'll think about it? He hurt you, and you have the chance to get justice for what he did, and all you say is that you'll think about it?"

I looked up to her, and before I can sign yes, Joseph said it for me. "Yes. Now leave the papers so she can read them and think it over. She'll contact you with an answer when she's decided on an answer."

Ruth hesitated then nodded and stood. "Make sure you make the right decision, Mirda." She spat out my name, and I flinched just slightly as she turned and walked away.

"Mirda?" Joseph whispered.

I looked to him then at Paul and Ebony, who were pretending that they hadn't just heard the entire conversation, then I looked back at Joseph, a slight plea in my eyes. He didn't say a word, just simply pulled me to him in a hug. He held me as we sat there, and for a moment, I forgot we were in a school's cafeteria.

For a moment, we were the only two people in the world.

CHAPTER 66

Ruth's proposal was on my mind for the rest of the day. The plan was to sentence him to jail for a year then for him to come back out and finish high school. If I didn't join in prosecuting Jonah, then Ruth's lawyer planned to drop the severity of the charges to six months imprisonment and simply change schools to finish high school. Either way, no Jonah for the rest of high school. I didn't think it was such a bad compromise. If I could change, he could change. However, Ruth didn't see that, and maybe more jail would allow that opportunity for Jonah to change. Or maybe not. I released a heavy breath then set the paperwork aside and looked down at the field to see Joseph waving hi. I smiled then waved back, before looking back down at the papers.

"You're still thinking about the proposal."

I looked up to see Paul walking across the bleachers toward me. I frowned and looked to Coach Peterson, then back at Paul. He shrugged. "We're just doing warm-ups right now, so he won't kill me yet."

I smirked as he sat down beside me. 'Where's Ebony?'

"There's a meeting for a club she's in, so she's not going to be joining you this afternoon."

I gave a half smile and signed, 'It's all right. I wouldn't be much for company today anyways.'

He nodded then looked out at the team. "I don't blame you, you know, for hesitating on this matter. Jonah's future balances in your hands." I nodded and he said, "But that's not why you're hesitating is it?"

I shrugged then signed, 'In part yes, but no. I... I've forgiven him, Paul.' As that realization hit, I finally realize why I couldn't say yes right to Ruth's proposal. Somehow, I had forgiven Jonah, and now all I wanted to do was to help Ruth do the same. I took a deep breath before signing honestly, 'I have no desire to seek revenge any more than I have the desire to turn away from God again.' Because although Ruth said justice, I knew she meant revenge.

"Why didn't you tell Ruth that?"

'Because she's still healing, and it's not fair that I've been healed, and she hasn't.' Biting my lip, I hesitantly signed, 'Maybe this is how she will be healed by prosecuting Jonah, maybe she'll find peace at last.' However, as I signed those words, I felt a great, big pit being dug in my heart, and I knew prosecuting Jonah wasn't the answer to the present situation. Pursing my lips together, I looked down as tears suddenly come to my eyes. *This is an impossible situation you've put me in, God. Why so soon, especially after I've just regained the faith?* A moment later, my answer came, but not in some great, thunderous typhoon but in the quiet voice of my best friend.

"God's with you now, Mirda, so you know like how I know that that choice is not the one for you."

Looking up at Paul, I saw him peering into my soul. He knew just as well as I that if I prosecuted Ruth with Jonah, the hard work that I had put in of seeking forgiveness, of forgiving myself, and Jonah…it would be all for naught. *So then what should I do?* I thought bitterly as I stared blankly at the field.

Once more the answer to that question came not from angels above but from an angel right beside me. Paul scooted over to me and bumped my shoulder getting my attention.

Looking at him, I saw him sign, "Maybe you need to go talk to Jonah. Get his side of the story, and then maybe things will be clearer."

My eyes widened, and I asked, 'Why are you signing?'

He hesitated then looked down at the field, "Because if I say the words out loud, I might not let you go. He hurt you, and although I only saw the damage a day later, it was bad, Mirda, and if it had been me that found you…instead of Joseph…I would have killed him. However, I feel like you need to hear this even if I can't say it."

Taking a deep, shuddering breath, I looked back at the field. *So this was your answer, God? To go see the boy who hurt me? What could he possibly say that Paul couldn't say for you now?* Silence filled the air for some time after I silently asked the question, and I knew in my heart that if I wanted to find out that answer, I would have to go and talk to Jonah myself.

Taking a deep breath, I looked to Paul and nodded, 'Thank you.'

He nodded then murmured, "The keys to my car are in my gym bag."

Smiling my thanks, I silently shook my shook my head. The drive would be over far too fast, and I needed the time to prepare myself before I saw him. Paul opened his mouth as if to protest but closed his mouth a second later.

Raising his hands, he signed, "Be careful."

I smiled then nodded, 'Always.' Glancing down at the field, I saw Joseph practicing his pitching and a soft smile touched my lips, before I looked to Paul, who had started walking down the stairs. I started to wave my hand to get his attention when he stated abruptly, "Don't worry. I'll let him know eventually just go do what you need to do Mirda."

As he said my name, he looked up at me and for a moment we were eight years old again meeting for the first time. Grinning, I gave a small salute before walking to the back of the bleachers and down the back stairs that led away from the field. Stepping around the gate that blocked the road from the field I started the trek into town.

Normally the walk seemed to last forever today it took minutes before I was in town, and not five minutes later, I was in front of the town's detention center for teens, aka juvie. Taking a deep breath, I stared at the door looming over me before flexing my hand then reaching forward and tugging on the handle. It swung open, and after nervously licking my lips, I walked in. The front waiting room was mostly empty the only person in sight the cop behind the front desk reading the paper. I recognized him, of course. I had met him at church on Sunday, but I was so nervous I had forgotten his name, but he hadn't forgotten mine. Glancing up at the sound of the door closing, he said with a note of recognition, "Afternoon. Mirda, right?"

Nodding at him, I took tiny steps forward. Recognizing that I was nervous, the cop smiled kindly as he gently reminded me, "I'm Officer Jericho."

Pulling out my phone, I wiped the sweat off my hands before typing, 'Afternoon, Officer Jericho. Can I talk to Jonah Haggart… Please?'

For a moment, Officer Jericho's face fell, and he asked, "Are you sure you want to do that, hon? If I recall the reason why he's detained is because he hurt you and one other girl, correct?"

I gave him a curt nod before typing emphatically, 'Yes, I want to see him.'

"All right. You just need to sign in." He placed a pen on top of a clipboard that I had failed to see on the front desk." Looking back at Officer Jericho, I saw him looking at me concern evident in his gaze. Nodding at him both to reassure him that I was all right and that I understood what he was asking, I managed to take one step forward then another. I walked to the front desk and picked up the pen.

As soon as I started writing my name, a profound sense of peace overwhelmed me, and I knew that in that moment I was doing the right thing. After I finished signing in, Officer Jericho reached behind his desk and briefly, I heard a buzz before the door to my left swung open. "I'll meet you on the other side," Officer Jericho muttered before going out a door at the back of his office.

For another long moment, fear and doubt paralyzed me, and I couldn't move, couldn't breathe, couldn't do anything.

Then a voice so quiet that had the room not been silent as the field I said my prayer in that I would not have been able to hear him reached my ears. "It's all right. Breathe." With those simple words, I took a breath and, in that breath, said a silent prayer, asking God for strength. Then I opened my eyes and marched forward through the open door.

Like Officer Jericho said I met him on the other side then followed him to another door where he typed in a password. The door swung open, and he grasped it holding it open for me. Signing thank you, I quickly walked past him and into an open room that I presumed was the visitor's center. There was a door opposite from me, and in between, there were six picnic tables scattered around the room, none of which were occupied. I said a silent prayer of thanks that no one else was visiting anyone in juvie at this moment, then I said an additional prayer that someone might come visit all those staying here sooner or later. Looking back to Officer Jericho for direction, he shrugged and gestured to the tables as if to say, *You pick.*

Taking a deep breath, I looked around the room before my hands landed on a table that was almost in the center of the room. A small smile touched my face and boldly I walked forward and set my backpack besides the table before sitting down with my back to the visitor's entrance. Placing my phone on the table, I looked up to Officer Jericho and nodded. I was ready.

Officer Jericho nodded then turned and left the room through the door opposite to the visitor's entrance.

He brought Jonah out wearing an orange suit, handcuffs, and all in all looking very disheveled. When he saw me, his eyes widened in shock as he sat down across from me.

I looked up at the cop as he stopped beside me. "I'll be in the corner if you need anything." I nodded my thanks, and he added, "Just let me know when you're done."

I nodded the pressed a button on my phone, 'I will.' It rang out. He nodded then turned and went to stand in the corner. I looked back at Jonah then.

We studied each other for a moment in silence before he asked bitterly, "Why are you here? To remind me of what I did? Of the punishment I am serving? Of the pain I caused?"

I gave him an odd look before pulling out the papers from under the table. I set them in front of him and let him read them. His expression changed from a bitter rage to a morbid fear. "Why are you doing this to me?" he whispered. "Do you enjoy seeing me in pain?"

I hesitated then typed into my phone, 'Did you?'

He looked at me and saw pain and absolute regret in his eyes. I hesitated then typed into my phone, 'When you were beating me? When you made fun of me, did you enjoy watching me suffer?'

His eyes lowered in shame before he whispered, "I did, until they read me my rights and I was sitting in my cell wondering what I had done that was so horrible. It took some time, but I finally realized that what I was doing to you was wrong. I was feeding my desires, yes, but I was feeding the wrong desires. I had let the natural man within me out, and I didn't know how to control him. I was terrified of myself, and suddenly, the blinders were ripped from my eyes, and I saw that what I had done was worse than wrong. It was criminal." Jonah squeezed his eyes shut then murmured, "And I know you can never forgive me, but you have to believe me when I say, I'm sorry. I'm seeing a therapist, and I'm in a help group, and I'm getting my emotions, desires, aggression under control. If you want to prosecute me, I'll tell my parents to not fight back. I deserve it, and you deserve justice." He looked up at me after he said the word *justice*, and I saw the sincerity in his eyes.

My mouth dropped open as I realized my silent plea that I had in my heart since Ruth had proposed her plan to get back at Jonah was answered. I didn't have to sign these papers. I didn't have to go to court against Jonah.

I gave a small smile before typing on my phone, 'I won't take you to court, Jonah. Ruth will, but I won't. Just promise me this one thing.'

He nodded then said, "Anything."

I took a breath before typing, 'Take into consideration that maybe part of your problem was the lack of God in your life.'

Jonah frowned in confusion. "What do you mean 'lack of God in my life'? I had God in my life. I mean, I went to church."

'I know you did, and honestly, everyone in this town does, but does that mean we actually have God in our life, and if we do, do we listen to him? Do we pay attention to what he has to say?' I shook my head. 'Most of the time no. I know I didn't, and as a result, I made some of the worse mistakes of my entire life. Don't do the same thing I did. Find God in your life again. He's there, always has been. You just were the one who took too many steps away, but thankfully, He has the patience and the mercy to wait for you. But He's still an all-powerful being, and there will come a time when He won't wait, so don't keep Him waiting.'

Jonah stared at me in shock before clearing his throat. "Wow. Did you practice that before coming here?"

I smiled then shook my head.

He looked at me then said, "I'm sorry I was such a jerk. I think if I hadn't been, we could have been great friends."

I shrugged then typed into my phone, 'We can still be, if you want.'

His eyes widened, and he said, "Are you certain?"

I shrugged. 'I can add a slot for another friend anytime I want to, so yeah."

"No, I mean, you want to be friends with the kid that beat you up and bullied you?"

'Yes. You did those things,' I typed before standing and grabbing my bag. I swung it over my shoulder before typing into my phone, 'But I forgive you.' Then I picked up Ruth's proposal and tore it in half.

Jonah opened his mouth in shock, and I saw a tear trickle down his cheek before a small smile touched his face. "Thank you."

I smiled back then tossed the papers in a trashcan by the wall before turning back to Jonah and typing into my phone, 'Same time tomorrow?'

He nodded, and I smiled before typing, 'Well then, I'll see you then.' I turned and nodded to the cop before exiting the visitors' center smiling.

I walked out to the parking lot still smiling when I saw a familiar Mustang parked across the way. My mouth dropped open, and I turned to see Joseph walking toward me still in his baseball gear.

"You just don't give up on anything or anyone…do you?"

I smiled then shook my head. He smiled then wrapped his arms around me and pulled me close. "So how did it go?"

I pulled away, smiling, and signed, 'I'm coming back tomorrow.'

He made a face and asked, "Is that a good idea?"

I took a breath then signed, 'He's different, Joseph.'

"How do you know?"

I shrugged. 'For one thing, he told me, and for another, I can just tell.'

Joseph sighed then said, "Okay, but I'm picking you up every day afterward, so that way, we can go get ice cream."

I smiled then signed, 'I would like that,' before I took his hand and walked with him to his car.

CHAPTER 67

With a nervousness that would even give anyone a cause to tremble, I gave Ruth my answer the next day. Simply put, I told her that I would not be prosecuting Jonah and I didn't think she should either. As I gave her my answer, peace filled my heart, and all the nerves I was feeling faded to the back of my mind. I found myself standing taller as she proceeded to yell at me and told me I was being an idiot.

I expected anger to fill my heart as I attempted to explain why I felt that it was best that I did not prosecute Jonah with her, but instead, empathy filled my heart and as I listened to her, and a silent prayer filled my heart. I prayed that she would find peace and find the strength to forgive Jonah for what he did. Granted, I didn't exactly understand what she went through so the pain could be ten times worse for her than me. However, I do know what the scriptures say, 'To forgive seventy times seven," aka to forgive forever and ever. God would take care of judgment when it's needed, but our job was to simply forgive and keep loving. It was a lesson that I had thought I had long forgotten but had rediscovered whilst flipping through my bible that Christ had returned in my vision. I remembered to mark it and had offered the scripture reference on a slip of paper to Ruth, but her heart wasn't open to that lesson yet. So as she spun on her heels and stomped away, I prayed that one day her heart would soften, and she would hear the lesson that I knew God wanted each of his children to learn.

Her prosecution of Jonah didn't stop me from visiting Jonah before and after his trial. Although I didn't attend the trial (at Jonah's request), I prayed the entire day that everything would work out the way it needed to.

The following day I went with Joseph to visit Jonah, and he told us that six months were added to his previous sentence of three months. My heart ached at the thought of him remaining in jail for almost an entire year, but when Joseph inquired with Jonah as to how he felt about his additional sentence, Jonah revealed that he was okay with it. After everything he had done, it was a small price to pay.

At that comment, Joseph squeezed my hand under his table, and tears threatened to come to my eyes. My prayer had been answered, everything had worked out the way it needed to. For Jonah, for Joseph, for Paul, for Caroline, for Ebony, for my father, and for me.

It was an answer to a prayer that I'd never forget (especially since I'd written it down, haha). From there Jonah steadily progressed and got better, but he told me it wasn't just because of all the people supporting him. It was because he decided to change. He wanted to be a better person by the time his sentence was up. Which as a friend (and only as his friend) made me feel pretty proud.

Although I visited Jonah consistently and many people (including Ruth) believed that meant I was cheating on Joseph, Jonah and I never became anything more than friends. He was starting to become a great guy, but even if I wanted to stop dating Joseph (which I didn't, btw) and started dating Jonah, we would end up clashing way too much. Granted that didn't stop the rumors. Luckily, Joseph didn't seem to mind, and he even encouraged me to go visit Jonah. Of course, I eventually asked him why he would let me go with all the rumors flying around, and he told me that he had asked God what he should do because the rumors did bother him. However, he had received a prompting that he should let me go visit Jonah and that everything would be all right, so that's what he was doing.

He was the best boyfriend I could ask for. Nonetheless, did we fight? Absolutely. In fact, I remember this one argument about not eating at lunchtime. It was a stupid argument, I'd admit, but he made some good points, so although I didn't start eating lunch, I made sure to steal a few bites of his lunch or bring a snack, and it did help prevent me from becoming hangry. However, just as often as I would humble myself and admit he was right, he would do the same thing.

I couldn't remember a day that we let the sun go down on our anger and that reasoning made all the difference for us. Our relationship…it was a dream come true. Only dreams last for so long, and you're forced to return to the real world. I kept telling myself this every day, and I waited for the wonderful dream to end. For things to go back to the way it was before, and for God to tell me this was all a mistake. I didn't deserve any of these blessings. However, he never did. He just kept giving me more.

It was a few months after Jonah's trial, and it was a completely ordinary day. I went to school, watched Joseph and Paul practice then went home to start making dinner. Only when I got home, I found my dad already sitting at the dining table with a woman that I didn't recognize. I tried to think of a logical explanation that would explain why she was here, but nothing came to mind except work. However, Dad always had his conferences in the city, not at our home. So why was she here? Swallowing the little spit in my mouth, I shut the door then walked toward the kitchen. As I approached my dad, he glanced up, and as his eyes landed on me, I saw a hope in them that I hadn't seen in years. Glancing at that woman I saw how put together she was, and I could almost see her in a white lab coat.

Looking back at my dad, I shook my head and signed, 'You promised.'

He bit his lip then signed, "I know, but please."

For a moment, I wanted to say no and run to my room like I was a kid again, but if Dad had broken his promise and gotten this doctor to come to the house, then he must really believe in her. Taking a deep breath, I shrugged then walked forward. I watched as my dad visibly sighed with relief then looked back to the woman. He said something quietly, and the woman turned around in her seat to look at me. She was pretty. Her hair was short and dark, and her skin pale but not unnaturally so. Her red lipstick stretched across her lips, and she stood and smiled. Pushing back her chair, she walked up to me as my dad came around the other side of the table.

"Dr. Dubois, this is my daughter, Mirda."

"Bonjour, Mirda," Dr. Dubois said, her French accent prominent as she said my name. "I have been looking forward to meeting you for quite some time." Raising an eyebrow, I asked a silent question.

'Why?'

Dr. Dubois smiled kindly at me before gesturing to the chair across the table. Taking a deep breath, I inclined my head in acknowledgement then walked around the table and sat down, crossing my arms as I leaned back in my chair. Dr. Dubois looked me up and down, clearly analyzing me. It wasn't something I was used to. Although it had been years, I remembered each doctor my dad took me to, to get my voice back, doing the same thing. Back when I was a kid, I would cower or act shy, but I wasn't a kid anymore. I had been through the fire, and I had been burned yes but the burns reminded me each time not to let my guard down.

Lifting my head defiantly, I met Dr. Dubois's gaze as she proceeded to introduce herself, "My name is Dr. Leah Dubois of the *Clinique de l'Alma*. I heard about your story from a colleague of mine, and I immediately was intrigued." She leaned forward clasping her hands. "I specialize in the internal workings of the human body, and I believe that I know how to get your voice back."

Before the potential hope behind that statement could get planted, I squashed it. Doctors had told me that before then they'd done further investigation and found it was impossible, so I wouldn't fall for her trick, not until there was some real proof.

Raising a doubtful eyebrow, I gestured for Dr. Dubois to continue. A small smirk of a smile touched her eyes before fading as she proceeded to explain, "I have a proposition for you, Mirda, and I know you've been to eight doctors in the past none of them succeeded, but I've developed a new system of monitoring the larynx and new tools to manipulate the vocal cords themselves. I would like you to come back with me to my office in France so I can do a few tests to guarantee that surgery I have in mind will work. However, I don't want to put you through any unnecessary pain, so if there's any time in the process that it's revealed to me that the surgery will not work, then I will be the first to tell you. No secondhand information and no prolonged interlude. I promise."

It was my turn to smirk. The doctors promised a cure for the Sickness, but it never came. The eight doctors promised they'd find a solution for my lack of voice, and it wasn't them who found solutions; it was me. As a person, I was sure Dr. Dubois word would have meant a lot to me, but her word as doctor meant nothing to me. So I raised my hands and signed definitely, 'No.'

My father translated, and Dr. Dubois nodded. "I had a feeling you would say that. She turned to her side and pulled from her lap a folder. She set it on the table then opened it and proceeded to hand my father and me two packets of paper. "These are contracts solidifying what I just said. Also, it says that you do not have to pay for a single thing. This is entirely funded by my company, whether or not it works." I took the contract, and unlike my father, who started flipping through, I kept my eyes on Dr. Dubois as she pulled some x-rays of a throat from the folder. "These are your x-rays, and these are from a person who has healthy vocal cords." She began to explain how she had gotten my x-rays from one of my past doctors and how she began to develop her theory. Apparently, she had been working on this for months, and although her ultimate goal was to change France's image for doctrinal practices, she did want to fix my voice. She seemed credible, and I meant, she had flown from France to talk to me personally in my home.

As I tried to fortify my mental box to keep the walls from falling, Dr. Dubois told me that everything would be paid for. My dad and mine's flight to and from France. The apartment we would rent (for the first three months). School in France. The surgery. It would be basically like a vacation.

How could I in good conscience refuse then she dropped the bombshell. "Even though I know you will most likely refuse, I did already purchase the plane tickets." She pulled them from a pocket of the folder and slid it over to me.

As I picked them up, my eyes widened as I saw the day of the trip. "They are for the day after tomorrow. However, I did talk with your father, and he said that you are pretty much done with school for the year."

Numbly I nodded as I stared at the plane ticket, the question echoing in my head, was this really happening? At my silence, Dr. Dubois murmured softly, "I don't need an answer now, but I'll give your father my number so that when you've decided you can give me a town. Also, please feel free to call me if you have any more questions."

I felt her gaze on me and I knew she was hoping for a yes, but I couldn't. I couldn't leave, I couldn't hope. However, I also couldn't say no. As I acknowledged that fact, the box I had closed almost ten years ago sprung open. I could get my voice back. It was possible. However, it wasn't. If it was, I would have had my voice back already. Unless…unless God had purposely let me continue living without a voice. I bit my lip as I thought about all the experiences I had and how different they would have been if I had my voice. Jonah wouldn't have had a reason to bully me. Paul might have still been my friend but not necessarily my best friend and Joseph…I might have never met Joseph with my voice.

So although it might have sucked for a time the loss of my voice had indeed become a blessing, so why? Why did God send Dr. Dubois now? Pressing my hand to my throat, I wondered for a moment what it would be like to have my voice back and for a minute I let myself embrace the hope that I had swelling inside me. Maybe getting my voice back was possible, and it was what God wanted. However, a second later, I heard my dad's voice, and the reality of the situation hit me once more. If I wanted my voice I'd have to go to France, miss out on my Senior year of high school, miss my best friend and Joseph. I couldn't do that to them, not after everything they had done for me, but I knew what they would say. They would want me to go, but I couldn't. What if the operation failed? What if something went wrong? What if something happened here? Another sickness and I couldn't get back? Panic swelled inside of me, and I couldn't seem to get enough air. Faintly I heard my father calling my name but despite wanting to reassure him that I was all right I knew I wasn't.

Shoving my chair back, I stood abruptly as my lungs tightened further. "Mirda?" I couldn't breathe. I needed air. Looking up I saw the slightly open back door. Taking a shallow breath, I darted around the table and threw the door open wider before running out the back door as my father called after me. Although, I knew he was worried I couldn't turn back, couldn't explain what was wrong, my body wouldn't let me, so I just kept running. Trying not to think, trying not to breathe. Eventually I had to stop or else my legs were going to give out. Doubling over, I put my head between my knees as the thoughts I had tried so desperately to push away came crashing down.

Everything I had built up was falling apart. I had accepted that I wouldn't get my voice back. That I would never be normal, but now that I had once again had the chance to, my world was caving in. Taking a deep breath, I glanced up to see I was kneeling next to a pond at the back of our property. A small smile touched my face as a happy memory found its wait through the panicked chaos of my mind. Paul and Caroline were swimming. I had known how to swim for years, but Paul and Caroline hadn't really ever had the opportunity to swim. The pool in their backyard was so big that it scared them, so I offered to let them use my little hideaway to practice whenever they wanted. It was small, barely six feet deep but for a kid it was the biggest bathtub we had ever had.

So until Paul and Caroline became used to swimming, we swam here. The first three weeks of the summer, they moved here. It was wonderful and one of my favorite parts of that summer. Summer. I put my head back in between my legs as I realized that if I went through with Dr. Dubois's crazy scheme in addition to potentially missing my Senior year, I would also miss summer. Tears came to my eyes, and I blinked them away. School was over in a week, and I had been looking forward to this summer. It was first with Joseph and the first that I was actually present. Sighing, I leaned back my head and looked up at the sky through the tree branches. *What should I do, Lord?* I asked silently. *What should I do?*

Closing my eyes, I waited, hoping for a simple answer of "Yes, stay" or "No, don't" when a voice I had known so long ago but had never quite forgotten filled my ears, "Why are you holding back?"

Despite the exhaustion starting to fill my limbs, from running all the way to the pond, I managed to find the strength to stand and turn around. It took me a second to find him as he was standing in a particularly bright patch of sunlight, but as soon as I spotted him, a smile came to my face and a tear trickled down my cheek. Standing amongst the trees and bushes, his hands in his pockets, a goofy grin on his face was my twin brother, Zacharias Johnson.

CHAPTER 68

Blinking my eyes several times, I found myself breathless again as I stared at Zach. He was not the little kid I remembered; rather, he looked around my age. He was tall and lanky with defined muscles. He looked well-groomed with no hair on his face, and his collared shirt was unbuttoned, revealing a plain T-shirt underneath. Nonetheless, he wore sensible boots and a well-worn pair of jeans, which ultimately led me to recognize him. No matter how worn his jeans were Zach always preferred to wear the one pair of jeans. No matter how many other pairs Mom bought, he always wore the same one pair. Guess even in heaven things don't change too much. A smile spread across my face, and tears streamed down my face as I raised my hands to confirm, 'Zach?'

Smiling at me, he gave a small wave. "Hey, Mirda! How have you been?" With his nonchalant answer, I knew the man standing in front of me was indeed my brother. A sudden burst of energy streamed down through my limbs, and I ran forward, throwing my arms around his neck, my tears pouring down my face. My brother was dead. He had been dead for a long time, but somehow, someway he was here. It could have been a hallucination. I know. My emotions and hormones were spiking, but as my brother's arms wrapped around me, I didn't care if it was a hallucination, and I found myself silently God for this moment. Eventually Zach chuckled and murmured softly, "Mirda. Always so dramatic."

A smile spread across my face, and I pulled away to sign, 'You would be too if it was you living and me who got resurrected.'

He shook his head. "Not resurrected, Mirda. Not yet."

I frowned then asked, 'Then how are you here?'

Zach sighed then shoved his hands in his pockets. "It's complicated, and unfortunately as much as I wish I could take the time to explain how I'm back, I don't have the time. So I'm just going to get straight to the point." He placed his hands on my shoulders and asked bluntly, "What's holding you back?" Knowing exactly what he was talking about, I shrugged helplessly. It was that I didn't know what was holding back, I knew what was holding me back, but I was afraid that voicing my fears out loud would make them real. That all my hope was for naught. Zach waited patiently for answer but when he didn't come, he smiled encouragingly, "You have a free chance to get your voice back. Why aren't you jumping at the chance to get the blessing God is freely giving you?"

I tried to find a reasonable explanation that would explain why I couldn't, but I couldn't, not without revealing all my fear and doubt. So I pushed back my reason and lied, 'I don't know.' Zach gave me a knowing look, and I glanced down unable to meet his gaze. Zach sighed a tinge of exasperation in his voice as he said, "We both know that's not the truth, Mirda."

I felt him tap my chin, and I automatically titled my chin up to look at him. I expected to see frustration for lying to him or not being able to tell him, my twin, why couldn't I commit, but all I saw was love. Smiling down at me, he wiped a stray tear from my cheek before placing both hands on my shoulders, "What's holding you back, Mirda?"

Biting my lip, I turned away as my fear began to overwhelm me. Wrapping my arms around my middle, I walked away then turned back and saw my brother looking at me with a slight smile on his lips. I couldn't help but smile back as I looked into my brother's eyes and found the courage that I had been searching for, for the last ten years. Taking a deep breath, and in spite of the fear I felt inside, I raised my hands and signed, 'I'm worried it's too good to be true.'

With that simple phrase out of me, I felt a pressure that I didn't know was resting on my chest lifted off. Suddenly it became so much easier to breath, and I fairly collapsed onto a log as my lungs began to function again. I took a deep breath and looked up as Zach walked around and silently sat across from me. I raised an eyebrow confused as to why he wasn't saying anything, and he rolled his eyes before gesturing for me to continue. Licking my suddenly dry lips, I hesitated then raised my hands and explained, 'In these last few months, I have gone from having nothing to having absolutely everything. I have a boyfriend. I have a relationship with Dad, with God, with people again. I forgave a man for hurting me, and I've found myself again.' I bit my lip then glanced down briefly before looking back up at Zach. 'She hasn't been around for a long time and just as much as Paul and Caroline missed her, I missed her. I missed being me, and I haven't been this happy since you, Mom, and baby Ben died.' Lacing my fingers, momentarily I closed my eyes then mouthed, 'And I'm worried that it's all too good to be real.' My lip trembled, and I leaned forward covering my face with my hands briefly before lowering them and signing, 'And I'm worried that if I reach out for another blessing, all the blessings that God has given me will disappear.' Shaking my head, I desperately signed, 'And I can't say goodbye. Not to me, not to Dad, to Paul, or Joseph.' A tear slid down my cheek and my chest heaved as a silent sob escaped. Pressing a hand to my face, I pressed my fist to my chest and signed, 'Sorry.' Zach didn't say anything, and I lowered my hand from my face to see his own tears running down his cheeks.

I watched in shock as he looked at me and signed, "No, I'm sorry. I'm sorry I wasn't there for you. I'm sorry that I couldn't grow up with you and remind you of how special you are and that God knows how special you are and will never take away your blessings. He will only give you more." At Zach's words, the fear in my heart vanished and was replaced with an overwhelming sense of peace, and the tears really started coming. At the sight of more tears, Zach took a deep breath, brushed away a few of his own residual tears before leaning forward, and placed a hand on my hands.

My hands automatically wrapped around his, and I looked at our clasped hands. This should have been us; he should have been here, but he was gone. Mom was gone. Baby Ben. I couldn't lose anyone else, but as I looked back up at Zach, I saw in his eyes that I was missing the point. He wasn't gone. He was right here. Right in front of me, "And in your heart," he said as he leaned forward and touched the spot just over my heart before tapping my chin. "You may have not expected this at all, but you've learned to flourish in spite of your challenges, Mirda. You're incredible, and although I'm sad I couldn't be physically present with you, and so is Mom for that matter, she, we are so proud of you."

I tugged my hands from under his and signed, 'Even in spite of my mistakes?'

Zach cocked his head, and a grin spread across his face, "Mistakes or happy accidents?"

Frowning, I gave him a look that said "You're kidding, right?"

Zach laughed then shook his head before saying, "God is all knowing, and although we have our agency, he has a plan, an amazing plan for everything." He looked up at the sky and shook his head once more. "I wish you could see all of it, but you don't need to." Then his face froze, and his grin faded to a more serious expression. He looked back at me then threw one leg over the log before looking me dead in the eye.

"Can I just be frank with you?" Meeting his gaze even though it honestly terrified me, I nodded. I watched as he took a deep breath then stated simply, "That's not how God works. He's not going to dangle a bone in front of your face and snatch it away. You've come so far, and he wants you to keep moving forward. However, as you are now without a voice, you can't progress. With a voice, though, you will influence so many people, because you understand. You can comprehend. You can empathize. It's time we break that shell surrounding you and let you step out into the real world."

'So the surgery will work?' I signed desperately, hope filling my heart.

Shrugging, he looked down, shaking his head before looking back up at me and honestly said, "I don't know, but I have faith that by God's will, it will." He patted my knee then threw his leg back over the log. He stood up then looked back down at me, and I saw in his eyes that he needed to get going.

Not wanting him to leave I shot to my feet and shook my head then mouthed, 'No, I need you.'

Smiling kindly at me, he opened his arms, and I rushed into them a couple tears that I didn't know were left trickling into his shirt. His arms banded around me, and I felt him press his head to the top of mine. I felt the rumble of his voice in his chest before I heard him say anything. "I wish I could be here with you, Mirda, but I've got my own work and life to get back to."

Understanding filled me, and I somehow found the strength to pull myself away, nodding, not meeting his gaze.

I heard Zach sigh then said, "It's your choice, but I think you should take the chance even if you are still uncertain."

Glancing up at him, I mouthed, 'Really?'

He nodded. "I know I have most of the facts, but even if I didn't, I'd trust that peace you're feeling in your heart. God is responsible for that, whereas that doubt you feel that's from the devil."

As he phrased it like that, the hope and peace that was flickering in my chest roared, and I knew what my decision would be, even if I started doubting again.

Stiffening my chin, I looked up at Zach and signed, 'You're right. Thanks, Zach.'

He smiled then signed, "I love you, sis."

Bittersweetly I signed back, 'I love you too.'

He smiled then shoved his hands in his pocket and started walking backward. "You know, your boyfriend is pretty cool. I think we could have been friends had I survived the Sickness."

Nodding with suppressed emotion, I smirked at the thought of Joseph and Zach hanging out before looking back at Zach who had paused at the edge of the woods, and I knew he was looking for a proper way to say goodbye. Shaking my head, I signed, 'Not goodbye. Farewell.'

Zach smiled then nodded and saluted to me before turning to walk into the woods. My heartstrings tugged to beg him to stay, but I knew he had to leave. Nonetheless, I had one more question for him. Rushing forward I grabbed his arm stopping him from leaving quite yet. He paused then looked back at me, a silent question in his eyes. Taking my breath, I took a step back so I could sign my question. 'Are you happy?'

One last time I saw a smile stretch across his face as he said, "Yeah. I really am." Glancing up to the sky, he commented, "Heaven is wonderful. You'll love it someday, but for now, enjoy Earth." His smile became sad as he murmured, "Enjoy life… It's a gift." He paused, then looked at me one last time before signing, "I love you."

Fresh tears streamed down my face as I signed back, 'I love you.' Then as he turned and walked away, I blinked. When I opened my eyes again, he was gone.

I stood there for who knows how long wondering if I had imagined it all, but I knew in my heart I hadn't, for the peace in my heart still lingered and my conviction to take that chance. Looking up at the sky which was slowly darkening I signed, 'Thank you.' Then I turned and followed the old path back to the house.

My father and Dr. Dubois were outside scanning the woods, I was certain, looking for me and as I approached a profound look of relief appeared on my father's face. Running forward, he called out, asking if I was all right. I held up a hand to signal I was fine. However, as he was my dad, he was satisfied until he had looked me over himself. After he did, I looked up at him to find chastisement in his eyes but instead I just saw curiosity.

"So did you decide?"

Nodding slightly, I held up my hands and signed, 'Will you translate?'

He nodded then turned back to the house with me. We walked up to Dr. Dubois, who was lingering back in an attempt to give us our privacy. As we approached, she took a step forward and said, "I'm so sorry, Mirda. I didn't mean to offend you or overwhelm you or—"

I held up my hand, cutting her off, then signed, 'I will come.'

My dad translated, and I heard the shock in his voice. Dr. Dubois smiled then clarified, "Does that mean you accept my proposition?"

Nodding, I signed, 'Yes.'

My dad translated once more, and a sincere smile spread across Dr. Dubois's face as she promised, "We will do our absolute best. I promise."

'Thank you.' Suddenly emotionally exhausted, I turned to my father, who signed, "I'm so proud of you." I gave him a small smile before signing, 'I'm tired. Can I go to bed?'

He nodded. "You're good. I'll discuss the details with Dr. Dubois."

Sighing with relief, I signed back, 'Thanks.'

He nodded then held out his arms. Walking into them, I hugged him back as his arms enclosed me in his embrace. I felt him press a kiss to the top of my head before he murmured softly, "I love you, Mirda."

Pulling back, I raised my right hand, 'I love you too.'

Then I turned and walked inside my house, up to my room. I shut the door before taking a deep breath and leaning against the door. Pressing my hands to face, my limbs trembling, I once again asked myself if that just really happened. Once I reassured myself that it really did, I collapsed to my knees and in the middle of my bedroom floor I offered a silent prayer. In that prayer, I thanked God for sending my brother to me and prayed for the courage to continue on in the path that I had chosen for myself. Then just before I ended my prayer a sudden realization hit me. I had no idea how I was going to break the news to my friends.

CHAPTER 69

Although I had prayed for guidance the night before as to how I should break it to my friends that I was leaving for France tomorrow, no guidance came. It seemed like God wanted me to try and figure things out for myself. Which was fine. So fine.

The next day I went to school, my heart was heavy with the news. I tried to bring it up all day, but the timing was never quite right. Then at lunch Paul reminded Joseph and me about the party at his house that night. It was to celebrate the fact that they won the playoffs and that we were almost done with our junior year. A light-bulb went off in my mind, and I smiled as the pressure of telling Paul and Joseph that I was leaving was slightly lifted. I would tell them tonight at the party then after go back home and pack. It was a solid plan, except for the fact that I would break Joseph's heart and ruin Paul's party. Granted that was the worst-case scenario, but knowing that did not stop me from thinking about it at random intervals throughout the day. Eventually I made it through school, the afternoon, and somehow found myself walking to Paul's house. (Joseph had offered to drive me, but I needed the time to compose myself.)

As I approached Paul's house, I took a deep breath and said a little prayer in my heart before walking up to Paul's house. Walking up the steps, I pushed open the door and walked in, grinning as I heard the baseball team cheering. Walking into the kitchen, I saw a couple of guys on the couch playing video games, some were playing a card game at the coffee table, and Paul's mom was managing food.

I waved to her and then signed, 'Where's Paul?'

She gestured with her thumb to the backyard, and I signed 'Thank you' then walked to the back door. Pulling it open I stepped out onto the back porch to see Paul and Ebony cuddled by the fire.

Grinning, I walked down the steps around the pool, out the gate and to the fire. Ebony looked over her shoulder and smiled as she saw me then murmured something to Paul. He released his hold on her, and she stood up, turned, and briefly helped him before running over to me. She threw her arms around me, and I hugged her back then let her go so I could hug Paul briefly. Afterward, he pulled back, grinning, "We did it."

Forcing my small smile to spread a little wider, I nodded. 'Yeah we did.'

"Now just to finish junior year," Ebony joked, and as Paul chuckled, my smile faded.

'About that…I've got some news.'

Paul's and Ebony's eyes went wide as I explained the situation and the decision I made. 'At best I'll miss summer, at worst, I'll miss senior year. Are you mad?'

Oddly enough, Ebony was the one who responded first. She smiled at me and said simply, "I've always wondered what your voice sounds like. Now I'll get to find out."

A grateful smile spread across my face, and with tears in my eyes, I signed, 'Thank you.' Then I looked to Paul. He was frowning, but it wasn't a mad or disappointed smile; it was the frown he had when he was trying to hold back emotion.

'Paul,' I tentatively signed.

Glancing down, he signed then looked back up at me, and I saw the tears in his eyes. "You better write every day."

Tears pricked the corners of my eyes, and I signed, 'Every day doesn't seem realistic, Paul.'

"You know what I mean. Email, letters, messages once a day, letting us know you're alive or I won't let you go."

Smiling, I tentatively signed, 'Really? You'll let me go?'

Sighing, he said, "What kind of best friend would I be if I didn't let you go to France to get your voice back. Besides," he affirmed, "if the procedure doesn't work, we'll still be here waiting for you to come home."

Touched I pressed a hand to my chest.

Paul smiled, "When do you leave?"

I made a helpless face as I signed, 'Tonight.'

He nodded sadly then said, "Well, you better go find Joseph and tell him the news." Then he reached forward and gave me a proper hug.

"I'll see you soon, bestie."

With tears in my eyes, I tightened my embrace to emphasize his message then pulled back and nodded before turning and hugging Ebony.

"I'll take care of him," she murmured into my ear before pulling away and smiling.

I smiled back then nodded my thanks before looking back to Paul to ask where Joseph was when I saw by the big oak tree at the edge of the woods surrounding Paul's house, a figure that I knew all too well.

I felt Ebony rub my back soothingly then murmured, "Go get him."

Nodding, I walked forward a couple steps before looking back and waving to Paul and Ebony. They waved back then turned to walk back to the house and touched by their attempt to give Joseph and me privacy I turned back to Joseph. He had moved from standing by the tree to standing behind an old swing that Paul's stepdad/uncle had built years ago to get closer to Paul. It was a sturdy thing and despite Paul, Caroline, and I using it for many years it had yet to break once. However, as I say that, I should probably knock on some wood.

Anyway, as I approached, Joseph looked up and smiled. "I was wondering when you were going to show up." I couldn't help but smile then walked up to him, the swing in between us. He smiled down at me then gestured to the seat of the swing. "I saved you a seat."

'Why, thank you,' I signed mirthfully before sitting down as he walked behind me. After I had grasped the ropes of the swing, Joseph pulled me and the swing back, then let go. I felt like I was a kid again, but instead of being here with Paul and his sister, I was here with the man I loved. It was a dream come true and as he pushed me back and forth, and for a moment, everything was perfect. There was no

French doctor, no troubles, or problems, no school, just Joseph and me. Then the swing slowed, and the moment ended. I opened my eyes to see Joseph standing in front of me.

Smiling down at him as I swung forward then back, he smiled up at me. "How did I get so blessed?"

I shrugged then wrapped my arm around the swing before awkwardly signing as the swing continued to swing. 'You brought me back.'

He shrugged then said, "You did all the heavy lifting. I just gave you a little nudge in the right direction." He pushed the swing a little as he finished the sentence, and my smile got bigger. Grinning, he reached out and snagged my swing, pulling me to a stop. Looking up at him, I watched intently as his eyes examined my face briefly before he held out his hand to me. Placing my hands in his, I let him pull me to my feet and into his arms. Tears threatened to stream down my face, but I pushed them back as I closed my eyes.

"You're leaving, aren't you?"

It took me a second to process what Joseph said, and when I did, I pulled away as shock filled me. Shaking my head, I stared at him, making sure the surprise was evident on my face. He frowned, and I thought he misinterpreted the expression on my face because he asked again, "Are you leaving me?"

Hesitantly I signed, 'Yes.' Then I shook my head as I attempted to understand how he knew. Finally, I gave up and just asked him, 'How did you know?'

He shrugged then said, "I could just tell." Raising an eyebrow to show that I doubted his words, he sighed then admitted, "The way you're looking at me now…it's as if you're trying to memorize my features." He touched my cheek and murmured, "As if you're not sure you'll get another chance." A tear trickled down my face, and he raised his other hand and brushed away the tear. I raised my hands and placed them on his wrists. Leaning my head forward, he met me halfway and leaned his forehead against mine. We remained like that for a few moments before he murmured, "You looked at me like this once before."

I made a face mentally wondering when I had felt like this which would prompt this particular face, and nothing popped up.

Joseph chuckled then gently murmured, "Right after you went in to talk to Jonah, you made the same face." He lifted his hands from my face and clasped mine, bringing them to his lips and pressing a kiss to them before letting go of my hands and asking, "Where are you going?"

I took a breath then signed, 'France. To maybe get my voice back.'

It was his turn to be shocked. His mouth dropped open, and he said, "I thought you had given up."

I nodded. I had but he had taught me hope was still there and that maybe I shouldn't have given up so soon. I raised my hand to protest, or explain, I wasn't sure, but his hand covered mine.

Lowering it to, he silently examined my face for some time then took a deep breath and stated firmly, "Okay. I'll be waiting for you when you come back." Tears of relief streamed down my face as he continued, "Although you've proven countless times that you don't need your voice to speak your mind, you need this trip, this experience. I can't say why, but I feel in my heart that this is what needs to happen." He took a deep shuddering breath, and I saw a tear trickle down his cheek. My heart clenched, and I fell in love all over again as he said, "I know how much it hurts…not always being able to express what's on your mind, Mirda. To not fully express what you are feeling, and I think this is God's will for you to get your voice back, so that way, you don't have to live in silence anymore."

He squeezed my hands gently then pulled me to him. I wrapped my arms around his neck and buried my face into the shoulder of his shirt.

As we lingered in each other's arms, a nagging feeling began to permeate the harmonious spirit. Pulling back slightly I allow myself to drop back down to the pads of my feet as I attempt to pay attention to that feeling. I felt Joseph press a kiss to the top of my head, and it hit me. Looking up at Joseph, I automatically opened my mouth to say what I felt when he beat me to it. "I love you. I have for a long time, but now, I love you more than enough to let you go."

My mouth dropped open, and I couldn't stop the slightly annoyed look I shot at Joseph. Joseph pulled back, "Sorry. I know that was bad timing, and you're leaving, but—"

Shaking my head, interrupting him, I raised my hand and signed, 'Yes, bad timing, but not for that reason.'

Joseph frowned, "Then why were you glaring at me?"

'Because I was about to tell you I love you and yet somehow you beat me to it!'

Grinning, Joseph I asked, "Really?"

Annoyed at his doubt and his smile, I pulled away, shaking my head. 'You're seriously doubting me? I thought it was the girl who's supposed to doubt the boy, but you don't see me doubting you.'

"I'm sure that will come eventually." Joseph smirked, and I gave him a look. He sighed then took a step forward and pressed a hand to his cheek. "I love you."

My annoyance faded, and my smile returned. Taking a step back, for emphasis, I did the full signing process with both hands and not just one. 'I love you.' He smiled then took a step forward and cupped my cheeks with his hands. Grasping his wrists, I held tight for a moment then took a step into his embrace.

His arms wrapped around me, and I heard the emotion clog his voice, "You so better write me."

Nodding against his chest, I tightened my grip on him momentarily before Joseph murmured, "All right, I have to let you go now, or I'm never going to let you go." Reluctantly, I agreed internally then together we pulled away from each other. Lowering my hands to my side, I watched as Joseph shoved his hands in his pockets. Taking a deep breath, he asked, "Do you need help packing?"

Shrugging weakly, I signed, 'Honestly, don't even know what I need or how long I'll be gone—' As I thought about all the things, I didn't know my brain began to go into panic mode. My breathing began coming out in short, choppy breaths, and I looked to Joseph helplessly. Taking his hands out of his pocket, Joseph took a step toward me and visibly took a breath. Copying him, I took a deep breath, calming my rapid heartbeat. After a long moment, I finally signed, 'No. It will just make it more difficult.'

Even though Joseph's face clearly reflected disappointment, he nodded, and I saw understanding flash in his eyes. "All right."

Nodding, I looked down, blinking back the tears, then when I realized it was fruitless effort, I looked back at Joseph with tears streamed down my face as I signed, 'Thank you.' My hands trembled as I promised, 'I'll write you, and I'll think about you every day and miss and…' I got up every ounce of courage I had and signed with trembling hands, 'I promise, whether or not the surgery works, I'll come back to you.'

A small gasp of relief escaped him, and I saw another tear trickled down his cheek before he pulled me back into his arms. I felt his limbs trembling with repressed emotion, and I smiled before locking my arms around him attempting to convey without words my faith in him and in God. Eventually I know the time has come, and I shifted in Joseph's arm. A sigh of regret escaped Joseph, but he loosened his hold, and despite the fact that I had ended the moment, I could see the smile in his eyes as he looked at me. Lovingly he reached out and brushed back a strand of my hair behind my ear.

After staring at me a moment longer, he murmured, "I love you."

I felt a soft blush rise to my cheeks, and I looked down at my hands as I pulled them from Joseph's before looking up at him and signing, 'I love you too. I always will.'

Joseph nodded, and I saw for a moment, my anxiety reflected in his eyes. Then as he began to blabber, I couldn't help but smile. "Everything will be fine. You'll see. All you have to do is put your trust in God, and everything will turn out all right." He averted his gaze. "Maybe not the way you wanted them to but—"

Before he could say another word, I pulled my hand from his and covered his mouth.

He looked at me, startled, and I smiled kindly at him before taking my other hand from his, and signing, 'It will work out.'

Then removing my hand from his mouth, I reached up and gently combed my fingers through his hair at the back of his head as I let him read my gaze, 'I love you.'

"I love you." He hugged me once more briefly before letting me go.

I turned and walked down the hill, my heart aching both from the effort of hoping that I was doing the right thing and from the realization that it would be most likely a whole year before I would see Joseph again. I turned back one more time and locked eyes with me. He raised his hand and waved to me. I waved back before turning back to the road and taking a breath knowing that if I looked back again, I would never leave.

CHAPTER 70

As soon as I got home my dad sent me upstairs to our attic to get down our suitcases, I passed them down to Dad then dropped down and took a few to my room. Glancing around helplessly, I began just grabbing clothes and stuffed them in the bags. Since I really didn't know what to take, I took a mix of just about everything. I ended up with a total of three suitcases and one backpack as a carry-on. (In my defense, my dad had two huge suitcases and a carry-on.) The airport was around seven hours away, so we went to bed early then woke around midnight to drive to the airport. Right before we left, I insisted that Dad say a prayer to not only bless our travels, but our house, and the friends that we were leaving behind. My dad had smiled at my insistence then nodded before saying a brief prayer. Afterward we took one look around the house, made sure we weren't missing anything, and threw away all our perishable foods then went to our packed car, hopped in, and drove to the airport. At the airport, we paid for long-term parking then checked in our suitcases before going through security.

It was around nine am, so we got some overprice airport breakfast then played a few card games while waiting for the flight attendant to call our flight. My dad and I didn't talk. I was determined to remain focused on the game and ignore my pent-up nerves. However, it was all for naught as when they eventually called for our flight to start boarding, and I began freaking out. Although outwardly there were very few signs, biting my lip, tapping my foot, and sweating, my dad still picked up on my tension. Looking to me, he opened his arms, and I rushed into them. He held me while my body shook uncontrollably.

A couple of minutes later, my dad broke the tension and asked quietly, "Nervous?" I nodded against his chest, and he smiled then said, "Have a little faith. Maybe twenty-fourth time is the charm."

Unable to put my fear aside, I was grateful for the attempted hope he gave me, but I was unable to find the strength to separate myself from his arms. I wasn't going to go back home. I was going to get on this plane. I repeated to myself again and again in my mind when my dad murmured, "And if it doesn't work, God will still be there for you. I'll still be there for you, and so will your friends." I gave a small smile before it faded as I thought about Joseph. "You're thinking about him.

I looked to him with questioning eyes to find him giving me a knowing look. Taking a deep breath, I nodded, confirming his statement. I heard my father sigh then pulled me close to his chest momentarily then murmured, "God wouldn't have sent him to you if he wasn't ready to handle a little separation."

Grateful for his reassurance but also plagued by my own anxiety, I pulled away from Dad and signed, 'This isn't a little separation, though, Dad. This is across continents.'

A look of understanding crossed his face, and he hesitated before offering me a small smile. "Did I ever tell you that for the first part of your mother's and mine's marriage, the first two years actually I was rarely at home?" Confused at his random thought, I made a face, and my dad smirked before stating simply, "We, your mother and I, didn't want to wait to have you kids, but unfortunately, my job at the time made that simply impossible." His face turned sour as he described the first two years at his now loved job. "I enjoyed the work I was doing, yes, and loved helping people, but it forced me to be away from your mother for long periods of time. We thought about moving, but we both loved our little house in the country so much we decided to attempt the long-distance thing." My dad gave another small, sad smile, but as the tears pricked the corner of his eyes, I saw in them the love he still had for my mother. A small sad smile touched my face as he continued, "Your mother was very patient with me and my inability to come home as often as she liked. Somehow, she even kept on loving me despite the fact that we were rarely together. Eventually, though, when your mom found out she was pregnant with you and Zach, I realized that enough was enough. I was going to be there for her no matter what my boss said, and I told him just that." My mouth dropped open as my generally nonconfrontational father admitted that he told off his boss. "After your mom gave me the news, I marched into my boss's office and told him that I would quit unless we could arrange a way that I wouldn't have to travel to the city so much. To my astonishment, he agreed with me, and we arranged it so that I would have to go to the office a couple of times a week and travel once a year. Twice if absolutely necessary. It was an answer to my prayers, and I headed home that day." My dad smiled lost in a memory. "I didn't tell your mom, so when I was back up at the house, she was dressed in her bathrobe. Her hair was in a messy bun. She clearly had just been handling a bout of morning sickness, but to me, she had never looked so beautiful."

I smiled then waved to get his attention before signing, 'And knowing Mom, she screamed in spite of the nausea.'

"Yep and jumped on me then demanded to know how we were going to pay for the house if I didn't have a job." My dad laughed, and my smile broadened.

It had been so long since we had talked about Mom, and somehow it felt like a huge weight had been lifted off my chest, like if we had done this years ago, then maybe we would have had a relationship sooner.

Eventually after my dad stopped laughing, he cleared his throat and said, "Now it's only years later that I realized us being apart wasn't entirely a bad thing. Though yes it was difficult it also caused us to grow stronger not only as a couple but as a person." He paused, speaking as the line shifted forward, and we moved a couple of feet before he turned back to me. "I have confidence that by God's will, you and Joseph will not only grow stronger as a person but as a couple. It will make the reunion that much...more."

I nodded then gave him a side hug. 'Thanks, Dad. That's what I needed.'

He smiled then gestured to the lady holding out her hand for my ticket. "Come on. We have a flight to catch."

Although it wasn't my first flight ever, it had been awhile, and I forgot how much I missed it. The sensation of flying, of feeling weightless, the shifting of the plane. It was soothing to my nerves, and I found myself nodding off within the first hour of the flight. I did fall asleep for a good portion of the trip as the flight was over seven hours, but about an hour before we landed, I woke up and found that I couldn't go back to sleep.

So I looked out the window and pulled out my art pad as I watched the sun descend. Casually I sketched the sun and found myself adding in the outline of a man. Before I knew it, I had drawn in the features and found myself looking at Joseph. A twinge of pain filled my heart, and I leaned my head back against the headrest of my seat, closing my eyes. Mouthing a silent prayer for peace and the knowledge that everything would be okay.

Next thing I knew, I was waking up as the tires of the plane hit that tarmac. We were landing just outside of Paris, and someone was supposed to be waiting for us to drive us into the city. Funny enough, it was Dr. Dubois waiting for us and who drove us to our rental house on the outskirts of the city about ten minutes from her office. It was a quaint place. A two-story apartment with two bed-rooms, an office, a kitchen (with a fully stocked fridge), and laundry in the basement. (Later I looked up the prices of apartments in Paris, France, and realized how blessed we were for not having to pay for the apartment.) Anyways, the first day I was so exhausted from jet lag that after I unpacked one of my suitcase I crashed.

The next day after a hearty breakfast, Dad and I went into the city to do a little sightseeing. We went to the Eiffel Tower, to Notre Dame, and to the Arc de Triomphe. I had read and studied these places in school, but actually being there in person was something else entirely. Nonetheless, as I took photos with my dad, I couldn't help but wish that Joseph or even Paul was here with me. However, just because they weren't didn't mean they couldn't be here in spirit, so I took plenty of photos then went home that night eager to begin, what would become my habitual letter writing. I wrote first to Joseph, a whole two pages, then Paul, then to Ebony, and finally Caroline. The first thing the next morning I dropped the letters off in the mail-box, before going to Dr. Dubois's office with my father.

To say I was nervous was an understatement, but God and my brother had reassured me that everything would be all right. Besides

I was here, and I wasn't planning on running now. She performed several tests on me via x-rays, MRI, physical, etc. The physical tests aka the speaking tests I totally failed, no sound came from my throat which although I expected I hoped that maybe by some miracle it would be fixed just by my faith to fly to France, but of course, it wasn't as I had more to learn while I was in France. When I could I zoned out during the tests as it was the best option at the time as when I paid attention to what she was doing I just tensed up which ended up forcing us to redo some of the tests.

Honestly, by the end of it, I was just so worried that she would change her mind and send me home, that I didn't care what she was doing. So as I tapped my foot waiting for Dr. Dubois to come back with my father with a verdict, I silently prayed that God's will would be done and that I would accept whatever that may be.

My father entered the room five minutes later, and I jumped to my feet with a question on my lips but unable to voice it. My dad looked at me, his face not revealing and gave a small shrug of his shoulders. My hope fell, and I bit my lip then looked down when there was a knock at the door. I couldn't look up as my dad opened the door. Hearing the soft clacking sound of heels, I knew without looking it was Dr. Dubois. Squeezing my eyes shut, I was ready for her to break the bad news to me when the three magical words filled my ears. "I can do it."

I started nodding automatically and grabbed my notebook, prepared to go back to the States with my dad when it registered in my mind what she said. "I can do it."

My eyes flashed open, and I just had to look at Dr. Dubois, see the sincerity in her eyes and hear her repeat, "I can do it."

Tears flooded my eyes, and I pressed a hand to my heart momentarily before signing, 'You're serious?'

Dr. Dubois looked at my dad for translation, and after my father did, Dr. Dubois smiled kindly at me before further explaining, "We can perform the surgery in two months when all the equipment I require comes in. I ordered it just before I left for the States hoping you would say yes and that you'll continue to say yes." Fervently I nodded, and she smiled. "Wonderful. Well, until the equipment comes in, there are other tests I would like to try that might nullify the surgery."

My eyes widened, and I signed, 'You really think that's possible?'

She bit her lip as my father signed before giving a curt nod. "For your sake, yes, but in all likelihood…no." Appreciative of her honesty and admiration for her unwillingness to give me false information, I nodded understanding. However, clearly, she wasn't able to read the gratitude in my expression because a twinge of doubt traveled across her face, and she asked again. "Do you still wish to continue working with me and my company?"

Smiling broadly at her, I signed and mouthed, 'Yes.'

For once Dr. Dubois didn't need to translate what I said, and her smile returned to her face. "Well then, I will see you a week from today."

Nodding, I signed 'Thank you' then looked to my dad who grinned cheekily. Playfully glaring at him, I put my sketchbook back in my bag before turning and walking out of the room. I heard my dad chuckle behind me then his rapid footsteps as he hurried after me.

As we exited the building I turned to my dad, an incredulous smile on my face. He grinned then leaned down and gave me a hug. "I told you things would work out."

A smirk touched my face, and I nodded before pulling away from my dad. Then like I was eight years old again I took his hand and half skipped my way back to the apartment.

I wrote a couple more letters that night and afterward while I was staring out the window a thought came to my mind.

Things were working out now yes, but nothing good in life ever came easy; soon enough, trials would come. With that grim thought I rolled my shoulders back and pushed aside the fear that came with the statement and instead replaced it with my testimony that God was real. That Jesus Christ was real. They would protect me. No matter what trials would come my way.

CHAPTER 71

To put it simply, trials did come.

First, the parts Dr. Dubois needed delivered to perform my surgery were delayed by another month.

Then I had a bad reaction to one of the tests Dr. Dubois performed so the surgery had to be pushed back another week.

On top of that my third and fifth letter to Joseph were sent back because I put the incorrect zip code on the envelope. (I put the France one instead. Facepalm.)

Now some good things did happen while all the bad things were going on too.

First, I started my senior year in France. It was extremely different from my American school and a little difficult since I knew barely any French, but I caught up rather quickly, and it ended up being a ton of fun. Although I missed my friends and home, I eventually made new friends. Despite the fact that I didn't have a voice, my new friends didn't judge me and were instead impressed by the app I made to speak English for me. (Honestly, though, I was more impressed when they took the initiative and helped me make my app French-friendly.)

They constantly took me on tours around Île-de-France and to the surrounding region: Burgundy, Champagne, Normandy, etc. It was all very different from home, and I was homesick on more than on one occasion, but I found myself falling in love with France and its people. I couldn't really explain it, but there was a beauty there that America had failed to grasp. Something about the food, the people, the traditions. Or maybe it was the simplicity or the history. I wasn't entirely sure, but in the short time I stayed in France, I gained a great respect for France and its people.

It was just before Thanksgiving that I got the surgery. I didn't remember much as I was asleep, but I did remember not being afraid. I should have been terrified out of my mind, but right before I went into surgery, I said a prayer with my father, and as we finished, I felt in my heart that everything was going to be okay.

When I woke up, my father and Dr. Dubois were by my side, telling me that the surgery went well and that I had to wait another three weeks for my body to heal from the surgery before I should try and use my voice. I had a giant bandage over my throat keeping my whole head mostly in place, so I simply raised my hand and signed, 'Yes.'

Since France doesn't celebrate Thanksgiving, I skipped a whole week of school and had lots of makeup work, which, for once, I was genuinely excited for. Mainly because it was busy work that distracted me from the time it took for Paul or Ebony or Joseph to write back. I'll admit it was hard being away from them, my best friends, but it was comforting to know they were doing well. I knew they each had their own trials and though they briefly mentioned them, they didn't go into detail. I knew they didn't want me to worry, but nonetheless I did, so each night as I sent my prayers up to heaven, I prayed that my friends would be all right. That angels would be sent to protect them. From the letters it seemed like my prayers were working, so I kept at it.

Another thing I kept at both before and after my surgery was going to church. My father and I found a church very similar to ours called the Church of Jesus Christ of Latter-Day Saints, and though it was different, they did testify of God and Christ. They made sense and gave me hope. It was one of the only places I felt at home despite being so far away from home and I made a note when I got back into the US to investigate more about this church.

Three weeks passed swiftly and soon enough I was back in Dr. Dubois's office. She was telling me to start with something simple. To say the Alphabet in English (since that's the language I was most used to.) So I tried, and tried, and tried again, praying the entire time that the surgery had indeed worked. Then as I went through the alphabet the third time, I felt something tickle in the back of my throat, however, it wasn't until on the letter *m* that I felt that something in the back of my throat turned into something.

Attempting to ignore the hopeful fluttering in my stomach I tried pronouncing the letter again, "Mmmm. Mmm. M." Then I realized I was using my vocal cords to produce those sounds. Dr. Dubois smiled and nodded encouragingly. Letting my small success fuel me, I formed the letter *n* with my mouth and attempted the same thing. "Nn. Nnnn. N. Ooo. O. Pe. P. Quuu. Q." Slowly I went through the rest of the alphabet, my voice getting stronger and more confident with each letter. By the time I got to *z*, I was crying, my father was crying, Dr. Dubois was crying, and all the other nurses in the room observing were crying.

Over the next month, I progressed from sounding out letters to saying simple sentences. Then after another month, I began saying more complicated sentences, and just for fun, I learned to speak French too. Though it was difficult at first, and rather confusing, somehow it eventually made sense; and by the time I left France, I could fluently speak English again, and I was fairly fluent in French.

Anyway, I stayed in France one more month, just to make sure that my voice wasn't going to give out on me any time soon. I expected to be home just after Valentine's day, but Dr. Dubois wanted to run a few more tests to make sure that my voice wasn't going to give out on me anytime soon. The tests came back positive, and I was able to go home right before Saint Patrick's Day.

We got home around eleven at night, and almost immediately when I lay on my bed, I fell asleep. I awoke late the next morning, around ten, and smiled as I saw the sun shining. With a small sigh, I got out of bed stretched then opened my suitcase and got ready for the day. Afterward I went downstairs and hunted around in the cupboards until I found the fixings for brown sugar oatmeal. After smelling it and making sure there were no bugs, I heated up some water and made the simple meal. As I was spooning the oatmeal into bowls, Dad walked down the stairs, smiling. I smiled at him as he walked over and pressed a kiss to the top of my head.

"Morning, Mira."

After I got my voice back, it was really hard for me to pronounce my name, Mirda. Mainly because I had to roll the *r* and *d* together, and each time I tried, my voice gave out. So I just decided to shorten it and go by Mira. (Besides, my French teachers could never get my name right anyways, so it didn't really matter.)

"Morning, Daddy." I placed the pot in the sink before grabbing two spoons as my dad sat in front of the bigger of the two bowls of oatmeal on the table. Handing one of the spoons to Dad, I sat in front of the other bowl and folded my arms as my father said a quick prayer blessing the food.

As we ate, I asked, "Are you going to the store today to get real food, or am I or we both…?"

"Whatever you want to do, Mira," my dad said as he took another bite of oatmeal. "I know you want to see your friends, so if you can't go shopping, I'll go, I do have to make some calls to the office to let my boss know that I'm officially back, but other than that, I have no plans."

"Okay." I contemplated what I should do and who I should see first when the doorbell rang.

My dad, who had just opened one of the stack of newspapers he had found on our entryway rug, sighed and set it aside, murmuring, "I got it."

I smiled then finished off my oatmeal before I stood and grabbed both his and my empty bowl before placing them in the sink. My ears perked up as I heard my dad walk to the front door then open it.

"Hi! It's so good to see you two! How are your parents? That's wonderful. Mira! You should come see who it is."

I sighed then turned from the sink and walked to the front door only to hasten my footsteps as I saw my best friend and his sister standing on my porch steps.

CHAPTER 72

As I approached the front door, my dad stepped aside, smiling lovingly down at me. Briefly I smiled back before looking at Paul and Caroline. They were silent for a moment, waiting for me to sign something probably, but I did no such thing.

Instead, I opened my mouth and said brightly, "Hey, guys! How are things?"

In sync, their mouths dropped open and after briefly looking at each other before looking back to me.

After another moment of silence, Caroline blurted, "You can talk."

I laughed then said, "Yes, I can."

She grinned then ran to me and hugged me. "I missed you so much. I missed my big sister. You're still her, right?"

I smiled then took a step back and signed just for her, 'Of course I am.' She smiled back at me then hugged me fiercely before letting me go and going to my dad.

"Mom said that you should come to our house for dinner today since you have no food in the house. She also said that she and Daddy will help you go shopping…" Caroline continued to jabber away at him, and I turned my attention to Paul, who was still standing on the porch his mouth gaping open.

"Surprised?"

He chuckled then smiled before nodding. "To say the least."

I nodded then walked forward and hugged him.

He hugged me back for a moment before he said, "Can't believe you didn't tell me."

I laughed then pulled away and said, "If it makes you feel better, I didn't tell Joseph or Ebony either." I walked out to the front porch and sat.

Paul sat down beside me, shrugging, "Little bit."

I chuckled then looked at him and asked softly, "How is Ebony?"

"She's great. We're great, going on almost ten months."

"She told me in her last letter that she's very proud that you've put up with her for this long." Paul rolled his eyes, and I teased, "Honestly, I'm proud and a little surprised that she's put up with you for this long."

"Ah, shut up," he muttered, pushing me good-naturally.

I smiled, then it faded as I said earnestly, "I did miss you, guys, a lot. I prayed every day that not only your relationship would last but our friendship."

Paul nodded then said, "So did I. Maybe not as earnestly or as faithfully as you, but I did pray a lot. For your voice, for you. I can't imagine how stressful the last eight months have been."

I shrugged then sighed. "They were stressful, yes, but knowing that my best friend had my back supporting me made all the difference."

He nodded, and we were silent for a moment appreciating our surroundings when eventually he asked, "Did your dad call you, Mira?"

I nodded, "Yep. When I got my voice back, I couldn't pronounce my name. It was too hard, so I shortened it to something I could pronounce."

"Mira." He paused as if tasting the name then finally he smiled and stated simply, "I like it."

A sigh of relief escaped me. "Thanks."

He nodded then bumped my shoulder gently with his shoulder, "So how was France?"

I took a deep breath then state simply. "It was amazing."

Paul grinned, and I knew this was the moment to give him his gift. I straightened up. "And speaking of France, I have a present for you."

"Oh?"

Nodding, I started to turn back to the house. "Give me a moment." I ran back inside and up to my room. I grabbed the gift that I had wrapped in newspaper and brought it outside. "For you," I said, handing it to Paul.

He took it, and I sat beside him and unwrapped it.

"A Boules Set?"

I nodded then explained, "It's a very popular game and or sport in France. If you want, I can teach you one of these days after school."

"School?" he asked.

Smiling, I stated simply, "I want to finish my senior year with you guys. Go to baseball games, have group dates, family dinners." I smiled then said, "I've spent most of my life not living, and now I don't want to waste another minute." He smiled then set his gift aside and reached over and hugged me. "So you like the gift?"

"It's perfect. I just hope you got something for Caroline?" he asked, pulling away.

I nodded, smiling, "I know how much she loves books, so I got her a pristine version of *Le Petit Prince*."

"I don't know what that book is, but if it's a book, she's going to love it."

I chuckled then asked hesitantly, "You hanging out with Ebony today?"

"Yeah, in about an hour, and on the way, I can drop you off at the auto body shop where Joseph works."

I grinned then confirmed, "He works at the car shop now?"

Paul nodded. "He didn't tell you that in his letters."

I shook my head. "He told me he started a new job fixing cars but"—I paused, raising my fingers to put air quotes around what I next said—"didn't want to burden me with the unnecessary details."

"That sounds like someone very familiar."

I rolled my eyes then playfully punched his arm. Paul rubbed his arm then asked, laughing, "What?"

I grinned then stood. "I'm going to go get ready to go. Don't vanish on me before I get back."

He grinned then said, "Never in a million years."

I got cleaned up in record time. Before I knew it, I was in Paul's car headed toward the auto body shop. I was trying to remain calm, but internally, I was screaming. I hadn't see Joseph in over a year. What if we had changed to much? Or if he didn't like my voice? Or if—

Caroline must have sensed my distress because she reached over the seat and patted my shoulder. I looked to her, and she smiled, comforting me.

"You got this."

I nodded and took a deep breath as we pulled up to the shop.

"Go get him."

I nodded then opened the door and started to step out before handing her the book wrapped in newspaper. "This is for you."

"Thanks, sis. Now go."

I smiled then looked to Paul. "Tell Ebony I say hi."

He nodded. "I will. Now stop stalling and go."

I nodded then turned to get out, but the nerves got the better of me.

Taking a shallow breath, I turned back, and both Paul and Caroline shouted, "Go!"

I smirked then, tension broken, and I turned then climbed out of the car. I shut the door and took a step forward as Paul drove away.

CHAPTER 73

I walked up to the auto body shop and saw Joseph's back as he worked on a Chevy.

I watched him work for a moment before I cleared my throat and asked loudly, "Is there a mechanic around?"

"Yes," Joseph said, his back to me. My heart fluttered at the sound of his voice, and it took all of my concentration to focus on his next words. "But I'm a little busy at the moment."

"Oh, that's all good." I bit my lip, stifling a little giggle. "I was just wondering if you could take a look at my Mustang."

"Sure. What year?"

"1964...I think the fuel pump is messed up."

"Well, I happen to have 1964 Mustang fuel pump in stocks."

I know, I thought, biting my lip again, stifling yet another laugh as I recalled his letter.

"So let me just finish up here...and... done." He stood and grabbed a greasy cloth. He wiped his oily hands on the cloth before he turned, saying, "I'm Joseph Wilson, by the way."

I smiled then said as his eyes aligned with mine, "I'm Mira Johnson...but you knew me as Mir-r-da." My tongue stumbled over the *r*, but I managed to say my first name the way it was intended to be said. It took him a moment for him to register what I said, but once he did, it was obvious.

"Mirda?"

Nodding, I replied, "Hi, Joseph, it's been awhile."

He stared at me in an amazement before whispering, "Yeah." He stared at me for another moment, obviously in complete and utter shock. I smiled nervously then clasped my hands in front of me as he continued to stare at me.

"Joseph?"

He blinked then took a few steps forward before freezing as if he was worried I would flee the moment he tried to approach me. Fearing the same thing, I took a few steps forward, matching him. As we both realized that neither of us was going anywhere, we both started walking forward and met in the middle. Once there we stared at each other for a bit before Joseph reached out and took my hand. I looked at our clasped hands before I looked back up at him to find him staring at me again.

As we stared at each other, I saw tears glistened in his eyes, and I felt my own tears rise up as Joseph asked, "You're really here? You're really home? I'm not imagining this?"

I glanced down then shook my head. He waited in silence as I looked back up at him tears trickling down my cheeks.

"Yeah. I'm really here."

He smiled, and I saw a tear trickle down his cheek before he reached out and pulled me into his arms. I had been imagining this reunion for over eight months, and I wasn't about to hold back. My arms wrapped around him, and for a moment, it was only us. It was unreal, the two of us finally together, after so long. My heart felt like it was going to explode, but I wouldn't have it any other way. I was home. I was being embraced by the man I loved. Everything was perfect. Eventually Joseph pulled backed slightly to look at me.

"I can't believe you're here..." He smiled at me, his fingers brushing some of my hair back behind my ear. "And you're speaking to me."

"Yeah." His smile faded after a moment, and I frowned, confused, "Joseph?"

"Why didn't you, in any of your letters, mention that your voice was back? Or that the surgery worked?"

My mouth made a little *o* as I smiled again. "I wanted to surprise you, and besides...you never asked."

He pulled back even farther, annoyance evident in his expression, but from the twinkle in his eyes, I knew he was teasing me.

"You never brought it up." Then more seriously, he said, "I thought the treatment might not have been working. I didn't want to make you feel bad."

I laughed then said, "Well, that's awfully sweet of you, but clearly, I'm fine. The treatment worked, and you no longer have to worry about me anymore because I'm not leaving you again. Okay?"

Joseph stared at me, stunned once again.

I frowned in confusion. "Joseph, what's wrong?"

He shook his head. "Nothing. It's just…" He smiled then said, "I've never heard you laugh before."

I blushed then said, "It's just a laugh."

"Not for me. And I don't think it's ever going to be just a laugh for you either."

I shrugged then sighed. He was right; it was never going to be just a laugh for either of us. It was going to be a symbol of hope. Of possibilities. Of a future. Joseph reached out again and pulled me back into his embrace. "You don't actually have a 1964 Mustang with you? Do you?"

I chuckled then said, "No, it was just an excuse to talk to you."

"Well, you always have an excuse to talk to me, being my girl-friend and all."

I pulled away smiling before I asked, "Really?"

"Really," Joseph confirmed.

My smile broadened, and I tightened my grip on his hands. "Good, because we have a lot to talk about."

CHAPTER 74

We held hands as we walked to the bench customers used when waiting for their cars. We sat down together, and I smiled as he brushed a strand of my hair back.

"When did you get back?" Joseph asked quietly, never taking his eyes off of mine.

"Late last night. Paul stopped by this morning and told me that you two were switching days to check when I had gotten home. Is that true?"

Joseph smiled then nodded. "Yeah. We knew that you would probably forget to text, and we presumed that you still couldn't call us. So we developed the system three months after you left. Last night I stopped by around seven."

I nodded then said, "We didn't get home until around eleven or so."

Joseph chuckled then said, "Yeah, that's a little late. How long have you had your voice back?"

"Two months or so. The operation occurred two months before that."

"Wow, and you didn't dare mention it to me in any of the letters you sent."

I sighed before shrugging. "It took a month before I could say my first words then another two and a half before I could talk normally, and the entire time, I expected my voice to give out and for me to go back to being a mute. I didn't want to give myself false hope any more than I wanted to give you false expectations."

Joseph nodded then said, "That sounds logical, and it's okay." He put his hand on my cheek. "I'm not mad, maybe a bit annoyed, but I'm not mad. I would have done the same thing." I nodded and watched as he ran his thumb along the back of my hand. It felt wonderful to be back with him, in his presence. I felt whole again. I took a breath and looked up at him as he asked, "So are you going to finish high school here? Or did you finish already?" I smiled then shook my head before leaning slightly forward, placing my free hand over his other hand.

I looked down at our stacked hands before saying, "That was my one wish before I left. That I could graduate here."

A smile stretched across his lips, "Looks like your wish has been granted." He raised one of my hands up and gently kissed the back of it before pulling me to him in a hug. "I'm glad you're home," he whispered into my ear.

I smiled then whispered back, "Me too." Then I giggled.

Joseph pulled away and asked, "What?"

I smiled then said, "Tomorrow is Sunday, right?"

His eyebrows furrowed with confusion as he nodded. "Yes?"

I smiled then said, "Well then, the church in France was nice, but it wasn't quite like the family we have here, so let's just say I'm a little excited for tomorrow."

Joseph shook his head chuckling, "You will never cease to amaze me." Then he leaned forward and pressed his lips to mine, for one perfectly blissful kiss.

CHAPTER 75

The next day Joseph came and picked me up early so that we could go for a walk before going to church. However, that walk became an extra-long walk, which nearly made us late to church. Then trying to get Joseph out of the car and into the building was like trying to convince a child to eat broccoli (practically impossible). I tugged Joseph's hand as I pulled him through the parking lot.

"Come on!"

"I'm coming," he said as we raced up to the church building. We burst through the front door and walked to the last row just behind where Paul, Ebony, and their families were sitting.

"Told you we'd beat them," I said, smiling at Joseph as he wrapped his arm around my shoulder.

"Yes, you did." Five minutes later, my father and Joseph's stepparents walked in and sat in our row just as the preacher got up to start the meeting.

"Nice timing," I whispered to my dad.

He smiled then winked at me. I smiled when I felt something tugging in the back of mind. Slightly confused, I turned slightly around in my seat and saw by the door of the church three people.

A woman with long brown hair braided down her back, her hand was clasped with a little boy who was maybe around seven. Right beside them was a man, whom I had seen a little less than a year ago. A man who convinced me that I should take the chance to get my voice back.

My breath caught, and tears came to my eyes as my mother, little brother, and twin all waved at me. I gave a little wave back, shaking my head in disbelief. My mother smiled then knelt and picked up the little boy before turning and walked through the door. My twin stayed a bit longer. He smiled at me then looked at Joseph before nodding as he looked back at me. His message was clear: Joseph was the man for me. I gave a slight nod of my head to indicate I was thankful for his approval. He smiled then gave a small bow before he turned and walked through the door. I took a deep breath then turned to face the preacher, silent tears streaming down my face. A second later, I felt a hand touch mine. I looked to my right and saw my dad smiling at me.

"I saw them too," he signed.

My breath caught before I bit my lip and managed to nod.

After church I was walking to Joseph's car after talking to Paul and Ebony when Joseph asked, "You all right, babe?"

"Huh?" I asked, looking up, slightly startled.

He gave a small smile then said, "Mira. You've been distracted all meeting, what's up?"

I shrugged, and he made a face. "Mira."

I sighed as he walked around the car to grasp the sides of my arms.

I sighed then said, "I saw my family. They were there today. My mother, my baby brother, and my twin. Who, strangely enough, approves of you, by the way."

Joseph chuckled, and I asked incredulously, "You believe me?"

He nodded then said, "Mira, you can't lie."

I laughed; that was true, I couldn't.

"Besides," he said, taking my hands, "you would never lie about something like this."

I smiled then said, "Thank you."

"I love you."

He smiled then pulled me into his arms as I whispered into his ear, "I love you too."

EPILOGUE

So that's my story. That's how I found out God was real and that he never lost sight of me. That everything that happened was for a reason and that I wasn't alone. It was a long and winding road. It's still long and winding, but this time, I'm not trying to face it on my own. I have my family, friends, and most importantly, I have God.

I ended up going to nursing school and becoming a nurse. I now work at our local clinic and have no plan to leave anytime soon. As for the rest of the people in the story, they each got an ending. Whether it was a happy ending will be for you, the reader, to decide.

Jonah got out of jail after five years and is now living in Ohio with his wife and daughter.

The doctor who fixed my voice ended up becoming really famous. She and I actually went onto some talk shows together, and every year in the spring, she flies back to the United States to see me. Every year.

My father ended up retiring at the ripe old age of sixty-two. Now he enjoys sitting on the porch and watching the sunsets.

Paul ended up going to college on a soccer scholarship. He came back eight years later with a teaching degree and now teaches at our old high school. He's also the soccer coach. He and Ebony… are still going strong. They broke it off when Paul went off to college, but when Paul came back…they got back together, and now three years later, Paul is texting me different pictures of engagement rings. I expect a wedding in the near future.

Now Joseph. Dear, dear Joseph. Just to be clear. He's fine. I didn't kill him, nor did Paul or anyone else, for that matter. He's still around and will be for a long time. After I got back from France, he waited five months (basically, until after we graduated from high school) before proposing to me. A year later, we were married right in my backyard. Ebony was my maid of honor with Caroline as my bridesmaid, and Paul was Joseph's best man.

Another year later, instead of having kids, we got a dog. By that time, Joseph had finished his basic training and went into the military. Though it was hard for us, we knew this is what God wanted. He served two tours before he came back home and became a cop. I can't begin to tell you how proud I am of my husband. He truly is the best partner in crime a girl could ask for. Now before I sign off, I have one more story to share with you. It's just after Joseph finished his second tour. I was waiting with Paul, Ebony, my dad, and Joseph's stepparents at the airport for Joseph with two surprises.

*****

"Where is he?" I said, biting my lip.

Paul chuckled. "Mira, his flight landed like seven minutes ago. Be patient."

I breathed out a sigh before looking down at my double stroller. I smiled as I saw my baby boy was awake, while my little girl was fast asleep.

I smiled then asked quietly, "You ready to meet Daddy?" My baby boy gave a slight smile, and I giggled before looking up to see Joseph walking through the doors. He was in his military uniform, his hair freshly buzzed. My hands went to my mouth, and tears streamed down my face as I ran to him. He dropped his bag to catch me as I threw my arms around him. He spun me around, and faintly I heard cheering, but I didn't care. Joseph was home. My husband was home. Eventually he sent me down, and I pulled away so I could gently kiss him.

"Welcome home," I whispered, pulling away once more.

He smiled then said, "It's good to be back."

I gave a small nod before I pressed, "You ready to meet them?"

"I was ready long before we even knew about them."

I smiled then walked back to the stroller as he knelt and picked up his bag. I reached the stroller just as Ebony was getting out Mari.

I nodded my thanks as I reached into the other side of the stroller and pulled out Zach. I turned back to Joseph as he walked up to us. "May I introduce Mari Ester Wilson and Zach Samuel Wilson. Your daughter and son."

Joseph stopped before me, and Paul took his bag before I passed him his son. Joseph held Zach in shock as I turned to Ebony and took Amelia. I held her close to my chest as I watched Joseph as tears dripped down his cheeks. He looked at Zach, Amelia, then me. "We made a couple of good kids. Didn't we?" He said, his voice chock-full of emotion.

I nodded, my voice also clogged as I said, "Yeah. Yeah, we did."

*****

There you go, one final memory. I hoped you enjoyed it and you enjoyed my story. Maybe you learned something along the way, maybe you didn't. Either way, I learned something that no one can take away from me, and that's a far greater prize than anything this world could ever offer.

AUTHOR'S NOTE

You may be wondering, other than the miraculous vision Mirda had, where Jesus Christ or God is in this book. Well, I'm here to tell you He's everywhere! Although this may have seemed like a simple romance story, it was more than that. Mirda, though she didn't understand it out that time, reached out to the universe for help, and in effect she was reaching out to God and to Christ, and when you reach out to God, He takes you as you are!

If you ask him, He will mold you into the best person you could possibly be. However, He's not necessarily going to do it overnight. It takes time, patience, heavenly and earthly angels! In Mirda's case, it was her best friend and the love of her life. For me, it's been my family, my best friend, and so many others.

If we but ask God, He will send someone to rescue us from ourselves, and then one day, you could be the person rescuing another (like how Joseph rescued Mirda). Heavenly Father knows who we can't say no to, and He will shamelessly use them. However, that's not because He's using us just to fulfill His plan. He's using them to help us because He loves us. So He uses the people we love, the people we can't say no to no matter how hard we try, to help us become the best person we could possibly be.

I didn't want to write this book. I didn't want to be that person writing realistic fiction, but my friend Vanessa gave me an idea, and I just ran with it. My family and best friend supported me in every step of the way, and though at times I wanted to give up, I couldn't.

I couldn't because I fell in love with my characters, with God, and with Jesus Christ. He is in this book! He is here, and you could read this just to have good time, and that's fine, but my goal when writing this was to help at least one person to come closer to Christ, and I can testify that one person already has!

I have come closer to Christ through writing this book, and I'm not only a happier person, but I'm also a better person. I love myself, and I testify that if you choose to come unto Christ, whether it's through my book or through other means, then you will be a happier and better person too.

I love you, and most importantly, God and Jesus Christ loves you.

Thank you for reading *Muted*. Have a marvelous rest of your day!

ABOUT THE AUTHOR

 Rachel started creative writing in response to her favorite TV series ending in a way she didn't expect. Encouraged by her friends and family, who liked what she wrote, she started rewriting other movie scenes so she didn't have to watch the entire movie to enjoy the scene. From there, she kept writing throughout her high school career to keep her mind focused on class, and it was in her AP English class that the idea of *Muted* was formed.

Presently, Rachel lives in Virginia's Blue Ridge Mountains, attending college. On the days that she is not swamped by schoolwork or writing, Rachel loves outdoor activities like horseback riding, going on walks, and participating in community service. When she needs some alone time and has to be indoors, she can often be found reading fantasy novels, binging Disney Plus, or cleaning the house. She is an active member of the Church of Jesus Christ of Latter-Day Saints and dreams of becoming an institute teacher.

Printed in the USA
CPSIA information can be obtained
at www.ICGtesting.com
CBHW032311271123
2181CB00006B/211

9 781684 985500